Pazoten

Pazoten

Jack McGinnigle

First published in 2021 by Highland Books,
1 Fairfield Close, Exmouth, EX8 2BN, England.

ISBN-13: 978-1-897913-55-0
ISBN-10: 1-897913-55-9
Ebook ISBN: 978-1-909690-55-4

Chapter 1

"3,476 times 59?"

'205,084.' The answer wiped soundlessly across his consciousness.

'Tch!' Otisk clicked his tongue in annoyance. These mathematical tests kept happening periodically and this had been going on for a long time. His answers were an automatic reflex, as his brain responded to a query that came from nowhere!

"30,926 divided by 47?"

'658.' He sighed inwardly. There it was again! His calculation was completed in a microsecond, without any volition from him. Yes, of course he had always been good at maths; always capable of impressive feats of computation.

'Why are these tests always in decimal?' He muttered querulously, 'hexadecimal is so much more flexible; even octal is not so bad.' Then he relaxed and smiled. 'Although I do admit to a weakness for duodecimal. So elegantly divisible. Really, duodecimal makes so much more sense for human numerical computation.'

"83 times 97 plus 73?"

'8,124.'

'Oh dear!' This time it was an involuntary exclamation.

'What's wrong?' Francel was unfailingly sensitive to his mood.

'Oh, nothing much!' As usual, Otisk was a little embarrassed. 'It's happening again, that's all. You know, the "mysterious maths". I don't know why it keeps happening. The annoying thing is that I just respond automatically. I just can't help myself.'

'Maybe the test calculations come from your brain,' Francel said quietly. 'Maybe it's just to keep you in practice?'

'Well, yes, I have thought of that before,' he conceded, 'it's certainly a possibility but I'm supposed to be in charge of my brain, am I not? And I don't particularly want it to practice maths on my rest day, right in the middle of this extremely pleasant ramble you and I are having. I'm strolling along a lovely, spacious path with the nicest girl in the world and I want us to relax completely. I mean, that's why we've come here, isn't it?' Now he grinned affectionately.

Francel agreed. 'It's really lovely out here, isn't it? It's the first time we've travelled quite so far west. I'm sure we've never been in this particular area before.' She paused and then sighed in contentment. 'Although it's always nice to be with the others back in the Town, I do find it essential to get away every so often. To be alone, you know?'

'But, Francel, haven't you noticed, you're not alone, you're with me!' Otisk was teasing her affectionately.

'Oh, come on, Otisk!' she reposted, 'you know I meant "to be alone with you". You know how I'm always happy to be with you—and isn't it brilliant that the Counsellors arranged for us to work together, too? That means we're almost always together, doesn't it?'

'Yes, I couldn't agree more,' Otisk responded. 'You know I always love to be with you. In fact, when I'm alone, away from you, I actually feel that part of me is missing. It's a very strange feeling; I've never felt like that before, you know. Never in my memory.'

Francel smiled. 'I'm so happy you feel like that. I feel exactly the same. Even the Counsellors approved of us being together almost as soon as we met, didn't they? All that seems such a long time ago, doesn't it?'

'Mm, yes. We were a bit worried at first but, right away, they approved of us being together and gave us absolutely everything we wanted.'

During the next half hour or so, they walked side by side, drinking in all the peace and beauty around them, occasionally climbing to a vantage point that would give them an even more extensive view. Eventually their steps took them to a clearing that was ideal for the picnic lunch they had brought with them. Now they spread out a cloth and arrayed their various items of food and refreshment upon it, eating and drinking until they were replete. Afterwards, made drowsy by exercise and food, they stretched out alongside each other, pressing together to enjoy that unique magical contact which men and women have enjoyed since humanity was created. Before long, gentle sleep took them away on its journey.

Francel was the first to stir, opening her eyes to see the mysterious azure of the skies. Slowly, she sat up, noting how much longer the shadows had become. Beside her, Otisk had become aware of her movement and was awakening to join her.

'Mm. That was lovely. I feel totally rested.' He sat up and stretched languidly.

'Otisk?'

'Yes?'

'I've been thinking about what you said a little while ago.'

'Oh dear! I hope it was something good! Intellectual, maybe?' He smiled affectionately.

'Well, no, if it was intellectual I don't think you meant it to be!' She returned his smile, then became serious. 'Listen, Otisk. You were speaking about being away from me and how it made you feel that a part of you was missing.'

Otisk nodded. 'Yes, and I meant every word of it.'

'Listen, Otisk, but I have been thinking about what you said after that. You said you had never felt like that before. *Never in your memory.*'

'Well, Francel, that's absolutely true. But why does that "make you think"? Am I missing something here?' Otisk was puzzled.

'Listen. You ended by saying: "Never in my memory."'

'Did I? So what?'

'What is in your memory, Otisk? We've been here in Pazoten for quite a long time now but, somehow, we've never really talked about our own memories in depth, have we? Of course we've talked about a few things in the past but we've never explored the big picture. You know, what we were actually doing before we came to Pazoten; exactly who we were, where we were, what we were doing. That's what I have been thinking about. I'm wondering what we can actually recall of our past lives. As far as our time in

Pazoten is concerned, I think I can remember all of that, especially my first meeting with you. I certainly remember that very well!'

Otisk grinned affectionately. 'I wholeheartedly agree with that, Francel. Meeting you is certainly the highlight of my Pazoten memories, too.'

They were silent for a moment or two, both reliving their separate experiences of the golden moment when they first met.

'Otisk?'

'Yes?'

'Can I just ask you some questions?'

'Of course, Francel. Fire away. I hope they're not going to be too difficult. I don't want to appear like a fool in front of you.'

'No, they're not difficult. Ready? Here's the first one. Can you remember everything that has happened to you since you came to Pazoten?'

He screwed up his eyes as he applied his mind to this question. 'Well, yes, I think I can, Francel. Maybe not minute by minute—but nobody can remember that sort of detail, can they? I can remember the sequence of events—especially the important items within the sequence. Is that good enough?'

'Yes, of course. But the important thing is—you sound pretty convinced that you can remember what happened to you here in Pazoten.'

'Yes, I believe I can.'

'So how long have you been in Pazoten, Otisk?'

'Oh, that's an easy one! Ah... Ah...' Otisk paused, his eyes beginning to register the beginnings of confusion. 'Ah... let's see. I must know this.' He paused again for a longer time. At last he spoke: 'I'm sorry, Francel, I'm actually sure I know this. At least, that's what I have always thought—but every time I open my mouth to tell you the answer, I suddenly think: "Wait a minute—that's wrong!" A moment ago, I was going to say six months but then I thought: "No, it's longer than that—maybe it's three years". But as soon as I thought that, I became convinced that was wrong, too.' Now Otisk looked totally confused at his failure to answer such a simple question.

Francel was solicitous. 'Otisk, please don't look so worried! You see, if you asked me the same question, I couldn't give you the answer either. I think we don't know the answer. Do you recall when you had that discussion about your age (with the Counsellor, remember?); it was suggested that Pazoten reality could be different from our expectations? Afterwards, we concluded that the concept of time might be different here. Does this help us in any way?'

'Different time? You know, Francel, I remember that conversation but I struggle with the concept. Because I understand time to be finite. A minute is a minute, isn't it? And a year is a year. It's fixed, that's the logic of it. These things are concepts of number—and I know all about numbers. I'm a bit of an expert, it seems.'

'Well, yes, Otisk, you certainly are a numerical expert. In pure logic, what you have just said is certainly the case. But think about this: I've known some minutes to flash past at lightning speed—and I've known others to drag on almost like hours. Haven't you had that experience?'

'Hm.' Otisk was thoughtful, 'that is a very wise thing you've just said, Francel. Lateral thinking, indeed. Of course I agree with you; I've certainly had that experience and I'm sure everyone has.' He paused and then added softly, 'so what I've just said about finite time is completely wrong.'

She shook her head. 'No, I don't think you're wrong, Otisk. I just think there may be room in reality for both statements—and maybe many others, too.'

Again, silence reigned for a time.

'Now can I ask you another question, Otisk?'

'Oh dear, I hope it won't be as difficult as the last one!'

'You will definitely be able to answer this one. I'm deliberately making it easy. Here it is: "Are you an adult?"'

Otisk looked down at his body. 'I think I can answer "yes" to that one, Francel. I think you could say "yes" as well.' As he said this he looked at her with admiring affection.

'OK, this is the follow-on question, Otisk. I'm sure you will find this one easy, too. Were you an adult when you arrived in Pazoten?'

His answer was immediate and confident. 'Certainly, Francel. And I would imagine that you would answer that question similarly?'

'Yes, I would, Otisk.'

"48 times 236?"
'11,328.'

"13,908 divided by 76?"
'183.'

"951.6 times 157.37?"

'149,753.29.'

'Stop it!' Otisk was very annoyed. 'I'm busy. Go away!'

'More maths, Otisk?'

'Yes. I've stopped it—I hope!'

'Right, Otisk. Here is my final question. It's to both of us, really. We both need to think about this one and answer it as best we can. Pool our knowledge, you know? Here goes, then. It's the question I asked a minute or two ago but with a sharper focus. Specifically, where were we before we came to Pazoten? Where were we as babies, as children, as teenagers? Who were our parents? What happened to us? Have you ever thought about these things, Otisk?'

'No, Francel, I haven't. In a way, that's very strange. I can't understand why I haven't.'

'OK, let's both think about it now and share our thoughts.'

Minutes of silence passed, then Francel spoke at last. 'I've thought about it as deeply as I can, Otisk, but I'm coming up with absolutely nothing. I simply don't know. I cannot recall any memory of my life before Pazoten. It's like I didn't have a life then—so there's nothing to remember. But I feel convinced about one thing. I must have been somewhere, growing up. I must have had birthdays but I can't remember anything about them.'

Otisk lifted his head. 'You know, I'm at exactly the same point, Francel. However hard I try, I have no memory before Pazoten. Absolutely nothing. But I agree with your analysis. I must have been somewhere but there's a block on my memory. Why?'

Both were silent for some moments more. Then he said, 'we're talking about the past, aren't we, Francel? Right now, I find I'm confused. I find I'm not actually sure what "the past" is.'

'Do you think we've lost our memories, Otisk? Is that what has happened to us?'

He thought about this. 'I suppose it could be. But somehow that doesn't seem to fit, does it? Because we seem to know things that must have come from the past, even if we can't remember the past itself; if, indeed, there was such a thing as "the past"!' Now he paused in consternation. 'Goodness, now I don't seem to be able to define what the past is. Can you?'

She reflected about this, then shook her head. 'No, I can't, Otisk.'

They sat quietly for a while, both deeply engrossed in their thoughts.

Finally, Francel spoke. 'I have an idea, Otisk. Maybe it would help if we told each other our story of how we became aware we were in Pazoten. Because that was the finish of the past we can't recall and the beginning of the past we can remember. Do you think that might clarify anything for us? Could it give us any clues?'

'Well, it might. I certainly can't think of any other strategy— apart from giving up, that is!'

They knew that Otisk had arrived in Pazoten first. However, they both thought that Francel had arrived very soon after him, because, when they first met, the felt they were very much new-comers in this amazing land.

'Right, Francel, I'll go first and you can record what I say. Then you give your account and I'll record it. Afterwards, we can listen to both accounts and examine the similarities. You never know, it might jog our earlier memories and take us forward—or should I say backwards,' he concluded with a brief smile.

Francel started the recorder and Otisk began to speak.

There really was nothing dramatic about it. Quite the reverse. He just became aware, gradually, that he was sitting in a large, rather pleasant room. Somehow, the ambience of the room was very comforting, reassuring. There were a few other people in the room, speaking to each other or sitting quietly. Everyone's move-ment was unhurried, quietly purposeful. They looked like ordinary pleasant people, men and woman of various ages. There were a few children, too, interacting calmly with the adults. Everyone looked serene, content, happy.

No-one in the room was making a loud noise; neither were there any annoying whispers. Conversations were neither muted nor strident; loud enough to hear if one put one's mind to it. At that moment, Otisk had no wish to hear what people were saying or to join in any conversation, so he let the comforting susurrations flow over him luxuriously. He looked around him, noting how the room was cleverly decorated and furnished to be comfortable yet stylish and pleasing. In his account, Otisk stressed that he had felt per-fectly at home there and had no ambition to stir himself from the very comfortable seat in which he was sitting. Then he told Francel of his first contact with his Reception Team

'Hello, Otisk.' A man and a woman approached him and spoke with wonderful, radiant smiles.

He looked up at them happily and returned their smile. 'Why do you call me Otisk?' he asked.

'Because that's your name,' the woman answered. 'Look, it's here, on your bracelet.' She indicated a slim, soft bracelet around his wrist, made of a translucent material. She turned it around so that he could read it. Sure enough, it said "OTISK" on it.

The woman held up her arm. 'We've all got them. I'm Branea.' She held up her wrist and showed him her bracelet. He read: "BRANEA" printed boldly upon it. She pointed to the man. 'This is Grabitzo but, quite often, we just call him Bitzo. He answers to that, don't you?' she laughed.

The man smiled. 'Yes, I seem to have a rather tedious name and it's quite convenient to be able to shorten it to some degree. It was Branea's idea. She's pretty clever at that sort of thing. We're your Reception Team here,' he concluded.

'What's a Reception Team?' Otisk enquired.

'We are the people who are here to meet you.' Bitzo answered. 'We are a team because some functions need two people, usually a man and a woman and,' he looked at Branea affectionately, 'we are paired up as a Reception Team. It's the way we're organised here.'

'OK, but what...?' Otisk began.

Branea held up a kindly hand. 'Just take it easy, Otisk,' she said warmly, 'you've just arrived. You're our latest incomer and we'll have a lot to tell you in due course. However, there's absolutely no hurry and it's important we cover everything properly, slowly and calmly. I know you'll want to know everything all at once but it doesn't work that way. For today, we need you to follow our directions and begin to get inducted. Our aim is to make your stay here totally enjoyable and positive in every way. Will you just work with us on that?' She regarded him with loving concern.

Otisk looked from one to the other. 'Yes, of course,' he responded with a hint of weariness, 'I'll do anything you say. You are the experts.'

'Good!' Bitzo was joyful. 'You should eat and drink this (a tray of food had appeared on a small table beside the seat) and then rest. We'll see you in a little while and then we can start on the essentials. Is that fine with you?'

By this time, Otisk had to admit he was feeling quite tired. He nodded his head and his two companions left him. The sight of the food on the table made him feel very hungry and he ate and drank everything on the tray with great enjoyment. Everything was very much to his taste and absolutely delicious! Immediately after he finished, he fell soundly asleep.

When he awoke, he was surprised, although in no way alarmed, to find himself lying on a soft, comfortable bed in a beautiful airy room with sunlight streaming through a large window. Rising from the bed, he crossed to the window and was uplifted by the attractive scene before his eyes. A large town square, immaculately neat and clean, bustling with people of all ages. He opened the window and heard the buzz of happy conversation interspersed with bursts of joyous laughter.

'What a glorious place,' he said to himself, 'I wonder where I am.'

A gentle knock at his door preluded the entrance of Branea and Bitzo, carrying a folder and a small box. 'Here we are,' they said, 'we've come to induct you, as we promised.'

'How did I get here?' Otisk asked, 'and what is this place. A hotel?'

'This is your home while you are here, so long as it is completely to your satisfaction. If it isn't, you just let us know what you would prefer and we will arrange it for you.'

Otisk looked around. 'It looks fine,' he said.

'That's good!' Bitzo said, 'we thought you would like it.'

'Let's all sit down around the table,' Branea said, 'so we can start the formal induction.' She turned to Otisk. 'Here is an info-reader that contains all the information you will ever need to know. I'm now going to give you the Spoken Outline. The whole of this Land is called Pazoten—this is how it is written. As you can hear, the spoken name has three syllables with the middle syllable emphasised—it sort of rhymes with "forgotten." The Land is in a very large beautiful valley with high ground surrounding it. Virtually everyone in Pazoten lives here in the Town—there are just a very few others outside, who live on farms, etc. There are many roads into the country and these are referred to by their direction—the West Road, for instance—it goes west! Everyone may go where they wish in the Land. You can choose any form of transport to travel—or none at all. You will learn about all this by your own explorations.'

'Now, somebody has to be in charge of this Land, to make sure that it continues to run perfectly. These are a small group of people called Counsellors –just six of them. All six Counsellors are highly experienced people who have been in Pazoten for a long time. They are our wise men and women and they have the authority to make decisions when required. The Counsellors are available to the people at all times and oversee everything in the Land. They are also responsible to the Leader who coordinates everything that happens in Pazoten.'

'When we have left you, please go out and just wander around to familiarise yourself with the centre of the Town. You will meet many people who will help you and look after you. They will know that you are a new incomer. Later on, you will have plenty opportunities to explore the country in any way you wish. You may call for us at any time. Just think our names and ask us to come to you and we will join you as soon as we can. However, soon, you will meet your Monitoring Team (another lady and gentleman) and their function is to look after you constantly while you are here. Do you have any questions now?'

Surprisingly, Otisk found that he had none. He felt completely relaxed and confident. And he knew that help was available, not only from Branea and Bitzo, but from the Monitoring Team that he would meet soon and from all the other people he could see outside. So he could just ask anyone anything and they would help. He felt wonderful!

'Thank you, both, for all your help,' he said to Branea and Bitzo, 'I'll try not to be a nuisance.'

Branea held him by his upper arms and looked deep into his eyes. 'Otisk, you are very special to Bitzo and me. We will retain an interest in everything you do. It is our function here.'

Now Otisk looked at Francel. 'And that's exactly what I did. I went out and wandered around. Many people stopped to talk to me and welcome me. Others helped me to find lunch and dinner, offering me their company. Everybody answered all the questions I had, making me feel completely at home. And my Monitoring Team, a really nice couple, came and introduced themselves to me. By the end of that first day, I reckon I knew all the basic stuff about the Town and quite a lot about the Land of Pazoten, too. The rest was just a matter of experience and I accessed a lot of other information from the info-reader. The most important thing that happened after that was meeting you, Francel. I recall that happening very soon after, probably the very next day after my arrival.'

Francel stopped the recording and spoke, 'My experience was really rather similar. I'll go through it as we agreed and you can record it.' When all was ready she started to speak, telling how she "woke up" in the room he described ('It wasn't really waking up— more like just becoming aware of a new location'). Like Otisk, she had felt comfortable and serene. After a while, she had been approached by a very friendly man and woman who had greeted her joyfully. They identified themselves as her Reception Team. She had been a little surprised to find that her name was Francel but had been shown her bracelet and theirs, too. Anyway, she couldn't think of any other name that was hers!

She did identify a slight difference of her experience. She had been taken to her beautiful rooms quite soon after her Reception Team came to her—although she couldn't really understand how she got there! On arrival, her friends had served her a delicious meal and she had slept soon after. On awakening, she had seen the lovely Town Square outside and felt very happy. Then her Reception Team returned and the induction briefing they gave her was very similar to Otisk's. Finally, they suggested she should go outside and explore. Shortly after, she met her Monitoring Team. She found everyone most helpful and kind and felt very happy to be there. While exploring outside, she met this lovely young man and they became inseparable companions. 'And, as you know, the rest is history!' she concluded with a knowing smile towards Otisk.

'Well, Francel, that's so interesting. We both had very similar personal experiences. The few differences that we have identified do not alter the similarity of the overall procedure, do they? And, after it, we both sailed along serenely, just like everyone else here seems to do. But at the same time, it's a bit puzzling, too, especially when we begin to address the sort of questions you were asking just a little while ago.'

'Listen, Otisk. Were you asking yourself these sorts of questions, too? I mean, I was the one to start, wasn't I? But were you doing the same?'

Otisk furrowed his brow. 'Well, yes and no. No, I don't think I was ready to ask your excellent questions. But I was perfectly happy when you did, because in some ways there is a sort of disquiet deep inside me, stirring within me. You know how I like to think of myself as logical? Well, I felt that my situation here was beginning to have elements of illogicality. Sorry! That's the best way I think I can describe it at the moment. Maybe I would have formulated your sort of questions in time. I don't think I was ready to do so but, as I have already said, I was very happy to participate when you raised the matter. Does all that make sense?'

Francel smiled. 'It makes perfect sense. Because that's exactly how I felt a little while ago. A bit worried (although "worry" is too strong a word for it), a bit off-balance, you know? Then, as I was thinking today, suddenly I just started to ask these questions. It wasn't planned, it just came out.'

Otisk looked into her eyes and nodded gravely. Then, suddenly, he jumped to his feet with a peal of joyful laughter, seized her slim figure and whirled her around in a wild dance. 'You know, I think you're wonderful!' he gasped, 'you know I love you very much, don't you?'

'Wow!' she screamed. 'Stop—you'll make me giddy. You know I love you, too.'

Otisk stopped and held her close with loving tenderness. After a moment, suddenly she felt his body jerk with sudden tension.

'What is it?' she cried, 'Is it the maths again?'

'No.' A softly whispered reply in her ear. 'Look.' He turned her around slowly and pointed. They both looked up towards the nearest mountain top. There, illuminated by the late afternoon rays of the sun, was a very large, squat grey building, incongruously merged into the rocks of the mountain peak. As they watched in riveted astonishment, after some minutes the building's entity began to fade in the changing rays of the sun, becoming progressively more diaphanous until it disappeared completely, leaving nothing but the hint of misty cloud where its presence had been.

During this time, perhaps a total period of seven or eight minutes, Otisk and Francel had not moved, he holding her in his arms, both of them unblinkingly focussed on the astonishing artefact that had captured their attention so completely before it had been withdrawn from their incredulous sight. Finally, wide-eyed, they turned to face each other.

'What was that?' she whispered.

'I don't know,' he answered, 'but I do know it wasn't there earlier.'

'Maybe we imagined it,' she said in a stronger voice, trying to inject some logic into the situation. 'I should have taken a photograph of it.'

He shook his head. 'No, Francel, we didn't imagine it. It was there—in some form, at least. This is going to require a lot of thought—and a lot of explanation, too.'

They stood silently for a moment. Then she touched his arm. 'Otisk, it's beginning to get dark. We need to get back to the Town. But first, I just want to take a few photographs. The light is so unusual, so beautiful.' Within a moment, she had produced her camera and was composing images in her viewfinder screen. After walking around to take photographs from various locations, she packed her camera away. 'I'm ready now,' she told him.

'Right,' he said, his tone practical, 'let's collect our belongings. We had a nice seven or eight mile hike to here, didn't we? I was looking forward to the walk back but it's too late now. We'll just need to relocate.'

Seconds later, they stood beside the quad bikes they had chosen as their vehicles for the picnic outing, parked neatly in the wooded clearing where they had left them.

'Let's just relocate these along with us, Francel,' he said. 'I know we were planning a nice ride back but we can always do it some other time. In any case, I think we will certainly want to return to that spot before very long, won't we?'

'I'm sure we will,' Francel agreed.

Then they and their quad bikes were back in the Town.

* * * *

Back at home, they sat quietly looking out of their large window that overlooked the Town Square, an early evening scene bustling with happy, contented people, all enjoying themselves. Without averting his gaze from the soothing scene below, Otisk spoke in a quiet voice.

'You know, I just can't do it, Francel. I know I said I would ignore all the inexplicable things that happen here and just enjoy the wonderful life that we have together.' He paused. 'But I can't... I really can't.'

He turned to look at her, waiting for a reaction to what he had just said, tense and just a little afraid.

'Neither can I, Otisk,' she whispered.

Chapter 2

Love at first sight. In human life, it seems to happen remarkably often! And when the love at first sight is reciprocated, it can blossom at truly lightning speed, becoming a totally arresting event for the two people involved. This is precisely what had happened to Otisk and Francel. Having begun to orientate himself the day before, his first day in Pazoten, Otisk was feeling more and more at home in this marvellous place. The people we so unfailingly kind and the facilities in the Town were absolutely fantastic. Otisk had already found that, whatever he desired, it was usually available somewhere in one of the many shops around the Main Square. If not, there were further shops in the streets that led away to other parts of the Town. Every street he investigated brought more interest and pleasure.

To his surprise, he found that physical money was not used for purchases anywhere; neither were payment cards of any type. The shopkeepers or their assistants merely helped him to find what he wanted and then his purchases were completed automatically, without any mention of cost. Characteristically, he had asked about the elegant system that controlled all this commercial activity when he made his very first purchase of some artists' materials. The shopkeeper explained that every shop was fitted with a system that automatically recognised the customer plus the item being purchased and linked them together. He didn't know how the system worked but he knew it was all handled in Central Finance, located at the Administrative Centre in the Town. He added that there was no need for him to know how everything worked and who organised it. All he knew was that it never went wrong. There was never any trouble with the sales he made from his shop, he said with a happy smile.

'What happens if the customer doesn't have enough credit for what they're buying?' Otisk had enquired.

The shopkeeper had frowned and seemed rather reluctant to talk about this. 'Well,' he said at last, 'that never happens. People always know whether they can afford what they want to buy before they enter the shop.'

'Really?' Otisk was surprised and puzzled. 'How does that work?'

Now the shopkeeper was visibly nonplussed. 'Ah... I don't know, I'm afraid. It's just the way things are in Pazoten,' he said weakly.

'I'm sorry,' Otisk pressed the man, 'but can you be a bit more specific? How does it work?'

Now the shopkeeper became increasingly upset. 'Listen,' he said in a high voice, 'I really don't know—and I don't need to know! All I know is that the system works extremely well. I suppose it's all handled by the Financial Authorities. I don't know. I'm only a shopkeeper here.'

Inevitably, Otisk wanted to probe the system further. 'OK. What would happen if I wanted to purchase every item in your shop,' he asked. He liked to test every situation to its limit!

At this, the shopkeeper's face changed to disquiet and confusion. He looked around at his extensive stock. 'I really don't know,' he whispered. After a pause, he continued in a stronger voice, 'but I don't think anyone in the Town would ever act like that, do you? I mean, it wouldn't be reasonable, would it? And the one thing about the Town and the whole of Pazoten, too, is that people will always be reasonable, kind and considerate.' Now the man began to look much happier! 'Anyway, I'm sure that a Counsellor would soon be around to investigate, don't you think?'

Otisk's ears had pricked up. A Counsellor would appear? What would happen then? Would this be a breach of the law? Would it indicate a serious problem that needed resolution at a higher level? Would this bring trouble and punishment upon the perpetrator? His questions tumbled out.

The shopkeeper relaxed and smiled. 'No, no, no,' he chuckled. 'Nothing like that. Nothing like that ever happens in Pazoten. No, the Counsellor would come to assist in the situation. He or she would establish what was happening and an outcome would be agreed to the complete satisfaction of all. There is never any strife in Pazoten. Never.'

Otisk persisted. 'Yes, but what if someone was unreasonable and insisted on their desire? What if they still insisted that they wanted to acquire every item in the shop?'

The shopkeeper looked at Otisk kindly. 'You're a very recent incomer, aren't you? The answer to your last question is just what I said a minute ago. No-one in Pazoten would ever act like that. It would be detrimental to the Land. It would be against the Will of the People.'

Even Otisk recognised that he had pushed this as far as the limit—and probably beyond! He thanked the man profusely and apologised for being an awkward customer.

The shopkeeper smiled kindly at him. 'No, no, you've been fine,' he said. 'You were just taxing my knowledge to the limit, that's all. And I was glad to help you in every way I could. It's the way we live here. Pazoten is an absolutely wonderful place. We're all so lucky to be here.'

The final surprise came when the shopkeeper wrapped his goods and set them aside instead of handing them over the counter. Seeing Otisk's surprise and remembering he was a recent incomer, the shopkeeper explained that the goods would be waiting for him when he returned to his house. 'The system knows where you live. Everything is made easy for you in Pazoten,' the man had said with a final smile—one tinged with relief as Otisk turned to leave the shop!

Somewhat shamefacedly, Otisk went on his way, thinking about all he had heard. 'It seems I have a lot to learn here. It certainly is a superb place. I mustn't let my questioning mind offend other people.'

* * * *

Some hours later, Otisk had completed a wide circle though the Town streets and had returned to the Town Square. Now he was sitting at a table outside a café, having eaten a delicious lunch. As he scanned around him, taking in all the pleasant sights, his eyes were drawn to a figure dressed unusually in a fluorescent orange jacket. This was a small elderly man who was wheeling a little cart around and examining all the litter bins that were spaced around the Town Square. The people of Pazoten wanted to keep their town neat and tidy at all times, so they always placed their litter and any other small items of rubbish in the litter bins. Otisk recalled seeing litter bins sited in the other streets at well. Obviously, all these litter bins had to be serviced and emptied. This man, dressed in his eye-catching orange, was obviously one of the crew who carried out this important task. Otisk watched the man with interest as he worked his way around the Square, carefully emptying the bins into his cart.

As the man came closer and closer to the café, Otisk noticed, with surprise, that everyone ignored him completely. They did not speak to him or smile at him; it was almost as if he wasn't there. Immediately, he felt sorry for this little man. 'I don't know why people are ignoring him,' he thought, 'politeness costs nothing and, in any case, kindness is very much the norm in Pazoten. When he comes to empty the bin in front of the café, I'm going to greet him. I know! I'll ask him to join me for a coffee.'

Now he watched the man carefully to check on his progress. He observed that it would not be long before he came to the bin just in front of the café. With a slight clatter of cart wheels, the moment arrived and Otisk stood up to speak to the man. However, his words of invitation were never uttered. Just as he opened his mouth, his eyes focussed over the little man's shoulder to rest upon an incredibly beautiful girl who was walking directly towards the café. Although she looked happy enough, he sensed a degree of nervousness and uncertainty about her. As she drew nearer, Otisk was increasingly transfixed by her beauty and natural elegance. It was love at first sight! The little man in his orange jacket was totally forgotten! When she was close to his table and about to walk past, he spoke her name softly.

'Francel?' What a beautiful name, he thought. So perfect for her!

Abreast of his table, she stopped and looked around in some confusion, meeting his soft gaze of admiration, respect and love. In response, a fierce wave of emotion swept through her. 'Wow, he's really nice.' A thought which catapulted joyfully through her senses. Love always recognises love!

She smiled uncertainly. 'How did you know my name?' Her voice was warm, though tinged with anxious concern.

'It's something we can all do in Pazoten,' he replied, somewhat breathlessly.

She looked at him wordlessly for a moment, then: 'You're Otisk?' She thought this was a fine masculine name that fitted him so well!

'Yes, I am, Francel. Please sit down and join me for lunch. Would you like to do that?'

She hesitated only for a fraction of a second and then sat down quickly at the table.

'She's even more beautiful close up,' he thought. 'I mustn't worry her in any way.' He signalled to a waiter and her order for lunch was taken quickly. Despite the fact that he had already eaten, Otisk ordered another lunch for himself.

'I'm rather new here,' she said, 'I'm afraid I don't know the ropes very well.'

He smiled at her. 'Don't worry, I will be delighted to help you, Francel. I think you have a very beautiful name.'

She frowned a little and he hoped he hadn't offended her. 'Do you really think so? Funny, I was a bit surprised when they told me that Francel was my name. I didn't really recognise it as belonging to me but then, as I thought about it, I couldn't think of any other name that's mine, so obviously I accepted it. In any case, it's printed on my bracelet here.' She held up her wrist with the familiar slim bracelet.

'Well,' he said, 'everyone here has a bracelet with their name on it. It's just part of the routine of living here. This is a wonderful place, Francel, you're going to enjoy it so very much. I'll show you around, if you'll let me, that is.' He hoped fervently that she would agree.

'Are you an old hand, Otisk? It must be great to be an old hand and to know your way around everywhere.'

He flushed a little. 'Well, Francel, I must be truthful (unfortunately, he thought), I arrived only recently. Yesterday, I think it was. I've been meeting so many people, discovering so many places and learning so many new things that I'm not really paying attention to what day it is. It seems to me I've been carried along in a sort of tidal flow of enjoyment, if you know what I mean.' Suddenly he became worried. Was he babbling? Would she think him odd? 'Well, at least, that's how I've been finding it, anyway. It can be a bit confusing,' he finished uncertainly.

She looked at him candidly. 'You don't strike me as the confused kind.'

'Well, I don't think of myself that way either,' he said, 'but I think it's what happens to everyone here. Maybe it's because we are all having such a delightful time, enjoying the place and the people so much, that we don't become slaves of the clock.' He paused and then added, thoughtfully, 'I think that's it, Francel. I've not really thought about it before but that must be it.' Now he felt much better.

'So what have you been able to see and do?'

'I've pretty well covered all the centre of the Town. There are many more shops down all of these side streets. No matter what you want, you'll find it here in the Town shops. I must have covered a circular area of at least a mile and there were shops and many other businesses all the way. Everything is so very well organised and it's always spotlessly clean. I'll take you on a bit of tour if you like, Francel. We could go this afternoon.'

'Let's see how we feel after we've finished our lunch, Otisk. Maybe we'll feel more like relaxing. Sitting and watching the world go by; forgetting what day it is, you know?'

He smiled at her and nodded his acquiescence.

* * * *

In the end, they had continued to sit at the table for some time after they had eaten. Francel continued to listen with avid attention as Otisk shared his knowledge of Pazoten. In fact, he would have been greatly flattered had he known that she spent at least some of that time examining him carefully, content to let his pleasantly modulated words flow over her. She thought that he was immensely attractive. 'How lucky I am to have met this lovely young man on my first day,' she thought. 'I hope we can continue to be friends. I did feel a bit lonely earlier on, even although everyone was so nice to me, but now I feel really comfortable with Otisk.'

'So would you like to have a little stroll around?' Otisk asked finally.

'Yes I would,' she replied, 'I've just remembered a few things I'd like to get.'

'I remember there's a department store just down this street. Let's walk down there and see if it has the items you want.'

As they started to walk, her hand slipped quite naturally into his. Otisk was a little startled but extremely pleased; he squeezed her hand gently and she flashed him a happy smile. Before long, they arrived at the department store.

'I can just go in myself, Otisk. I'm sure you don't want to be stuck in the ladies' underwear department!'

Otisk was a little embarrassed! 'Ah... OK,' he spluttered, 'Francel, just remember how the system works. You take what you want to the shop assistants and it will be debited to you automatically. You don't need to do anything. Also, unless you want to carry your purchases around with you, they will send them directly to your home. That's another thing that happens automatically.' He looked around. 'Look, there's a chemist shop just over there. I need to get a few toiletries. I'll go and do that and then wait for you there. Don't worry, I won't run away and desert you!'

'Thanks, I know I can trust you,' she replied, teasingly.

* * * *

Otisk entered the chemist's shop. It was a large well-lit store with shelves displaying all sorts of personal items. There were a number of other customers in the shop; every time he met them, they greeted him pleasantly with a nod or a word of welcome. He walked up and down, scanning the shelves as he went and gradually collected the toiletry items he needed. Then he stood at the end of the shop with a slightly puzzled look on his face.

'Hello, Otisk. You're looking puzzled.' A middle-aged couple stood before him, smiling.

'Well, yes, I suppose I am.'

'What's the problem?' the man asked encouragingly.

'I'm just wondering where the medicines are.'

The smiles left the faces of the man and woman. They both looked at him with worry and concern etched on their faces.

'Medicines?' the man repeated, in an uncertain tone.

'Yes, that's right. Medicines. Painkillers, antiseptic creams, you know? Things like that.'

The man and woman looked around them, clearly perturbed. 'Sorry,' the woman said, 'we don't understand your question. Everything you might want from a chemist's shop is here, isn't it?' Her companion nodded warmly and the smile returned to his face. 'Yes, that's right, Otisk. Everything is here. If you can't see what you want, I'm sure one of the assistants will help you. They will be very pleased to do that.' At this, the man and woman turned and hurried off.

Otisk was extremely surprised. 'How strange,' he thought, 'I'll just have to ask someone else.' He looked around and found, to his surprise, that he was now the only customer in the shop. 'Oh, well,' he thought, 'I'll just enquire at the counter.'

A moment later he stood at the counter which was located at the end of the shop. Here, a smiling young lady awaited him. She took the toiletry goods from him, while enquiring after his wellbeing.

'Thank you, I'm fine,' Otisk said, 'how are you?' The young lady smiled and placed his items in a stout bag before passing it through a hatch behind her. 'I'm very happy,' she replied, somewhat surprisingly. 'Is there anything else I can do for you?' she enquired.

'Well, yes, there is,' he said. 'Could I ask you a question? I'm quite new here.'

'Of course you can,' the young lady replied with a smile, 'we are all here to help each other and, while I'm on duty here, I'm very happy to deal with customer enquiries and I'm sure I will be able to answer all your questions completely.'

'Thanks. Are all the chemist's shops in Pazoten like this one?'

She looked rather puzzled. 'Well, yes, they are. I mean, they're not exactly the same. Some are bigger and some are smaller. And, of course, they are different shapes. Some have more than one floor. Isn't that what you would expect?'

'Sorry if my question confused you. Maybe I should have expressed it more clearly. I meant, do all the chemist shops in Pazoten sell the range of goods you have here?'

'Well, yes, I think so.' The young lady looked happier. 'There may be one or two differences, because the chemist manager of each shop chooses what stock the shop will sell but I think most shops will come to much the same conclusions about that. Does that answer your question?' She looked at him encouragingly.

'Where are the medicines?' Otisk asked.

Her face fell. 'Medicines?' she said rather faintly.

'Yes, medicines. Drugs – you know – tablets, capsules, creams…'

The young lady said nothing but continued to look at him, distinctly discomfited. After ten seconds or so had passed, she said 'Will you wait here, please. I'll just get the chemist manager to speak to you.' Without waiting for an answer, she disappeared through a door behind the counter.

After a minute or so, a hearty voice boomed out. 'Otisk? Hello. I'm Farob. I'm the chemist manager here. You're asking my assistant a tricky question, a question that she feels she cannot answer?' The manager was an older man, burly and confident.

'Yes, Farob. Where are the medicines? Don't you keep medicines in a chemist's shop in Pazoten? I certainly don't see any here.'

There was a long pause while Farob looked at Otisk with a neutral expression. At last he said:

'You're absolutely right. No chemist in Pazoten has medicines in their shop.' Then he added, 'whatever they are.'

Otisk was startled. 'Did you just say "whatever they are"?'

The man was serious as he replied. 'Yes, Otisk, I did. What are they?'

'You know, drugs, antiseptics, pills, creams. Items prescribed by a doctor.'

'Sorry, you will not find any of these items in any chemist shop in Pazoten. What is a doctor?'

Otisk was dumbfounded! 'A doctor is a person who looks after the sick. Treats them, cures their ills, you know.'

'Ah, I see.' Farob looked happier. 'Well, we are all "doctors" in Pazoten. We all look after each other and ensure we are all happy and healthy. Except that we don't call each other doctors.' He looked at Otisk brightly. 'Does that answer your query?'

Otisk was transfixed in astonishment. Finally, he gasped. 'Thank you, Farob. Sorry to bother you with these questions…'

'It's no bother at all; we are here to help you. That's what chemists do, wherever they are.' He paused and smiled broadly. 'So now I wish you well. Come back anytime.' He waved a cheerful goodbye and disappeared.

'Thank you for your custom, Otisk,' the young lady said mechanically, looking distinctly upset.

'Thank you very much. You have been most helpful.' Otisk tried to smile encouragingly.

'Goodbye then,' the young lady said in a very relieved voice.

As Otisk walked towards the shop door, Francel entered.

'Hello, Francel, am I glad to see you! I've just had a most peculiar experience. Let's get out of here and I'll tell you all about it.'

They walked down the street and came to a small ornamental park with bench seats placed around it.

'Let's sit down here. I asked a question of some people in the chemist's shop and it caused consternation!'

'Really, Otisk? I would have thought that was impossible!'

'Well, all the customers ran out of the shop!'

'Gosh, you had better tell me what it is, then.'

'This is the question I asked: "Where are the medicines?"'

Francel continued to look at him expectantly. When he said nothing else, she said 'Yes—and what did they reply?'

'That's just the point, there was no reply. The people I asked didn't seem to know what I was talking about. And there was no pharmacy in the shop. No medicines, painkillers, healing balms, etc. Nothing. So then I asked the shop assistant the same question. She was nonplussed and called the chemist manager. He didn't know what I was talking about either! What do you think of that, Francel?'

'I would certainly expect to find a pharmacy in a chemist shop,' she replied slowly, 'and I would expect to find medicines on sale.'

'But that's not all. I mentioned doctors as being the people who looked after those who were ill. The chemist manager didn't know what a doctor was! When I explained, he insisted that everyone on Pazoten is a doctor, because here we all look after each other and ensure that everyone is healthy and happy—what is your reaction to that?'

'Well, Otisk, I would certainly expect there to be doctors to help people with their medical problems and that they would prescribe the medicines to deal with these problems.'

'Hm.' Otisk was silent for a moment. 'So you are the same as me.' He grasped her hand. 'No wonder we get on so well. It looks like we're the same as each other but different from others here—at least some others, anyway. We seem to have knowledge that they don't have.'

They looked at each other sombrely. She began, 'I wonder what it all means? This is such a fantastic place and we should be so happy to have met each other. Everyone here seems so lovely, so dedicated to each other and the community. It's an ideal way to live, isn't it?'

'Yes, it is. I think maybe we should just forget all about this. Just accept that this is what Pazoten is like and enjoy our life here to the full. Anyway, now that I have met you, I feel that my life is complete.'

They left the park and walked back to the Town Square, hand in hand.

'Where is your house, Francel,' he asked.

She pointed. 'It's over there, just by the side of the square.'

'You mean this one?' His voice was one of rising excitement.

'Yes.'

'Brilliant! My house is next door. We're neighbours and we'll be able to see a lot of each other. I hope you feel as pleased as I do about that.'

She took his hand. 'I really do, you know. I'm so glad I met you—is it only today that we met? Really, just a few hours. Yet it seems like a lifetime already!'

"4,298 times 26?"
'111,748.'

"230 times 159 plus 723?"
'37,293.'

"9,541 divided by 29 plus 62?"
'391.'

The answers flashed effortlessly across his consciousness.

'How annoying,' he muttered. 'Not you, of course, Francel,' he added, seeing her startled face.

'Who is annoying you?' she said, looking around.

He was embarrassed. 'Oh, I get these maths tests every so often. You see, I'm very good at maths and I can do complex mental calculations at lightning speed. Since I arrived in Pazoten, I've been getting occasional maths problems flashing into my brain. I just automatically do the calculations instantly. I've always been able to do that sort of thing.'

'So you're a maths genius? That's very impressive.'

'Well, genius is a bit strong. But I certainly can do maths. It can be a bit annoying, of course.'

They had reached their houses. He turned to face her. 'Francel, will you come to my house this evening and have dinner with me? Please say "yes".'

'Of course I will. I was hoping you would ask me—otherwise I would have dragged you into my house! Having found you, I certainly don't want to lose you.'

* * * *

They found plentiful food and drinks stored neatly in kitchen cabinets.

'Do you know how to cook, Otisk?'

'Well, I wouldn't say I'm a great cook but I can follow the instructions on these packs, can't I? Or, of course, we can go out and eat in a restaurant. Would you prefer to do that, Francel?'

'No, I wouldn't, Otisk,' she replied softly. 'I want to have dinner alone with you.'

So they had chosen the dinner they would like to have and laid out the various items on a table in the kitchen.

'Look, Francel, here's a nice starter for us. Savoury tartlets. They just need to be heated up.'

'Yes, Otisk, this chicken dish looks really tasty. We could have that after the starter.'

'And here's a fruit gateau for dessert,' he said. If it's anything like the picture on the front, it will be wonderful! So let's organise all that for ourselves.'

As these items were being prepared, Otisk found a cooler cabinet of white wine and bottles of water. 'What sort of white wine do you fancy, Francel? Looks like there's everything here.'

She came over to look. 'This Chablis looks nice,' she said. 'Shall we have that?'

'Good choice!' He congratulated her. 'I'll open it when we're ready, along with a bottle of water.

In due course, their meal was ready and proved to be delicious. Afterwards, sipping the last of the wine, they sat at the table beside the window overlooking the Town Square and Otisk told Francel about the many other facilities available in Pazoten.

'Before I met you today, I was looking into the information files that are available on my info-reader. As far as I can see, Francel, they've got everything here in Pazoten. There are buses and hire cars to take you anywhere you want to go. You've probably seen some of these in the Town today. You can get your own car if you want. Motorcycles and quad bikes are also available as well as ordinary pedal cycles. There are boats that cruise on the lakes—we'll have to find out where they are. There's every sort of entertainment, too. Cinemas, theatres, concert halls, sports arenas, libraries, art galleries, etc. All the culture and entertainment you could ever want. There are sports halls covering every sort of sports activity as well as ordinary exercise gyms. And, of course, you've seen a few of the many shops, cafes and restaurants. The shops provide anything you want. If a shop doesn't have what you want, the staff will direct you to where you can get it or it will be ordered and obtained for you very quickly. And, finally, there's a school, a college, a cinema, a theatre and a large church, too, set on top of a hill. However, I have to admit I don't know much about these places at the moment. Anyway, isn't it all breath-taking, Francel? Whatever you want, it seems to be here in Pazoten! I'm really looking forward to exploring some of these things! He grinned at her happily.

'Well, I must say, Otisk, it all sounds absolutely super.' She thought his boyish enthusiasm was most attractive.

'Yes, doesn't it…' After a pause, he continued: 'Of all the things you've seen, Francel, what do you fancy the most?'

'You,' she answered quietly and clearly.

He was dumbfounded. 'What?' he whispered hoarsely, after a pause.

'You,' she repeated, looking at him tenderly. 'I love you.'

His face drained of colour as he looked at her, shocked.

'But…' He was speechless. She could see his confusion clearly. It was written all over his face. Suddenly, fear gripped her with an icy hand. She had made a mistake! He was shocked, terrified by her declaration of love. Maybe even disgusted by her. She should never have been so forward. She should have realised that you cannot meet such a wonderful, handsome man and throw yourself at him like a lovesick child! Oh, why had she been so stupid. Now he would want nothing more to do with her and she would be left alone in this strange place, surrounded by well-meaning people but separated forever from the most important person she had ever met. Desolated, she dropped her eyes and tears ran down her face to drip from her chin.

'But you can't love me…' He had found his voice and spoke these words so softly she could hardly hear them.

'I do. I'm sorry, I shouldn't have spoken,' she whispered without lifting her head, tears still streaming down. A minute expanded across uncharted dimensions of time.

'But I love you too,' he exploded. 'You are the most fantastic person I have ever met. I have loved you from the very moment I saw you in the Town Square. I can't believe you love me. I'm nothing special. Absolutely nothing special like you are.'

What was this? What was she hearing? Was she hallucinating? She looked and there he was, smiling at her. 'I love you, I really do. I have since the moment I saw you,' he repeated.

The next morning, they woke up in each other's arms.

Chapter 3

'Bad news!' Otisk had appeared in the kitchen, looking serious. 'I've just heard that my Reception Team is coming to visit. It all sounded very serious and formal. They don't waste any time, do they? I suppose we shouldn't be too surprised. I think we might be about to discover that they don't like their inhabitants linking without permission. "Falling in love is not allowed!" Anyway, I told them they could come after we have had breakfast. I said come at ten o'clock.'

'Well, I don't care about them coming. And I don't care what they think about us being in love with each other.' Francel was defiant. 'I love you so very much and there's nothing they or anyone else can do about it.'

He smiled fondly at her. 'I love you too. I wonder what they will have to say, though. Like you, I don't care what it is. It isn't going to make any difference to our love, is it? No-one can stop you loving, can they?'

Francel became down-to-earth and practical. 'Anyway, let's have breakfast. We'll soon find out how disapproving they are of our relationship and what they intend to do about it. I will just sit here and listen quietly to them and then, when they're finished, I'll say: "I love Otisk and he loves me. We want to be together. How do we arrange that?"'

Otisk looked at her with shining, admiring eyes. 'Wow, Francel, you're really sharp! I like your approach very much. Go in for the attack—that's a great strategy. That should give them a shock. Maybe a shock big enough to recognise that our love is real and forever.'

Nevertheless, despite all their bravado, breakfast was a quiet, rather subdued affair as they both considered what might happen to them. Would they be censured and reprimanded severely? Was falling in love and being together against the rules of Pazoten? (It could easily be!) They didn't know but certainly no one had mentioned to them anything about relationships with the opposite sex. Would they be forbidden to see each other again? This they would certainly defy... Then a terrible thought came to Francel. Would they be physically separated in such a way they could not see each other? Maybe sent off to live at opposite ends of Pazoten? That would be catastrophic! Francel bowed her head and could not help starting to weep at the thought of such a terrible punishment.

'Francel, why are you crying?' Otisk seized her hand to comfort her.

'Maybe they'll send one of us away so that we never see each other again,' she wailed.

'Listen, Francel, if they do that—or anything like it—we'll fight it every inch of the way. You'll see. I'm pretty ferocious when I get going. Don't worry, we'll beat this. Love cannot be beaten.' Otisk was quietly determined.

As time crept past, they clung to each other in a misery of despair. Imperceptibly, agonisingly, the clock wound around to display '1000 hours'. The entrance doorbell chimed.

'Here they come.' Otisk's voice was quiet and resolute as he operated the door release. Quickly, Francel dried her tears and they waited, poised for battle. Branea and Bitzo entered the room. Both were serious and unsmiling as they greeted Otisk and Francel with handshakes.

'Good morning, Francel and Otisk,' Branea said with a brief, neutral smile. 'I'm glad you are both here, because what we have to say concerns you both.' Francel and Otisk glanced covertly at each other and forced pale smiles. 'The Counsellors have met to discuss you both. They have looked carefully into your records and studied your behaviour since you have been here. They have reached a decision about you both and that is why Bitzo and I are here to see you this morning. We are authorised to be their official messengers.

I am now going to set out for you the detail of their proposal for you both.' She stopped and looked at each one of them with serious formality.

'I think it would be useful if I gave you a word of background at this point. As you may already have concluded, the Reception Teams (people like Bitzo and I) have one of the most important roles in Pazoten and it is essential that the right people are chosen to carry out this task. The Reception Teams receive new incomers, process them, settle them and induct them, after which the incomer becomes the responsibility of a Monitoring Team. However, Monitoring Teams may need to approach the Reception Teams for advice and action if a serious problem develops. That is the background you need to know.'

'There is now an immediate requirement for another Reception Team to be formed. So, here is the Formal Proposal of the Counsellors that I am instructed to communicate to you this morning—I ask that you listen carefully to my words. The Counsellors propose that you, Otisk and Francel, should form a new Reception Team. Although you are young and recently arrived, the Counsellors are convinced that you both have the right qualities and abilities to carry out this very important task. Incidentally, it is a task that will earn you many credits in Central Finance. If you require time to think about this, we can give you a few hours but the Counsellors need to have your decision as soon as possible. If you agree, you will start the Training Phase right away. May I say that Bitzo and I will be delighted if you feel able to join us as professional colleagues.' Now she smiled fondly at both of them then turned to her partner. 'Have I covered everything, Bitzo? It's the first time I have been instructed to carry out such an important communication task for the Counsellors. I felt really nervous about it.'

'Yes, Branea, I am sure you have covered everything about the Reception Team Proposal. However, you will recall we have also been instructed to ask about one other unrelated matter,' Bitzo said quietly. He turned to address Otisk and Francel. 'This concerns a very personal matter but the Counsellors have instructed us to ask it, so I hope you will forgive my impertinence. In view of the fact that you have fallen deeply in love with each other, the Counsellors wish to know if you would like to live together in the same house. If you agree, your separate houses will be remodelled immediately into one larger house. That completes our communication here to you and we await your response to both propositions.' He stopped and stood silent and still beside Branea.

After a moment, Otisk turned to Francel, astounded but with eyes shining. He spoke very quietly, in a tone audible only to her. 'Francel, I am sure I would like to say "yes" to both the questions we are being asked. However, would you prefer to defer our decisions for a few hours, so that we can have a discussion? I'd be perfectly happy to do that.'

Without taking her eyes from his, Francel shook her head immediately. 'There's no need to wait, is there, Otisk? I feel strongly that what is proposed is absolutely right for us. I think it would be a great honour to form a Reception Team with you, as well as an incredible pleasure. My answer to that is a definite "yes". And, as for sharing a house with you, Otisk, my answer to that is "Yes, please!"'

'You're quite sure?'

'Absolutely.'

'Shall I speak for both of us and give our reply?'

'Yes, please, Otisk.'

Otisk turned back to Bitzo and Branea. 'You have four "yesses" from here to your two questions. Taken all together, they make one resounding and very loud "Yes, please!"' He smiled widely at them.

Bitzo and Branea responded with genuine delight. 'Thank you, both,' Bitzo said, 'and welcome to the Reception Team Organisation. We have just informed the Counsellors of your decisions. You will start to train immediately, later today, I expect. You will find the Reception Team a most rewarding activity and there is no doubt it is one of the most important tasks in Pazoten.' He looked around. 'As you see,' he continued, 'your house has now been enlarged and remodelled. We hope you like it but, of course, you can alter anything that is not to your taste. We will leave you now. We should all celebrate and I am sure you have much to say to each other.' With a cheerful wave, Bitzo and Branea faded and disappeared as they transferred away.

Otisk and Francel hugged each other with pure delight.

'We thought we were going to be disciplined!' Francel shrieked with laughter.

'Severely reprimanded and sent to the opposite ends of Pazoten!' Otisk gasped in laughing reply.

Now he looked around in amazement. 'Hey, look, Francel,' he said, 'the house is really different. Much bigger, wow! It was a lovely house before. Now it's even better.'

They walked around, examining everything critically. 'They have obviously turned our two houses into one. See, here in the hallway. This was where our entrance doors were. Now there's just one door into this house. This is very clever stuff, isn't it? Instant remodelling with no rebuilding. I wonder how that is done.' He thought for a bit, then smiled happily. 'You know, Francel, I don't care how it was done. It's just delightful that it has happened. I think there are so many wonderful things that happen here in Pazoten—things that should just be accepted. And that's exactly what I'm going to do from now on. Accept that I am living here with this absolutely wonderful person whom I love. That's the real miracle in all of this, you know.'

'I'm so glad to have met you, Otisk. It's great that we can be together like this. And now we're going to work together, too, in a very important Pazoten function. Life is truly wonderful, isn't it?'

* * * *

That afternoon, after they had eaten lunch, they received a message:

Counsellor Begiet will be pleased to see you at the Administrative Centre at 1500 hours.

They looked at each other gravely and then dissolved into nervous laughter. They felt exactly like schoolchildren summoned to see the Headmaster!

'Looks like we're going right to the top, Francel.' Otisk chortled.

Francel controlled herself. 'Yes. We must be serious, though. It will be fascinating to meet a Counsellor, won't it? They seem to be the people in charge here. The big bosses! What do you think? I reckon it has got to be a very old man with a big bushy white beard, dressed in a long white robe—oh, and sandals, rather than shoes.'

'Hey, where did that image come from, Francel? I don't recall ever meeting anyone like that.'

She thought for a while. 'You know, Otisk, I really don't know where that picture came from. Like you, I've never seen anyone like that or even read about an old bearded man wearing a robe. Must have come from deep in my subconscious. Or perhaps I'm going a little crazy?'

He put his arms around her. 'Well, Francel, if you're going crazy, it's a craziness I really like. So don't stop being crazy, will you?'

She smiled at him. 'Yes, Otisk, I promise. That will be an easy promise to keep.'

Otisk now turned practical. 'Right. I'll just have to check where the Administrative Centre is.' He consulted his info-reader. 'Ah, yes. Here it is. Look, Francel, it's not very far from here. Seems to be up a bit of a hill. The route takes us along some roads we haven't explored before, so that will be interesting, too. We are not asked to bring anything with us, so it looks like we'll just present our plain, unadorned and wonderful selves to your "old-man-with-a-beard". I expect this will be a sort of "meet and greet" operation. A preliminary briefing, leading into the real work. It could take some time to train us to be an effective Reception Team, couldn't it? It seems like a pretty tricky job. There must be a lot of aspects to it—and it must be so important to get it right.'

'Well, after today's initial meeting, we'll probably have an idea of what the training will be and how long it will take. Gosh, I hope the training won't include any maths. I've always been hopeless at maths…'

Otisk squeezed her hand. 'Just leave the maths to me. I'm an expert. So expert that I'm doing complex mathematical calculations at times I don't want to. It's very annoying!'

* * * *

They left the house and, hand in hand, began to walk towards the Administrative Centre, giving themselves plenty time to meet their 1500 hours deadline.

'Look, Francel! There are some very interesting shops along this street. Look at this model aircraft shop: they cover every sort of model—and every size, too. I wouldn't mind building and flying some of these models. That would be really good fun, don't you think? And look, there are model boats, too. We'll have to find out where the lakes are and then I can sail some model boats on them. This shop is a great find, isn't it, Francel?'

She looked at him affectionately. 'Yes, of course it is, Darling, although maybe I have a tiny preference for some of these designer clothes shops on the other side of the road. And there's a lovely photographic shop over there, too. I love photography. I must get a camera.'

'You're a photographer, eh? I do a bit of painting, you know—mainly watercolours. You see? We fit together in yet another way. We'll need to get you a camera as soon as we can.'

'That's a deal, Otisk. I'll take you with me when I go to buy it.'

'Fine, Francel. Although I warn you I don't know much about cameras.'

Ahead of them, they could see a large elegant building, built on the highest point of a hill. A few minutes later, they had walked through a large ornate gateway, beside an artistic sign that proclaimed "Administrative Centre". Inside, a smooth pathway ran between well-tended gardens, bright with attractive flower displays. Finally, a large, elegant doorway was identified as the "Entrance".

'Good afternoon and welcome, Francel and Otisk.' A smiling man in a formal uniform had stepped out of an office just inside the doorway. 'Welcome to the Administrative Centre. You have actually been here before, you know—but you won't remember. All the Reception Rooms are here in this Centre. It's where everyone starts their lives on Pazoten.'

'Good afternoon,' Otisk responded, then he frowned, 'I'm sorry, I don't seem to be able to greet you by name. I can't sense it—don't know why.'

'Oh, that's very easily explained,' the man said pleasantly, 'when I'm on duty as a doorkeeper, my official duty takes over my identity. So you only see me as the Doorkeeper. On duty, my name is irrelevant to all the visitors who come here. In Pazoten, all official duties are handled in this way. Of course, if you met me off-duty, you would be able to access my name as normal. The system stops information overload, you see?'

'Thanks for explaining that,' Otisk said, 'although, I must say, I prefer to address people by name.'

'That's very kind of you, Otisk,' the man said. He consulted a display screen in his office. 'You are asked to proceed to Room F3-46,' he said, 'where Counsellor Begiet will see you.' He pointed down the corridor. 'The transporter will take you there. Just through these doors. Have a pleasant visit.' The doorkeeper re-entered his office and closed the door gently.

Francel and Otisk walked down the wide corridor. Ahead of them, there were double doors which slid open as they approached. As they walked through, the doors closed behind them. Otisk looked around for a set of controls to instruct the transporter but there were no controls to be seen. The walls were entirely blank.

After a brief second, another set of doors ahead of them slid open. Through these doors, they could see a short corridor and, facing them, a large door marked "F3-46". As they watched, the door swung open soundlessly.

Otisk looked at Francel with raised eyebrows. 'Wow, that was pretty elegant! I wonder how they do that. I suppose it must be programmed by the Doorkeeper.'

'Or maybe the system just picks it up from us?' Francel mused. 'You know how sophisticated everything is around here. Anyway, however they do it, it's extremely efficient! I'm not like you; I don't need to know how everything works.'

They walked through the door into a spacious room, richly carpeted and comfortably furnished with large, deep armchairs and sofas plus a few tables and upright chairs. They walked in and the door closed softly behind them. There was no-one else in the room; however a large data screen faced them, proclaimed a message:

```
Good afternoon, Otisk and Francel. Please sit
down and relax; Counsellor Begiet will be with
you shortly.
Current time: 1500 hours
```

They chose to sit down together on a very comfortable sofa and held hands.

'Otisk?' A soft whisper.

'Yes?' A whispered reply.

'I feel I ought to be nervous but, somehow, I don't. I'm feeling relaxed. In fact, I'm feeling more relaxed by the second.'

'Well, I certainly feel very relaxed too, Francel. It's very comfortable here. Reassuring, somehow. It fills you with confidence.'

They sat, cocooned in pleasant, contented reveries as uncounted time glided past. Suddenly, both were startled into full consciousness as the restful silence was violated by the gentle "swoosh" of the door opening. In pure silence, the gentlest of sounds becomes a deeply shocking disruption! A slim, young blonde girl entered the room, walking soundlessly on the thick carpeting. Otisk saw that the clock on the data screen now said "1503"—just three minutes had passed since they entered the room. 'Astonishing,' he thought, 'I would have thought we've been here much longer than that.'

The young woman sat down on an upright chair facing their sofa and placed several slim files on the small table in front of her.

'Good afternoon and welcome, Francel and Otisk. Sorry to disturb you but I see you have successfully completed. ('I wonder what that means,' Otisk thought.) Now I'm preparing to move you on to the next phase.' She opened the files and examined them gravely.

In the full light of the room, Otisk examined the young woman. Who was she? She had not introduced herself. Could this be Counsellor Begiet's Personal Secretary? Do Counsellors have secretaries? He didn't know but there must be a lot of administration to do in the Administrative Centre. He smiled momentarily. A lot of administration done in the Administrative Centre! That's a good joke—he must tell Francel later!

He looked once again at the young woman. She looked about the same age as Francel, he thought, maybe even younger. 'She's probably just an Administrative Assistant sent to prepare the basic paperwork for the Counsellor,' he concluded. 'She's probably too young to be his Personal Secretary. I'm sure that would need someone who was more mature.' Satisfied by his conclusions, Otisk sat back and waited to see what would happen next.

'Right,' the young woman said in a quiet, well-modulated voice, 'let's get started on our chat. You will be able to ask me questions after I check your training.'

Otisk felt he must intervene at this point and sat forward in his seat. 'Sorry to interrupt, but who are you? I am not able to sense who you are. What position do you hold here? And could you tell us when we will meet Counsellor Begiet? That is why we have come here this afternoon.'

'Sorry, Otisk. It's all my fault,' the young woman said, 'I haven't activated my system. I'm Counsellor Begiet.'

During a shocked pause, Otisk's face registered his confusion and embarrassment. 'Ah... Ah, I'm very sorry, Counsellor... I didn't know...' he said finally.

The Counsellor smiled broadly at him. 'Of course you didn't, Otisk! We Counsellors are aware that most people in Pazoten expect to meet a dignified old man! You know, someone with a long white beard and dressed in a long white robe to match the beard!'

Francel gasped. 'That's exactly the picture I gave Otisk this morning! We thought it was... ah... a joke,' she finished weakly.

Counsellor Begiet laughed uproariously. 'Well, there you are, then! That just shows how well you are tuned into Pazoten society!' She began to scan some papers.

'Now, I just want to check your functional understanding of the position you now hold,' she said. 'Can you tell me in what category you are going to be employed?' The Counsellor looked at them brightly.

Otisk sat forward. 'I'm sorry, Counsellor, I don't understand your question. But I would like to ask you some questions, please. When do we start our training? How long does it take? Is there an on-the-job phase afterwards and, if so, how long will it be before we are fully accepted as a functioning Reception Team? Obviously, Francel and I are anxious to contribute as quickly as possible but we understand that the preparation for such an important function has to be done with great care and with complete thoroughness. We would be most grateful for all that information.' He paused and then said, 'We are an Adult Reception Team. An ART.' As he said this, his face registered wonderment and consternation!

'I agree with Otisk. We are in the Adult Reception Category,' Francel added, almost mechanically.

'Very good,' the Counsellor smiled and then addressed Otisk. 'You are not the first person to ask these questions. I suspect you now know the answers but here is a confirmation. Your training is complete. The Training Package was downloaded to each of you in the minutes between your arrival in this room and my entry. There is no other training. You now know everything you need to know to function as an ART and you will be on duty tomorrow morning from 0900 to 1500. There will be a CRT on duty with you. As you know, that is a Child Reception Team to receive our younger incomers. Your age range starts at…? She looked at them quizzically.

'Twelve,' they responded together.

The Counsellor smiled again. 'As you know, you are supported by the Administrative Centre for all the facilities you need for each incomer. How you apply your skill is your responsibility. Do you have any questions about your Reception Team work?' She looked at them both.

'I don't,' Otisk said in a rather surprised voice, 'I feel I know everything about the function.'

'So do I,' Francel said.

The Counsellor beamed at them. 'So, welcome to the Staff,' she said, 'Can I help you with anything else before we finish?'

'Well, yes,' Otisk said, 'but I don't know whether I should ask this. I don't know if it's allowed.'

The Counsellor looked at him kindly. 'Everything is allowed, Otisk. I know what your question is and I will answer it. The only thing is that I don't know whether you will find my answer satisfactory.' She paused. 'You want to know why I am a Counsellor when I am so young?'

Otisk flushed and nodded. 'I thought it might be impertinent...' he faltered.

The Counsellor laughed. 'But that didn't stop you, Otisk, did it? I must admit it is quite an unusual question. Normally, if I am asked anything, it's about some detail of my life as a Counsellor in Pazoten. You, on the other hand, want to go for the jugular!' She laughed again, then, noting his embarrassment, said, 'I don't mean that unkindly, Otisk. You see, everyone is different. You have an exceptionally enquiring mind and that's one of the reasons that you have been chosen as a Reception Team member. Such people have to be completely free-thinkers.' She turned to Francel, 'you, too, have this quality, Francel, though your application of it is rather more subtle! That is why, together, you will make an exceptional Reception Team.'

She paused while regarding them impassively. 'Now,' she said finally, 'how to answer your question...?' She sat, deep in thought for a moment. Then, looking earnestly at them both, she began. 'Most people in Pazoten regard Counsellors as very important, highly privileged, senior people—hence the old-man-with-beard analogy. We are thought of as people who make rules and give out reprimands and punishments. As people who sit on high and make judgements. But that is, in fact, completely wrong. My fellow Counsellors and I have a responsibility to the Leader to serve the population of Pazoten completely and constantly. The small team of Counsellors to which I belong is here for just that one purpose— to serve the people of Pazoten during every single moment of their lives, to look after them, to solve their problems and keep them happy and contented. Although (as you have noted, Otisk) I am quite young, I have actually been here for a long time and have learned many things about Pazoten and about the way that people need to be supported. That is why you find me as a Counsellor. That is my answer.' She looked at Otisk.

'Yes, thank you,' he said, 'but what can you tell me about the Leader?'

She sighed. 'I knew you would ask me that, Otisk. I can tell you nothing about the Leader, apart from this. He is the Leader of

Pazoten and that is his responsibility. We Counsellors serve him by serving all the people who live in Pazoten. We all have been given our areas of responsibility and we carry out the work in these areas constantly. There is no need for me, or any of the other Counsellors, to meet the Leader. However, the Leader knows constantly what we are doing.' She smiled at Otisk. 'So, Otisk, if you ever meet the Leader, you can ask him or her your questions. I have no doubt that you would do that! However, I have to say that I have never known anyone who has met the Leader but – who knows? – perhaps you will be the first!' She collected her papers. 'And now I must leave you, Blessed People. You know when and where to go tomorrow and you will discover the times of your other duties then. We will no doubt meet again and I give you my blessings for the momentous task you are about to start. These blessings come from all the Counsellors and from the Leader himself. Goodbye.' She left the room silently, leaving Otisk and Francel silent and thoughtful.

* * * *

Half an hour later, they were sitting in the sunshine outside a pleasant café.

'In one way, I feel as if I have been catapulted on to a pinnacle,' Otisk said. 'I don't know whether to be elated or frightened! Who would have thought the training would have been completed in three minutes! Now, I call that real efficiency. This Leader person must be someone exceptional. Superhuman, perhaps I should say.'

'Yes, you're right, Otisk. A full Reception Team training course imparted in three minutes is certainly an extraordinary thing to achieve. And, the thing is, I feel totally confident that I know everything I should. I know I will be able to deal with every situation I might come across in the Reception Room and elsewhere. I think that's absolutely wonderful, don't you?'

He took her hand. 'We'll make a great team, won't we, Francel?'

'Of course we will. After all, we're free-thinkers, aren't we?'

'Not too free, I hope,' he smiled. 'I think it can get you into trouble.'

'Not if you're subtle, darling!'

Chapter 4

They awoke early, excited at the prospect of their first day as an ART. As Otisk bathed under the pleasant spray of a hot shower, he wondered what lay ahead of them on their first spell of duty. He hoped that all would go well and that anybody they received would be brought gently to the essential knowledge about Pazoten that it was the ART team's solemn duty to impart. Although he knew this was an enormous responsibility, he knew with certainty that the training they had received had prepared them for any eventuality. The training had made them sensitive to the needs of the incomer and how they dealt with them would instantly be tailored to give them the best experience of "arriving". He smiled as he luxuriated under the flow of water.

"45,521 divided by 23?"
'1,979.1739.'

"298 times 64?"
'19,072.'

"27 times 4,751 plus 320?"
'128,597.'

"4,378.95 divided by 37?"
'118.35.'

Otisk's brain supplied the answers at lightning speed and without any deliberate effort from him. He didn't mind the maths on this occasion. He was comfortable under the shower and happy at the prospect of his new function, especially since he would be working with Francel. 'If my brain wants to keep my maths in practice, that's all right with me,' he thought amiably, 'as long as it doesn't come when I'm working on something difficult. I would be pretty annoyed if that happened.' However Otisk knew he had no control over the maths. As he had told Francel, it was something that had been happening to him ever since he arrived in Pazoten. Had it been happening to him before that? He pondered this. He didn't know, because he couldn't remember anything about his life before Pazoten. 'If I ever had any life before Pazoten, that is,' he muttered darkly.

Feeling completely clean and refreshed, he stepped from the shower, dried himself vigorously and dressed quickly. Minutes later, he joined Francel in the kitchen where the table was laid for breakfast. Fresh coffee bubbled in the coffee maker.

'That smells nice,' he said to Francel, who was already seated at the table. 'And so do you,' he added, kissing her lightly.

She flashed him a smile. 'I've been thinking,' she said, 'how do you think we should get to the Administrative Centre? I'd quite like to walk there but I don't want to tire myself out before I start. I want to make sure I'm completely ready and fresh for my first incomer. What do you think?'

'Well, I know what you mean, Francel. I think I'd like to walk because it gives us time to chat and think. It would feel a bit disquieting if we just relocated there. I feel a bit nervous about doing it that way. We could leave early and give ourselves plenty of time for a leisurely stroll to the Centre.'

Francel nodded. 'Let's do that. We'll arrive in a more relaxed state of mind, I'm sure.'

'OK, so we'll leave here at 0830 hours. That will give us plenty time.'

* * * *

Soon they were on their way and strolling hand in hand along the pleasant streets that led towards the Administrative Centre. As they turned to walk up the hill, Otisk's attention was drawn to a flash of orange some distance away. He identified this as a man wearing an orange jacket, busily emptying the contents of the litter bins into a wheeled cart. He immediately told Francel the story about the litter bin maintenance man in the Town Square, how he was about to greet him and invite him for a coffee when he was "blown away" by her sudden appearance. 'You know, I had forgotten all about him; I mustn't forget to invite him to join me for a coffee at the next opportunity. I hope I can recognise him again. After all, I'm extremely grateful to him. I might not have seen you otherwise.'

'You're absolutely right, Otisk. You should keep your promise, especially as everybody seemed to be ignoring him. Why were they doing that? It isn't what usually happens in Pazoten.'

'I've wondered about that too. Maybe there's some rule about not disturbing people when they're working. Remember how we couldn't sense the name of the Doorkeeper up here at the Administrative Centre? He explained he was made anonymous while he was working. Maybe the maintenance people are like that, but more so. Maybe you shouldn't talk to them while they're working. Anyway, I think it's impolite to ignore someone, especially in a place like Pazoten, so I'm going to speak to him when the opportunity presents itself.'

By this time, they had passed through the gates, walked through the gardens and were now in the Entrance Hall. As they passed the office, the Doorkeeper raised a hand to acknowledge their presence—they were "staff" now and could come and go as they pleased.

The transporter whisked them directly to Reception Room RR5, which was located on the top floor of the building. The door opened as they approached and, somewhat diffidently, they entered the large room.

'Hello, Francel and Otisk,' a warm, friendly voice greeted them. A man and women rose from some comfortable chairs nearby and came to shake their hands. 'I'm Kanen and this is my partner Tarinc. We're ART5 and we're very glad to see you, especially since you're taking over from us,' the man joked. 'As this is your very first visit, let me show you where the Duty Schedule is. It shows when your shifts are. It's in the Duty Office over here.' They entered a smaller room and stood in front of one of the large data screens. 'I take it you know you're ART9?' Otisk nodded. 'Well here you are on the Schedule. Here's today's shift 0900 to 1500 hours. At 1500 hours, you're replaced by ART12. All the duty periods are six hours, covering 24 hours, of course.'

'Are you kept very busy here, Kanen?' Otisk asked. 'I mean, how many incomers do you usually get during a shift?'

'It's very variable, Otisk. Sometimes there's none—for instance we haven't had any during the shift we've just done. Most often it's one or maybe two but we have had as many as three, haven't we, Tarinc?'

She smiled. 'Yes, it can get a bit exciting when that happens. In an extreme, you need to split up. It isn't ideal but it's sometimes necessary. If you get more than three, you should call for the Standby Reception Team. You can see from the Schedule that we all have these Standby Duties at times. On these, you just wait in readiness. Then, if you're called, you relocate here immediately and start working right away.'

'When you're on standby,' Francel asked, 'do you need to stay at home?'

'No need for that, Francel, though some of the Teams do. It doesn't matter where you are or what you're doing, when you're called out, you just relocate here as quickly as possible. Your call-out means that there's an emergency here. Don't worry, it doesn't happen very often.'

'Thanks for that information, Tarinc.'

They walked back into the Reception Room. 'You're on duty with CRT15,' Kanen said. He indicated a man and a woman at the other end of the room, 'As you see, they are busy with a child incomer. I don't think you'll see much of them during this shift. Once you have an incomer to deal with, it takes up all your time. As you know, the others in the room are the Duty RT Administrators. They are here to assist you when you are arranging the facilities and requirements for your incomers. They will also help you personally—you know, everything from advice to coffee! And finally there are the Technicians. They keep the equipment running. Talk to them if there are any technical problems.'

They all walked to the door. 'When is your next shift?' Otisk asked Tarinc.

'We have two days clear, now, then we're back for an evening shift. Of course, we have to keep in contact with our new incomers and give them information and advice anytime they want it. This is specially important until their Monitoring Team take over.' she replied. 'Of course, all these activities generate work credits for us,' she added.

Now they turned to the door. 'So that's it, ART9.' Kanen was jovial. 'Enjoy yourself and our blessings upon you both. Goodbye for now, we're just relocating home.' With that, Kanen and Tarinc faded and disappeared, leaving Otisk and Francel as the responsible ART in the comfortable environment of RR5.

Feeling the weight of responsibility, they sat down together on a sofa facing a display.

'We can relax at the moment, Francel. We know that the system will tell us if an incomer is due. Meanwhile, I think it would useful if we looked at some of the incomer statistics. I'm interested to see the distributions.'

Otisk instructed the system and various tables and graphs were displayed.

'Look at this, Francel. The average number of incomers is 5.87 per day. That includes all incomers, including babies. In the adult age range, the average is 4.09. You can see the distribution curves here. It seems that their extreme has been nine incomers in one day, six adults and three children. Wow! That must have been an exciting day. I hope that doesn't happen today.'

'I'm with you on that,' Francel replied. 'However, I would like there to be one incomer for us. I'd like to go home today knowing that I have been able to cope with the job.'

'Yes, I hope we have one to test us out. That will show us where our weak spots are.'

'I wonder if Pazoten ever gets full,' mused Francel. 'I haven't thought about it before but there may be a limit that the Land can support. Maybe incomers have to go somewhere else then? To another Pazoten, maybe?'

'Possibly, but perhaps the system is much more complex than that. Maybe we shouldn't apply normal reasoning to Pazoten. Perhaps the Land is not finite.'

Francel was puzzled. 'Not finite? What does that mean?'

Otisk smiled. 'You're good at asking difficult questions. I don't really know how it could work. I'm just making it up as I go along! All I'm saying is—maybe Pazoten doesn't work with the logic we understand. You know, dimensions—length, breadth, height, time, etc. Maybe it works some other way. An infinitely stretchable piece of elastic? Anyway, there are certainly a lot of people in Pazoten but there's no sign of overcrowding, is there? I have a feeling we might never know the truth of this.'

A soft chime interrupted their interesting discussion. The screen announced:

```
Incomer procedure is commencing
One adult manifestation is proceeding
Data will follow
```

They both stiffened. 'This is it, Francel. This is what we're here for.' His voice was filled with a blend of bravado, fear and concern.

Francel looked pale. 'I hope we can do it properly. It's so important to get it right.'

Otisk became more resolute. 'Listen, I'm sure every new Reception Team has the same worries. Just remember that we've had the full training. We know everything we need to know and we have been specially selected for this most important task. I think we've just got to trust the people who run this place.'

'I'm sure you're right, Otisk. But I can't help feeling just a little frightened.'

They waited, eyes fixed on the display in front of them. When it came, the soft chime sounded deafening!

```
Manifestation is now at Stage 6
Name of incomer: GORTL
Data: Male, Age 16 years Arrival Location:
RC3
```

The display changed to an image of RC3 (Reception Capsule 3). At the same time, they could see a ceiling indicator glowing over one of the Reception Capsules at the other end of the room. They knew they would both go there after manifestation was complete and the incomer was ready to begin Personal Interaction. Meanwhile, they could monitor progress from their display and would know when the time was right to approach the incomer. To help them, data on the incomer would continue to be provided on their display, showing the development of his awareness profile. Francel and Otisk knew from their training that the timing of this last stage was highly variable; some incomers raced through the awareness stage, others proceeded much more slowly.

'Slowly does it,' Francel murmured, 'we just need to wait.'

So they waited, eyes never far from the screen. At last, a gentle chime accompanied the information that would spur them into action:

Incomer GORTL, Male, 16
Awareness has reached Level 10

PI is now appropriate.

Immediately, they both rose and made their way to RC3. They found a slim young man, very boyish in appearance, sitting calmly in the extremely comfortable seat that is the major part of a Reception Capsule. He turned a mildly quizzical gaze upon Otisk and Francel as they approached and lifted a hand to greet them.

'Hello!' he said, 'I knew there were others here. I could see and hear them. I was just beginning to wonder what would happen next.'

Francel and Otisk smiled at him. 'Hello Gortl,' Francel said, 'We're really pleased that you have come to us. We are your Reception Team. I'm Francel and this is Otisk. We are here to look after you. How are you feeling now?'

Gortl considered this. 'Well, I think I'm all right. Although I do feel as if I've been through the mill, if you know what I mean?' Again he smiled, demonstrating the freshness and beauty of youth. 'But what name did you call me a moment ago?'

'Gortl,' Otisk said. 'That's your name. Look at your wrist band.' He pointed to the young man's right wrist, encircled by the familiar translucent bracelet. 'You'll see your name printed there—look, there it is "GORTL". Here, we've all got wrist bands just like yours with our names printed on them.' He held out his own wrist and showed his printed name.

The young man turned to Francel. 'Listen, what is this place, where is it and what am I doing here?' His tone was calm and unperturbed.

Francel smiled gently at him and held up her hand. 'Whoa, Gortl. Slow down! We just want you to relax at the moment. There'll be plenty of time to answer all your questions once we get you inducted. Meanwhile, I bet you're hungry and thirsty, aren't you? Look, here's a tray with your favourite food and drink. (This had appeared on a table beside the boy.) 'Please eat and drink all you want. Afterwards, there will be plenty time to talk and answer all your questions. We'll stay here with you. Don't worry, we are here to make sure everything is fine for you.'

'Yes, you're right,' Gortl responded. 'I am very hungry and thirsty. And you're right again, this really is my favourite meal.'

Francel and Otisk sat down and watched Gortl as he ate and drank heartily. Afterwards, it was patently obvious that he had become very sleepy. He sat back in the comfortable seat and his eyelids drooped.

Francel spoke softly. 'Just close your eyes, Gortl. You're tired after your journey here. It will do you good to have a rest. When you waken up, we'll get you sorted out. Don't worry. Everything will be just fine.'

The boy nodded. As he closed his eyes, he murmured, 'Thank you for being my friends. I really appreciate that.' Then he fell soundly asleep.

'Right, Francel, we need to start making decisions about him. While he was eating, I checked with the Duty Administrators for an accommodation proposal and the suggestion is that he should occupy a student flat. Nothing too fancy but a simple place where he lives with other young people around his age. There's always some degree of accommodation supervision at these places. I can't see anything wrong with that suggestion. Do you agree?

'Yes, I do. If the Duty Administrator suggests that, we have no reason to go against it, have we? Sixteen is a bit of an awkward age. Not quite adult but no longer a child. So shall we confirm that we accept that proposal? Then, when we're ready, we can relocate him.'

'Agreed, Francel.'

'Did the Administrator suggest anything for his activities?'

'Yes, I checked that, too. They suggest he should be a student. The data reports there are quite a few students who are studying in Pazoten. He will be surrounded by others like him so that should fit in pretty well. I think we can accept that, too?'

'Certainly.' She looked at Gortl, deeply asleep in the seat. 'I think we should relocate him to his accommodation quite soon and settle him down for the night. Then we can visit him first thing tomorrow and complete the induction.'

'Certainly. There's no need for him to do any more at the moment. We don't want him to become confused or agitated.'

'Otisk, I think you should relocate him and put him to bed in his student flat. Sounds like a man-to-man thing... I think Gortl might be embarrassed if he thought I had been involved in putting him to bed!'

'Good thinking, Francel, although we know that the transition to bed is just another relocation event. Nothing overtly physical happens! Anyway, if he enquires about it tomorrow morning, I can tell him what happened.'

'OK, I think we should start disengaging him from the Reception Capsule and then you can relocate him. You shouldn't be away for long, should you?'

'Definitely not. But even if we started to receive another incomer, I would be back before the active phase started. Anyway, you would advise me and I would return as quickly as possible. Meanwhile, I'll get him organised and arrange that he doesn't waken until 0730 hours tomorrow. That will give him time to sort himself out before we come to do the induction. He'll wake up knowing that we're coming, of course. All that agreed?'

'Agreed, Otisk.'

'See you soon, then.' Otisk linked to the Reception Capsule and made the disconnect. Then he placed his hand on the young man's arm and they both faded and disappeared.

The student flat was a compact living area, comprising a medium-sized lounge, a bedroom, a small kitchen and a bathroom. It overlooked a pleasant street with an attractive park beyond.

'This is nice,' Otisk thought, 'just what is required for a sixteen-year-old student.' Gortl was sound asleep in a comfortable lounge chair. Otisk relocated him to the bedroom, clothed him in pyjamas and tucked him up comfortably in bed. He knew that if Gortl had any problems in the night, he would know about them and relocate back to attend to him immediately, so he had no qualms about leaving him now. He scheduled the 0730 hours wake up and left a message to say that he and Francel would arrive at 0900 hours to induct him and answer all his questions. After a final check of the flat, he relocated back to RR5.

Francel looked up as he reappeared. 'You were quick! All quiet here. All well with Gortl?'

'Sleeping like a baby,' he smiled. 'He'll waken at 0730 and he'll know that we are coming to see him at 0900 hours. This gives him plenty time to wash, dress and have breakfast.'

'Perfect,' she said. 'All good so far?' They smiled at each other, part pride, part relief, part love.

* * * *

They had spent a rather restless night, inevitably disturbed at times by the new experiences of the day before and by their responsibility for Gortl. However, they knew they were tuned in to him, so if he had any problems during the night, they would be aware and ready to go to him if required. In the event, nothing happened.

Francel was up early, preparing for the induction.

'Just getting us organised,' she said to Otisk as his yawning figure appeared at the door of the kitchen. 'Checking to see that we have all the material and equipment that we need to give him.'

'There isn't a lot, is there?' He enquired. 'Just the same as we received, isn't it? The info-reader and the schedule reminder pack. It's very clever, that. You learn by your own experience. The most important thing is to send him out to explore and let him meet people, especially his fellow students. We'll just make sure he does that.' He continued to stand in the doorway. 'You know, I've been thinking, Francel.'

'Not too deeply, I hope!' She quipped.

He smiled briefly. 'Listen, Francel, I suddenly asked myself: "What age am I?"'

'Yes? What about it?'

'I discovered that I don't know what age I am. I tried my hardest to recall it but I can't remember! Do you know what age you are, Francel?'

'Eh, yes. Ah... it's...' she was silent for some seconds. 'I don't seem to know either!'

'There you are—you're just like me: you can't remember your age.'

'Well, I admit that does seem a bit peculiar. You would have thought we would know that, wouldn't you? Anyway, maybe nobody here knows their age.'

'But listen, we know Gortl's age; we know he's sixteen.'

She was silent for a moment. 'I see what you mean,' she said thoughtfully. Then she became brisk. 'OK, I think we've got to concentrate on Gortl at the moment. That's our primary responsibility. We'll return to the subject of our ages later.'

* * * *

0900 hours found them outside the large building that contained the students' flats. They had enjoyed the short walk from their house overlooking the Town Square.

'It's Flat 5-34C,' Otisk said, 'on the 5th level and overlooking the street and the park. Very pleasant. I hope he's pleased with it.' The elevator whisked them smoothly upwards and they found Gortl waiting for them at his open door. He looked happy and rested.

'Hello, Gortl,' Francel greeted him with a big smile. 'Here we are as promised. As you know, we've come to induct you this morning. That means we're going to give you an initial briefing about life here in this wonderful Land. When we've finished, you can ask us any questions you like. Meanwhile, how are you?' She put her arms around him and kissed him on the cheek.

Gortl seemed pleased by this attention. 'I'm absolutely fine, Francel. It's very nice to see you and Otisk. I slept very well and I feel really good. And this is a super flat. It's got everything in it that I need and, this morning, I have already met the two girls that live in the flat opposite. I heard them on the landing earlier and opened my door to see who it was. They were very friendly and they have promised to have a coffee with me this afternoon in the Town Square, wherever that is.'

'Don't worry,' Otisk said, 'we'll make sure you know where to go this afternoon to meet your new friends. Meanwhile, can we sit down and tell you the essentials about your life here?'

'Yes,' Gortl said, 'that would be great. I've made some coffee for us. I hope it's good. I just switched on the machine and it did it all automatically. Pretty neat, I thought!' He smiled.

'We'll be very pleased to have some of your coffee, Gortl. Bring it on!' Francel said.

They sat around a table. Otisk started the induction. 'First of all, this place is called Pazoten.' He wrote the name. 'It's pronounced like I just said it—three syllables, like the word "forgotten". It's a very large area of beautiful land, set in a valley between mountains. There are rivers and lakes too. Almost everyone in Pazoten lives here in the Town. Roads lead to all other parts of the Land; these radiate out from the Town and are known by their direction of travel—for instance the East Road runs east. Everyone in Pazoten can go anywhere they want and there are many forms of transport you can use. Furthermore, if you are in a hurry, you can choose to "relocate"—in other words you can transfer yourself instantly to wherever you want to go. However, you'll find that most people take a more leisurely approach to their transportation!' He nodded to Francel.

'Gortl, this flat is your home during the time you are in Pazoten. If there is anything you would like altered, this can be done without problem. Just let us know. As you are quite a young man, I can tell you that you will be a student in Pazoten. You may already have guessed that this is a building of student's flats and that all the people who live here (like your neighbours) are students. In due course, you will be contacted about your study schedules. As you know, Otisk and I are your Reception Team and we will retain an active interest in you. However, you will be looked after by a Monitoring Team from now on and they will contact you very soon. They will ensure you have everything you want and they will be available to you constantly.' She placed a small piece of equipment on the table. 'This is an info-reader. You just talk to it and it will supply you with information about Pazoten and your life here.' She looked at Otisk. 'Will you do the organisation brief, please?'

'Yes, of course,' he said. 'Gortl, the person in overall charge of Pazoten is the Leader. That's where all the policy decisions come from. However, Pazoten is run by six Counsellors, who are very experienced people in our community. They are our wise men and women who make administrative decisions for the Land and all the people in it. They keep watch over everything and intervene when required. You may meet them from time to time. That is the end of the induction briefing.'

'Do you have any questions, Gortl?' Francel asked.

Gortl looked at them both. 'You know, I thought I would have lots and lots of questions. But somehow, I feel you've covered everything. I'm really surprised.'

'That's great, Gortl, it means that we are doing our job properly.' Francel smiled at the young man. 'We would like you to go out after we leave and wander around the Town. Remember, you can go anywhere. By the way, the Town Square is quite near here. Go out the entrance of your building, turn right and keep walking until you come to it. You can't miss it. Your friends will no doubt be going to the large café in the Square. When you go out, you will meet many people who will recognise you as a new incomer and offer to help you. Once you know the Town, you can begin to explore the country—but there's plenty time for that. You are very important to us and it is our function to make sure you have no problems.'

'Thanks, Francel and Otisk. It's really good to know you as my guides and friends. I'll look forward to meeting you again soon.'

Otisk and Francel smiled at each other, knowing that Gortl's thoughts were already fixed on his meeting with the two girls who were his close neighbours!

* * * *

As they left the student accommodation, they made contact with Gortl's Monitoring Team and suggested that they should meet at the café in the Town Square. Within fifteen minutes, they were all sitting in the sunshine around a table in front of the café, refreshing themselves with cold drinks. The Monitoring Team, a young man and woman, received all Gortl's details and the responsibility transfer was completed smoothly.

'You know where we are if you need us,' Otisk said finally.

'Yes, but I doubt there will be any problem,' the pair replied. 'We find that this age group settles down well and usually link up with members of the opposite sex before long. That focusses their interests positively!'

'Well, it works for us!' Otisk said with an enigmatic smile.

'And us!' the man and woman looked at each other fondly, 'so why shouldn't it work for them, too.' Shortly after, the Monitoring Team had excused themselves and left Francel and Otisk. 'Just got to do our rounds, you know. Goodbye, a pleasure to meet you.'

* * * *

It was lunchtime and they were at home.

'Otisk?'

'Yes?'

'If we're free this afternoon, I would like to go shopping for a camera. Photography is my hobby, you know.'

'Hm, that's interesting. A hobby that comes from your past life, just like my painting? I know I haven't done any painting as yet but I know it's something I enjoy. As you know, I did buy some equipment soon after I arrived here and I'll certainly want to use it in the future. I'm sure there are some very interesting pictures to be painted around Pazoten.'

'Equally,' she said, 'I'm sure there are some very fine photographs to be taken, too.'

'Do you know what sort of camera you would like, Francel? There are so many different types. I wouldn't know what to buy.'

'Well, I know I want a good camera. One with a good digital resolution so that the print can be enlarged. You know, Otisk, cameras used to be solely optical, with images recorded on celluloid film. But now, digital cameras are extremely good and I definitively intend to go for that type. The old optical cameras wasted a great deal of film, you know, whereas with digital cameras you just discard all the images you don't want—erase them, you know?'

'Right, Francel, you seem to be something of an expert on photography, so I'll be fascinated to see how you get on. Shall we go to that camera shop that's on the way to the Administrative Centre? They had a really large display of cameras in their shop window.'

'Yes, I think we'll go there, see what they have and listen to what is suggested.'

It did not take them long to reach the camera shop. They paused by the large display window to look closely at the many cameras and other photographic equipment artistically displayed inside.

'Francel, do you remember I told you about my very first purchase and how I asked the shopkeeper awkward questions?'

Francel smiled. 'Yes, I do remember, Otisk. After that, I think you concluded you would need to be a bit more careful. And more diplomatic!'

'That's right, Francel, I did; but the shopkeeper said that people never asked to buy what they couldn't afford, remember? He implied that this information was automatically given to them by the Pazoten Financial Authorities. He didn't know how—and he didn't want to, either! In fact, he didn't want to talk about it at all.'

'So...?' She looked at him quizzically.

'Well, as you look at this display of cameras, do you feel you have any financial restriction? I mean, if you look at the most expensive camera in this window, do you feel that you can afford it?'

'Ah, that's interesting,' she said, 'just give me a minute.' She scanned the window. 'No, Otisk, I have no feeling or communication from anywhere that there are cameras here that I cannot afford.'

'Excellent, Francel! That's significant, isn't it? I know that our Reception Team function is reputed to be a "well-paid" one—we were told that at the briefing, weren't we? But it's certainly very interesting to test it out.'

She embraced him affectionately. 'Poor old Otisk—always testing the system!'

He grinned. 'Well, you know I like to know how things work.'

Arm in arm, they entered the shop, to find they were the only customers.

'Hello Francel and Otisk.' A jovial middle-aged man came from the rear of the shop with outstretched hand. 'I'm the shopkeeper here. How may I help you today?'

'I am thinking of buying a camera, Janest.' Francel said, sensing his name as he had done with them.

'Well, my friends, you've certainly come to the right place. I reckon I have the very best selection of photographic equipment in Pazoten. And, if you want any advice on what type of camera you're thinking of, I should be able to help you. What do you want to do with your camera? Is it for you, Francel?' She nodded. 'Is it just for taking nice snaps of people and places? Perhaps a nice little camera to slip into your handbag? I've got all the makes here— Olympus, Sony, Panasonic, Cannon, Nikon... and many others; I've got all the model ranges, too. Now, let me see...' he looked at her appraisingly, 'I would probably suggest a Panasonic Lumix or a Sony Cyber-Shot for you.'

With well-practiced movements, the man lifted two small cameras from glass shelves behind him and placed them rather triumphantly on the counter in front of Francel. 'Both of these are well built, small and light, good lens and digital resolution...; or you might prefer a Nikon Coolpix—slightly bigger but an excellent little camera, too. Shall I...?' The man gestured towards a display case.

'Have you got a Leica S?' Francel's words stopped the shopkeeper in his tracks! His face went pale. 'What?' he said faintly.

'A Leica S. Have you got one? And what lenses have you got for it?' Francel's voice was calm.

'Ah...' the man was totally taken aback. 'Ah... well, I do have one but it isn't on display,' he said finally. 'No-one has ever asked me for one before...' He looked at Francel doubtfully. 'You do know it's very expensive?'

'Yes, I do,' she replied resolutely. 'Can you show it to me?'

They waited until he returned with a large impressive box. From layers of plastic and moulded packaging, he unpacked the substantial black camera body reverently, a vision of smooth ergonomic curves. Deftly, he installed the battery and then unpacked a lens which he snapped into the camera body. 'This is the Vario-Elmar 30-90mm ASPH lens and the fixing is the latest bayonet system,' he said as he handed the completed camera to Francel. Otisk was surprised and very impressed to see her examining the camera critically and professionally, testing the operation of the various controls, checking the image on the screen and through the viewfinder, taking a number of photographs and studying the result gravely.

'Very nice, excellent quality and spec of course,' she said as she handed the camera back to Janest, 'but far too heavy for my purposes. I want a camera to weigh much less than this. However, I need a good digital resolution and a really flexible lens. What would you recommend?'

The shopkeeper looked at her with considerable respect. 'Well, the Canon EOS range is very good, although the high-spec models can still be quite heavy. What sort of resolution are you looking for?'

'I would be happy with 25 megapixels if the weight was around 500 or 600 grams,' she replied.

The shopkeeper began to pore over tables of specifications on his data screen, working his way through many camera descriptions. 'Ah,' he said finally, 'perhaps you should look at a Nikon. It's 24 megapixels so it's a very high-spec camera. And I think it's the lightest of the cameras with that specification. It comes with a Nikkor AF-S 18-55mm lens—a good flexible lens. Shall I show you?'

Francel tested the camera carefully, operating all its functions and taking some photographs which she studied very carefully. 'I think this is perfect for my purposes,' she told the delighted shopkeeper. 'Thanks very much for your advice, Janest. I'll take this, thank you. Now, I need a case, a tripod and some other accessories...'

Meanwhile, Otisk had been examining some binoculars on display. 'Could I just take these outside to test them?' he said to the shopkeeper.

'Yes, of course—but which ones are those? Ah, yes, these are a very good specification, 10x50 which gives you ten magnification with a good wide field of view. Furthermore, they are waterproof, designed for extreme conditions. Coincidentally, you have chosen Nikon, same as Francel's camera.'

Otisk went outside for a few minutes. When he returned, he said, 'Yes, these are what I want. I'll take them.'

They left the shop, joyfully carrying the range of items they had bought.

'Let's go home right away, Otisk. I can't wait to read all the instructions and specifications and become the complete expert!'

Otisk smiled at her fondly. 'Looks like I won't be seeing much of you this evening,' he joked. 'I hope there will be room on the table for the delicious dinner I'm going to cook for us.'

She stopped and kissed him on his cheek. 'There will always be room for you, Otisk. Just tell me to move if I'm in your way.'

'Well, I might have to—but I will be very diplomatic.'

Chapter 5

Otisk and Francel had really enjoyed the evening before. After poring over instruction books and specification sheets for hours, Francel was now a true expert on her Nikon camera.

'It's absolutely wonderful, Otisk. Easily the best camera I have ever had!' she had said.

'That great, Francel. But can you remember any other camera you have had?'

She paused and looked at him gravely. 'No, I can't. Isn't that astounding? I obviously know a lot about cameras and taking pictures, yet I cannot remember anything about the past. Anything before Pazoten, that is. This is what we've been talking about before, isn't it?'

'Yes, it is. But let's forget that for now, because I'm about to serve you the best dinner you have ever had—I hope,' he added.

'I'm sure it will be masterful,' she replied as she cleared all her books and equipment from the table. 'I'm starving.'

After breakfast the next morning, they turned their minds back to the question that Otisk had posed the day before.

'Francel, we know that you can't remember anything about your previous cameras, even though it is obvious you are an expert on photography...'

'Hey, just a minute, I'm not so sure about expert—but, yes, you're right, I have no specific memory at all but I do know about cameras and taking photographs. Strange, isn't it?'

'Certainly is,' he agreed. 'However, let's get back to the more fundamental questions I was asking yesterday. I think we had a good starting point there. Let's ask you again, Francel. What age are you?'

Francel screwed up her face in thought. 'For just a moment there, I thought I might be twenty-six but now I don't think so. That number sort of came to me as a flash of information and then disappeared immediately.'

'So do you think you might be older or younger than twenty-six?'

'Sorry, Otisk. I really don't know. I could be any age, really.'

'Well, no, I don't think that's true. You couldn't be sixty, for instance; nor twelve.'

'Thank goodness for that! I don't want to be older or younger than I am! How old do you think I look?'

Otisk's heart sank! He knew there was danger in that question! He looked at her, trying to calculate the odds on the success of his reply! 'Ah... I would say that you are in your twenties,' he said truthfully, hoping this would be acceptable. He was relieved when she smiled.

'I think you are in that age range, too,' she said, looking at him fondly.

They sat for a minute or two, engrossed in thought.

'OK, we can guess at our ages but that doesn't take us any further forward,' Otisk said. 'I know, I'll ask my info-reader. That's probably a sensible place to start.'

He connected to his info-reader and gave the command:

'Display my age.'

"Your age is not available." An instant reply.

'Explain.'

"It is not included in the Level-1 data store."

'Access my full database.'

"Full database accessed."

'How many items are there in the full database?'

"263"

'In what categories?'

"All categories. Past, Present, Future. Physical, Psychological, Intellectual, Spiritual. Then many sub-categories below."

'From full database, display my age.'

"Your age is not available."

'Explain.'

"Your age is barred information."

The door chime sounded and Francel permitted the caller to enter, after noting with surprise that it was Counsellor Begiet. She entered the room silently.

Otisk disconnected from the info-reader. 'Good morning, Counsellor,' he said warmly. 'This is a great pleasure. Can we offer you a coffee?'

'Yes, thank you, Otisk, you are very kind,' the Counsellor smiled serenely in reply.

Soon, they were all sitting comfortably, sipping their coffees.

'How may we help you? Is this ART business? I hope you found our work with Gortl satisfactory?' Otisk was a little worried. Had the Counsellor found them wanting in some way?

Counsellor Begiet smiled. 'Your first incomer was handled beautifully,' she said, much to their relief. 'No, this is not ART business. I understand you have been searching for your age?'

Otisk was startled! This was the last thing he expected. This is what he had been engaged upon at the very moment she arrived. 'Goodness, that was quick,' he thought.

'Er... yes,' he faltered, 'neither Francel nor I can remember what age we are and, since everyone's age is important to them, we thought we would like to find out—be reminded of it, you know. After all, we know Gortl's age. It seems extremely peculiar that we should know our incomer's age but not our own, don't you think?' Otisk finished on an upbeat note of triumph: surely Counsellor Begiet could not disagree with the logic of his case?

The woman sat silently for a moment or two; then she lifted her head. 'You put your case very well, Otisk, but you're forgetting one thing. You are here in Pazoten. And, in Pazoten, things are different. I know you have already headed towards that conclusion, because you have discussed it with Francel. You are very well-matched, you two!' She smiled quickly at Francel and turned back to Otisk. 'You suggested that dimensions, by which you mean parameters, may be different in Pazoten. In fact, you used the words "not finite" which, as you know, may be interpreted rather differently from its apparent word twin "infinite". I must say, I thought that was very clever of you, Otisk. Furthermore, I have to say that not many of those who come to Pazoten ever suggest that such ingenious elegance is possible. Now, I must tell you right away that it is not appropriate for me to go into the reality of Pazoten. That is only in the aegis of the Leader. However, I can say that that the reality of Pazoten is different from any other reality that either of you will have experienced before.'

Now she paused for a moment before continuing. 'So I would ask you to listen carefully as I turn to the question of your age. You know from your info-reader enquiries that your personal database contains 263 parameters allocated to a comprehensive range of categories. All these data are used by the Leader to ensure an optimum path for you while you are in Pazoten. Because of the unique reality that attaches to Pazoten, some of the parameters are not only irrelevant to the individual but conform only to the reality of Pazoten. Age is one of these. That is why the value is withheld.'

Otisk was silent for a time as he considered everything that the Counsellor had said. 'OK,' he said finally, 'Of course I accept what you say, although I cannot comprehend the concept of "unique reality"—not yet, anyway. However, I can appreciate that things are different in Pazoten. Francel and I have already accepted that obvious fact.' He paused, then continued: 'So, thank you very much for your explanation and for coming here personally to explain all this to us. It was really nice to see you again.'

'Right, Otisk and Francel, I give you my blessings and I know you have already become a very fine Reception Team. So I will leave you now. I have work elsewhere and I must relocate there immediately.' As soon as she had finished speaking, the Counsellor faded and disappeared.

They sat looking at each other. Francel was the first to speak. 'So what do you think, Otisk? Are you content with that explanation?'

'Well, I do think it was nice to have an explanation from such an important source.'

'So you're happy to drop it? Forget about what age you are?'

'Certainly not!' He turned to her with an impish grin. 'I would still like to know what age I am, wouldn't you?'

'Yes,' Francel said doubtfully, 'but that information is not available to us.'

'Yes it is.' He was still smirking.

'How?' She was incredulous.

'From Branea and Bitzo, of course. My Reception Team,' he exploded. 'I may not know how old I am—but they do! They got that information from the manifestation warnings. I'll call them and ask if we can get together with them later today. We had better not use the café in the Main Square—Gortl might be there with his lady friends and he might think we're spying on him. I think we had better go to the café down by the river. Then, after I have discovered what age I am, we'll do exactly the same with your Reception Team. Then we'll both know. Won't that be nice?'

* * * *

In the warm afternoon sunshine, Otisk and Francel were sitting in the tranquil setting of the café by the river. Earlier, Otisk had contacted Bitzo and Branea. 'Francel and I would love you to join us for a drink at the café by the river. I have an important question to ask you. No, it's not a difficult question. It's an easy one! But it's something I need to know.' So Bitzo and Branea promised to come to the café that afternoon.

Soon they were exchanging stories about their work in RR5. Branea and Bitzo had had a very exciting time on their previous shift. Two incomers had manifested almost simultaneously. Of course they had split up and carried out Single Reception Procedures ('not as good as normal two-handed teamwork but the best we could do in the circumstances.' Branea's aside to Francel.) Then, just as they were getting on top of the relocating phase, another incomer began to manifest and they had to call in the Standby Reception Team.

'That's the very first time we've ever had to do that,' Bitzo laughed, 'but there was nothing for it. There was no way we could handle a third incomer at that moment. I must say, the SRT could not have more charming, even although it was the middle of the night! We gave them our thankful blessings before we left. I must say, we both slept very well after that shift.'

'I'm glad that all our shifts are not like that!' Branea added with a grimace.

Bitzo now turned to Otisk. 'Now, Otisk, what was this easy question you wanted to ask us?'

'Oh, Bitzo, it's really simple—what age am I?'

Bitzo looked thoughtful as he looked at Otisk with a steady gaze. 'What age are you, Otisk?' he repeated thoughtfully, without taking his eyes off him.

'Yes, how old am I, Bitzo?'

After a short pause, Bitzo said: 'Sorry, Otisk, I don't know what age you are.' He turned to Branea. 'Do you know what age Otisk is, Branea?'

She thought for a moment. 'No, Bitzo, I'm afraid I don't. Is it something we should know? I've never been asked that before.'

'Bitzo turned back to Otisk. 'Sorry, Otisk. Neither of us know. Why don't you ask your info-reader?'

'Bitzo, the info-reader won't tell me. It's barred information, it says. But listen, Bitzo, you *must* know. It's part of the basic information that Reception Teams are given when manifestation commences.'

'Is it, Otisk? I must say I don't remember.'

Otisk turned to Branea who was deep in conversation with Francel. 'Sorry, Branea, could I interrupt? When a manifestation starts, the display gives the Reception Team the age of the incomer, you know? You must have seen it plenty times.'

'Does it, Otisk? I'll take your word for it but I must say I really don't remember. Bitzo, yesterday, when we started our manifestations, did it give us the age of the incomers?'

Bitzo pondered. 'It might have, Branea, but I don't think so,' he said finally.

'I don't think so, either. Sorry, Otisk.'

'Listen, my friends, I can assure you that it does. For instance, we looked after our first incomer yesterday and he was a young man of...' He paused and looked embarrassed. 'Francel, sorry, what age is Gortl? You know, it was displayed in the basic manifestation data.'

'Oh yes, we were told his age. It was...' she stopped. 'That's weird, Otisk. I can't remember. We know he's quite a young man. A teenager, I would say. But now I cannot seem to recall his exact age.'

Otisk looked stricken. 'Neither can I, Francel.'

'Right, both,' Branea's decisive tones now broke the short silence, 'if that was the important question you wanted to ask, I'm afraid we don't know the answer. Sorry about that. Anyway, not knowing your age is hardly the end of the world, is it? After all, Branea and I don't know our own ages either. It's not a matter of concern to us. We're quite happy as we are. I suggest you just forget about it. Now, I'm afraid we need to go to another meeting.' Branea and Bitzo got up. 'Hope to see you soon. Goodbye for now.

Thanks for the drinks. Our blessings upon you.' They waved cheer-fully and relocated.

Otisk and Francel sat disquieted and wordless. After some minutes Otisk spoke very quietly. 'OK, Francel, maybe I'm just beginning to understand how they do it. Yes, we do see the age of the incomer as basic data and then use it for our approach and, specifically for the accommodation and occupation procedures. Then, when our incomer has been inducted and is content, his age information is wiped from our memories. Within a short time, we are made to forget it! This means that age is irrelevant in Pazoten. That's essentially what Counsellor Begiet told us. But I don't see why it should be.'

Francel took his hand. 'That sounds right to me, Otisk. Look, I know you can get wound up about things like this but, really, it's not worth it. If that's the way things are in Pazoten, then we just need to accept it and forget it. Move on, you know?'

Otisk smiled at her. 'Thanks, Francel, of course you're right. But it is annoying, isn't it?'

She squeezed his hand. 'Let's go home and have a relaxing evening... and night,' she added.

* * * *

The following day was a rest day for them. Immediately after breakfast, they remote-checked Gortl and found him happy and contented. As an attractive teenager, he was already well-integrated with his fellow students, most of whom lived in the student flats around him. Also, he had registered for courses at the College nearby and was about to go there for lectures and instruction. The two girls across the landing were going to show him the way. Gortl was very pleased about that!

'I think we can safely leave him alone,' Francel said with a smile. 'His Monitoring Team will already be in full contact with him. I feel sure that Gortl will not be disturbing them or us today!'

'Yes, it's good to see that he's doing well. I suggest we have a day of exploration out in the country, Francel. My info-reader tells us that it should be possible for us to rent a car and go for a nice long drive. How would you like to do that?'

'I would love that. Shall I get a picnic to take with us, Otisk? I'm sure we should be able to find a nice spot to enjoy ourselves far away from the Town bustle. Of course I'll take my camera.'

'And I'll take my artist's equipment, too. I might try a country scene.'

Half an hour later, they approached one of the large car dealerships that was located not far from the Town Square.

'I don't know what the procedure is here,' Otisk said, 'let's go in and make some enquiries.'

They entered the lavish car showroom which had marble floors and acres of tinted glass all around. Gleaming high-quality motor vehicles of every size, style and colour covered the huge floor area. The range covered everything from small compact vehicles to massive stretch limousines. Every style was there; saloons, estates, hard and soft-top coupes, gorgeous sports cars, majestic SUVs, etc.

'Wow!' Otisk murmured, 'these are pretty smart-looking cars! They walked around and looked at the various makes and models. 'You know, Francel, these are the top models from most of the quality motor manufacturers. They really are gorgeous. All of these are obviously brand new. They must be for sale, although I don't see any price displays on them. I imagine you need a great deal of credit to afford one of these.'

Francel was also looking around. 'Yes, these are top-of-the-range cars, obviously. However, I've been thinking. I can't remember the make and model of any "ordinary" cars, can you?'

Otisk look slightly crestfallen. (Men like to be very car-knowledgeable!) 'Well, no, neither can I, just at this moment. However,' he continued firmly, 'I'm sure that we aren't looking for one of these gorgeous vehicles. We're looking for a rental car. Rental cars are usually well-worn and more than a little battered! Look, there's an office over there. Let's go over and find someone to help us.'

They walked between the rows of gleaming models and approached the office. Inside, two men were watching their approach from behind large elegant desks.

'Can you help us?' Otisk called out as they arrived at the door.

'Yes, of course we can.' One of the men sprang to his feet and approached to shake their hands cordially. 'Welcome to Town Auto One. I'm Morseb, the Principal Manager here. We are honoured by your visit, Francel and Otisk. We are the biggest and best car dealership in the Town and you are making the best choice if you deal with us. We have the best range of cars. We have the best service, too, and we cannot do enough for our customers. Whatever you want, we will supply it. You will always be extremely pleased if you deal with us, I promise you that: 100% satisfaction is guaranteed – that's our motto.' Finally the man stopped and cocked his head invitingly, waiting for Otisk or Francel to speak.

'Well,' Otisk responded, 'we haven't been here before and so we are not familiar with the procedure.'

'Yes, of course we recognise that you are new customers. That's why we didn't approach you right away. We thought you would want to have a good look around first.'

'There are certainly some lovely vehicles here,' Otisk said, looking around admiringly.

'Yes, we pride ourselves on have the best model range in the Town,' the man said. 'Did anything catch your eye?'

'Well, there are at least a dozen cars here I could easily take home!' Otisk joked.

'Of course, everything is possible,' the man said smoothly. 'If you wanted a number of cars, we could certainly meet your requirements. Were you looking to buy some cars?'

'No, no – sorry – I was just joking. I was just complimenting you on your stock. We just want to rent a car for the day.' Otisk felt rather small as he admitted that.

'Of course,' the man was smiling broadly. 'Very few people actually buy the cars. Really, our buyers are people who want to take the vehicle home and lavish constant care and attention upon it. Wash it, polish it, sometimes every day. Study the detailed engineering. Some customers even have hydraulic lifts put in their garages so that they can examine the underside of the car. And, of course, they spend considerable amounts of time sitting in the car and dreaming—that sort of thing. Most of our customers just rent a car for whatever period that suits them. Which car would you like?'

'Could you advise us about the car rental range?' Otisk asked.

'Sorry,' the man looked puzzled. 'I don't understand…?'

'Well, you're not renting these cars, are you?' Otisk said crisply. 'Where are the details of the rental fleet?'

The man looked puzzled. 'Sorry, Sir. Rental fleet? There is no rental fleet.'

'I mean—the cars you *rent*. You do rent cars from here, don't you?' Otisk was becoming exasperated.

'Yes, of course we do. We rent these cars.' The man swept his arm around to encompass the showroom.

'But all these cars are brand new and high-quality models,' Otisk said, rather faintly.

'Of course, Sir. We only have the best. Which one would you like to take? It is absolutely your choice.'

The formalities had been incredibly simple. Otisk had consulted Francel and they had chosen a thrilling Mercedes SL500 Roadster, a vision in sparkling silver.

'Will you be the official renter for the records?' the man asked Otisk.

'Yes, I will, thanks.'

'Fine,' said the man. 'It's done. You may both drive the car. We know you are both capable drivers. Here are the keys. Most of the locks are remote and automatic. The car is waiting outside, fully fuelled. There is a map of Pazoten in the car. I suggest you go on the North Road. The scenery is very good in the north. Enjoy your-selves. We'll see you this evening when you return.'

'Do you need any other information from me? Do I need to sign anything?' Otisk asked.

The man shook his head. 'No, Sir. We already have all your details, Sir, and they have been recorded.'

They had gone outside and found the car, roof cleverly folded away, sitting in the bright sunshine, to their eyes a perfect piece of automotive sculpture.

'Goodness,' Otisk was bowled over. 'I thought we would be driving out of here in some sort of old banger, not in a brand new super-expensive sports car. Pazoten is great, isn't it?'

'Yes, it really is, Otisk. Although, now that I think about it, the few vehicles I have seen in Pazoten have all been in pristine condi-tion. That goes for the public vehicles, too. I think old and battered cars may not exist, here.'

'Would you like me to drive, Francel?'

'Yes, please. I shall just sit here and look superior.'

The engine started with a sophisticated purr. 'Hm, that's a V8 if I ever heard one,' Otisk said happily, 'they make a distinctive sound. This is a very powerful car, you know. However, I don't plan to do any fast driving, I think you will be glad to hear!'

'Well, Otisk, just remember that I don't know what sort of a driver you are. So I think you should try to impress me.'

'So it's up the road at 100 miles an hour, is it?' he joked.

She emitted a little fake scream. 'Just the opposite, please!' She unfolded the map of Pazoten. 'Just a moment, Otisk, let's check where we should go.'

They both scrutinised the map carefully. 'Ah yes,' he said, 'we are here,' he pointed. 'We turn right and keep going until we arrive at this circular road. It's called the Ring Road and it encloses the Town. All the other roads radiate outwards from the Ring Road. So if we turn left on to the Ring Road and keep going round until we turn right on to the North Road. Are you happy with that, Navigator Francel?'

'Looks simple enough, Captain! Let's roll!'

Otisk slipped the gear lever into Drive, released the parking brake and the car whispered forward. He then turned right and headed for the Ring Road. A few moments later, they had to pause briefly at traffic signals before joining the Ring Road. Traffic was quite light and the car glided serenely over the smooth surface. After they had crossed several intersections, Francel indicated that the next major intersection in the Ring Road should be their right turn to North Road. A large sign gave them warning of their turnoff in good time and soon they turned smoothly into North Road. Before long, houses gave way to farmland. In the far distance, they could see a range of mountains. Otisk increased the car's speed to around 60 mph.

'This really is the life,' he commented, with a happy smile of satisfaction, 'driving along in a wonderful open top car in the warm sunshine with the person you love sitting beside you. I would say this is just perfection, wouldn't you, Francel. I'm so glad that we thought of doing this on our free day. It's absolutely magical.'

Well, Otisk, this was your idea and how very pleasant it is! Who would have thought we would get such a splendid car? Could there be a better car than this one? It's so smooth. And even though it's an open sports car, there's no wind buffeting.'

'Well that's because it's so aerodynamically designed, Francel. Everything is designed to be perfect.'

At first, the road had been straight but now it curved around the various contours of the ground, carrying them ever closer to the high ground in front of them. They met very few vehicles and there was little activity at the farms they passed. Once or twice, they saw a tractor working in the fields while in many fields, contented animals could be seen grazing or resting on the warm ground.

'Francel stretched luxuriously. 'You know, Otisk, it really is perfection out here. I'm enjoying this so much.'

He glanced across at her. 'Do you want to drive, Francel? I really recommend this car. It's easy to drive.'

'Maybe later,' she replied, 'I'm just enjoying being a passenger so much.'

Eventually, the car had climbed to higher ground although the mountains were still in the distance. At this point, the road turned roughly parallel to the range of mountains and took them west.

'Look up there, Francel,' Otisk called out, 'there's a little road that leads up to a clearing that should have an excellent view across the valley. Shall I drive up there and have a look? If we like it, we can have our picnic lunch there.'

'Oh, yes. That looks nice. Let's try it.'

It proved to be the ideal spot for a picnic. Otisk parked the car in the shade of a large tree. He operated the roof control and the panels of the roof extended from the boot to click perfectly into place and lock. Otisk was very impressed: 'What an elegant piece of engineering,' he thought.

'Look at this, Francel. It's not only an open top roadster. Now it's a closed coupé—and it looks wonderful as both!'

'Yes, of course it does, darling.' (A woman's reaction!) 'Why did you close it up?'

'To keep the insects and animals out of the car,' he said, adding, 'and I did want to see how the automatic roof worked. Impressive.'

'Yes, Otisk, I'm sure it is.' She was making ready the picnic. 'Come and eat.'

They had eaten and drunk their fill. They had relaxed and dozed off a little. Now they both sat up, looking at the panorama before them.

'How beautiful it all is,' he said. 'How superb! You know, I'm going to stop questioning all this. I'm just going to accept the wonder of it all. After all, in life, we aren't supposed to be able to understand everything, are we?'

Francel smiled tenderly at him. 'No, Otisk, my love, we aren't.' She knew he would never stop questioning. 'And neither will I,' she thought. Then she stood up purposely.

'What's up, Francel? You going somewhere?'

'It's photograph time, Otisk,' she said, 'time to exercise my new camera and burnish my photographic skills. Comb your hair, my darling, because you will certainly be in some of the pictures. In fact, you will *be* the picture at times. I will always want to be reminded of you when you're not with me.'

'Goodness, I'd better get myself tidied up,' he said. 'Must put my best foot forward.'

Half an hour later, Francel had taken many photographs of Otisk and their surroundings. Now she reviewed her work seriously, deleting many frames as she did so.

'Hey, Francel! You'll have none left!' Otisk joked. 'Maybe you shouldn't be hasty.'

'I'm not being hasty, Otisk,' she replied serenely, 'I'm being professional. I know which ones are likely to be successful and I'm keeping all these. The others are flawed or inferior so they should be disposed of.'

'Goodness,' he said, 'you're a real professional. I would keep everything!'

'That's just what amateurs do all the time!' she teased.

'I think I'll try a little oil painting from that spot over there, Francel. I'm not sure whether I'll be able to achieve much. I don't feel very confident. Anyway, here goes:' he set up his equipment and soon was hard at work, sketching the scene before him, while she watched him affectionately from her chair.

'Come and have a look at my first attempt, Francel. Don't expect anything very great, however. I feel that I'm handing the paint very clumsily.'

Francel was pleasantly surprised when she saw his work. His painting was in a very modern style, using unusual colours and bold brush strokes. Overall, the effect was dramatic and striking, while accurately capturing the feel of the scene before them. 'That's extremely good, Otisk. I really mean it. You obviously have considerable talent. I'm really surprised. You had me convinced that you would produce something very unskilled. This has a unique, bold and professional touch about it. Congratulations on being so skilled and talented.'

He flushed deeply with pleasure. 'Stop, please! You'll make me conceited.'

She kissed him lightly. 'I mean it, Otisk. It's really good. But you know that, don't you?'

He looked at the painting critically. 'Well, it's OK—but it could be better.'

* * * *

Now they prepared to leave their idyllic spot. She had cleared up their picnic. He had packed away his artist's equipment. He lowered the roof of the car, once again marvelling at its elegant operation! Soon, they were ready to leave.

'Do you want to drive the car, Francel?'

She considered this. 'Well, I suppose I should. It's not difficult, is it?'

'Very easy,' he said. 'It's automatic. It changes its own gears—all seven of them! You don't need to do anything except press the accelerator and brake. And steer of course; you'll love it.'

She did love it. It was so smooth, easy and well-behaved. 'I can't remember what cars I have driven in the past,' she said as they bowled along, 'but I'm sure they were nothing like this.'

'That's what I think, too.' Otisk looked at her with admiration and love as she drove the car with smoothness and expertise. 'You are obviously a wonderful driver,' he said.

'So are you,' she said, 'and I'm handing this lovely car back to you now. According to the map, this road meets the Northwest Road in about 10 miles or so. If we turn left there, that will eventually take us back to the Town.'

Early evening saw them back in the Town, handing in the car at Town Auto One.

'I trust everything was satisfactory?' Morseb asked unctuously.

'Excellent. We'll certainly come to you when we want a car again,' Otisk smiled.

'As you know, Sir, "100% satisfaction is guaranteed." It's our motto.' Morseb said proudly.

* * * *

Dinner together had been delightful and they sat looking out of their large window at the bustling scene in the Town Square below.

Otisk stretched languidly. 'I'm just going to enjoy all this,' he said contentedly. Then he looked at Francel. 'And, especially, I'm just going to enjoy you!' His smile was radiant. 'And—you know what—I'm not going to worry about anything. I'm a changed man, I promise.'

She smiled back at him.

Chapter 6

Otisk and Francel had settled very comfortably into their important roles as members of a Reception Team, where they found their functions completely absorbing and fulfilling. At the same time, they took full advantage of their off-duty times, visiting various places of entertainment (cinemas, clubs), keeping fit by going to the gym and sometimes attending church on Sunday when free (somehow, the church appeared to provide for all religions). Of course they also continued their exploration of Pazoten. And, within all these activities, they continued to enjoy each other's company—very much.

Their duty times in RR5 came round three or four times a week, when they covered their six hour shifts during various spans of day or night. Of course, these hours were not the only work they had to do. There were also the incomer aftercare duties, the induction procedure and the handover to the designated Monitoring Teams. On most shifts, they received one or even two incomers; usually, the two incomers were spaced sufficiently far apart to give them no problems. On the other hand, there had twice experienced a much closer spacing and had been compelled to split up and apply Single Reception Procedures. Both agreed that Single Reception was rather less satisfactory for the arrivals.

'The incomers are more reassured when they see two people,' Francel had opined. 'I think it gives them a more balanced welcome.'

'I think that's true,' Otisk had agreed, 'and it spreads the load for us. It means we can be more sensitive to the incomer's needs because one of us is always in Observation Mode while the other is in Active Procedure.'

'I sometimes wonder what the other Reception Teams do. The training doesn't cover this specifically—it just leaves each team to work out what they believe to be the best procedure for the incomer's arrival,' Francel said. 'But I do wonder. I suppose we could always ask at handover?'

Otisk thought about that. 'Well, I suppose there's no harm in it,' he said finally, 'but I think the teams are left alone to arrange their procedures in the best way that works for them and the incomer. That means variability and flexibility, doesn't it?'

'I suppose so,' Francel said; 'better forget it, I think.'

Today, they were reviewing the work they had done. They agreed that the vast majority of their incomers had been no problem—just like their very first, the student Gortl. As their very first incomer, they always remembered him with affection! As time passed, they had found that their techniques, imparted to their minds by their initial download training, had been refined as they learned the very best way to function together.

'The main thing is to keep them calm and reassured. You just watch their eyes and body language and act quickly to stop them imaginatively travelling somewhere that would be detrimental for them,' Francel said. 'If you're able to do that, a successful reception is pretty well guaranteed, isn't it?'

'Yes,' Otisk agreed, 'observation and sensitivity is the key. Being tuned in.'

'Certainly.' She nodded. 'There is also a lot to learn from the few difficult cases we have had, though.'

'What do you count as your most tricky reception, Francel?'

'Definitely Uforta. Remember her? She was very young, just into our category, I suspect. What's yours?'

'It's got to be Brocks. He was quite a hard nut to crack, wasn't he? But for a different reason.'

* * * *

They were still relatively inexperienced when Uforta arrived. When the system advised them that that the incomer had reached Level 10 Awareness, they knew that Personal Interaction should commence. When they arrived at the Reception Capsule, they found a young, thin girl who was far from calm. In fact, she had not only left the Manifestation Seat but was attempting to break out of the capsule. Of course the force field made this impossible. She was extremely distressed. Her mouth was wide open and it was obvious that she was screaming and crying.

'Otisk, we have a serious problem here,' Francel said worriedly, 'I suggest you stand by out here where she can see you. I'll go in and apply calming techniques and we'll see how far I can rectify the situation.'

As soon as Francel entered the capsule, the girl stopped screaming and shrank against the back wall, shielding her face. 'Go away,' she shouted, 'you are evil. Don't come near me. I'll hurt you if you do. I know how. Don't come near me.'

Francel sat down on Seat 2 which was directly opposite the Manifestation Seat. 'It's fine, Uforta, it really is. You're safe here and nothing will hurt you, I promise. I'm Francel and that's my partner outside. He's called Otisk. We are your Reception Team. We're here to look after you and make sure that you have a very nice time while you're here with us. Come and sit down here and we'll have a chat. You can tell me what your problems are and I'll sort them out. I promise I will.' She gestured to the girl and pointed to the seat. 'Please come and sit down.'

'No, I won't,' the girl screamed in fury. 'Where am I? What is this place? Wherever it is, I don't want to be here. You have no right to bring me here and I'm going to complain about this and you'll be punished. Anyway, what's all this Uforta stuff? What's Uforta?'

'Uforta is your name. Look at the bracelet you are wearing around your wrist. You'll see it has your name printed on it. See? "Uforta". There it is. Look at this. This is mine. I'm Francel and here is my name printed on my bracelet. Just like yours.'

'Don't call me that! That's not my name. You've no right to call me that. I'm going to complain and...'

'So what is your name, Uforta?' Francel's voice was calm and soothing.

The girl was quiet for a few seconds. 'I don't know my name,' she said finally. 'But it isn't Uforta. I know that.'

'It *is* Uforta. It's on your bracelet. That's why you're wearing a bracelet. The bracelet is to tell everyone your name. We've all got them here. Everyone. Look—my partner Otisk has got his. It's exactly like yours and it's got his name printed on it. Come and sit down here. We can talk and I'll help you with all your problems. That's my job, Uforta.'

'I told you. My name isn't Uforta.' A quieter voice, now tinged with weariness. Clearly, the girl was tiring now, increasingly drained emotionally.

Observing this development, Francel rose to her feet and walked towards her.

'Don't come near me!' the girl screamed 'you're not allowed to come near me. It isn't allowed. If you do, I will complain and...'

Ignoring her words, Francel grasped the girl's thin arm gently. 'Come and sit here, Uforta. We can talk. I can sort everything out for you. Everything will be fine. I promise you.'

In response, the girl tore her arm from Francel's grasp and collapsed in a heap on the floor, pressing herself against the rear wall of the capsule and making herself as small as possible. 'No,' she screamed, 'I won't! Get away from me.'

Francel sat down on the floor, close beside her. She judged it was time to apply a different technique. 'Listen, Uforta, you have to get up and come back to the seat. You'll feel better when you do. I promise. And, listen to me carefully, I guarantee that I'll sort everything out for you. Everything will be fine. I'll make sure of that. I'm your friend.'

'Go away. I won't do it. Leave me alone.' A hysterical scream.

Francel was silent for a moment or two. She thought: 'Time for action.' She rested her hand on the girl's arm and said: 'Uforta, you cannot stay there, you know. I'm going to ask Otisk my partner to come in and he will lift you up from the floor and carry you over to the seat...'

'NO!' The girl screamed the word as loudly as she could. 'He mustn't. It's not allowed. He's not allowed to touch me or come anywhere near me. If he does I will complain and...'

Francel interrupted once more. 'Then get up, walk over and sit down on the seat, Uforta.'

Time passed. 'Otisk, would you come into the capsule, please. I need this girl to be carried to her seat.' Otisk entered. As soon as he appeared, the girl jumped to her feet and scuttled fearfully to the

Manifestation Seat where she sat down gingerly. Without a word, Otisk sat down in Seat 3, which was some distance from the girl.

'Thank you, Uforta,' Francel sat down in Seat 2, close to her. She took the girl's unresisting hands in hers. Then she applied her power. 'Now I just want you to relax and be good. You're feeling much happier now because you're among friends here. We are going to look after you and you are going to have a lovely time here. Right now you're feeling very sleepy, Uforta. So go to sleep. You'll feel wonderful when you wake up.'

Within a short time, the girl's eyes closed and she fell deeply asleep.

'Phew!' Francel looked across at Otisk and then closed her eyes too. 'I feel exhausted. I had to use all my power there to overcome her. I never thought I would need to use that technique but I'm very grateful I had it available.'

Otisk smiled at her. 'You were great, Francel. Absolutely wonderful.'

As Uforta slept heavily, they consulted with RT Administration and accommodation was agreed. Uforta would live with a family who had children around her age. She would attend their school.

'I'll take Uforta over there right now, Otisk. She'll sleep the rest of the night and she'll soon settle down under their influence. I'll let them know that she'll probably need a lot of loving at first but that she should soon be fine. I'll get back here very soon—as soon as I can.'

Francel placed a hand on the sleeping girl and relocated.

The following day, they were extremely relieved when a transformed Uforta met them at the family's house. They inducted her successfully and subsequently passed her over to her Monitoring Team. Francel was right. Uforta settled in well and was happy and contented in that loving family.

'Goodness, I remember Uforta well!' Francel concluded with a grimace. 'Your man Brocks was rather more recent, wasn't he? A new test for you!'

Otisk smiled ruefully. 'Yes. In many ways diametrically opposed to your Uforta. A completely different challenge, just to test us out; both of us, I think.'

* * * *

The usual chime had altered them. Brocks was commencing manifestation and was identified as an older man. (Of course, they could not remember the specific age now.) He was arriving in RP12. They prepared themselves and waited for the Level 10 Awareness Notification. Soon they were approaching the Reception Pod. They could see Brocks sitting in the seat. His eyes were closed and he was smiling. They entered the pod and the elderly man opened his eyes slowly, fixing his gaze on Francel.

'Ah,' he said in a gentle voice, 'you have arrived. I thought someone would be coming soon. It's very nice to see you although, I must admit I was perfectly happy here with my musings. I muse quite a lot, you see—it helps to pass the time.' He stopped and looked at them with a kind smile.

Otisk was gentle. 'I'm Otisk and this is Francel, Brocks. We are your Reception Team. We are here to look after you and ensure that you will be happy here with us. We are your friends.'

The man listened with close attention. 'Well, I must say, you are very kind and I am most appreciative. You seem like a very nice young man, Otisk, and your partner is very beautiful. That's the thing about young girls, they are so beautiful. I have always thought so, you know.' He addressed Francel. 'Francel, it is a great pleasure to meet you. You have a lovely name and I can feel you have a sweet and loving nature.'

Francel smiled, a little taken aback. 'Well, Brocks, I must say that you're the first incomer to tell me that! It's very nice of you.'

'Think nothing of it, my dear,' the man said, 'you are a pleasure to look at. Are you two lovely people married to each other?'

They looked at each other, a little lost for words. 'Well... ah... listen, Brocks, we certainly are together as a couple. We're not married however. We only met each other here.'

The man looked at them serenely. 'I understand,' he said kindly. 'You are true lovers, aren't you?' He looked at Otisk. 'I must say, I envy you, Otisk.' He paused and sighed deeply. 'Now, I hear you keep calling me "Brocks" and I have already spotted that name printed on this bracelet affair that I'm wearing, so I imagine that must be my name, is it?'

'Yes, Brocks, that's right. That's your name. You see, we all have our names on our bracelets. Everyone here has a bracelet identical to yours, except that it's got their name printed on it.' As he spoke, he showed Brocks the printed name on his own bracelet.

The man nodded serenely and sat back in the chair.

'Now Brocks, we just want you to take it easy before we move on to the next stage...'

Brocks opened his eyes sharply. 'The next stage, Otisk? What's the next stage?'

'Well, after you've rested for a while, we're going to look after you. Arrange where you're going the live, here, etc. Get you sorted out, you know. Just leave it all to me. Meanwhile, would you like to eat something? You must be hungry.' A delicious meal appeared beside Brocks' seat.

He looked at it. 'Well yes,' he said, 'now that you mention it, I am rather hungry and thirsty, so I accept your kind offer with pleasure.'

'That's it, Brocks, you eat and I'll go to work on your settlement here.'

'Otisk?

'Yes?'

'Could Francel stay here with me and talk to me? I would really like that.'

Otisk looked at Francel. 'Yes, OK,' she replied, 'if that's what you really want. I'll stay with you while you eat and then you can rest.'

'Fine,' the man said, 'I'll do anything you say.'

Otisk left them and Francel chatted to Brocks as he ate his meal.

'Just rest now, Brocks. We're going to look after you now.'

'Francel? Will you take my hand as I go to sleep?'

She hesitated. 'Well, OK, Brocks. Just this once.'

After consulting the Admin staff, Otisk returned to find Francel disengaging herself from Brocks' hand. 'He asked me specially and it seemed unkind to refuse,' she explained, somewhat discomfited.

'I've sorted out his accommodation and I'll relocate us over there in a little while. Meanwhile, Francel, I see we have another incomer on the way. First indication was about five minutes ago, so we've plenty time to deal with Brocks.'

They turned towards the man and found that he was sitting with his eyes wide open.

'That was nice,' he said quietly, 'I'm glad you're still here, Francel. So you have other work to do, Otisk. That's perfectly all right, Francel and I will just stay here. I'm perfectly content.'

'Well, that's nice to hear, Brocks. But I will shortly take you to a very nice house. This house will be yours for as long as you stay here with us.'

'You mean us three will be living together in this lovely house?'

'No, sorry, Brocks, I didn't mean that. When I said "us", I didn't mean Francel and I, I meant all the other people who live in this land. There are a lot of other people who live here, in a town. You'll find them all very nice and kind. All these people will be your friends.'

The man was silent for a few moments.

'I'm just going to stay here with Francel. I don't want to go anywhere else. I just want to be with her. She is an absolutely lovely girl and I'm very fond of her. You can just go away and do your work, Otisk. Francel and I will stay here.' He sat back and closed his eyes.

Otisk shook his head. 'I'm sorry, Brocks, you can't do that. This is the Reception Centre. You just arrive here and then you need to move on so that others can arrive. We are your Reception Team right now but, in a little while, we will be the Reception Team for someone else. In fact, that person is in process of arriving right now. So you see, it's impossible for you to stay here.'

Brocks lifted up a hand. 'No, Otisk. I really appreciate what you're trying to do for me but I'm staying here. Don't worry about me. I'm not going anywhere. I'm just staying here—with Francel. She's absolutely lovely, you know. I'm really smitten with her.'

'Listen, Brocks. Francel can't stay here with you. She has other work to do.'

The man looked pleadingly at Francel. 'Don't leave me, Francel. I'll be so lonely without you.'

'Brocks, Otisk is right. I can't stay here with you. It's absolutely impossible.'

The man was silent for some time. 'OK, I understand. I agree you should go and do your work. I'll just stay here and you can come back to me as soon as you can. I want to hold your hand again. I want to embrace you. In fact, I want to be with you for ever…'

The man drifted off to sleep as Otisk applied his power. He looked at Francel with a stricken expression. 'What do we do, Francel? There's nothing in the training to cover this! I want to do what's right for Brocks but my mind is a blank. OK, I can relocate him to his house and keep him asleep but it's very likely he'll wake up shouting for you. No-one will know what to do with him! It will cause a serious problem.'

Francel was also very worried. 'Look, Otisk, we have another incomer in about ten minutes. At least one of us has got to be here for that. We can't call in a Standby Team for that. We would not be fulfilling our responsibility.'

Otisk sat down with his head in his hands. 'Think, think! There must be a solution to this.'

'Well, if the worst comes to the worst, we'll need to apply a temporary solution and try to solve it tomorrow but that's a poor outcome for Brocks,' Francel said. 'I don't know what to do!' Her voice was filled with despair. 'I've never envisaged anything like this happening to me.'

'I know.' A cry of triumph from Otisk. 'A surrogate. That's what we need—a surrogate. I need to find someone to replace you. He's become imprinted on you. We need to switch the imprint! I'll get on to this right away. You better go and begin to deal with the new incomer and I'll join you as soon as possible.' He disappeared rapidly.

Francel looked at him softly. 'And you did it, didn't you, Darling? You solved it perfectly. You relocated him to his accommodation and installed a surrogate. She was a very nice woman and she was more than happy to help. In fact she admitted to feeling rather alone even when she was surrounded by friends. You arranged for the imprint and Brocks fell in love with her right away. They were wonderfully happy together. Furthermore, you were a bit of a hero, weren't you, Otisk? Because your solution to the problem is now included as a module in the training procedure for new Reception Teams. You received a special thank you notification from the Counsellors.'

Otisk looked at her with affection. 'Well, I knew I had to solve it, my love. I might have lost you to Brocks, otherwise. That was certainly a test for me.'

Eventually, she rose to her feet. 'Otisk, I have some shopping to do. Clothes, food, that sort of thing,' she smiled. 'You can just chill out here.'

'That's fine, Francel. I would only be a hindrance to you. Maybe I'll drop over to the café and watch the world go by for a while.'

* * * *

He sat relaxing at a table in front of the café, sipping a coffee and languidly watching the people go by. Occasionally, someone would greet him and he would reply with a smile and a wave. You met a lot of people when you were in a Reception Team and they always remembered you!

"362 times 476?"

'172,312.'

"54,117 divided by 63 minus 65?"

'794.'

He clicked his tongue in annoyance and waited for the third one. Seconds ticked by. Nothing.

'Maybe my brain got a little tired,' he grimaced wryly.

Suddenly his eye was caught by a flash of orange and there he was, the Litter Bin Man, working his way around the Town Square, checking the bins and emptying them when necessary into his cart. As usual, although the Square was busy, nobody paid any attention to this small man, who carried out his solitary maintenance task as if no-one else was there. People swirled around him as if he was a static lifeless artefact.

Otisk sat forward purposely. 'Second time lucky,' he muttered. 'This time I won't miss him. In any case, I'm really grateful to him. If it wasn't for him, I might not have seen Francel and my life would have been immeasurably poorer. I can't imagine life without her!'

As the man worked around the periphery of the Square, Otisk had another thought. 'I wonder if it's the same man. I think I have seen members of this maintenance team working in other streets.' He strained his eyes towards the man, trying to make out the detail of his features and see whether this tallied with his earlier recollection. As the man approached, Otisk began to see his face quite clearly. He saw an elderly, very tanned and lined face, an impassive expression and eyes that never met anyone's gaze. A man absolutely focussed on his task.

'No good,' Otisk muttered, 'I can't remember what the first man looked like. This could be him—I really don't know. Anyway,' he resolved, 'this is the man I'm going to invite for a coffee.'

Now Otisk began to experience the human tension that preceded a task that was judged to require accurate timing and effective execution. He was aware of an increase in his heart rate, matched to the man's progress towards him. He must get the approach right— the right timing, the well-chosen words, the correct tonality in the voice. He began to rehearse what he would say, projecting silent words in his consciousness and mentally trying them out in his mouth. Then the final countdown commenced, as the fluorescent orange jacket became worryingly within touching distance.

'Hello.'

Otisk was horrified! His single word of greeting reverberated around his skull, appallingly thin, cracked and hugely disappointing. The man ignored him, peering intensely into the litter bin. 'Hello!' he repeated, another inappropriate, disappointing effort, hardly any better. Still nothing. He steeled himself to stand up and touch the orange shoulder lightly. The man reacted immediately, spinning around and, in the same movement, lifting the lid of his cart.

'Put it in here, please.' A very quiet, hoarse voice. Uninflected. No eye contact.

'Ah... no... sorry!' Otisk was confounded. 'I just wanted to invite you to have a coffee with me. Right here.' He pointed nervously to the table beside him. At last, his voice sounded rather more like his own.

The man lifted his eyes and looked into Otisk's face for a brief moment. 'Can't, I'm afraid,' he said shortly.

'Why not? You deserve a break.' At last, Otisk was gaining in confidence.

'It isn't allowed,' the man said, turning away.

Otisk smiled at him. 'You can blame it on me. Please sit down. I want you to relax.'

The man stood stock still for more than ten seconds, his eyes now fixed on Otisk's face, a blank and neutral gaze. Then, suddenly, he stripped off the orange jacket, revealing neat brown overalls below. 'I will,' he muttered, 'just this time. I'll think of a reason.'

Coffee was ordered by Otisk and delivered. They both sipped the steaming, brown liquid.

'You're Otisk. Reception.' The same flat, neutral tone.

'How do you know that?' Otisk was surprised. The man did not answer, continuing to look across the Square.

After a pause, Otisk enquired. 'What is your name? I can't sense it.'

The man looked down into his coffee. 'I don't have an official name. They call me Lonei.'

'Well, that's your official name, isn't it?' Otisk said brightly. 'Is that what's printed on your bracelet?'

The man paused, looking into the distance once more. 'No. There's nothing on my bracelet.'

'I thought that was impossible,' Otisk commented. 'Are you sure? Could you show me, please?'

The man extended his arm. Otisk twisted the familiar translucent bracelet around. Nothing. He looked closer. No sign that there ever had been printing on its smooth surface. 'Was there ever any printing on it, Lonei?' he asked.

'No.'

'What about the other maintenance workers like you? Do they have names on their bracelets?'

'There are no other maintenance workers like me. I work alone. One is enough.'

Otisk was silent for a while as he thought about what the little man had said. He found that he was becoming very sorry for him. He seemed so alone, with nothing in his life except low-level manual labour. Meanwhile, everyone else was enjoying themselves in so many ways—and completely ignoring this man as he served them. It wasn't fair! 'I must do something about this.' Otisk's thoughts were stirring him up considerably!

'There's nothing you can do about it.'

The soft, hoarse voice of the little man surprised him. 'He must have guessed my thoughts,' Otisk concluded. He looked at the little man, still grasping his coffee cup and looking across the Square. 'Well, Lonei, it doesn't seem fair to me. I think everyone here has their work or study to do, but they all have plenty time off to enjoy themselves. There are so many pleasurable things to do here in Pazoten.'

'For you, yes. For them, yes. But not for me. These things are not for me.'

Another silence, while Otisk thought about this.

'Where do you live, Lonei?' His next question.

'I have a flat near the edge of the Town, in the south.' He gestured.

'Is it nice there? Who do you live with?'

'I live alone. The flat is OK. I'm rarely there. I'm out working all the time.'

'Don't you ever have time off? Days off, you know?'

'No. The work has to be done every day.'

'But that's ridiculous, Lonei. No-one should be required to work every day, all day. It's wrong.'

'It's wrong for you, Otisk, but not for me.' The man drank the rest of his coffee and stood up. 'I've got to go now. I have work to do.'

'Have you been in Pazoten for a long time, Lonei?'

The man paused and thought for a moment. Then he turned to Otisk and, for the first time, looked at him steadily in the eyes. 'Yes, a very long time,' he said. 'Now I've got to go. Thanks.' He gestured towards the empty coffee cup.

'We'll do this again, Lonei. Soon.'

Lonei ignored this as he donned the orange jacket again and fastened it up. Otisk watched the small cart being wheeled away, guided purposely towards the next litter bin. 'It isn't right, I'm sure. I must make enquiries about this,' he thought. But who to ask? He didn't know. Pazoten didn't seem to be set up for questions like that.

* * * *

They were back together in the house.

'It was very strange, Francel. It turns out that he is the only man who does that job, so it definitely was him that I saw the first time—that wonderful time when I found you. But it's not only strange, it's completely unfair! Do you know anyone else here who never gets a day off? Who doesn't use all the facilities here to enjoy themselves? That's right! I don't either. I've decided to ask some questions about this but I really don't know who I should ask. Do you have any suggestions?'

Francel thought. 'Well, I don't think our Reception Team Organisation is likely to be of much help, do you? Branea and Bitzo weren't much help when you asked the age question. They weren't interested, either. I think it's got to be Counsellor Begiet, don't you? We don't know any of the other Counsellors.'

'Right, Francel, thanks for that suggestion. I'll try that next time we're at the Centre.

Chapter 7

Otisk and Francel had a daytime duty (0900 to 1500 hours) at the Administration Centre two days later.

'After that duty would be an ideal time for me to pursue the matter of our friend Lonei,' Otisk said to Francel. 'What do you think?'

'Yes, I think that's a good idea. Is it possible to arrange it before-hand?' Francel asked.

'I don't know. I'll see if there's anything in the info-reader.' He scanned the screen for a while.

'Absolutely nothing, Francel. We give incomers a verbal brief-ing about the administration of Pazoten, telling them about the Counsellors and the Leader, but what we say is minimal, really. In the briefing, there's no attempt to suggest any contact mechanism. Now that we're thinking about it, that's a bit strange, isn't it?'

'Well, let's approach it when we get there. We can start with the Doorkeeper and see if he has any further information to offer about contacting the Counsellors.'

* * * *

The Doorkeeper raised a hand to acknowledge their presence and was surprised when Otisk knocked at his office door.

'Good morning, Otisk and Francel. This is an unexpected pleas-ure!' The Doorkeeper was smiling encouragingly. 'We haven't spoken since that first day you came; since then, I just see you flashing past from time to time. How may I help you today?'

'I want to speak to Counsellor Begiet after my shift today. How can I achieve that? How do I make an appointment?'

The Doorkeeper immediately became serious. 'Counsellor Begiet, eh? I'm afraid that is something I cannot help you with. That level of activity is well beyond my area of responsibility. I suggest you speak to the Administrative Coordinator. She should be able to advise you. She is authorised to operate at the highest administrative level in this building.' The Doorkeeper smiled, distinctly relieved to be shifting on the burden.

'Could you call her?'

'Sorry, no, I can't.'

'Why not?'

'I know she hasn't arrived yet.'

'So how can I communicate with her?'

'You can't. I will communicate with her and she will communicate with you. I am instructed to operate the system in that way. I'm not allowed to do anything else.' Now the man looked worried.

'Fine, I understand,' Otisk reassured him. 'You know who we are and we're working in RR5 from 0900 to 1500 hours. Would you inform the Administrative Coordinator that I wish to speak to her as soon as possible about setting up a meeting with Counsellor Begiet later today? Ideally around 1600 hours when we should have completed the handover at the end of our shift.'

'Yes, Otisk. I'll certainly do my very best for you.'

Otisk was a little taken aback. 'Sorry. What do you mean: "you'll do your very best for me"?'

'Well, the Administrative Coordinator is a very busy person.' The man was apologetic.

Otisk was silent for a moment. 'Please inform her that I *expect* to hear from her today,' he said finally. 'As soon as possible,' he added pleasantly.

* * * *

Francel and Otisk had dealt with one incomer that morning. It had been an uncomplicated case, a pleasant lady in her thirties, who had been processed without problem and was now resting in her new home. They would visit her the following day to induct her. At around 1300 hours, Otisk's phone bleeped and he answered.

'Otisk?' an impatient female voice enquired.

'Yes.'

'This is the Administrative Coordinator. You may come to see me in fifteen minutes. I have cleared ten minutes for you.'

'No.'

'What?'

'I said, no.'

'Look, Otisk, I'm fitting you in with great difficulty...'

'Reception Team members on duty need to stand by at their stations. They cannot wander off to other parts of the building when they feel like it. I thought you would have known that. You may come to see me, if you wish. I'm in RR5.'

Silence. 'What is it you want, anyway? I warn you I have many requests to process and it can often take considerable time...'

'I want to see Counsellor Begiet, today, at around 1600 hours, if possible. How do I set that up?'

'It is not permitted to approach Counsellors directly, I'm afraid.'

'So how do I achieve a meeting?'

'I must carry out appropriate enquiries and make the link...'

Otisk sighed. 'So will you do that, please? It is an important matter and I would not like to report that it had been delayed unnecessarily.'

Silence. Then: 'You will be informed of the outcome.' Click. The connection was broken.

Around fifteen minutes later, Otisk's phone bleeped again. He answered.

'This is the Administrative Coordinator's Department. Assistant Clerk Level One speaking.' A hesitant young female voice. 'I have a message for you directly from the Administrative Coordinator herself. The message is: "Counsellor Begiet will see you at 1600 hours in Room 2-43." Goodbye.' The phone went dead.

Otisk smiled at Francel. 'It wasn't easy but it seems I have an appointment to see Counsellor Begiet at 1600 hours.'

Francel returned his smile. 'Bravo!' she said.

* * * *

Their shift had ended and they were leaving RR5 around 1540 hours.

'Do you want to come with me to see Counsellor Begiet, Francel?' Otisk asked.

'No, thanks, Otisk. The Counsellor's meeting is with you and I am not involved. I'm perfectly happy to wait for you in the garden outside. It's a lovely, sunny day. I'll look forward to hearing all about your discussion.'

The transporter took them to the front entrance. Francel pointed to a seat in the warm sunshine. 'I'll sit over there and relax. Just take your time. I'm in no hurry. It'll be nice to sit and just do nothing.'

'See you soon then,' he said, as he went back into the building. He was surprised when he emerged from the transporter opposite Room 2-43. The corridor here was gloomy and grim with many dark coloured doors on each side. The door of Room 2-43 swung open to reveal another surprise—a small, poorly furnished room with a single small window which lit the room with a dim, grimy light. The furniture consisted of a simple desk and several small, upright chairs. As he walked into the room, Counsellor Begiet strode in behind him.

They shook hands. 'Sit down, Otisk,' she said cheerfully, taking one of the small chairs beside the desk, 'you're looking a bit glum. Is there a problem?'

'Well, no. I just thought that Counsellors would have big, lavish offices—as befits their status, you know.' He finished with a rather pale smile.

She looked around and grimaced. 'It isn't very nice, is it? But this isn't my office. This is a general purpose interview room. There are a lot of them here on Floor Two.'

'Ah, that explains it, then. Your big lavish office is somewhere else, then?'

'No, Otisk. Counsellors do not have offices. We're on the move all the time, so we just use what is available at the time. We don't need a big lavish office; that would be completely at variance with our purpose here. We are here to serve the people of Pazoten constantly. You remember I told you that once before, don't you? Well, it's true and you can't do that effectively if you're sitting in a big lavish office somewhere! Now, please, let's get down to business. I sense you have come to me with something difficult.'

'Counsellor, I have come to you about Lonei's situation.'

'Lonei, Otisk? I had already sensed that as the subject but you have me at a disadvantage. Who or what is Lonei? I don't recognise the word.'

Otisk looked at her with surprise. 'Do you know the maintenance man who empties the litter bins in the Town? He's a small elderly man who always wears a fluorescent orange jacket and pushes a small cart.'

The Counsellor looked at him doubtfully. 'Well, Otisk, I suppose I do. I mean, I suppose I have seen him from time to time. He's not the sort of person you pay much attention to. As far as I know, I have never had any dealings with him, or, come to that, with whoever manages him. Perhaps one of my fellow Counsellors have. I can check. Anyway, is there a problem there? What is your concern? I certainly haven't been aware that there was anything going wrong in the Litter Bin Squad, or, indeed, in any of the other maintenance operations in the Town and beyond.'

Otisk paused for a moment without taking his eyes from the Counsellor's face. Then he spoke in a firm voice. 'Yes, Counsellor, I do have a significant concern. And, yes, there is a problem, in my opinion. I believe there is not a Litter Bin Squad, as you suggest, there is only this single man and he works completely alone. I have observed that everybody ignores him totally, while they are being kind, generous and considerate to everyone else. In other words, like you, they just don't see Lonei as a fellow citizen of the Town and the Land of Pazoten.'

'Observing this, I made it my business to speak to him. In fact, I intercepted him and invited him to join me for a coffee at the Town Square café. At first he refused and said he was not allowed to have a break from his work. However, I persuaded him. During the time we had together, he told me that he lives alone in a small flat somewhere near the southern perimeter of the Town. He told me that he works all day, every day and that he never is allowed any days off—or even part of a day. He says that the work he does has to be done continuously. I do not understand how this can happen to anyone in Pazoten because, as far as I can see, everyone else has days off when they can enjoy the many pursuits and pastimes that are available here. I cannot see why it should be any different for Lonei. Obviously, I do not know who he works for but, of course, this information will undoubtedly be available to you. Therefore, on Lonei's behalf, I seek justice for him.'

Counsellor Begiet was impassive as she replied. 'I will investigate this, Otisk and we will meet again. I have no record of anyone called Lonei. This is all a bit of a puzzle. I will need to speak to the other Counsellors and see what can be discovered. So, Otisk, we will meet again.'

'Thank you, Counsellor Begiet, I will look forward to that and for some improvement in Lonei's life. In any event, I intend to continue my friendship with him. He deserves it.'

They shook hands and Counsellor Begiet immediately faded as she transported away. Otisk was glad to leave the depressing interview room.

'How did it go?' Francel's first words, squinting up at him in the sunshine.

'Puzzling. She didn't even know who Lonei was. She's going to make further enquiries and says she will come back to me. I don't know when but at least the matter is under investigation.'

'What are you hoping to achieve, Otisk?'

'Well, I see no reason why Lonei cannot be treated like everyone else in Pazoten.'

'Do you know how everyone else in Pazoten is treated, Otisk?'

Otisk was silent for a moment. 'That's a good point, Francel. I should have thought of that. The answer is: No, I don't—but if there are other people being treated similarly, that makes my intervention even more appropriate, does it not?'

'That's quite right, Otisk. You could be benefitting a whole Pazoten underclass!' She was smiling.

'I know why you're smiling, Francel. It does seem unlikely that we have a "Pazoten underclass", doesn't it? But in any event, I think an underclass of one is unacceptable.'

She nodded. 'I wholeheartedly agree. Everyone seems to be so well provided for in Pazoten. It's really shocking to hear of someone who isn't.'

'Well, we'll see what happens,' he said. 'I won't give up, though,' he added.

She looked at him fondly. 'I know you won't,' she said softly.

* * * *

The following day, they had inducted the incomer of the day before. She was delighted with her new house and was looking forward to exploring the Town as they had recommended she should do. They gave her their usual briefing. Meanwhile, she could call on them if any problems arose.

Shortly after, they had met with her Monitoring Team and transferred her over to them. This left them with the rest of the day free (barring any emergency calls) and they decided to ride out into the country. Cycles were soon rented and they rode out on the long, flat East Road that led along the length of the valley. A pleasant picnic spot eventually caught their eye and they stopped there for rest and refreshment. As they sat at a rough-hewn picnic table, they could see the length of the road they had cycled and they amused themselves by following the progress of the occasional vehicles that sped along from time to time.

"58 times 621?"
'36,018.'

"3212 divided by 34?"
'94.47 approx.'

"29 plus 98 times 123?"
'15,621.'

Francel had noticed his sudden faraway expression. 'Maths?' she asked.

'Yes. Just the usual tests. I just supply the answers without thinking. I wish I could find out where these tests are coming from!'

'Well, my darling, it keeps you in practice, doesn't it? Maybe it's a skill you will need in the future?'

'Hm.' He did not sound convinced!

They sat, sweeping their eyes around the pleasant landscape in front of them. Suddenly, Otisk noticed a flash of movement far away on the road towards the Town. He narrowed his eyes to achieve focus in the bright light. 'Look at this cyclist, Francel! Wow! He's travelling really fast!'

In the very far distance, a brightly clad cyclist, fully helmeted and suited in professional cycling attire, had come into view. Even although the cyclist was far away, it was clear that he was travelling at a considerable speed. As the decreasing distance enlarged the image, it was possible to see muscular legs pumping up and down rapidly and polished pedal cranks whirling around at great speed.

Otisk was highly impressed! 'He must be doing close to forty miles per hour,' he gasped. That's probably over twice the speed we were doing, Francel.'

'Well, never mind, Otisk. We're not racing cyclists. What do you think? Is this person some sort of professional cyclist? Do we have cycle races in Pazoten?'

'I've not heard of them. But why shouldn't there be? I'll look into that when we get home. It might be fun to do some cycle racing!'

Francel smiled. 'It wouldn't be fun, Otisk. It would be extremely hard work and would take up all your spare time. You wouldn't have time for me anymore.'

He embraced her tightly. 'OK, you win! I don't want to replace you with anything.'

Now the cyclist, still moving at high speed, was approaching the picnic area. Otisk could see that the cycle was a very high-quality racing machine constructed from the finest carbon fibre materials.

'A professional cyclist, if I ever saw one,' Otisk thought.

Both were extremely surprised when, at the very last moment, the cyclist performed a very steeply banked turn from the road into the picnic area, headed straight for their table at speed and finally executed a perfect 180 degree skid to stop close beside them.

Otisk stepped forward. 'That was an incredible piece of riding. You are a real expert. I'm Otisk and this is...' the words died in his mouth as the cyclist removed the brightly coloured racing helmet, revealing the smiling face of Counsellor Begiet!

'That was really good,' she said with a happy smile. 'I enjoyed that! I rarely get a chance to do that nowadays. When I saw that you and Francel had ridden out here, I seized my opportunity for a bit of illicit pleasure.'

Otisk was dumbfounded! 'What... how...' he spluttered.

'I've come for a discussion with you,' the Counsellor said, 'following on from yesterday's conversation.'

Otisk began to retain his speech. 'But... you're as good as any professional racing cyclist... you're really fast!'

'Well, yes, Otisk. It is something I enjoy very much. These days, I rarely have time to do it. I must say it was a very pleasant change from my normal schedule.' Suddenly she laughed. 'Actually, I don't know why I'm saying the word "schedule". The point is, we Counsellors never have a schedule, because we just respond to the problems of Pazoten, wherever and whenever they happen. As I said to you before, Otisk, we are here to serve—constantly.'

Francel got up. 'I'll just leave you alone so that you can have your meeting...'

'No, Francel, please join us. I'm sure Otisk has discussed this problem with you, hasn't he?'

'Well, yes. He has given me an idea what it's about.'

'So join us then. You are most welcome.' Francel sat back down.

'Now, Otisk, I have had a meeting with my fellow Counsellors and we've all made further enquiries. I think we have a satisfactory outcome which I will detail to you in a minute. But first I have to say that my colleagues and I have been greatly puzzled by your friend Lonei. It seems he has been here in Pazoten for a long time and, somehow, has been omitted from the current records we hold. This is why I knew nothing about him when you raised the query. However, everything you told me is absolutely true. We have confirmed where he lives and his situation is precisely as you have described. As far as we can see, the reason he is given no time off is that he does not appear on any of the normal work schedules or databases. We have looked at the management trace and find that, although Town Maintenance is aware of Litter Bin Operations as a listed task, none of the Level Four Managers have that task in their area of responsibility. All four mangers think that one of their other colleagues is in charge of it. So, although all are aware of Lonei as a Town Workman and see him at the depot from time to time, it seems that no-one actually manages him.'

Otisk interrupted. 'What does Lonei himself say about his management structure?'

'Yes, I'm just coming to that now. Lonei himself has been consulted about his work situation and he says that he received his instructions many years ago from a manager whose name he cannot remember. Since then, he has carried out these instructions every day. He says he is happy in his work and does not want to do anything else. So that seems to be the explanation for this very peculiar state of affairs.'

'So what is to happen now, Counsellor?'

'We immediately authorised that Lonei should have two days off per week. When he was advised of this, he objected strongly. He said that two days off per week was excessive and he was adamant that the work would suffer. When we proposed that someone else would be allocated to cover the task on his days off, he refused very forcefully; he said he did not wish his work to be contaminated by another.'

'Did he actually use the word *contaminated?*'

'Yes, these were his actual words.'

'A strange word indeed. So how has this been resolved?'

'Well, we asked him what we should do and he proposed that he should take two half-days off per week. This would give him enough time off and still enable him to meet his full duties with the litter bins. He was certain that this was what he wanted. In view of this, we agreed with some reluctance but told him that his situation could be changed at any time if he wanted to extend his time off. He appeared to be content with that new arrangement when he left us.'

'Well, I think that seems like a fair outcome for him,' Otisk said, 'I'm very glad I raised the matter with you. It's a question of social justice.'

Counsellor Begiet smiled. 'So we Counsellors had better watch our step?'

He flushed. 'No, no. I didn't mean that at all. But it was a surprising thing to find out, wasn't it? I had thought that everything in Pazoten was perfect.'

'Nothing is ever perfect, as long as people are involved,' the Counsellor said dryly. 'Is there anything else, or have we covered everything?'

'What about Lonei's bracelet, Counsellor? Why isn't his name printed on it?'

'Yes, we did talk to him about that. We offered to change it for a new one with his name printed on it but he didn't want us to do that. He said the bracelet had always been like that ever since he came to Pazoten and he didn't see any point in changing it now.

'So how long has he been here?'

'We don't know. He wasn't in the consolidated records, even in the historical section. We've listed him now but we had to create a special sub-category for him because he didn't seem to fit into any of the normal slots. It's a funny thing, that. However, it's all solved now, thanks to you.'

'I'm pleased for Lonei. At least he can start to have a life here that's nearer to the norm.'

The Counsellor fastened her cycling helmet. 'So I'll be off, Francel and Otisk. It's been nice to see you again. I'm really looking forward to my ride back to Town. I intend to better my time, if I can.' She brandished the stopwatch on her wrist. 'Goodbye, then!'

For a moment, she held herself poised astride the cycle before clicking the start button of the stopwatch and simultaneously racing away to join the road in a cloud of dust, before accelerating rapidly towards the distant Town. They stood and watched the bright, dwindling figure with awe and admiration.

'Who would have thought it? A racing cyclist Counsellor! Paz-oten is certainly full of surprises.'

They sat down again at the table. Otisk was looking thoughtful. 'You know, Francel, I think we should find out when Lonei is having his first half-day off and invite him to come out into the countryside with us. What do you think?'

She put her arms around him. 'I think you're wonderful to think like that, my darling. Of course we should do that. Maybe we could visit one of the lakes and go boating, unless that's something Lonei doesn't want to do. We've never tried that yet and I rather like the sound of it.'

'Well, I'll ask him about that when I offer the invitation and see what he says.'

* * * *

It was two days later before Otisk had the opportunity to speak to Lonei. He and Francel had had a couple of very busy days with quite an influx of incomers. However, Otisk had looked out the window after lunch and observed Lonei working in the Square.

'Lonei! Hello, it's Otisk. I live just over there and I saw you working down here. Francel and I would like to invite you to come with us for a visit to one of the lakes—maybe do a bit of boating? We would be very pleased if you would come. I'll rent a car. What do you say?'

Lonei leaned on his cart and looked at him impassively. 'The Lakes,' he said finally. 'I knew The Lakes, you know, a long time ago. I used to go there. There was a really big lake for boats that you could hire and take a trip around and then there was a smaller lake for sailing model boats.' His eyes became wistful. 'I had a big model boat. It was the best one there—everybody said so—and I certainly didn't disagree with them, because they were telling the truth!' His face was transformed by the memory, becoming soft and wistful. Then, quite suddenly, his expression changed and he resumed his normal blank look. 'I've no idea where that boat is now. It's a long time since I had it. I must have lost it.' A sad, disconsolate voice.

Otisk seized his arm. 'Listen, Lonei, we'll get another one. There's a shop that sells model boats not far from here. Why don't we go and have a look? See what they have in stock?'

'Sorry, Otisk, can't do that. I'm working, you know. I've got to complete my cycle and I won't do that if I go swanning off, looking for a boat.'

'I understand, Lonei. Tell me, how big was the boat? Show me. And what sort of boat was it? I'll check out the shop and see if they have anything like it in there.'

Lonei paused and looked at him. 'It was about this size,' he held his arms apart, indicating a model boat about three feet long. It was a tugboat, he said. 'A proper, powerful little boat. Hard as nails, it was. A very fine model.' He paused and added wistfully, '"Juno", she was called.'

'Do you still know where these lakes are, Lonei? The place where you used to go to sail your boat?'

Again, Lonei was deep in his memories for some moments. 'Yes, I do,' he said eventually, 'it isn't something you forget. It's a lovely place.'

'So will you come?' Otisk looked straight into the little man's eyes. 'Please do!'

'OK,' the man whispered. 'I will. It would be nice to see The Lakes again.'

'So when is your next half-day off, Lonei?'

'Saturday. I finish my work at 1230 hours.'

'That's absolutely fine. Francel and I are not at work on Saturday. Could we pick you up at 1300 hours? From your house?'

The man looked at Otisk's enthusiastic face. 'I don't understand,' he said in a flat voice. 'Why do you want anything to do with me? Why did you help me? Why are you being nice to me? I'm nobody, here. Nobody notices me, ever. Nobody pays attention to me.'

'Well, I did. I noticed you. I paid attention to you. And the answer to your first question is: "We are all here to help one another." Don't you know that? It's the most important thing we do in our lives. That's all I'm doing. I'm helping you and you're helping me by coming to The Lakes and enjoying yourself. Now, give me the address of your house, please.' He recorded it. 'We'll see you at 1300 hours on Saturday. I may or may not have a boat for you to sail. I hope I will. Then you can show me how an expert does it. I would really like that. Goodbye for now, Lonei.'

Otisk strode away, heading back to his house. Lonei's eyes followed him. Then he turned away, muttering. 'That boy is different. He has something extra in him. Something very special. Justice and truth, that's what it is. Justice and truth.' He paused. 'And love,' he added, his voice so quiet that no one else could possibly have heard it.

* * * *

The following day, Otisk and Francel stood in the model shop that was not far from the Administrative Centre. Otisk's eyes gleamed with pleasure as he scanned the displays that filled the shop.

'Look at these model aircraft; they're absolutely marvellous! Look, I recognise this one. It's a Piper Cherokee; wow! And look at this one, Francel. It's an amazingly detailed model of a Learjet—I don't know the exact model—and here's a Boeing 737: aren't they all incredible? I really don't know how to choose…'

'Otisk! You're not here to buy an aircraft, remember? You're here to buy a boat. A boat for Lonei.'

'Ah, yes, thanks for that, Francel. Momentarily, I had forgotten that. But these model aircraft are so absolutely wonderful…'

'Yes, they are, Otisk. We can look at them another time, though. Let's look at the boats.' They walked towards the back of the shop where various boats were displayed. 'Do you see anything that is remotely like what Lonei was describing?'

Otisk scanned the wide range of large and small yachts, cabin cruisers in many sizes and speedboats of many designs. 'No, Francel, I don't see any tugboats here on display.' He walked a little further. 'Wait a moment!' His voice was filled with rising excitement. 'This looks more like it—I've found a model tugboat here at the back. It's certainly very pretty.'

Francel looked at the model in Otisk's hands, no more than a foot long. 'It's not very big, is it?' she said doubtfully. 'Didn't you say his tugboat was much bigger than that one?'

Otisk was visibly deflated. 'Well, I suppose you're right, Francel. This is a nice little model but it's nothing like the one Lonei described. Do you think it might do? I mean, at least it is a tugboat.' He looked around. 'I don't see any others. It looks to me as if this is the only model tugboat they have in the shop.' They looked at it rather sadly.

'Ah, I see you've found the tugboat. It really is rather pretty, isn't it?' The shopkeeper joined them from an office at the back, speaking in the joyous, positive tones of a salesman. 'It's extremely detailed, you know. Everything is there and it all works as it should.

We don't sell many of these, because most people go for the dramatic fast boats, the speedboats or the powerful cabin cruisers. And of course the sailboats are ever popular with the yachting community—they can spend hours trimming the sails!' he laughed. 'In fact they spend far more time on that than actually sailing the boats on the water! Anyway, I very much share your taste. I like the tugboat very much and I think you've chosen the best boat in the shop.' He paused. 'Shall I go and get the box for it?'

'Well, actually, I wanted something a bit bigger.'

'A bit bigger? Hm.' The shopkeeper looked around. 'I don't think we have a bigger tugboat. You can get them, of course and if you tell me what size you want, I'll look into it. Meanwhile, there's only this one...' His voice faded, then strengthened again. 'Just a minute, though. When you say "a bit bigger" how big would you want it?'

'Well, at least twice the size of this—or even bigger.'

The shopkeeper's eyes gleamed. 'Ah! Come with me please.' He took them through a door at the back of the shop into a large storage area. He began to move a large pile of boxes that were stacked at one end of the room, clearing them away to one side.

'So,' he said triumphantly, 'what about this: it was a special order but the gentleman declined to take delivery. He said it was too big! And, to be fair, I think it's too big as well, although I suspect that he couldn't afford it! I think that was the real reason. Now I really don't know what to do with it. That's why it's here in the back area of the shop. It's been here for some time.' He stepped aside to give them a completely clear view.

The model of the tugboat was over four feet long and nearly two feet wide. The finish was beautiful. The detail on it was magnificent. It was an accurate scale model of a very powerful tugboat and every system had been faithfully replicated. The shopkeeper resumed his sales pitch. 'This is not like all these other boats, you know. They are all powered by electric motors. This model has two miniature diesel engines, electronically controlled of course. And then there are all the usual remote-control systems to control its every movement and all the equipment aboard—you know cranes, capstans, pumps, etc. And, (his eyes shone with enthusiasm) it has a special propulsion system—just like the best real tugs. It really is an absolute marvel of model engineering.'

Otisk said nothing as he continued to look at the large model with astonishment. It was easily the finest he had ever seen!

'Listen,' the shopkeeper said, 'I know it's too big. However, it is quite magnificent isn't it?' Now he sounded more hesitant. 'Anyway, if you'll consider having it, I can offer you an exceptionally good price on it. I'm sure you could have excellent fun with it, once you get it into the water, that is. I reckon it will need two strong men to lift it in and out. You would certainly have the finest model boat in the whole lake. What do you think? Are you interested?' The man was beginning to sound quite desperate.

'How much?'

He man produced a notebook and made some calculations. Eventually he turned over a page and wrote. Finally he handed the notebook to Otisk. 'I have discounted it considerably,' he said, 'it's a really good bargain!' He stood back and waited.

Otisk glanced at the notebook, looked at Francel and squeezed her hand with a delighted smile. 'Fine,' he said to the shopkeeper, 'I think I know someone who would like this very much. I'll take it. I accept your price. It's very fair.'

Chapter 8

It was Saturday. In the morning, Otisk had made a purposeful visit to Town Auto One and returned to the Square with a large black Toyota Hilux pickup truck.

'You see, Francel, it has a double cab that makes it like a car inside and then it has a five feet square loading deck behind—and it's got a roof over the top. So we can fit Lonei in the cab and transport the tugboat on the deck behind. It's a very nice vehicle, too; drives just like a car. Although there is an automatic version, I chose the manual gearbox, which I think is better for "all-terrain" operation. Of course, it has large wheels and tyres as well as four-wheel drive to deal with any soft ground we might come across. Pretty neat, eh?' Otisk was very pleased with himself!

'Great choice, Otisk!' (Men should always be praised for their car choices!) That certainly should do the trick for us. What's the schedule? Picking up Lonei first or going to the shop for the model boat?'

'Well, I thought we would pick up Lonei and then go to the shop for the boat. We'll need two strong men to lift the boat into the truck. Also, we must make sure we have everything we need to get the boat going—fuel for the engines, batteries for the controllers, etc. Everything will need to be set up.'

'Where are we going to find these two strong men?' Francel joked.

'Could be a problem, Francel. We'll probably need you to carry one end!' Otisk riposted.

* * * *

They had enjoyed a light lunch and now the pickup truck had come to a standstill outside Lonei's house. His address was in a compact block of flats, one of a number of similar buildings that were spaced out along a street with ornamental gardens in between. Children played in the parks, riding bicycles, playing games or just dashing about with the energy that all children have.

Lonei must have been waiting for them, because he emerged immediately from the entrance of his block, neatly dressed in clean white overalls and wearing a red baseball cap.

Otisk climbed out of the pickup and opened the rear door. 'Hello, Lonei. Great to see you. You're looking really smart. I got us a pickup and there's plenty room for everybody. Jump in and make yourself comfortable.'

Lonei climbed in. When Otisk had resumed the driver's seat, he spoke briefly. 'Nice car, Otisk. Good choice.'

'Thanks, Lonei. Have you always lived here? It looks nice.'

'Yes, ever since I can remember.'

'Who lives here, Lonei? What work do they do?'

'Maintenance people mostly. Roads, parks, public buildings, that sort of thing.'

'Are you happy here, Lonei?'

Lonei thought about this. 'Yes,' he said finally, 'it's OK, I suppose.'

'We've got something to pick up, Lonei. We're going into the Town Centre to do that first. Which road do we go on after that?'

'You go out the Southeast Road, Otisk. That passes by "The Lakes".'

'Right. But first we go to the Town.'

As they drove along, Lonei began to speak. 'I've been thinking about my boat—you know, the tugboat I told you about. I must have lost it many years ago and, no matter how much I rack my brains, I can't remember what happened to it. I did have a search around but it's definitely not in my house. In any case, there isn't room in my house for a big model boat like that. Anyway, Otisk, I'll just enjoy going to The Lakes. It's many years since I've been there and it'll be good to relax in the countryside. Make a nice change. I wonder if there will be many people with model boats there. There always used to be. It doesn't matter that we don't have one.' An echo of sadness, however!

'Well, actually, we do have one, Lonei. We're on the way to pick it up.'

'A model boat? We're going for a model boat? Where is it?' Now Lonei's voice had a tinge of excitement.

'You remember I told you about the model shop. It's there. I've bought it and you can show us how to sail it when we get to The Lakes.'

'Listen, Otisk and Francel, I should warn you. I don't want you to be disappointed, after you've been so nice and friendly to me. If it's a little sailboat, I was never much good at fixing these sails. I mean, I'll do the best I can.'

'It isn't a sailboat, Lonei. It's got an engine. You'll be fine.'

'OK, that's good to hear. I hope you haven't forgotten the batteries. These boats need batteries to power the engine, you know. My boat—the one I told you about—it needed a very big battery to drive the engine. People were always surprised how big the battery was. You need to have the right size of battery, you know, or the boat won't work.'

'Don't worry, we'll make sure we have everything. Anyway, you'll be there to make sure we're doing everything right!'

The pickup came to a stop outside the model shop and they all entered. The shopkeeper was dealing with another customer and they waited for him to finish with them. Lonei left them and began to prowl around the shop, carefully examining the fine displays of model aircraft and muttering to himself. When he arrived at the display of model boats, he became silent, bending down to examine each one with great care, working out how each control system operated.

The other customers finally made their decision and the purchase of a model aircraft was completed. The shopkeeper gave them the box and the customers left the shop with mutual expressions of good wishes. He now turned to Otisk and Francel.

'Hello again,' he said joyfully, 'come for the best model in the shop, have you? I have everything ready. I've set it up on its hull supports through here and tested every one of its systems fully. I've fuelled it up and run the engines, too. They're really smooth. You've got absolutely everything you will need to get it sailing on the lakes. It'll cause a sensation, I promise. Come through here, please.'

Lonei had found the large tugboat. He stood totally motionless and silent several feet away from it, totally mesmerised, his arms limp at his sides but his eyes scanning every detail of the structure. As Otisk came forward to stand beside him, the older man spoke in a whisper. 'I've never seen anything so beautiful. So wonderful. So perfect. It's just like my tugboat but bigger, much better. And—let me tell you something amazing—this tugboat has the Voith Schneider Propulsion System!' Now he turned a serene and happy face towards Otisk. 'Let me tell you something. Whoever is lucky enough to become the owner of this boat will be the star of the model lake. I could never afford this. This will be the best model that anyone has ever seen. I tell you, it's absolutely wonderful. It's a privilege to have seen it.' He turned away reluctantly. 'Anyway, Otisk, which boat are we having? I noticed there was a very nice little tugboat in the shop out there. Nicely made and very detailed, too. I was thinking that might be that one you've got for us? I was sort of hoping it would be.'

'No, we aren't having that little tugboat out there.'

'No? So have you gone for one of these cabin cruisers?' he pointed.

'No, Lonei, I've gone for a tugboat. That's what you wanted, wasn't it? A tugboat like you used to have?'

'That would be nice. But where is it? I see only that little one but you tell me that's not it.'

Otisk grinned. 'No, you're right, it's not that little one. It's this *little* one.' He tapped the large tugboat's hull gently.

It took some minutes for Lonei to recover! He stood, shaking his head in disbelief and saying: 'it really is so beautiful' over and over again. Eventually he recovered his normal self and became devastatingly practical, questioning the shopkeeper carefully about the tests he had done and the equipment that accompanied the model. While Otisk completed the purchases, Lonei studied the manual carefully to ensure that he knew how all the systems were controlled. Eventually, the great moment arrived. The large tugboat was swathed in a protective cover, Francel was sent outside to open up the rear load area of the pickup while Otisk and Lonei carried the large boat out of the shop and placed it diagonally across the load area. Then they secured it with soft cotton tapes that were then fastened to eyelets on the floor. With the rear closed up and locked, they were ready for their adventure at the lake. Like children going on holiday, they piled noisily into the cabin of the pickup. Even Lonei was smiling!

Otisk drove carefully to the Ring Road and they began their journey towards the intersection with Southeast Road. There, the signpost read "Southeast Road" and, below, "Recreation Lakes SE" with the outline of a boat, floating on water. Soon they were bowling along Southeast Road towards The Lakes.

The Lakes were very popular on a Saturday with many people coming to enjoy sailing their model boats or going for boat trips on the much larger lake.

'You go left here,' Lonei said. 'This track leads to the smaller lake. The right fork takes you to the big lake where you can hire a boat and take a trip.'

Otisk bore left and the model boating lake soon came into sight.

'Gosh, it's really big, Lonei! I thought you were talking about a little lake for model boats but this is really huge. It must be really deep as well.'

'Yes,' Lonei confirmed, 'I think about half a mile long and pretty wide, too. I know it's very deep in the middle, too.'

Otisk drove along the track beside the lake until he reached a good launching point for a large model. Here, he reversed the pickup to a conveniently sloping area quite near to the water's edge. The tugboat was released from its bonds and placed carefully at the water's edge. Lonei then checked that all the control systems worked (the radio controller was impressively complicated, with many buttons, levers and coloured lights). Finally, Lonei was satisfied with the control system and set about fuelling and starting the two miniature diesel engines. Each one started with an impressive buzz accompanied by puffs of smoke.

By this time, a large audience had gradually assembled around them. Everyone agreed that this was the biggest, most impressive model boat they had ever seen on the lake. Otisk and Lonei were plied with many questions about it. Otisk did his best to answer them but Lonei, totally engrossed in his preparation work, ignored the spectators completely.

'I reckon we're ready, Otisk. Can we launch?'

Otisk lifted the bow and Lonei took the stern. They squatted down at the water's edge and lowered the model into the water, where it bobbed impressively. Lonei lifted the control unit and placed the support strap around his neck. He blipped both engines, one after the other. They sounded wonderful—powerful, willing and ready to go! Another deft movement engaged the drive to the propulsion system. Water bubbled around the tugboat and it began to glide forward, turning away from the bank as Lonei advanced the throttles and operated the steering mechanism. Gathering speed, the large model moved smoothly away, a vision of purposeful muscularity.

The round of applause from the large crowd of spectators developed into a rousing cheer. Everyone was delighted with this remarkable craft and looked at Lonei as something of a superman! He stood at the water's edge, legs astride, concentrating totally on the tugboat, controlling it with deft movements of his powerful hands on the banks of controls before him. He was oblivious to the crowd—well, almost! No-one is ever totally oblivious of adulation.

Otisk was absolutely delighted. Lonei was clearly enjoying himself since that had been the purpose of the day out. It was wonderful to see that he had been able to forget his daily work for some hours and that he had been able to recapture a little of what he used to do a long time ago.

'I wonder how long ago,' Otisk mused. 'There's something different about Lonei. He doesn't seem to be like any of the other people I have met in Pazoten.' He paused and thought some more. 'Maybe it's all to do with his constant working. I don't think anyone else in Pazoten works all the time. That's certainly what he was doing—just working, all of the time. That's bound to make you different, I suppose.' He turned around to speak to Francel and found her busy at work with her camera, taking many photographs of the boat, of Lonei and other scenes around the lake.

'How's it going, professional photographer?' he greeted her.

'Pretty good,' she answered, without stopping her activities. 'I'm sure I'm getting some really good images here. Once I edit them and blow them up I think I may have one or two quite spectacular shots.'

Otisk was impressed as he looked at Francel. 'You know, Francel, I think you might have been a professional photographer. Your whole demeanour is completely expert.'

She stopped and looked at him thoughtfully. 'Well, I certainly don't need to think about the mechanics of what I'm doing,' she said slowly. 'And this means I can just concentrate on the result I'm trying to achieve. I agree that I must have handled a camera before—but before we make me a professional, let's just wait and see what sort of results I can produce!'

'I'm sure they will be splendid, Francel.'

She flashed him a smile. 'You're a great encourager, you know. I love you so much.'

Suddenly, they were aware of a growing commotion a little way along the lake. A young man's model speedboat had raced down the lake and collided violently with a tall, majestic yacht right in the middle of the lake. The yacht had come off considerably worse. The heavy collision had damaged its hull and it was taking on water. In addition, the main mast had been broken and its large sails were now spread out on the water. The shamefaced young man had gone to speak to the owner of the yacht, an elderly man who was regarding the wreckage of his pride and joy with considerable horror.

'I say, I'm really sorry about that,' the young man began, 'I'm afraid I lost contr...'

'Steam gives way to sail.' The older man interrupted, without turning around.

The young man did not understand. 'What?' he said, in some confusion.

'Steam gives way to sail,' the older man repeated dully. 'Don't you know that?'

'Sorry, I don't know what you mean.'

Now the older man swivelled around and looked at the young man sadly. 'Powered boats give way to sail boats. Don't you know anything about the laws of the sea?'

'Oh, I understand now. Look, I lost control of my boat. I'm really sorry. Of course I'll replace your boat. The collision was my fault.'

'Irreplaceable.' The older man said bleakly, his eyes fixed on his foundering yacht.

'Sorry?'

'Irreplaceable.' The older man repeated. 'It's an antique. It's irreplaceable.'

'Well, then, we'll recover it and get it repaired by the finest craftsmen.'

The older man shook his head. 'You won't. She's sinking. By the time you get out there she will have sunk to the bottom. It's very deep out there, you know. You won't be able to recover her.

She's gone. A perfect example of fine craftsmanship. And my pride and joy.' The last words a whisper.

There was a heavy silence as both men continued to look at the stricken model sinking ever lower in the water. A gloom of hopelessness enveloped the scene.

'Maybe I can help?' A new voice. Lonei's voice. He had walked closer to them and had heard the end of their conversation.

'You could if you had the right boat. But nobody has the right boat here. You need something really big and powerful. Something with lifting and towing gear on board. A salvage vessel,' the older man said disconsolately, without taking his eyes from the dying throes of his stricken craft.

'I have a tugboat. A big one. I can try, if you like. I don't guarantee anything but I may be able to do something. It may work.'

Now the older man's eyes left the wreckage of his yacht and he turned around, first to look at Lonei and then to focus beyond him to the squat, purposeful form of the approaching tugboat. A light of hope kindled in his eyes. 'That's beautiful,' he said, feasting his eyes on the tugboat, 'it's just what we need for a shipwreck. Thank you so very much. Please go ahead. You can't do any harm now. It's our only chance.'

Lonei positioned himself at the lakeside and guided his tugboat towards the wreck of the yacht. As it approached the yacht, Lonei reduced the tugboat's speed progressively, so that it stopped close to the yacht without causing any dangerous waves.

'Is that a large cleat I can see near the bow?' he asked the older man. 'Would that be a suitable towing point if I could get a hook on to it?'

'Yes, I think it would,' the yacht owner whispered, greatly overcome by the drama and tragedy of the scene.

With a myriad of tiny control movements, Lonei turned the tugboat around within its own length until the squat, low stern was facing the bow of the stricken yacht. The crowd, now swelled to a considerable number, gasped as the tugboat started to edge towards the yacht, which was now almost submerged in the water. Eventually, the stern of the tugboat touched the yacht's bow lightly, without upsetting its precarious equilibrium in any way. Now Lonei began to lower the tugboat's towing hook towards the cleat on the yacht's deck. As the hook approached the deck, it became clear that it was too far forward to engage with the cleat.

'Maybe I can set the hook swinging and make contact that way,' Lonei said to the yacht's owner. 'I'll try it and see what happens.' Lonei achieved the beginning of a swing on the hook by moving the tugboat gently backwards and forwards. However, the resulting waves began to wash dangerously over the bow of the yacht and he had to discontinue the attempt after a few minutes.

'Oh, dear,' the yacht's owner said plaintively, 'it really does look as if we'll lose her.' Tears began to form in his eyes.

'Just a minute,' Lonei said, 'I'll manoeuvre round to the side of the bow. I will try to attach the towing hook from there. From there, it should be a shorter reach to the cleat.'

It was a complex operation to move the tugboat to its different position. By the time Lonei was satisfied with the tug's position, the yacht was dangerously awash.

'I don't think we have much time left,' the owner said to Lonei. 'I think she'll sink very soon and then there's nothing we can do.'

'Yes,' Lonei agreed grimly, 'but if I can attach the hook to the cleat, my tugboat is big enough to hold it up even if it is sinking. So here goes!'

This time, the tugboat's towing hook could reach the cleat. Even so, it was necessary to make a number of attempts to hook it on, because the cleat was small in comparison to the tug's hook.

'She's going down,' the owner cried hoarsely. 'Look, the bow has gone under. She'll soon be on the bottom. We've lost her.' As he spoke, the tip of the towing hook slipped into the cleat and arrested the sinking. Lonei tested the strain and began to winch the cable in sufficiently to stop the yacht from sinking any further.

'Got her!' he cried excitedly and a loud cheer went up from the spectators. Lonei's hands flicked across the control console and the tugboat moved at "dead slow" towards the bank, with the stricken yacht hooked securely behind. Ten minutes later, the owner had recovered his precious yacht with all its broken equipment still attached. He pumped Lonei's hand vigorously.

'You are an absolute hero, Sir,' he said. 'You deserve a reward for this. You were amazing!'

Lonei was pleased but adamant. 'I need no reward, Sir. I just happened to have the right equipment for the job. Anyway, you should thank Otisk, here—it's his tugboat.'

'No it isn't, Lonei.' Otisk was equally adamant. 'It's your tugboat. I bought it for you. It's a birthday present.'

'But, Otisk, it isn't my birthday!'

'I don't care!' Otisk was smiling broadly.

The young man now joined the group. 'I'll have your yacht rebuilt in the best craft workshop in Pazoten. I'm Grangel and this is where I live.' He gave the older man a card. 'I'll contact you tomorrow and we'll get the repair put in hand immediately. Your yacht will soon be fully restored and I promise to be more careful in future.'

The older man shook his hand and smiled. 'No-one plans accidents, Grangel,' he said, 'especially in Pazoten. And, when they do happen, we soon put everything right. But just remember this— "steam gives way to sail."'

'I know what that means now,' the young man said with a smile, 'it's engraved on my mind!'

The older man turned to Lonei. 'Please come and have a drink with me.' He indicated a picnic table and chairs set up nearby. 'I want to ask you about your wonderful tugboat. It's the best I have ever seen and I would like to know everything about it.'

Lonei looked doubtful. 'I don't know if I can, Sir…'

Otisk intervened. 'Of course you can, Lonei. Francel and I are going to stroll over to the big lake and maybe we'll take a quick boat ride. We'll see you here when we get back.'

* * * *

The large lake was a very extensive stretch of water. There were many different kinds of boat available for hire, everything from simple rowing skiffs to powerful motor cruisers. A line of people were waiting to rent the boats and Otisk and Francel joined the line.

'We'll just take a short trip in a powered boat. I'm sure Lonei will be enjoying himself with his new friend, telling him all about the tug's construction, facilities and systems! You know, I really fancy one of these beautiful red cruisers they have here. We'll get one of these.'

However there was disappointment when they arrived at the front of the line. There were no red cruisers available. The two that had been moored there had been taken by people ahead of them in the line. Now, a few small rowing boats were all that appeared to be available. Seeing the disappointment on Otisk's face, a lake staff member (his badge identified him as the Boat Master) approached them. 'Good afternoon, Francel and Otisk, do we not have what were you looking for?'

'Well, I rather wanted a powered boat,' Otisk replied, 'but it seems there are none available. We'll just have to take what you have.'

'What sort of powered boat did you want?' the man asked.

'I rather fancied one of these smart red cruisers—like the one that left just a few minutes ago.'

'Wait a minute, Otisk. That's no problem.' As he spoke, a powerful engine was heard to start up and a gleaming red cruiser appeared from a small, inconspicuous boathouse a little way along the lakeside. This impressive craft powered down to them and pulled in at the jetty, its twin exhausts crackling impressively. A cheerful young man jumped off and held the boat against the jetty. 'Here you are!' he said. 'Jump aboard. Are you familiar with the controls? The throttle levers here control the two engines—usually, you move them together unless you want to use separate power for turning. The gearbox control is here; forward engages forward drive of course and pulling backwards puts you into reverse. And, of course, the wheel controls the rudder for steering. Just use low power until you're clear of the jetty and be careful of the small boats. Once you are out in the centre of the lake you can open her up. This is quite a fast craft, you know. Enjoy!'

'How long do you want it for, Otisk?' the Boat Master enquired.

'We'll just take half an hour, I think. We don't want to be away too long.'

Otisk settled into the padded seat behind the wheel and Francel sat close beside him. He eased the throttle levers forwards and steered the craft away from the jetty towards the centre of the lake. Once there, well clear of any of the smaller boats, he increased the power and the boat accelerated forward, its engines growling impressively. Soon they were moving at an exhilarating speed.

'Wow, Francel, this is awesome! I've never driven such a powerful boat. This is really fantastic.'

After they had been cruising along the lake for almost fifteen minutes, Otisk throttled back and brought the boat around in a big circle. 'We need to watch our time, Francel. We don't want to desert Lonei for too long. That's why I made our ride just half an hour long. Here, you take over and try driving the boat. You'll enjoy it, I guarantee.'

Francel was a bit reluctant at first but was persuaded eventually. Soon they were bowling along. 'I never knew it could be such fun,' Francel gasped, 'It's quite an amazing experience.'

They switched control once more and, shortly after, Otisk eased the craft towards the busy jetty area. The Boat Master seized their tether and tied them up.

'Hope you enjoyed that,' he said to them. 'This is our fastest craft, you know.'

'It was absolutely great,' Otisk reassured him. 'Next time, we'll take it for much longer.'

'I look forward to seeing you again soon,' the man said with a smile.

They stood by the jetty. 'Francel, before we go back to Lonei, there's one thing I really must do.'

'What's that?'

'Just walk down the lakeside a little way with me,' he said, somewhat mysteriously.

He took her arm and they walked towards the small boathouse. When they reached it, Otisk said in a low voice. 'Francel, I really must have a look inside this boathouse. How did they manage to produce our craft from here so quickly? It's puzzling me and you know how I like to solve mysteries. Could you have a look around to see if anyone is watching us? Let me know if you see anything suspicious. I'm going to try and have a look inside if I can.'

'Be careful, Otisk. Maybe there are things we aren't allowed to know.'

'Well, I'm going to have a look, anyway.' He disappeared down one side of the boathouse while she scanned around for onlookers. As far as she could see, no-one was observing them. He was gone for just a few minutes and then he returned.

'Right, Francel, let's go. I'll tell you what I found later.'

* * * *

Lonei was having a wonderful time with his new friend. They were deep in animated conversation when Otisk and Francel arrived, empty wine glasses in front of them. Eventually, Lonei spotted them and waved, rising to his feet and bidding a very friendly farewell to his companion.

'You're back, then. We were having a lovely chat about boats and many other things. He says I must come again and talk to him some more—and I've promised to do that. Shall we pack up the tugboat and get it stowed in the truck?'

'Yes, I suppose it's time we went home, Lonei. It's getting quite late.'

Soon they were bowling along smoothly in the pickup, the tugboat packed safely in the load area behind them.

'Not only have we had a great time sailing the tugboat but we saved the day as well! Or, at least, you did, Lonei!' Otisk was jubilant.

'Well, I must say it was really nice to be sailing a boat again— and such an outstanding boat, too. Then, it was good to be able to help people who had come in contact with bad luck.' Lonei was serene.

'Whoa! You call it bad luck, Lonei? That young man was acting recklessly with his speedboat. The collision was all his fault and the result was severe damage to a beautiful antique yacht. People shouldn't have such fast speedboats on the lake if they can't control them. That's what I think.'

Lonei was silent for some moments. Finally he spoke quietly. 'You know, people make mistakes, Otisk. We all do. We always will because not one of us is perfect. What matters is what our attitude is. What matters is how we react to our mistakes; what do we do afterwards, you know. Now, that young man made a mistake but he had bad luck, too. He said he lost control of his boat and that's why the collision happened. We don't know why he lost control. Maybe it was completely his fault but maybe there was a malfunction in the signal transmission or in the switchgear of his control console. We don't know. But he immediately owned up to his mistake and offered to put everything right, to the absolute satisfaction of the owner of the yacht. I think that's a fine example of what people should do, don't you?'

Otisk was silent and still as he drove along and Francel became worried that he had been offended by Lonei's words. Would Otisk interpret Lonei's words as a rebuke?' She hoped not. She wondered if she should try to say something to defuse the tension that she felt was building up—but she couldn't think of the right thing to say! So she sat silently, becoming increasingly miserable as the seconds plodded by in an increasingly hopeless procession.

'You're right.' Otisk's voice was soft and filled with wonderment. 'What you have said is very wise, Lonei—and it needed to be said. My judgement was hasty, superficial and harsh—as well as wrong! Of course you're right. Accidents will always happen and it's the subsequent events that define the quality of the outcome.

Thanks for your words, Lonei. I've learned something important from you today.'

'Listen, Otisk. I'm sorry. I shouldn't have spoken. I was just thinking out loud and I shouldn't have done that...'

'No,' Otisk voice was warm, 'you did absolutely right. You're a philosopher, that's what you are. You taught me something today and I love learning new things, especially things that improve me.'

'It's nice of you to understand but I'm sorry just the same.'

They arrived outside Lonei's flat.

'Thanks, Otisk and Francel for a terrific day,' Lonei said, preparing to get out.

'Hey, just a minute, don't forget the tugboat! I'm coming to help you carry it in.'

'Listen, Otisk. It's too good a present for me. In any case, no-one ever gives me presents. You must keep it. I'm happy to sail it with you any time I'm free.'

'No, we want you to have it. It's yours, if you want it, that is.'

'Of course I want it. It's so beautiful, the finest model I've ever seen and the best I've ever sailed. But...'

'Then take this end. Let's lift it into your house. I've told you it's yours.'

Lonei was silent as they carried the tugboat into his house and laid it down gently on its hull stands in front of his sitting room window, taking pride of place in the room.

'It's so great to see it there. It's so beautiful.' Lonei said again with utmost seriousness.

'Well, there you are. Happy birthday!'

'But it isn't my birthday; I told you before.'

'It's a present for your last birthday, then,' Otisk smiled. They shook hands. 'I must go now but I'll see you soon and we'll go boating again. Meanwhile, you can go boating with any of your friends anytime you're free and we aren't.'

'Otisk?'

'Yes, Lonei?'

'Can I call her "Juno II"?'

'Of course you can. I think that's a marvellous name for her.'

* * * *

'I finally persuaded him that the tugboat was his!' Otisk was driving along, Francel by his side. 'He asked if he could christen her "Juno II". Of course I said "yes".'

Francel smiled. 'That's a lovely name for her—and a meaningful link with his previous boat, too,' she said.

Soon they were relaxing at home, having returned the truck to Town Auto One.

After a thoughtful pause, Francel spoke again: 'So what was in the boathouse? What did you see?' Her curiosity had been aroused.

'Well, I checked the back wall and down each side but there were no windows. I looked around the front where it faces the lake but the big double doors were solid wood and shut fast. Maybe there are skylights in the roof but I couldn't see that high.'

Francel was disappointed. 'So you didn't manage to see inside?'

He grinned. 'Well—you know me! I eventually found a crack in the boarding in one wall. It wasn't very wide but I managed to look inside. It was really dark in there and I had to wait for my eyes to adjust.'

'So what did you see? Tell me!'

He smiled. 'I saw nothing.'

'But you told me you were able to see inside…'

'Yes, Francel. That's what I'm saying. I saw nothing. There was nothing inside that boathouse. Nothing but the water from the lake and a narrow walkway around the sides. Nothing else. No boats, no equipment, no lighting that I could see. Nothing! Looked like it had been empty and completely disused for years.'

She looked at him, wide-eyed. 'But how…'

'I've absolutely no idea, Francel. It's a mystery. Another Pazoten mystery—just like the brand-new rental cars at Town Auto One—we just need to accept it.'

Chapter 9

They had chatted comfortably at breakfast. Now there was silence as they both pursued those random paths of idle thought that are a speciality of human relaxation, their thoughts totally unconnected with anything they had been talking about before.

"48 times 236?"
'11,328.'

"13,908 divided by 76?"
'183.'

"951.6 times 157.37?"
'149,753.29.'

'Hey, that's cheating!' Otisk cried out, the sharp suddenness of his voice startling Francel.

'What? Whatever has happened to you?'

'Well, I've just had one of my maths tests and the calculations are ones that I have been asked before. Maybe some weeks ago but I do remember them. So I'm just telling the originator of the tests to make up new calculations if he or she must do this to me.'

Francel smiled. 'The "he" or "she" might be "you". Your own brain, you know.'

Otisk was silent for a moment. 'That's a very interesting comment, Francel. If it was my brain doing this I don't think it would be repeating the calculations. It would be formulating new ones. Because that's the sort of thing I would do—and it's my brain, I'm in control.'

'Well someday maybe you will find out the truth. Meanwhile, it's keeping you in practice, isn't it?' Francel thought it best to put a "positive spin" on Otisk's maths tests.

'Hm, maybe,' he flashed a smile at her, knowing she was trying to help. 'Listen, Francel, we don't have a shift today but we need to catch up on our incomer reviews. Do I recall that you wanted to spend some time editing the photographs you took yesterday? Why don't I get on with the review and you do your photographs? If there are any problems, we can discuss them later.'

'That's kind of you, Otisk. Yes, I would like to do that. Once I've deleted all the photographic rubbish (and there will be plenty of that) and then edited the rest, I'll be ready to go to print. If any are really good, I may get them blown up really big at the photographic shop. The shopkeeper has all the latest processing and enlarging equipment there.'

'Fine. Let's get started on our tasks, then.'

Later in the morning, Francel had appeared with several large photographs just as Otisk was finishing the reviews.

'No problems with any of these reviews, Francel. All our incomers are doing well and have settled in happily.'

'That's good to hear. I thought we might have problems with one or two—I'm sure you can guess which ones—but we seem to have won at the moment, anyway.'

'Are these the professional photographs of the epic day out?'

'Yes. I brought the final selections for you to have a look.'

Eight large photographs were spread out on the table, showing various scenes from the lakes.

'Hey, these are really good, Francel. I mean it. I am sure you must have had a connection with professional photography in the past. Professional photographs always look so different from the pathetic snaps that we mere mortals take.'

'Well, Otisk, I know you're being really encouraging and I thank you—but I'm really pleased with this group. They capture exactly what I was attempting to do and the colour and composition balance has worked well. I'm really very impressed by that Nikon camera I bought. I know it wasn't the most expensive in the shop—I'm pretty sure that was the Leica S—but the Nikon was a really good choice for me. It seems to fit into my hand so very well and the weight is just about right.'

'Well, your photographic friend at the shop certainly did a lot of work to find you the right camera. He was glued to that data screen for ages, but it seems that all his work paid off.'

'That's what it's like when you're an enthusiast—I'm sure you know that. The shopkeeper would not have thought of all that searching as a chore. He would have enjoyed every minute of it. He was demonstrating all his knowledge and expertise to us and that's bound to be enjoyable.'

'Yes, of course you're right, Francel. We can all get caught up completely in our enthusiasms, can't we? Are you going to get these enlarged further?'

'Yes, I thought I might go round to the photographic shop now. I can get them projected much larger and make a decision on which ones to turn into large picture-size. Do you want to come with me?'

'No, Francel, I'll let you go alone. I have a strong feeling that you and the expert at the shop will be indulging in a lot of technical "photographer-speak". I would just be a hindrance. I'll clear up my review work here and then wait for you over at the café. It will be very nice to watch the world go by for a little while.'

'There's something else I want to do at the shop, Otisk. I've decided I need to add to my camera equipment. I need a good telephoto lens. There are times when I just need to get a bit closer to my subject than I can at present. I'll discuss this with my expert friend but I intend to have a look at the matching Nikkor telephoto lens; I think they do a really useful 55-300mm model that is in the same series as my standard lens. That might be very suitable for what I want. No doubt it will be a bit chunky but almost all telephoto lenses are. Anyway, I'll see what my friend at the shop has to offer.'

'Fine, Francel, that sounds great. I'll see you later. You'll find me daydreaming at the café—just wake me up gently!'

* * * *

It was almost lunch time when Francel joined Otisk at the café. He saw her approaching. 'Hello, you're just in time for lunch. How did your visit to the photographic shop go? Did you get the photographs enlarged?'

'Yes, I had three of them made into a large picture size. Here they are. I also bought a good telephoto lens—the Nikkor 55-300mm I was talking about. That was my friend's recommendation for my camera. So now I'm ready for all eventualities.'

The large photographs, printed on heavyweight matt paper, were extremely impressive. There was a scene of the large lake, one of all the activity at the model boating lake and a final one with Lonei rescuing the stricken yacht with his tugboat.

'These are spectacular, Francel, truly professional; I'm really impressed.'

'So am I.' A new voice. The café proprietor had come to their table and was looking at the photographs with great admiration. 'Listen, Francel, would you sell these to me? I've been looking for some really good pictures for the café walls and these would be perfect. If I can have them, I'll get them framed and put up as soon as possible on that wall over there.' He pointed.

'I could let you have the two scenes,' Francel said. 'I want to give the tugboat rescue picture to the owner of the tugboat.'

'Done! I'll be happy to have these two,' the café proprietor said. 'Free lunches for a week? Any food and drink you want. Would that be satisfactory?'

'Accepted!' They shook hands smilingly. 'So we'll order our first lunches right now.'

As they were eating their food, Francel said. 'When we're finished here, Otisk, I'd like to get the tugboat picture framed up and sent to Lonei. I'm sure he would enjoy having it in his house. Shall we have a stroll around to that art shop that you deal with? We can choose a suitable frame and have the picture sent over to his house right away.'

'That's a good idea, Francel. Let's do that.'

Half an hour later, they stood in the art shop.

'What sort of framing would you like?' the shopkeeper asked. 'I keep a large selection here.'

'You've been in Lonei's house, Otisk. What kind of frame do you think would fit in?'

'Just something plain. A nice slim light-coloured wooden frame would be best, I think. Maybe ash or beech?'

'Here are some frame samples,' the shopkeeper said, producing a sample display board from an extensive rack. They pored over it, placing the photograph next to the frame samples.

'What wood is this one?' Otisk enquired.

'That's beech,' the man said. 'That certainly would complement the colours of the print, in my opinion.'

'We'll have that, thanks,' Francel confirmed. 'However, we don't want the picture to be transported to us. It's a special present for the man in the picture. Here's his address. If I give you a gift card, would you include it with the package?'

'Yes, of course I will. I'll have the framing done this afternoon and then it can be packed and transported over to his house right away. Just leave it all to me. Thank you for your custom.'

They completed the purchase and thanked the man.

'Let's just go for a short stroll now,' Francel said. 'It's a lovely afternoon. Then we can have a quiet evening so that we'll be ready for our overnight shift. As you know, we've copped the ever-popular 0300-0900 hours slot!'

'You know Francel, I quite enjoy walking to the Administrative Centre in the middle of the night. With no-one around, everything is so quiet and calm. I find it so much more restful in comparison to relocating straight to RR5.'

'Yes. I enjoy the leisurely walk too. So shall we leave about 0215 hours and walk over, hand-in-hand, like lovers?' she smiled.

'Why not,' he replied. 'That's what we are, isn't it?'

* * * *

It was a warm, still night and their stroll from the empty Town Square to the Administrative Centre had been very pleasant. Walking in the silent stillness was a welcome change from the normal bustle of the Town. As they entered the Administrative Centre, they greeted the Duty Doorkeeper with the usual wave and were transported to RR5. Here, a surprise awaited them. They knew from the Rota that they were taking over from ART7 but the couple who greeted them rather nervously were unknown to them.

'Hello, Laneo and Fargee,' Otisk said, sensing their names, 'we're ART9, Otisk and Francel, taking over from you. We were expecting to see ART7. I think that's what it said on the Rota the last time we were here. Is there a problem with them or have we misread the Rota?'

'Er, no, Otisk.' The man was rather nervous. 'We are ART7. We're a new team, just completing our very first shift. We've replaced the people who were ART7. I hear this happens from time to time. They've—ah—left.'

Otisk nodded. 'Ah, yes, I understand, Laneo. Sorry to be so dense; it must be because it's the middle of the night. So how did your first shift go?'

'Well, it went fine,' the woman said quietly, 'but absolutely nothing happened.' She looked at her partner. 'We don't know whether to be pleased or worried. What's the usual pattern here, Otisk? Does an incomer usually arrive sometime during the six-hour shifts?'

'Well, it's variable, Fargee. Yes, one incomer is quite normal for a shift. That's what the statistics tell us. However, sometimes it's no arrivals and occasionally it can be two. You will find that two can get a bit hectic if they start to manifest close together in time. Then you need to go to Single Reception Procedures—I'm sure you know all about that, don't you?'

Both members of ART7 nodded but continued to look distinctly worried. 'We were hoping we could put our training into practice,' Laneo said rather sadly. 'We feel… a bit redundant.'

'Presumably you trained fairly recently?' Otisk asked.

'Yes, it was just two days ago. We were asked the day before to be a Reception Team because a vacancy had occurred. We ourselves have only been in Pazoten for a short time. For some reason, I can't remember how long. Can you?' Laneo looked at Fargee with a raised eyebrow.

She shook her head. 'No. I'm like you, Laneo. I can't remember either. I don't know why.'

'Listen. That's nothing to worry about,' Otisk reassured them, 'you'll find that time is a bit different here in Pazoten. Just relax and enjoy yourselves. Go with the flow, you know—that's what we all do.'

'And as far as your first shift experience goes, Laneo,' Francel smiled at him, 'just being here and getting familiar with the place has given you valuable and essential experience. You're just being eased in gently. Don't worry, you'll receive an incomer or two soon enough. Anyway, I'm sure you're both tired now and ready for a good rest.'

Laneo returned her smile. 'Thanks for these words, Otisk and Francel. You're quite right, we have plenty of time to gain experience. And, yes, we are pretty tired so, if it's all right with you, we'll hand over to you now and relocate ourselves back home. By the way, your Child Reception Team is CRT4. I haven't seen them receiving an incomer either. They're up there in their reception area. I understand that their shift timings are different from the ARTs?'

'Yes, that's right, Laneo. I think the management is quite right to stagger the shifts. It gives better coverage of the overall situation. Anyway, thanks for your briefing. We'll take over now. Are you back soon on another shift?'

'Our next shift is in two days; it's daytime from 1500 to 2100 hours.'

'That's good. Gives you a day to relax and assimilate.'

'Good night, then.' Laneo and Fargee shook hands with Otisk and Francel and then faded and disappeared as they relocated.

Otisk and Francel immediately moved across to their reception position and scanned their display. 'I see the last incomer was during the shift before theirs, so, statistically, we're quite likely to receive tonight.'

They sat down together with a hot drink.

'Francel?'

'Yes?'

'That unexpected replacement of ART7 has made me think again about people leaving here. It seems to happen so suddenly—and without warning. One minute the people are there, just acting normally, and the next minute they've disappeared. We never see them again. And no-one seems to bother about it. They hardly seem to register it. They just state it as a fact and continue their life here as if nothing has happened. We seem to be the only people who ever question it!'

Francel was thoughtful. 'Well, Otisk, we've certainly talked a lot about people arriving. And, as a Reception Team, we've certainly got plenty of experience of the actuality of it. We have tried to fathom out the meaning of our own arrivals, haven't we? But we couldn't come to any conclusion. We couldn't remember anything significant and it seems that we are not supposed to recall anything of that nature.'

'Yes—but there we were, just a few days ago, handing over to ART7, to people we've known for quite a time—and suddenly, they're gone. Suddenly, ART7 has become two new strangers. Nice people, of course. But I find it distinctly unsettling. What has happened to our friends who were ART7? Where have they gone and why?'

'Obviously, I don't know, Otisk, but your question links back to all our previous discussions on the past, on what age we are, on what our life was before Pazoten, if we had a life, that is. I suppose all we can say about this situation is—we come to Pazoten, we stay a while and then we go away. We don't even know whether we go back to where we came from or whether we go off to a different place. It's all completely unknown. Anyway, Otisk, we agreed we would just go along with it all, just like everyone else seems to, and enjoy our wonderful life here in this amazing land.'

'You're right to remind me of that, Francel. Because wracking your brains on this subject never seems to get you anywhere. So, I'm going to be quiet now and just enjoy you and Pazoten!'

Francel smiled, knowing that Otisk (and she) would always struggle with these matters to some degree or other. However, it would seem that they were destined never to make progress on their impossible questions.

A familiar soft chime made them turn their attention to the screen:

"Incomer procedure is commencing One adult manifestation is proceeding. Data will follow"

He grinned at her. Here we go again, Partner: ART9 will spring into action when the time is ripe!'

She leaned over and kissed him. 'I'm so glad that you are the other half of ART9, darling Otisk. We are so very lucky to have been chosen for such a vitally important function.'

* * * *

After their shift, they had relocated home and slept for a few hours. Now they were settled at a table in front of the café to have a late lunch. Francel was delighted to see her framed photographs gracing the walls of the café. People were very interested, leaving their tables and going for a closer look and making very complimentary comments about the quality and beauty of the images.

'You know, your photographs look even better when framed and displayed,' Otisk said warmly to Francel. 'What a very clever and artistic person you are.'

'Have you looked at the new pictures?' One of the customers at the next table leaned over and addressed them. 'They really are superb. The proprietor said he just put them up today and they're certainly causing a lot of interest. I see they were taken at the Southwest Lakes. The scenery is very good out there. You know, these must have been taken by a really talented photographer. I know a bit about photography myself but I couldn't equal the skill and artistry of these. They're just signed with "F"—you wouldn't know who that was, would you?'

Otisk looked at Francel with raised eyebrows. 'Well, I don't know…' she began hesitantly.

'So, Francel, your pictures are causing quite a stir.' The café proprietor beamed down upon her as he stood by their side and spoke these words loudly and joyfully. 'They really look great, don't they? And everyone likes them.'

The man at the next table rose to his feet. 'Hey, everybody,' he said commandingly, 'Francel here took these photographs!' As he spoke he pointed out her location at the table beside him. 'Isn't she absolutely great?'

A hubbub of congratulation and admiration filled the café, followed by loud applause. Eventually, a rather pink-faced Francel stood up. 'You're all very kind,' she said, 'it's so easy to photograph Pazoten—everything is so beautiful. I'm sure you could all do it but, anyway, thank you very much.'

She sat down to another round of applause. 'Well, that's it, Francel, you're properly famous now—and you deserve to be.'

'You know, Otisk, all this has made me think of my past once again. I feel I must have taken photographs before because I don't need to think about the mechanics when I'm doing it. All that just comes automatically and I find I can concentrate totally on the artistic aspects of my subject. Anyway, we've tried to get through to the past several times now and have always failed despite our very best efforts. So I think I'll just have to enjoy what I seem to be able to do here.'

'Yes, Francel, we've agonised over this before. Let's just accept it and enjoy it.'

They looked at each other seriously and then burst out laughing. 'Have you noticed, Otisk, we keep saying that to each other—quite often.'

'It's absolutely true, Francel. One or other of us keeps going back to the same set of puzzles—ones that it seems we can't solve! We really must learn to behave.' They laughed again.

'Hello, Otisk and Francel.' A very quiet voice. Lonei stood before them in his orange jacket, his cart parked nearby. They had been so absorbed in their interaction with each other that they hadn't noticed his approach.

'Hi, Lonei, welcome; come and join us for a drink and a snack.'

Lonei looked doubtful but tempted. 'I don't think I should...' he began.

'Oh come on, you can spare ten minutes surely! Sit down and relax. Take a break.' He gestured to the waiter. 'What would you like?'

'Well, I'll just stay five minutes. I'll have a coffee and a biscuit. Just a plain one,' he added.

Otisk ordered this. 'Listen, Otisk and Francel, I just stopped by to thank you for the wonderful picture you sent me. You are a very skilled photographer, Francel. It's really good and it's giving me a lot of pleasure. I've hung it in my sitting room where I can see it all the time when I'm there. But listen, Otisk and Francel, you mustn't spend so much of your credits on me. I'm just a low-level worker here and I don't deserve the lovely things you've given me.'

'That's not true, Lonei.' Francel was adamant, 'and you mustn't say such things. You are a very good worker for Pazoten and you deserve to be happy. It's a great pleasure for me to give you a picture that you enjoy and we were delighted to give you the tugboat as the first present you've received for many years. And I think her name is lovely.'

'No,' Lonei said, 'I didn't deserve the tugboat. It's too expensive a gift for me.'

Otisk snorted. 'Nonsense, it's a birthday present; in fact it's a birthday present for all the birthdays you've had here in Pazoten.' He grinned at the little man.

'Well, Otisk, you have a very persuasive way with you. Anyway, I love the tugboat and I love the picture. So thanks, both.'

They sat quietly for a moment, watching the people enjoying themselves in the Town Square.

'Lonei? Can I ask you a question?'

'Of course.'

'Have you had many birthdays in Pazoten?'

Silence while Lonei looked inscrutably across the Square. 'I think I have,' he said finally.

'Can you remember how many?'

'Don't think so. Why do you ask?'

'Lonei, last week when I said the tugboat was a birthday present, you said it couldn't be because it wasn't your birthday.'

'That's right, it wasn't. That's why I said it.'

'So does that mean you know when your birthday is?'

Lonei thought about this. 'No it doesn't. It means that I know when my birthday *isn't!*'

It was Otisk's turn to pause in thought. 'But surely this means that you must know when it *is*' he rejoined, piercingly.

Lonei looked straight at him and Otisk was surprised by the directness in Lonei's eyes. 'No, Otisk, I'm sorry. I know why you're saying that. You're applying mathematical logic. But that doesn't apply in this case. I only know when my birthday *isn't*. You just need to believe that.' He rose to his feet. 'And now I'm afraid I must go, Otisk and Francel, otherwise I'll fall behind my schedule and I mustn't do that. Thanks for everything. Goodbye.'

He walked away quickly without a backward glance. Wordlessly, they watched his orange-clad figure working its way around the Square until he disappeared down one of the streets.

Finally, Otisk turned to look at Francel. 'I suppose he's right. I mean, he certainly was right about the mathematical logic. This is another case of Pazoten rules apply. I suppose we just have to accept it.'

She took his hand and laughed. 'Here we go again! We keep saying that, don't we? We've said it so many times already and I suppose we'll need to say it many times more.' She paused. 'Listen, let's have a full day out tomorrow. We have a completely clear day. Which way do you think we ought to go? Let's go somewhere we've never been before.'

He thought for a minute. 'I've got an idea for a bit of an adventure: let's rent a couple of quad bikes; I've seen a few of these around so we must be able to rent them. Quad bikes can go to places that you can't take a car. If we get the bikes, we can go out the West Road and then go off on one of the tracks through the forested areas that I've seen on the map. We can park the bikes somewhere convenient and go for a nice long hike. Somewhere really remote. What do you think of that?'

'That sounds like a splendid idea but I'm a little worried about riding a quad bike. That's something I've never done before. Do you think I'll be able to do it?'

'Of course you will! You can drive a car so you know how to drive a motorised vehicle and you can ride a bike can't you? Well, a quad bike is easier that either of these. The gearbox and clutch systems are automatic and, of course, it's got four-wheel stability, unlike a pedal cycle. You'll find it extremely easy, I promise.'

'Hm. I must say you make it sound very easy. And I think it sounds very exciting and completely different from the things we have done before. Let's do that. I'll trust you and risk it. After breakfast tomorrow, I'll get a picnic together and we'll see if we can get suitable quad bikes from Town Auto One. I'll make sure I take all my camera equipment with me so that I can test out my new telephoto lens. I can take some distant mountain shots and zoom in on features of interest.'

'Maybe I need to become a mountaineer, Francel, and then you can take heroic pictures of me brandishing my ice pick from a craggy peak!'

She looked at him teasingly. 'I doubt whether you would ever need an ice pick in Pazoten. It's always so warm here and the mountains don't look very high.'

'Hm.' He pretended to be disappointed. 'I've always fancied myself pictured on the top of a jagged, snowy mountain, impressively holding my trusty ice pick.'

'Well, Otisk, who knows what we will find during our adventure. Anyway, you should take your painting kit with you in case you're inspired.'

'Good idea—I think I'll take a sketch book. I can develop the canvases later.'

Chapter 10

They awakened the next morning in high spirits. The opened curtains revealed the perfect day, sunny, calm and already warm.

'It's a wonderful climate here in Pazoten,' Otisk called to Francel. 'Obviously, we need to have rain sometimes but this usually happens during the night. Sometimes we experience it on our nighttime shifts, don't we? When it's wet at 0300 hours, we could walk to or from work under our umbrellas but we usually just relocate, don't we? It's quicker that way—and you do stay dry!'

Francel smiled. 'Yes, I remember once we thought we would walk home at 0300 hours in the rain. As we walked it became heavier and heavier and the wind was blowing, too. We were soaking wet by the time we arrived home. We thought we would just relocate the next time it was wet! Anyway, Otisk, let's have breakfast as quickly as possible, then I'll prepare the picnic for our adventure. I'm really looking forward to this, you know—although I'm still just a little nervous of this quad bike you're putting me on. I hope I can ride it safely. I certainly hope I won't fall off.'

'Look, Francel, you'll be fine, honestly. They're really easy to ride and we won't be doing anything extreme, I promise you.'

'Well, OK, I trust you—I think.'

Within an hour they had breakfasted and made all their preparations. Now they arrived at Town Auto One. Otisk looked around. 'I've never seen any quad bikes in the showroom—or even motor bikes. If they have them, they must be kept in another part of the building.'

They walked across to the office. 'Hello, Morseb, how are you today?'

'Otisk! Nice to see you again. What can we get for you today?'

'Do you have any quad bikes?'

'Yes, of course we have.'

'Where are they? I don't see any in your showroom.'

'They're in Showroom 2, along with the motorbikes, etc. We'll go there in a minute. I would just like to check what you need; there are several types, you know. Basically, there are sports and utility quad bikes. As you may guess, the first are used for sporting activities only—track racing, hill climbing, etc. The utility type can be "road legal" and go off-road as well. What sort did you have in mind?'

'We want "road legal" to cruise west and then go off-road on the forest tracks. Nothing too rough, though.'

'I understand. It's no problem. Let's walk through to the showroom.'

The large room was filled with motorbikes of all type and size, everything from light scooters to large very powerful machines. At one end, a range of quad bikes were displayed.

'Do you want to ride solo or are you both going on the same bike? The larger machines take two very comfortably,' Morseb said.

'We'll have one each,' Otisk smiled, 'we're planning to be adventurous!'

'In that case, I would recommend these.' He pointed to a group of brightly-coloured machines, all with large wheels and deeply treaded tyres. 'These models have a good wheelbase, so they ride comfortably. It's a 350cc engine, electric start, automatic CVT transmission, selectable two- or four-wheel drive and really good suspension for rough surfaces. I think they are what you want. You can take them outside to the yard and test them out. What colour would you like, Francel?'

'I'll like the dark green one. It looks really nice.'

'I'll have the aggressive red,' Otisk said with a grin, 'designed to suit my personality!'

The quad bikes were taken outside. Otisk started his machine, engaged gear and rode around the yard smoothly. 'This is really fun,' he said to Francel when he returned. 'Really easy.'

She mounted her machine. Otisk showed her the various hand and foot controls. Then she started the engine and rode slowly around the yard with increasing confidence. 'You're absolutely right, Otisk, it really is fun,' she said when she braked to a stop beside them, 'I'll be able to manage this—I'll just be careful, especially at first.'

'Right, Morseb, we'll have these, please. Will you sort out the essential riding kit for us?'

'Yes, Fine, Otisk. Let's go over here. You need a suit and a helmet. The helmets have an intercom, so you will be able to speak to one another as you go along.'

Shortly after, they had been fitted out and were ready to start. The machines were fuelled up and ready at the front of the showroom. Otisk had strapped their rucksacks to the carrier grid on the back of his machine.

'We'll see you later, early evening, I think,' Otisk called as they prepared to leave.

'That's fine, see you then. Enjoy yourselves.'

They had traversed the Ring Road and turned left into West Road. Now they increased their speed and bowled along the smooth surface at around 40 mph.

Otisk called on the intercom radio. 'Francel, this is really wonderful. Are you all right? Over.'

'Yes, Otisk, I'm really enjoying this. It's a really different experience. Over.'

'We'll keep going until we reach the forested area that we've seen on the map. Then we can review what tracks there are available and see what we want to do. OK by you? Over.'

'Agreed, Otisk. Over and Out.' Within her helmet, Francel grinned. *I've always wanted to say "Over and Out" for real – An ambition fulfilled*, she thought.

The forest area was reached and they stopped to confer and study the map. It was clear that there were many tracks and trails that criss-crossed the forest.

'I think we should stick to the main trails and still head westwards.' He studied the map. 'Look, I think this is the major track going west. Shall we go this way? It's marked "Track W10".' They looked around and observed that one of the forest tracks was identified by a rustic sign announcing "W10".

'Yes, let's do that and see what happens. The map suggests it will take us to the western edge of the forest and then there are footpaths going west. That's what we want, isn't it?'

'Let's try it, then.' Otisk remounted his bike and Francel followed suit. Soon they were riding through the forest. The track was reasonably well marked but some sections were rather rough and they had to slow down and take care. Nevertheless they were enjoying the experience completely.

Francel called Otisk on the intercom. 'This is really good. I've never done anything like this before. These quad bikes really can go anywhere! Over.'

'Yes, Francel, it's really exhilarating. Come on—I'll race you to the clearing ahead. We'll stop there and check the map. Right? Go when you're ready. I'll give you a head start. Over.'

'Received. Over and Out.' She couldn't help grinning again as she accelerated away! Several minutes later they had reached the intersection and stopped beside each other.

'Wow, Francel, congratulations! You won the race. That's the last time I give you a head start.' Laughing, they pored over the map. 'I see where we are—here.' He pointed. 'It isn't far to go to the western edge of the forest. I see there is a clearing marked just here. Shouldn't take us long to get there.'

They remounted and continued down the main forest track for another ten minutes or so. Eventually, they rode into the large clearing that marked the end of the track. They crossed over to the western edge and parked their quad bikes near the start of the well-marked footpath that snaked away westwards in the bright sunshine.

Otisk unstrapped the rucksacks from his quad bike. 'Let's get our rucksacks on and start our hike along this path. This will be a great day out. The countryside here is so spectacular and it's a perfect day for walking.'

They spent a few hours tramping along the path and admiring the views. Once on the journey, Otisk's attention was diverted by one of his involuntary maths tests. Noting his annoyance, Francel soothed him by pointing out that the tests kept his unusual ability in practice and this mollified him to some degree. 'Anyway, it's really lovely out here, isn't it?' she said, changing the subject. 'Although it's always nice to be with all the others in the Town, it does you good to get away. To be alone, you know.'

'But, Francel, haven't you noticed?' Otisk was grinning at her affectionately, 'you're not alone, are you? You're with me!'

'Oh come on, Otisk, you know I meant "to be alone *with you*". You know how happy I am to be with you—and isn't it a boon that the Counsellors arranged for us to work together, too? That means we can be together almost all of the time...?'

'Yes, I think that's great' Otisk responded, 'you know I always love to be with you. In fact, when I'm alone, away from you, I actually feel as if a part of me is missing. It's a very strange feeling; I've never felt like that before, you know. Never in my memory.'

Francel smiled. 'I'm so happy you feel like that. I feel exactly the same. Even the Counsellors approved of us being together almost as soon as we met, didn't they? All that seems such a long time ago, doesn't it?'

'Mm, yes. I remember we were a bit worried at first but, right away, they approved of us being together and gave us absolutely everything we wanted. I think that's been absolutely ideal!'

Periodically, Francel stopped to take photographs. 'You could climb up that ridge, Otisk, and I could get a good shot of you from down here. You'll just have to imagine the ice pick, though!'

A little later, Otisk asked if he could pause at a particular spot. 'I just want to make a quick sketch of the scene towards the range of hills, there. I think that could develop into an interesting painting later.' He did this quickly and efficiently and soon they were on their way again.

After a good long hike, they arrived at an idyllic spot and decided to "set up camp" there. Their picnic lunch was produced from rucksacks and provided delicious food and refreshment. Then, tired out by exertions followed by food, they lay down and drifted off to a blessèd sleep.

Several hours later, Francel woke up with a question in her mind. 'Otisk, I've been thinking about what you said a little while ago, just after lunch.' Then she questioned him about the meaning of his words: "Never in my memory."

'What is in your memory, Otisk? We've been here in Pazoten for quite a long time now but, somehow, we've never really talked about our own memories in depth, have we? You know, what we were actually doing before Pazoten; who we were, where we were. That's what I have been thinking about. I'm wondering what we can actually recall of our specific past. As far as our time in Pazoten is concerned, as you know, I think I can remember all of that but the bit I can remember most vividly was my meeting with you!'

He agreed warmly. 'Meeting you is certainly the highlight of my memory, too.' They were silent for a moment or two as they both relived the details of their meeting.

Then she turned back to him. 'Otisk, could I ask you some questions?' He agreed and she asked a whole series of questions about his life on Pazoten. Could he remember *everything* that has happened since he came to this Land? He thought he could—maybe not every detail but certainly the broad sequence of events. However, when she asked him how long he had been in Pazoten, he became confused and could not answer. She admitted that she was unable to answer that question either.

'Otisk, don't look so worried; I think neither of us know the answer. Do you remember when you had that discussion about your age (with the Counsellor, remember?), it was suggested that Pazoten reality could be different from our expectations? So we concluded that the concept of time could be different here. I'm wondering if that helps us in any way.'

'Different time?' he replied. 'You know, I remember that conversation and I struggle with that particular concept. Because I understand time to be finite. A minute is a minute, isn't it? And a year is a year. It's fixed, that's the logic of it. These things are concepts of number—and I know all about numbers. I'm an expert!'

'Well, yes, you certainly are a numerical expert. In pure logic, what you have just said is certainly the case. But think about this. I've known some minutes to just flash past at lightning speed. And I've known others to drag on almost like hours. Haven't you had that experience?'

'Hm.' Otisk was thoughtful, 'That is a very wise thing you've just said, Francel. Lateral thinking, indeed. Of course I agree with you. I've certainly had that same experience. I'm sure everyone has. And that means that what I've said about finite time is wrong, doesn't it?'

She shook her head. 'No, I don't think you're wrong; I just think there is room in life, room in *reality*, maybe, for both statements— and probably many others, too.'

She went on to ask him if he was an adult person. He agreed he was and identified her similarly, with a suitably admiring look! They agreed also that they had arrived in Pazoten as adults.

Francel said that her final question was addressed to both of them. It was: 'Where were we before we came to Pazoten? Where were we as babies, as children, as teenagers? Who were our parents? What happened to us? Have you ever thought about these things in depth?' She asked.

'No, Francel, not in depth. In a way, it's strange, that. I can't understand why I haven't.'

'I agree. Let's both think about it now and then we can share our thoughts.'

After a period of silence Francel admitted: 'I've thought about it as deeply as I can, but I'm coming up with absolutely nothing. I simply don't know. I cannot recall any memory of my life before Pazoten. It's like I didn't have a life then—so there's nothing to remember. But I feel convinced about one thing. I must have been somewhere, growing up. I must have had birthdays but I can't remember anything about them. I find that rather sad, don't you?'

Otisk looked up. 'You know, I'm at exactly that same point: however hard I try, I have no memory beyond Pazoten at the moment. Absolutely nothing. But I agree with your analysis. I must have been somewhere but there's a block on my memory. I wonder why?'

They both were silent for some moments more. Then he said, 'we're talking about the past, aren't we, Francel? Right now, I find I'm confused. I find that I'm not actually sure what "the past" is.'

'Do you think we've lost our memories? Is that what has happened to us?'

He thought about this. 'Well, I suppose it could be. But somehow that doesn't seem to fit, does it? Because we seem to know things that must have come from the past, even if we can't remember the past, if, indeed, there was such a thing as a past. Goodness, now I don't seem to be able to define what the past is. Not in the terms we have been talking about. Can you?'

She closed her eyes for a moment or two then shook her head in negation.

They sat quietly for a while, both deeply engrossed in their thoughts.

Finally, Francel spoke. 'I have an idea: maybe it would help if we told each other our story of how we came to Pazoten. Because that was the finish of the past we can't recall and the beginning of the past we can remember. Do you think that might give us any clues?'

'Well, it might. I certainly can't think of any other strategy—apart from giving up, that is!'

They then spent some time telling each other the exact details of their arrival in Pazoten, describing a situation that was now so familiar to them as Reception Team members. Their accounts ended when they met each other in the Town Square and fell in love at first sight.

Otisk summed up. 'Well, that's very interesting. We both had very similar personal experiences. The few differences that there were did not alter the overall procedure, did it? And, after that, we both sailed along serenely, just like everyone else here seems to do. But at the same time, it's quite puzzling, especially when we begin to address the sort of questions you were asking just a little while ago.'

'Listen, Otisk. Were you asking yourself these sorts of questions, too?' she said. 'I mean, I was the one to start this today, wasn't I? But were you actually doing the same?'

Otisk frowned in concentration. 'Well, yes and no, Francel. No, I don't think I was ready to ask your excellent questions. But I was perfectly happy when you did, because in some ways there is a sort of disquiet deep inside me. You know how I like to think of myself as logical? Well, I felt that my situation here was beginning to have elements of illogicality. That's the best way I think I can describe it at the moment. Maybe I would have formulated your sort of questions in time. I don't think I was ready to do so but, as I have already said, I was very happy to participate when you raised the matter. Does all that make sense?'

Francel smiled. 'It makes perfect sense, Otisk. Because that's exactly how I felt a little while ago. A bit worried, a bit off-balance, you know... Then, as I was thinking today, suddenly I just started to ask these questions. It wasn't planned, it just came out!'

Otisk looked into her eyes and nodded gravely. Then, suddenly, he jumped to his feet with a peal of joyful laughter, seized her slim figure and whirled her around in a wild dance. 'You know, I think you're wonderful,' he gasped, 'you know I love you so much, don't you?'

'Wow!' She screamed, 'stop—you'll make me giddy! You know I love you, too.'

Otisk stopped and held her close with loving tenderness. After a moment, suddenly she felt his body jerk with sudden tension.

'What is it?' She cried, 'what's wrong? Is it the maths again?'

'No.' A softly whispered reply in her ear. 'Look.' He turned her around slowly and pointed. They both looked up towards the nearest mountain top. There, illuminated by the late afternoon rays of the sun, was a large, squat grey building, incongruously merged into the rocks of the mountain peak. As they watched in riveted astonishment, after a few minutes the building's entity began to fade in the changing rays of the sun, becoming progressively more diaphanous until it disappeared completely, leaving nothing but the hint of a misty cloud where its presence had been.

During this time, perhaps a total period of seven or eight minutes, Otisk and Francel had not moved, he holding her in his arms, both of them unblinkingly focussed on the astonishing artefact that had captured their attention so completely before it had been withdrawn from their incredulous sight. Finally, wide-eyed, they turned to face each other.

'What was that?' She whispered.

'I don't know,' he answered, 'but I do know it wasn't there earlier.'

'Maybe we imagined it,' she said in a stronger voice, trying to inject some logic into the situation. 'I should have taken a photograph of it.'

He shook his head. 'No, Francel, we didn't imagine it. It was there—in some form, at least. This is going to require a lot of thought—and a lot of explanation, too.'

The light was fading and it was time to leave. Francel wanted to take some photographs as the shadows lengthened and took these quickly and efficiently. Although they had planned a pleasant hike back to the forest clearing, they now agreed that it had become too late for that. The practical solution was to relocate back to the quad bikes in the forest clearing, then link to them and relocate back to Town. Soon they were standing in Town Auto One.

'Did you enjoy the quad bikes?' Morseb wanted to know.

'Yes, indeed,' they both assured him. 'We'll definitely want them again. They're a rewarding way to travel around and really see the countryside.'

Morseb was pleased. 'Come again anytime and we'll get you sorted out. We are the best, you know. 100% satisfaction is guaranteed. That's out motto, you know.'

Otisk and Francel exchanged amused glances. 'Thanks again, Morseb. See you soon.'

Back at home, they sat quietly looking out their large window overlooking the Town Square, observing an early evening scene that was bustling with happy, contented people, all enjoying themselves. Without averting his gaze from the peaceful scene below, he spoke in a quiet voice.

'You know, I just can't do it, Francel. I know I said I would ignore all the inexplicable things that happen here and just enjoy the wonderful life that we have together.' He paused. 'But I can't do it... I really can't.'

Then he turned to look at her, waiting for a reaction to what he had just said, tense and just a little afraid.

'Neither can I, Otisk,' she said simply.

They continued to be quiet and still for some time, aware that what they had just said to each other had altered their perception of the reality of Pazoten. For a long time (and how long had that time been?), they had persuaded themselves to accept the Land as it was presented to them. This was extremely easy to do, because there was no doubt that life in Pazoten was an absolutely amazing and joyful experience. A life that guaranteed happiness, contentment and fulfilment for all people, in all things; a life that offered everyone, everything, in abundance. They had both recognised this as an unique and ideal state for mind and body and this was precisely why they had adopted a mind-set of acceptance and compliance. After all, surely happiness, contentment and fulfilment make a pinnacle of achievement for life? Add to this their powerful love for each other and the result must be a vision of all-encompassing perfection!

But some human minds are different, even in Pazoten where serenity and acceptance were the norm. A very few minds cannot stop being questing, probing and testing, always observing everything narrowly and logically evaluating the minutiae of their reality. Otisk and Francel were prime examples of this. This was *their* reality, embedded in the midst of Pazoten's reality.

Finally, Otisk broke the silence. 'OK, Francel. Here it is. The whole thing, as I see it. We arrived here from somewhere but we can't remember where. We can't remember anything about our past lives. We can't remember what age we were or, indeed, are. We live in this wonderful land where we are happy and fulfilled, with all our wants and needs looked after completely. We know there is never any sickness, illness or strife here. Using relocation, we can move ourselves instantly at will from one place to another, anytime we want. Physical things (e.g. cars, boats) can created instantly; houses can be remodelled immediately. When we meet someone, we are usually able to sense their name. We can buy unlimited (it would seem) goods and services without money or knowledge of value, although it is suggested that there are personal limits. Even rental items always seem to be new. We seem to be free to do what we want but we have noted that we are monitored to some degree; for instance, the Counsellors knew immediately about our relationship. We know that complex training is acquired directly and speedily without personal effort. Finally, we know people leave Pazoten but we have no idea why or where they go. As a description of Pazoten and our lives here, have I left anything out?'

'No, Otisk, I don't think you have left anything out but let's just recall what we know *instinctively* from our past, because that must be relevant to our situation now. We know that illness and strife *exist* although there is none here in Pazoten. We know about physical money and how it *is* finite. We know that training is normally a relatively long process of learning—that's why we were so surprised to receive all our Reception Team training in three minutes. We arrived, both knowing how to drive a car; I knew about cameras and you knew about painting, so these are things we must have done before. We had to be told that we could relocate instantaneously so I don't think that's something we could do in the past. And we were surprised (and pleased) that physical objects could be modified immediately or created instantly—I don't think that happened where we came from, either. However, I would stress that we have been happy to receive and use all these features and facilities as a part of our life this beautiful land of Pazoten. Do you agree with all that?'

'Yes, all that is correct and we accepted all these things gladly, Francel. I think all that we've just said provides a comprehensive summation of our situation. Now we come to the final game-changer. Today, this afternoon, we saw that strange building built incongruously on top of a mountain. Right on its peak. We both felt that it had extreme significance for us. Quite simply, we are agreed that we need to act on this. We need to have that building explained. Maybe there's a very simple explanation but we need to find out.'

'I agree absolutely.' Her words sealed their pact with a clear sense of finality.

Chapter 11

They had worked out a strategy. They would go back to their picnic spot when they had a day free and see if their "vision" was repeated. Certainly, Francel would have her camera at the ready! Meanwhile, they would start questioning people about the other things they couldn't understand. They knew they would need to approach this delicately. Otisk remembered his early experience in the chemist's shop when he asked about medicines. All the friendly helpful customers had been so appalled by his questions that they had run out of the shop in a panic! Now they discussed how they should approach their general investigations. They decided upon a starting point. They would enquire about all those who suddenly "left" Pazoten.

'After all,' Otisk said, 'everyone here knows that people suddenly leave. We'll ask people who have been here for a long time, because they will have seen it happening many times. Maybe they will have enquired about it and been given some sort of an answer.'

'Who do you think we should start with?' Francel enquired.

'I might have thought of starting with Branea and Bitzo—my Reception Team, you know—but I don't think I'll bother. I'm sure you remember their reaction when I asked them about my age. Let's try the experienced Reception Teams that we work with. There's no point in asking the new RT7 that we met on our last shift. Although they know that they replaced the former RT7 people, I'm sure they won't know anything about them. We were told nothing about the people we replaced, were we? And we still know nothing about them.'

Francel agreed. 'We can ask our questions at handover or take-over. Also, if the shift is quiet, we could ask our Children's Reception Team colleagues who are on duty with us. We know that some of them have been working in RR5 for a long time.'

* * * *

Their next shift started at 1500 the next day. They took over from a relatively inexperienced team and decided not to ask them any questions about the departure of people from the land of Pazoten.

Francel checked the Rota in the Office. 'I see that ART15 will take over from us at 2100. I think they are one of the longest serving teams here, Otisk. They've certainly been here a lot longer than we have. We could try talking to them. Also, we're on duty with CRT12. I think they've been operating here for quite a long time as well.'

'Fine, Francel, if we have a quiet period during the shift, we might take the opportunity to have a chat with our CRT colleagues. And we can talk to ART15 at 2100 hours if the moment seems appropriate.'

Almost immediately, they received their first warning of an adult incomer. In due course, the middle-aged man had been received, welcomed and processed satisfactorily without problem. Otisk returned from settling the incomer in his house and leaving him sound asleep.

'I told him we would come and see him tomorrow at 1000 hours. That gives him time to get himself orientated around his house.' He looked towards the CRT area. 'I see our colleagues are having a coffee break down there. Shall we join them? We'll see whether it's appropriate to have a chat about departed teams, etc.'

A moment later, they had joined their colleagues in the Refreshment Area.

'Quiet night, Rodeth and Wadea?' Otisk greeted them. Sipping their coffee, the CRT team nodded in acquiescence.

'Not like our last shift,' Wadea said with a smile, 'we had two incomers less than an hour apart! Tricky ones, too. I think we deserve a quieter shift this time.'

Otisk was sympathetic. 'Can be difficult, eh? But you managed to cope, didn't you? That's the advantage of experience, isn't it?' He poured coffee for Francel and himself.

'I saw you have already had one tonight,' Rodeth said. 'All OK with that?'

'Yes, all went well, I'm happy to say.'

'That's good—and very good for the incomer.'

Otisk nodded in agreement and then asked: 'You've been here for quite a while, haven't you? One of our most experienced CRTs, are you not?'

'Yes, I think we're the longest serving CRT right now.'

'You should get a special badge for it,' Otisk smiled, 'a Long Service Medal.' He paused for a moment. 'Did you ever know the names of the team you replaced?' Otisk's casual question.

Rodeth looked at Wadea. 'Did we?' he asked.

She shook her head. 'No, I don't think so. Why do you ask, Otisk?'

'I just wonder what happens to them. Where they go—and why.'

Rodeth pondered, then shook his head. 'Don't know, Otisk. Not our business, really. They went—we came. It's a simple as that. Rather neat arrangement, eh?' he said, laconically.

'Have you known of many other people leaving Pazoten?'

'Why yes, of course, as I'm sure you know, it happens quite often. All the time, in fact. You know what it's like, don't you? You've been seeing someone around the Town for...' he paused, 'well, I don't know for how long—then, suddenly, they leave. Happens quite often. Part of the process.' Rodeth smiled.

Otisk sat forward. 'Process, Rodeth? What process is that?'

The man frowned. 'Well, it's just the way things are, Otisk. You must know that. You know, there's "come" and there's "go". That's it, really. There's nothing else. Just part of the process.'

Otisk looked at Rodeth carefully. The man looked back with a half-smile, his eyes showing a degree of disquiet.

'Yes, of course you're right, Rodeth.' Otisk was warm and reassuring. 'Thanks for your company, both. We had better get back to our area. Bye for now.'

Back in the ART area, they sat close together.

'Well, we didn't get much out of that, did we?' Francel spoke in a low voice.

'Nothing really. It seems they have no curiosity about this. And I had the strong feeling that they didn't want to talk about it. I wonder why?'

'Well, Otisk, maybe we can try again at 2100.'

* * * *

ART15, a pleasant elderly couple, arrived at 2045 hours. They were briefed comprehensively by Francel and Otisk and acknowledged they were ready to take over.

'As usual, we're ready for anything.' they said jovially. 'We've certainly dealt with a lot of incomers during our time here.'

Otisk recognised the perfect opportunity. 'How long has it been?' he enquired casually.

'Oh, a long time. More than…' He stopped. 'Well, a long time, anyway. Years, maybe. Or months. I don't know.'

'Both of you must have seen many departures, then?'

'Departures, Otisk? Oh, you mean, people leaving Pazoten? Oh, yes, of course we've seen plenty. By the way, I don't mean "seen"; they just leave. Go, you know.'

'Where do they go and why?'

ART15 became quiet, looking at each other in some alarm. 'Ah… No-one has ever raised that sort of question before, Otisk. Why are you asking us that question? Do you have a special reason for your enquiry?'

'No, it's just that you've been here a long time. You've seen many things. We know you are very experienced.'

They smiled in relief. 'Yes,' the man said cordially, 'you're right, we have. We've seen it all. If it happens, we've seen it!' Relief generated just a tinge of hysteria in his voice.

'So where do the leavers go? And why?'

Immediately, they both became still and serious again. After a pause, the man replied. 'Yes, that's right, Otisk. Some come and some go. That's what happens. We can all see that. It's the way things are here. It's perfectly natural and nothing to worry about. Now I think we really must settle down to our shift. It's been lovely talking to you tonight. Good-bye. See you soon.' They turned away towards the ART area.

Shortly afterwards, Francel and Otisk were strolling down the street from the Administration Centre in the soft light of the setting sun.

'Let's drop into the Town Square Café and have a drink before we go home, Francel. I think we both need one.'

They had sat down at their usual table. An unfamiliar waiter came to serve them and they ordered their drinks. When the man returned with the drinks, he said, 'I believe you are the professional photographer, aren't you, Francel? He pointed to her photographs on the café wall. 'I think your pictures are very striking. I would like to have two more for the opposite wall of the café. Would that be possible?'

Puzzled, they looked up at him. 'Well, yes, I suppose so,' Francel said doubtfully, 'I can certainly bring some possible scenes but shouldn't the proprietor...'

'I am the proprietor,' the man interrupted smoothly. 'I have just taken over here. However I have been informed about your free lunches,' he concluded with a smile.

'But... where is the former proprietor?' Otisk asked.

'He has left,' the man said perfunctorily.

This reply was so unexpected that Otisk was momentarily confused. 'Sorry, left?' He said, 'what do you mean "left"?'

'He has left Pazoten. Gone, you know.'

'But where has he gone?' Otisk's inevitable question.

The man shrugged. 'Who knows where he has gone? We all come and we go, don't we? He came and now he has gone. And now I am the proprietor here. Enjoy your drinks.' He walked away noiselessly.

Otisk was silent, wrapped in thought. Then:

"589 times 741?"

'436,449.'

"72,756 divided by 129?"

'564.'

Francel noticed a change in his expression. 'What is it, darling?' she asked, 'you look as if you're in another world.'

He smiled briefly. 'No, I'm not. Just a little bit of maths taking me over.' They sat quietly for a moment then, suddenly, he turned to look at her intensely. 'That was so perceptive of you.' His eyes were blazing.

'Wow, stop!' she said, taken aback by his intensity. 'Don't frighten me.'

'Sorry,' he said, reverting to his normal expression, 'but you did say something very significant.'

'What was it?'

'You said: "… you look as if you're in another world."'

'Yes, that's right. That's how you looked.'

'Well,' he said, looking at her meaningfully, 'maybe that's where I was! Maybe the maths tests come from another world. Maybe it's the world I was in before I came to Pazoten. And—maybe the link to that other world is the building we saw on top of the mountain. What do you think of that?' he finished triumphantly.

She looked at him, wide-eyed, her thoughts racing. 'I do see what you mean, Otisk. We've become convinced that your maths tests came from inside you—from your brain—as a product of your unusual mathematical abilities. But, now that I come to think about it, surely it must be possible for the maths tests to come from somewhere else? It's very peculiar that we have never really thought about this, because this thought can actually be applied to everything here! We have accepted Pazoten as it is—a wonderful land where everything is perfect.' She paused for a second. 'Well, perhaps I should say *almost* perfect, because the presence of people means it can't be perfect! People will always introduce some elements of imperfection, don't you think? However, overall, we have agreed that Pazoten is a most extraordinary place to live. Look at us. We're having a marvellous time here. We're ecstatically happy with everything we have and everything we do, aren't we? And we recognise that we could live an existence that would be less happy, although we cannot picture how that might look and feel.'

Otisk had been listening raptly to Francel. Now that she had paused, he said: 'everything you have said is brilliant, Francel. And it's absolutely logical, too. I think there's something about life in Pazoten that encourages you to accept all things without question and I think that is precisely what almost every person does. That's why they become agitated when you ask questions that are outside the "rules" of Pazoten. Now, inevitably, there will always be one or two people whose thought processes are different to the vast majority. Perhaps I should call them the "psychological mutants"? They are the people who question. They are the people who "rock the boat". He paused and took her hand. 'And you know who I'm talking about, don't you?'

She looked into his eyes. 'Yes,' she whispered, 'you're talking about us. I wonder how many more there are like us.'

They sat wordlessly for some time. 'Not many,' he said in an undertone. 'Maybe none.'

After a while, they finished their drinks. He took her hand. 'Time for bed,' he said, 'we're going boating tomorrow afternoon.'

* * * *

They woke up early the next morning to another fine Pazoten day.

'When are we picking up Lonei?' Francel asked at breakfast.

'We're picking him up with the boat at 1200 hours. I'll go round to Town Auto One and get a pickup for us.'

'Fine. I'll get the picnic lunch together. I'll need to make a quick visit to the supermarket across the Square. There are a few items I need to get.' Francel sat making a list. 'Will a small table and three folding chairs fit into the pickup?'

'Certainly. That sounds a lovely idea. We can sit by the lake, relax totally and have a leisurely lunch.'

Breakfast over, Otisk appeared at Town Auto One. He made his way to the area where the pickups were displayed and examined the range on display.

'This Ford Ranger looks very nice,' he thought. 'I'll try one of these today.'

'Good choice, Otisk:' Morseb was always effusive, 'new model, you know. Very nice. As you know, we are number one for all rentals. 100% satisfaction is…'

'That's great, Morseb. I know. That's why I come here so often. Thanks a lot. See you later.'

'That looks very pretty,' Francel said, glancing out the window, 'I particularly like that shade of metallic blue. It really suits the shape of the vehicle. The effect is elegant, yet strong and purposeful, isn't it?'

'A fine description, Francel. It's really nice to drive, too. Its specification is rather like the Toyota I had the last time. Very torquey diesel engine, all-wheel drive and six-speed manual gearbox.'

'Torquey?' she teased him, 'is that English? Is it in the dictionary?'

He smiled back. 'Well, if it isn't, it should be. It means the engine has a lot of torque. Torque means "turning force". Torquey engines produce a lot of power when they're running quite slowly. These days, most diesel engines are like that. It makes the engines very flexible. You see, when…'

'Stop, stop!' She laughed, 'I wish I'd never teased you.'

Lonei was ready and waiting when they arrived at his flat.

'Hi, Otisk, nice pickup,' he said, apprising the vehicle with an expert eye. 'Nice colour.'

'Francel thinks so too,' Otisk said. 'She likes blue. Let's get the tugboat in.'

'She's all packed up ready,' Lonei said, 'come on in.'

'Ah, I see you have Francel's picture of you and the boat prominently displayed. It's really nice there, isn't it?'

'Yes, it is,' Lonei replied, 'shows all the details of Juno II.' Then lifting one end of the boat, he added, rather embarrassedly, 'it was kind of you.'

'It was a pleasure, Lonei.'

Soon the tugboat was safely secured in the back of the pickup and they were ready to go.

'Are you happy to go to the same place, Lonei?'

'Yes, certainly. I might meet my friend there, you know, the man with the antique yacht.'

'Ah, yes. You and he got on very well, didn't you?'

'Yes, he was very interested in model boats and I know quite a lot about boat construction so he was seeking advice on a quite a number of things to do with model boats.'

'Oh, that must have been nice for you, Lonei,' Francel said. 'It's good to find someone who shares your passion.'

'Well, I don't know about passion,' Lonei replied quietly. 'That sounds a bit strong to me—but I'm certainly very interested in boat construction.'

Otisk's ears had pricked up. 'How do you know so much about boat construction, Lonei? Until very recently, you've always seemed to be working at your job all day, every day, without a break.'

Lonei was silent as they sped along smoothly. 'Well, I learned all that before,' he said finally.

'Before, Lonei? Before what? You mean, before Pazoten?'

Again, silence. Then Lonei stirred. 'I've always thought the countryside out here was very nice,' he said, very quietly. 'Peaceful, you know.'

'Yes, but...' Otisk stopped as Francel prodded his ribs with her elbow. He looked at her and she shook her head imperceptibly. He leaned back in his seat. 'Yes, it is nice,' he agreed.

The pickup drove along the lakeside to the spot they had found suitable for launching the tugboat on the last visit. Otisk swung the vehicle around and parked it conveniently near the water. The boat was unfastened from its fixings and Lonei made it ready for launching. An admiring crowd gathered, complimenting Lonei on the size and detail of the model boat and asking him questions about various items of equipment. Soon he was deep in conversation with several "serious" model boat mariners.

Meanwhile, Otisk helped Francel unload the table and chairs from the pickup. 'I don't think Lonei needs the presence of an amateur like me,' he laughed. 'I'll just help with the domestic chores.'

'We can set the table and chairs up on this level ground here,' Francel said. 'It'll give us a perfect view of the boating lake and we can relax and watch the serious sailors. Listen, Otisk, I hope I didn't hurt you when I elbowed your ribs in the pickup. I just thought Lonei didn't want to answer your question and I didn't want him becoming upset.'

Otisk laughed. 'Yes, I got the message and thank you for it. It just seemed too good an opportunity to miss but Lonei certainly didn't want to answer, did he? So it was a good thing that you stopped me.' He looked over at Lonei, deep in conversation with his new friends. 'Shall we go and have another boat trip on the big lake, Francel? I'm sure Lonei doesn't need my presence. He's too busy with his new mates! Anyway, I have a plan. I want to try something; test them out, you know.'

Francel looked at him doubtfully. 'Don't do anything to upset anyone, you know your enthusiasm can get the better of you at times. Some people can't take the shock!'

'No, I don't think this should upset anyone. It's just the system I'm testing.'

'Well, if you're sure...' Then she brightened. 'Anyway, it would be very nice to go sailing again. Maybe you should just check that Lonei doesn't need you for anything. If he doesn't, we can rent a boat for a little while.'

'No that's fine,' Lonei smiled. 'I'm quite happy here sailing Juno II. My fellow sailors here will help me if I need anything.'

'Fine, Lonei. We'll have some lunch when we get back. We shouldn't be very long.'

Soon they were at the large lakeside. It was much less busy this time and they were the only customers on the jetty at this time. They approached the Boat Master who was in his small office.

'Ah, yes, Otisk. I remember. You want one of the large red cruisers, don't you? We don't have one moored here at the moment, but just wait a minute.' As he spoke a powerful engine came to life in the small boathouse not far away and the doors on to the lake opened.

'Ah... Could we have one of the smaller motor boats this time?' Otisk said quickly, his eyes focussed on the boathouse. 'I think they were blue.' Before he had finished his sentence, the powerful hum of the engine had been replaced by the much quieter sound of a small engine and a small blue motor boat emerged from the boathouse to power its way towards the jetty.'

'Here you are,' the cheerful young man said as he stopped expertly beside the jetty.

Minutes later, they were cruising slowly along the lake.

'I know why you did that,' Francel said, laughing.

Otisk grinned. 'Well, I really had to test the system out. And you must admit it was faultless! The large cruiser was changed instantly into the smaller motor boat. Really clever, eh? When we get back, I'm going to ask the Boat Master about it. It will be interesting to hear what he says.'

Francel was doubtful. 'Do you really think you should?'

'If we don't ask, we'll never make any progress. But I'm guessing that we won't have the system explained to us. All that seems to be a secret, doesn't it?'

They enjoyed their leisurely trip along the lake. 'You know, Otisk, I think I prefer to go at this speed. I know the big cruiser was much more exciting but it didn't give you much time to enjoy the scenery.'

'Yes, I see what you mean. I suppose there's room for both types, depending on how much excitement you want.'

In due course, they returned to the jetty and handed the motor boat back to the duty staff.

'Can I ask you a question?' Otisk addressed the Boat Master through his office window.

The man looked up from paperwork. 'Of course you can; what would you like to know?'

'How do you manage to meet everyone's requirements for a particular type of boat, no matter how busy you are?'

The man smiled. 'Easy – we keep a large stock of all boats and we've always got enough for everyone's needs, whatever they are.'

'You mean if fifty people came to the jetty and each wanted a large red cruiser, you would be able to meet all their requirements in a short space of time?'

The man's smile was replaced by a slightly worried expression. 'Ah… yes, of course we would. We never fail to meet the customer's requirements. But such a large number would never…'

Otisk interrupted. 'Let's imagine that it's happening right now. Where are the fifty cruisers?'

The man paused for a moment. 'In the boathouse. That's where everything is kept when it is not required.'

Otisk pointed. 'Are you talking about this boathouse, just along the lakeside?'

'Yes.'

'It's much too small. You could hardly get one cruiser in there.'

'Ah, no. Believe me, the boathouse is much larger than it looks. It meets all our demands without fail, I can assure you.'

Otisk looked at the man who smiled back encouragingly. 'Right, thanks for answering my questions,' he said finally. 'We'll see you again soon. Goodbye.'

As they walked, Otisk began to rationalise their situation. 'You know, Francel, why doesn't he tell the truth? Clearly, this is one of Pazoten's "mysteries". Somehow, everything is produced without the necessity of storage. It's like the car, the pickups and the quad bikes that we rent. All brand new and unmarked. It's like all the other items we buy in apparently unlimited quantities. Obviously, this is the way Pazoten works. But why? That's what I want to know. Because I feel that's not the way life works. What do you think?'

'Otisk, I think people here are programmed to accept all these mysteries and to enjoy them to the full. We tried to do that, didn't we, but we seem to think a bit differently from most people. We've talked about this before.'

He nodded in agreement as they approached the boating lake. Lonei was just mooring the tugboat beside the bank.

'Lonei? Are you ready for some lunch?' Francel called. He waved back and nodded.

* * * *

They had eaten a hearty lunch and now they sat back, regarding the scene in front of them with fulfilled pleasure.

Now Otisk spoke quietly: 'Lonei, you've been here on Pazoten for a long time, haven't you?'

'That's right, Otisk. I told you before.'

'Have you been here longer than anyone else?'

Lonei thought about this. 'Maybe,' he said, after some time.

'So you've seen many people come and go?'

'Obviously.'

'So what do *you* think about Pazoten, Lonei? How do *you* understand it?'

There was silence for a while and Otisk thought that Lonei was going to ignore his question completely. 'It's just like everywhere else,' he said eventually, in a low voice.

'Sorry, Lonei. Could you explain that?'

'People come, people go. It's the same everywhere.'

'I really don't see...'

'Listen, Otisk. People come, they're born. People go, they die. Life and death, you know. People come and people go. You understand?'

'Yes, but where are they before they're born? Where are they after they die?'

'We don't know that, Otisk. Nobody knows that, although people do have ideas about it. In religions, for instance. You hear about it in churches—that sort of place. Maybe you should ask the leaders there?'

Otisk shook his head. 'I've tried that, Lonei, but somehow I never managed to achieve a serious one-to-one conversation with any of the church leaders before or after a service there. There was always such a crowd around them; they always seemed to be busy with so many important matters. I never managed to get a one-to-one conversation with any of them.'

Silence as he continued to ponder. 'Just a minute, though... Pazoten really is different, isn't it, Lonei? People aren't born here. People don't die here, yet they still "come" and "go". So they must come from somewhere and go away to somewhere. So where were they before they came? And where do they go to when they leave?'

Lonei was silent and still as he stared across the lake. Without moving, he spoke very softly. 'It's what I said before, Otisk. People come and people go. We don't know where they come from or where they go to. It's just not one of the things we know. And we don't bother with it, either. We just get on with our lives. Wherever we are, whenever it is, we've just got to live our lives where we are. That's what you're doing. That's what I'm doing. That's what we're all doing.'

In the silence that followed, Francel produced her camera and spoke brightly to defuse the tension that had built up. 'Look,' she said to them both, 'I've got some interesting shots of you, Lonei, and some of Otisk and me on the big lake.' They sat close together as she displayed the images on the camera screen and scrolled backwards through the frames she had taken, often commenting laughingly on each one. Finally she said: 'I think that's the first one I took here. 'I'll just check.' She was right. The next frame was a telephoto shot of the mountain top where they had seen the large building two days before. 'No, that's the lot I have to show you,' she confirmed.

'Just a minute.' Lonei's quiet voice. 'Can I see that, please?' She handed him the camera and he examined the image on the screen with great care. 'Where is this?' he asked.

'Along the valley to the west, maybe thirty miles,' she said, 'it's one of the mountains you can see if you look south-west from there. We had a bit of a ramble out that way. Why do you ask?'

He continued to look intensely at the image. Finally, he handed back the camera. 'Just thought I recognised it,' he said laconically. Then he rose to his feet. 'I must have one last sail of Juno II before we go home. And one of my friends down there wants to ask me some technical questions about it.' Without a backward glance, he left them.

Otisk and Francel watched his retreating figure, his words racing around their consciousness, desperately seeking to extend their knowledge of the Pazoten mysteries.

'I keep hitting a brick wall with my questions,' Otisk said. 'Lonei's replies have exactly the same elements as all the others we have heard. Everyone sees all these things happening, everyone knows they're happening but nobody ever gets beyond the most superficial of explanations. It's all very strange and frustrating, isn't it? At least Lonei talked about birth and death but that doesn't apply in Pazoten, as far as I can see. Nobody gets born here, do they?'

Francel nodded. 'You're right. I hadn't thought of that.' She sat silent for a moment and then placed her hand on his arm. 'Listen, Otisk. As you say, Lonei was taking about life, birth and death and eventually he attempted to link these things directly with Pazoten. But, as you said at the time, that isn't what happens here—and that's why his explanation doesn't work for here, at least. Anyway, we've now explored all the mysteries of Pazoten as fully as we can—except one! The building on the mountain top. Are we the only ones to see it? At the moment, we don't know if we are. However, I thought Lonei's reaction to the mountain top photograph was very interesting, didn't you? There's nothing to see on the photograph—no building, that is. He wouldn't explain his interest in it, though. That was a bit strange.'

'You're right, Francel. You've summarised everything succinctly. It's the building that we need to concentrate on now. Let's take a few days to let our ideas germinate and then we'll see what we can come up with. Maybe I'll just skirt around the subject with Lonei on the way home. You never know, we might just get a clue from him. He might know something about it. After all, he's been here a very long time—and then there was his reaction to the photograph.'

'Yes. As I've said, there's nothing to be seen on the photograph. Not even a vestige of what we saw at the time.'

While Lonei sailed his tugboat, Otisk set up his easel and painted a picture of the scene with broad confident strokes of surprising colour and texture. When Lonei finally came back, he was surprised. 'Didn't know you were an artist, Otisk.' He studied the painting gravely. 'I see what you're doing here. It has great emotional impact.'

They both looked at him in astonishment. 'I didn't know you had an artistic bent, Lonei,' Francel said, looking at him with new respect.

'I haven't,' he grunted, 'I just know what I like and I can see what Otisk is doing here.'

* * * *

An hour later they had packed up at the lakes and were driving back to the Town.

Otisk broke the silence. 'Lonei, have you travelled around the whole of Pazoten during your time here?' An innocent question.

'Yes. I check all the roads at times to keep all places tidy, you know. It's part of my job.'

'So you know the countryside pretty well?'

'Better than most, I would say.'

'Have there ever been any buildings built on the mountain tops you can see out west along the valley? For instance on the mountain in that photograph you were looking at in Francel's camera?'

They had the distinct impression that Lonei stiffened. He turned and looked at them impassively. 'Not that I have seen,' he said, very quietly. Then, after a long pause. 'Do you reckon you've seen something?'

'Yes. A big building on the mountain peak. We both saw it. After a while, it disappeared as we looked at it.'

Lonei was silent again as they entered the Town and drove to his house. Wordlessly, he and Otisk carried the tugboat into the house. Then he stood absolutely still and looked fixedly at the younger man. 'There's nothing up there in these mountains,' he said quietly. 'Trick of the light, that's all. Thanks for the afternoon.'

Chapter 12

Unusually, they found they had been allocated Reception duty shifts on the two consecutive days after their visit to the lakes. They discovered that the increased frequency of their shifts was due to the departure of no less than three experienced Reception Teams. Obviously, this left a substantial gap in the service; it was clear that this situation would remain until new teams could be selected, trained and deployed. The first of their consecutive shifts had been an overnight one, finishing at 0900 and the second started 24 hours later starting at 0900 on the following day.

As they sat in their Reception Area on the second of their shifts, monitoring their display for notification of any impending arrivals, Francel noted that Otisk was looking unusually serious.

'Is there a problem, Otisk?' She said, 'you're looking a bit glum.'

His expression did not change as he looked up at her. 'I've been thinking about the teams who have left, Francel, and I've just thought of something quite worrying. While we've been here, we've seen a number of Reception Teams leaving and, somehow, we have always assumed that both members have gone at the same time. I think that's what everyone assumes. But a few minutes ago it suddenly occurred to me—is that assumption correct? Do both members of a team depart together every time? Is it not possible for one member of the team to leave without the other? After all, you and I didn't *arrive* simultaneously, did we? Admittedly, you were close behind me, the following day, we think, but we certainly did not arrive at the same time. Surely departures could be at different times, too. So now I ask myself: When just one team member goes, what happens to the other who has been left behind?'

Francel was shocked and silent for a while. Finally, she said in a small voice: 'you're right, Otisk. I've never thought about that—and it is very worrying. You might have thought that a remaining team member would be paired up with someone new, wouldn't you? But I don't think that ever happens. Maybe the teams are selected because they have a special bond between them—we certainly were, anyway. That bond plus completing the training together may be the way the system is designed to work. So, in a single departure situation, maybe the team member who's left behind cannot be paired up again and needs to be allocated to do something else. That's all I can come up with at the moment. Incidentally, I bet we wouldn't get the answer to this problem if we asked the question, would we?' She lapsed into unhappy silence.

He nodded mutely and now they looked at each other, stricken.

'Listen, Francel,' he spoke close to her ear, 'I don't ever want to leave you and I don't want you to leave me. I want us to be together always. It's a terrible thought that we will be forcibly parted if one of us leaves Pazoten and the other doesn't. We might never meet again.'

'Then we'll just have to make sure that doesn't happen,' she said in a more determined, practical tone. 'You know, Otisk, this realisation makes it all the more important that we should solve the mystery of Pazoten—or, should I say, the *mysteries* of Pazoten.'

He was sombre. 'You know, I think we've solved most of the mysteries, Francel. I mean, not solved them exactly—for instance, of course I cannot understand how boats and cars, etc., can be created instantly, but I know and accept that it happens. And there are so many other things in Pazoten that are like that. The mystery we need to solve is the biggest mystery of all. What is Pazoten? Why is it here? Why is it organised like it is? And, at the moment, the only clue we have is that building on the mountain top. We need to solve that—and we need to solve it *together*. From now on, this Reception Team is sticking together like glue!'

'OK, Otisk, we have a clear day tomorrow. Let's make it a day of investigation. Let's get quad bikes, drive out west and get as near as we can to the mountain with the phantom building on top.

I'll take plenty photographs and we'll see what we can record. If we leave early, we might even have time to climb up that mountain. We must have a look at the map and see if we can work out the distance. If we could actually get up to the peak, or even some way up it, surely we must find some serious evidence there?'

'Good idea, let's do that. We'll rent the quad bikes today so that we can leave really early tomorrow morning. That means we should be in the area of our picnic spot before mid-morning. Then we can press on westwards, going as far as the bikes will take us. From that point, we can try to locate a path to the mountain.'

Their shift completed, they walked to the café in the Town Square and sat down for a drink.

'You haven't forgotten the pictures, have you, Francel?' The proprietor stood by their table.

'No, I haven't,' Francel replied rather guiltily, 'unfortunately we've been kept rather busy of late. Shortage of staff at Reception, you know. I'll try to sort out a few pictures for you to have a look at. I'll bring them in as soon as I can.'

'Thanks, I'll look forward to that,' the man said. 'Drinks on the house,' he added with a smile.

When the man had gone, Francel said, 'I mustn't forget to do that.'

'I'll try to remind you the next time we're coming here.'

When they had finished in the café, they walked to the Town Auto One showroom.

'Hi, Morseb,' Otisk called, 'we've come in for a couple of quad bikes again. We'll take them now. We want to make a nice early start tomorrow and have a full day in the country.'

'Fine, Otisk. Do you want the same models as you had the last time? There are bigger and more powerful ones if you prefer.'

'No, we were very happy with the ones we had. They seemed perfect for buzzing along the roads and they coped off-road very well. We'll have them again.' This time, Otisk chose a striking orange and Francel opted for silver green. 'Off we go, then,' Otisk waved, 'see you tomorrow evening.'

'Enjoy yourselves! You have the best quad bikes in Pazoten. 100% satisfaction is...' Morseb's voice faded away as they powered away up the street. Minutes later, they had parked the quad bikes beside their front door.

'Let's go in and examine the map,' Francel said. 'I've never really looked at the countryside in detail. We've just been looking at roads up till now.'

Soon, the map was spread out on the table and they were tracing their route westwards from the Town. 'Look, Francel, here's the forest. You can see the track we took through it. But this time, I suggest we don't waste time going through the forest. It'll be much quicker to stay on the road. You see, it runs along the southern side of the forest and it looks pretty straight and clear.'

'Yes, I see. There's the forest clearing. The road seems to be much more winding after that. That means it's following the contours of the land. I think this is our picnic spot, about here.'

'And there's the river below and the farmland stretching away westwards. The road continues west, although it gets more and more winding, doesn't it? Look, it's marked "rough road".' He turned his attention to the southern side of the farmland. 'Look at this, Francel. The map shows a belt of woodland south of the farmland pastures. Then, south of that woodland, there is no detail at all—the map is just blank. Further south again, it does show the mountain ridge but, again, there is no detail, no suggestion of heights or gradients. Also, no indication of pathways, either. It all looks rather blank, doesn't it? It gives one the impression of a *"no-man's land"*. We'll just have to get out there and see what the terrain is like. Go as far as we can on the bikes and then get our walking boots on.'

All that decided, they had a quiet and relaxed evening together and went to bed earlier than usual, in preparation for their "day of investigation". Otisk was on the point of sleep when:

"45,521 divided by 23?"
'1,979.1739.'

"298 times 64?"
'19,072.'

"27 times 4,751 plus 320?"
'128,597.'

As usual, he had supplied the correct answers instantly and without conscious effort. 'Repeats!' he thought sleepily. 'I've definitely had these before. They should make up new ones, whoever they are.' Immediately afterwards, he fell deeply asleep.

As planned, they rose very early and prepared everything they would need for their full day away. After a hearty breakfast, the quad bikes were loaded up and they were ready to go at 0645 hours. Apart from an occasional pedestrian, the Town Square was empty.

'No engine revving,' Francel warned. 'We don't want to wake everyone up.'

'I've just had a really good idea,' Otisk smiled, 'I don't know why I didn't think of it before. Let's just relocate ourselves with our bikes to the forest clearing out west. You know, the one where we parked our bikes before. Then we can start from there.'

Francel smiled at him. 'Why didn't I think of that? What a good idea—and that certainly won't wake up the neighbours!'

A second later, they were standing in the forest clearing beside their machines.

'Useful trick, that,' Otisk said introspectively. 'Saves us a lot of time. Look, we can ride down that track over there. I'm sure that should lead down to the West Road.'

The quad bikes were started and, minutes later, the West Road was reached and they turned right to head west along its smooth surface. Within two miles, they came to a road intersection where a prominent sign indicated a left turn to a road that linked West Road with Southwest Road. By contrast, straight ahead advised "West Road, no through road" and "Road becomes unsuitable for motor vehicles in three miles". They stopped at the intersection.

'Calling Francel. We'll continue west as far as we can or until we're due south of the mountain peak. That should be our closest point to it. If the map is correct, it looks about ten miles to that point. After we park up, we'll see what we can do on foot. No point in just relocating, I think, because we want to see and experience everything that's going on. Over.'

'Received, Otisk. Tally-ho! Lead the way. Over and out.' As usual, she smiled.

They rode much more carefully along the narrowing, winding road which undulated considerably as it wound around the many hills. As they progressed, the road surface deteriorated, eventually becoming no more than an uneven, stony track, which the quad bikes coped with splendidly. Progress, however, became quite slow. After five or six rather tiring miles, they reached the area where they had picnicked the week before.

Francel called Otisk. 'Calling Otisk. Let's stop here. I want to take more photographs of the mountain from this point. Over.'

'Received, Francel. Stopping now. Over and out,' Otisk responded and stopped in the mainly flat, grassy area that had been their picnic area.

Here, Otisk examined the mountain top carefully, using the powerful binoculars that he had purchased at the same time Francel had bought her camera.

'Can't see anything unusual on the peak,' he said, handing her the binoculars.

'Neither can I. I've been using my telephoto lens to bring things closer. Anyway, I've taken a number of frames. We'll see what they show when I enlarge them. I've recorded the images at maximum camera resolution so I can blow them up really large.'

'Good idea,' he answered, 'I'll just make a few sketches here. I have a strong feeling that there is a painting to be created from this.'

After a short break, they continued their journey westwards at an increasingly slow speed. After a few miles, the track became a narrow path and they stopped the quad bikes. 'This is it, Francel,' said Otisk, dismounting. 'It's on foot from now on.' Parking their bikes by the side of the path, they donned their boots and walking gear and set out briskly along the path.

'If the map is correct, I think we should arrive at the point closest to the mountain in about two miles. At that point, the peak should be due south of us. I'll keep checking my compass and see how that works out.'

'What does the compass show now, Otisk?'

He stopped and checked. 'We're heading west, although the path snakes around a bit. We can see the mountain peak over there. It has a bearing of 210 degrees at the moment, approximately southwest. You know, Francel, that mountain doesn't look too far away. Maybe only three or four miles. If we can find a path heading towards it, we have a chance of climbing it today. We've got plenty of time in hand.'

Francel was more cautious. 'Let's not be too ambitious, Otisk. We shouldn't try to do too much in one day.'

They had been walking for about an hour now and had made good progress. Suddenly, Otisk stopped. 'Look ahead, Francel. There is a track that runs almost due south between these two fields. Looks like a farming track. We must be coming close to our nearest point. The compass places the mountain peak almost due south of us now.'

As they paused beside the farm track, the silence was broken by the metallic, pulsating sound of a tractor. At first they were unable to spot its location but the increasing noise of the engine made it clear that the vehicle was coming closer. At last, a flash of bright red focussed their search down the stony track between the fields. As they did so, a large, purposeful tractor came into view and powered its way up the slope towards them. They stood aside to give the vehicle room to pass but it came to a noisy, lurching stop beside them, filling the air with clattering noise and waves of hot, diesel fumes. They waited rather nervously as a large man in a brightly-checked shirt climbed down from the enclosed cab with the ease of one who has made this move many times.

'Company!' He said loudly, with a wide smile. 'Otisk and Francel. Don't often get company out here. Out walking, are you? Nice day for it.' He enveloped them in welcoming cheerfulness.

Relieved, Otisk responded. 'Yes, this is the first time Francel and I have hiked out this way and we're enjoying it very much. Sorry, if we're interrupting your work. I'm afraid I can't sense your name and I see you're not wearing a bracelet on your wrist. You're the very first person I've met in Pazoten who isn't wearing a bracelet.'

'Zadorb, that's me,' the man bellowed cheerfully. 'I've got a bracelet, of course, but it got damaged. Caught up in machinery. Chewed up! I haven't had time to get it replaced yet. Thanks for reminding me that I need to do that. Listen, you're not disturbing me at all: it's nice to meet new people. I'm the Resident Farmer of this area and I hardly ever see anybody. I would be delighted if you would come over to my farmhouse for some refreshment. It's just over there, behind that hill. It's not far. I would really enjoy your company. Why don't you hop up into the tractor and we'll be there in a couple of minutes?'

'Well...' Otisk looked at Francel doubtfully and she nodded her head imperceptibly. 'Fine, thanks, Zadorb. You're very kind.'

A few minutes later they sat around a large kitchen table with a cold drink and some sweet biscuits in front of them. Otisk looked around. 'You live alone here, Zadorb?' his voice betraying some surprise.

'Yes, I do. Been here for quite a time. More than...' he stopped. 'Well, a long time. I'm not sure how long. Anyway, the farm keeps me busy all day, every day.'

'What do you farm?'

'Everything, really. Grain and vegetable crops. I have animals, too.'

'Really?' Otisk leaned forward. 'Does all your produce go to the Town? Who picks it up? How often? What…?

The farmer interrupted. 'They pick it up when it's ready,' he said briefly. 'Where are you heading for? Maybe I can direct you.'

'We're interested in climbing the mountain,' Francel said.

The man became still. 'Climb the mountain? What mountain? No mountains here. Just hills. None of them very high.' His voice had become flat and discouraging.

'We're heading towards that mountain to the south.' Otisk pointed out the window where the peak was visible. 'Can we walk down your track between the fields? Is there a decent path through the woods at the bottom?'

Now the atmosphere in the room had changed. The man was silent as he continued to look at them. 'No-one ever goes down there, apart from me,' he said finally, averting his eyes as he spoke. 'No point. That track leads only to my fields.'

'But I can see that the track goes right down to the edge of the woods,' Otisk said. 'Surely there's a path that goes beyond? Takes you through the woods?'

'There's no path. No-one walks through the woods. It isn't possible. It's too dense for walking. You're going the wrong way if you go down there. You should keep walking west and go for a ramble in the hills up there. Nice countryside up there.' He waved an arm towards the north-west.

'Thanks very much for your advice.' Francel's voice was soft and reassuring. 'We'll probably do that. We don't want to keep you from your work, Zadorb. It was really nice of you offer such welcome hospitality.'

The man turned to her gratefully and the tension in the room disappeared. 'That's all right, Francel. It's really nice to have company for once. Don't see many people out here. Can I offer you another drink? Another biscuit? Or something else, if you like?'

'Thank you, it's very kind of you but we had better continue our hike. We've got our lunches packed in here. We've got everything we need.' Otisk indicated their rucksacks.

The man was visibly crestfallen. 'OK, I understand. It's been nice to have company for a little while. It makes a nice change for me.'

They went back outside. 'I'll get on with my work then,' the man said, 'I have to go out to my western boundary and check some stock. Just go west on the road for about half a mile and then you can begin to climb into the hills. The path is very obvious. I guarantee you'll really enjoy it. Goodbye, may you be safe and in power.' He made a sign with one hand and climbed into his tractor, driving off in a cloud of heat, dust and noise, heading west along the farm track that was the extension of West Road. They watched the tractor disappear and it was not long before its noise faded away too.

Francel turned to Otisk, who was busy scanning the mountain peak with his binoculars. 'That was pretty strange, wasn't it? It was like he was warning us off. What do you think we should do?'

'I still can't see anything untoward on the mountain peak, Francel. Maybe you should take a few high-resolution photographs from here; this is the nearest we've been.

After the photographs had been taken, Otisk said: 'I think we need to walk down here and look for paths through the woods. Until we can see what's on the other side, we won't know whether we can get on to the mountain itself. Let's start right away.'

About thirty minutes later they were coming close to the end of the farm track and approaching the edge of the woodland. Sure enough, the man had told the truth. The track ended with gates on each side leading into the fields. A thick, very high thorn hedge barred their way forward. It looked impenetrable and somehow unfriendly.

'There's no way through this,' Francel said, 'unless you had a chain saw. Even then, I doubt whether you would get through. It's extremely thick and very wide, too. I can't see the other side of it.'

Otisk looked left and right. 'Let's go into the fields and walk along the hedge. Maybe we'll come to a gap that we can get through. Which way shall we go?'

'Let's go right, somehow it looks a bit more promising.'

They started walking along the unbroken, dense thorn hedge. Several times, they stopped and tried to peer through a part that they thought might be a little less dense but, on each occasion, they could see nothing.'

'It just looks black in there,' Otisk said, 'that's peculiar, isn't it? Surely some light should penetrate through the trees, even if they are very densely packed? Trees cannot exist without light.'

They continued to walk but the wall of prickly leaves and branches remained unbroken. Suddenly Otisk stopped.

'What is it? Have you seen something?'

'No, Francel. That's just the point. It's just dawned on me. There's nothing here in this field. No crops, no animals. Nothing. And no sign that there ever has been, either.'

She looked around at the overgrown grass. 'Yes, I see what you mean. It is peculiar. Another Pazoten mystery, perhaps?'

'Anyway, how can one man working alone look after a large mixed farm with crops and animals to attend to? It's impossible, in my opinion.'

'Well, I agree, Otisk, but I don't think we should get too hung up on that. We can't seem to make any progress towards our objective, can we?'

He looked at her seriously. 'You know, Francel, this isn't what we expected, is it? We thought we would just come out here, find the wooded area, walk through it, traverse the "no-man's land" beyond and climb up the mountain as far as we could—hopefully to the peak. The fact is, we are being prevented from doing that, aren't we? We can't find a way through this barrier and the wooded area beyond looks so dense that it may be impassable. Furthermore, before we even started this part of our journey, we meet Zadorb the farmer, who definitely warned us off. I am rapidly coming to the conclusion that we cannot go south from here. Or, to put it another way, we are not being *allowed* to progress towards the mountain.'

They sat down on a convenient grassy mound and were silent for a while as they thought.

'I know, Otisk. I think I've got it! Couldn't we just relocate through all this?' She waved at the hedge and the woods beyond. 'I know we didn't plan to use relocation for this part of our journey because we wanted to see and experience everything as we travelled. But now that we think we cannot do it that way, let's just relocate…'

Otisk though about this. 'You know, there might be a complication about that,' he said thoughtfully. 'With relocation, I suspect you need to know exactly where you are going to. In other words, you must have been there before, physically there—so that you arrive in precisely the right spot. We have a problem with that, Francel, because we have never been through the woodland or the land beyond, so we can't specify it. I like your idea very much, though. But how are we going to specify where we want to go? How can we get sufficient detail?'

They sat silently, applying their whole minds to the problem.

'The peak!' Otisk's shout was triumphant. 'We've seen the peak of the mountain! We know what that's like, don't we? Could we relocate straight to that? Might that be possible? If it is, that would take us exactly to the spot we wish to visit.'

Francel was cautious. 'It's a great idea but I'm not sure it will work. I think you're right about accurate specification. If we haven't ever been there, how can we specify it accurately enough? That's the big problem. Of course we can try it but let's think it through completely so that we have the best chance of success. When we try it, we can't be sure what will happen.'

'You're right. First of all, we need to go back to a spot where we can actually *see* the peak clearly. We can examine its detail through my binoculars.'

'Better still,' Francel was joyful, 'I can display my best peak photograph at super-high resolution! We can both study the detail of the terrain and commit it to memory. That's our best chance of getting our relocation to work, I think.'

Otisk leapt to his feet. 'Let's do it, Francel, let's walk back to the West Road track and get started on your scheme.'

Soon, they were standing on a high bank above the West Road track, with a clear, well-lit view of the mountain peak several miles away. Otisk studied the terrain through his binoculars while Francel took high-resolution photographs. Then they sat down and studied the detail of each photograph until they had assembled a complete picture of the peak's rocky land surface.

'I think I have it, Francel,' he said quietly. 'How is your perception?'

'As good as it will ever be, Otisk. Let's do it.'

'I suggest we should aim for this reasonably flat rocky ledge. That looks quite a safe place to land. We should both be aiming for the same place.'

'Should we hold hands so that we'll be linked together?'

'I think that would be best. I don't want to lose you.'

'OK. Let's do it.'

They stood and held hands, eyes fixed upon the mountain peak and applied the familiar relocation technique they had used so many times before. Nothing happened. They tried several times more. Nothing.

'Let's check the system,' he said. 'Let's relocate to the bottom of the farm track beside the thorn hedge. They readjusted their mental focus and immediately found themselves at the bottom of the track.

'Right,' he said, 'so we know the system still works. Now let's relocate to the other side of this thorn hedge. Ready?' They refocused applied their technique. Nothing happened.

After a moment, Francel spoke. 'It's no good, Otisk. Either we can't relocate to places we have never visited physically or we are prevented from relocating outside the "permitted area".'

'Or both,' he said grimly. 'We need to think about this. Let's relocate back to our quad bikes. We can ride them back to our favourite picnic area and have lunch. I think we deserve a rest and we need to keep an eye on the peak. I have a strong feeling that we'll see that building again. Next time, you must take many photographs.'

They started up the quad bikes and soon arrived at their picnic site. After eating lunch, they reviewed everything that had happened to them, while keeping a close watch on the mountain peak, its craggy shape innocently lit by the strong sunshine.

'We've been through it in detail, Francel, and I think our conclusions are right. We were prevented from making progress beyond what I will call the "boundary" of Pazoten. Although we can see that mountain, we are not allowed to go there. The reaction of Zadorb confirms this. Is it possible that he is some sort of "guardian"? Placed there to warn people like us?'

'Well, although he was very nice and welcoming, he changed completely as soon as we told him we intended to go to the mountain, didn't he?'

They sat quietly, again deep in thought. 'You know, Francel, I'm feeling really tired. I think it must be old age! Shall we have a little doze for a while? Keep one eye on the peak, though!'

They lay down together and slept as the sun lowered in the sky. Then, just like the first time, Francel was the first to wake. She touched Otisk lightly to wake him 'Come on, lazy bones,' she said, laughingly, 'time to…' her voice faded away. 'It's there,' she whispered. He jerked around, suddenly wide awake. There, unevenly lit by the slanting rays of the sun, was the large, grey building on the mountain peak.

'It's so much clearer this time,' she said, scrambling for her camera and swinging it up to take many photographs. Beside her, Otisk strained his eyes through his binoculars.

'Look, Francel. The wall isn't completely blank. There are some very small square openings on its surface. They could be small windows or maybe even doors. There's absolutely no sign of life, though. Never any movement to be seen. We'll continue to watch this for a long as we can.'

Totally fascinated, they continued to observe and photograph the building until it began to fade in the failing light. Just like the first time, they saw it dissolve before their eyes until there was nothing more to see. At last, they packed away camera and binoculars wordlessly and looked at each other, wide-eyed and exhausted by the experiences of the day.

He spoke very quietly. 'Relocation back, I think?' She nodded.

* * * *

Quad bikes returned, they sat by their window, looking at the busy evening scene in the Town Square below.

'I think we've proved it to be real,' she said.

'How?' he asked.

'I've been able to record it as a photograph. So it was real at that time, anyway.'

'Hm,' he mused, 'I agree, Francel, although maybe we need to redefine what "real" means. Our "real" means it exists all the time but that building doesn't. That's another Pazoten mystery we have yet to sort out.'

They fell silent again and the minutes ticked by.

'I've had another idea, Francel, on a completely different tack. I reckon it's him.'

'Who?'

'Zadorb.'

'What about Zadorb?'

'I reckon it's him. It's got to be.'

'Sorry, Otisk. Could you explain to us mortals what you're talking about?'

'It's him. He's the Leader.'

She jerked upright. 'What?'

'He's the Leader. Zadorb. The Leader has got to be somewhere, just like the Counsellors, only more secret. But I reckon it's him.'

'Why?'

'No bracelet, for a start.'

'Well, he explained that.'

'And also because of what he said when he was leaving us.'

'What did he say?'

'He said something very strange to us. Something no-one else has said, not even Counsellor Begiet.'

'What was it? I don't remember.'

'I think he said: "… may you be safe and in power," and he made a strange sign with his hand. No-one else has ever said or done that. It sounds like a sort of incantation, almost. I think he must be the Leader.'

She was silent for a few moments. 'You know, you could be right,' she said introspectively.

Chapter 13

'We're not on shift until 2100 hours this evening, Otisk. I thought I would work on my photographs this morning; seeing what's worth keeping, you know. And processing what needs to be enlarged.'

'That's fine, Francel. I'm feeling a bit artistic this morning. I want to look at these sketches I made when we were out on our investigation and see whether any of them would translate into paintings. I'm really looking forward to doing that. I feel quite excited about it! I think I may have a few good ideas there.'

'Oh, that sounds very sensible, Otisk. Get going while the fire is strong in you, eh?'

He stood up decisively. 'I'll get set up then and we'll see what happens. By the way, you have some photographs to sort out for our new friend over at the café. I understand his name is Purserf. We'll probably have lunch over there, so you can take anything you've sorted out to show him then, if you're ready to do that.'

'Thanks for that reminder. It had slipped my mind once again! So much seems to be happening in our lives just at the moment.' She settled down in a corner of the room with her camera and projector.

Otisk set himself up near the large window and began to examine his sketchbook carefully. He could see immediately that a few of the ideas he had sketched would make effective paintings. Colours and textures began to swirl around in his mind as he envisaged how he would turn his rough sketches into works of artistry. The room became completely quiet as they both concentrated fully on the tasks before them.

"298 times 64?"
'19,072.'

"27 times 4,751 plus 320?"
'128,597.'

"4,378.95 divided by 37?"
'118.35.'

He shook his head. 'All repeats,' he muttered.

'Did you say something, Otisk?'

'Not really, just had three sets of maths, that's all – repeats! I only seem to get repeats these days. It's very annoying. Why ask me the same thing over and over again?'

She shook her head abstractedly. 'Sorry; no good asking me.'

He turned back to his sketchbook and suddenly became transfixed. Eyes now blazing, he fixed a medium-sized canvas on his easel and set to work mixing colours on his palette. The picture on the canvas began to take shape and then, increasingly, acquired magical vibrancy. He worked like a driven man, totally absorbed in the entity that was developing on the canvas before him, brought to life by his positive and powerful brush strokes. The minutes then the hours slipped by without registration. His pace and intensity did not slacken.

'Wow, darling,' Francel stood behind him, 'that's fantastic. Easily the best you've ever done. It just captures the spirit of the scene. I can almost see it—the building, I mean. We absolutely know it's there, don't we?'

His painting showed the mountain peak, mysterious and rather menacing in its deep shadow, contrasting with the bright, soft greens and yellows of the foreground and the deepening blue of the sky, pierced by shafts of low sunlight. They were silent, she in admiration, he in exaltation mixed with exhaustion.

'Look, Otisk, it's lunchtime and you need a break. Let's go over to the café now.'

'In a minute, Francel. I must make one final adjustment. It's absolutely essential that I do.' His voice was hoarse and urgent.

'Fine. I've sorted out some photographs for Purserf. I'll go over there and show them to him. You come over as soon as you're finished. You won't be long, will you?'

Totally absorbed, he did not answer. She recognised the depth of his concentration and left the room quietly.

* * * *

She stood beside the proprietor in his café. 'I've sorted these photographs out for you, Purserf. I have four pairs to show you. If you like any of these, I'll get them enlarged to the same size as the others. If you would like to see other alternatives, I can sort that out another time.'

Purserf examined each pair carefully. 'All these are superb photographs, Francel. I must say, I envy your skill with a camera. I think I would choose this pair, because I think they make a nice contrast with the others that are already displayed.'

Francel compared the chosen pair with the ones already hanging on the wall. 'Yes, I see what you mean. They are very much in the same genre but the colour combinations are quite different. Different time of day, you see? Shall I go ahead on these?'

'Yes, please, Francel, that would be really satisfactory.'

She turned and found Otisk by her side. She examined his face carefully. There was excitement there, as well as serenity. 'Finished it?' she enquired gently.

He smiled. 'Yes, for the moment. A painter is never finished with his work, though!'

They ordered lunch and sat holding hands, viewing the tranquil scene before them. 'Purserf has chosen a pair of my photographs. Shall we walk around to the shop and get them enlarged?'

'Yes, we can do that when we're finished here. It will be a nice little stroll for us.'

An hour later, the enlargements had been ordered and they were walking down by the river, soothed by its gentle flow.

'I've been thinking, Francel. Yesterday, we failed. That really surprised me because I didn't expect we would be prevented from walking through these woods. I had thought our problem might be time—not having enough time to climb the whole of the mountain. I know we've gathered more evidence about the building—or whatever it is. For instance, we have good images to study but I have a feeling that we won't be able to glean a lot from these.

Also, even if I'm right about Zadorb being the Leader, I really can't imagine where that is going to take us. Let's imagine the situation. I turn up and say: "You're the Leader, aren't you?" and he says: "No" – which almost certainly he will – what do we do then?'

Francel replied thoughtfully. 'Would it be worth raising the matter, delicately, if you like, with Counsellor Begiet? After all, she has been pretty open with us up till now. She did tell us that we were a very unusual pair. It seems that most people don't raise the sort of queries we do. Is that worth a try?'

'You know, I think that sounds like a possible way forward. After all, if she says she cannot answer our questions, we haven't lost anything. And, you never know, we might get a few snippets of information that will help us to evaluate the information we've managed to gather up till now.'

'Yes, even if she doesn't answer directly, our devious minds might be able to figure out something from what she says—or what she doesn't say.'

'OK, then. When we finish our shift tomorrow morning at 0900, I'll visit the Dragon in her den.'

'The Dragon? Who's that?'

'The Administrative Coordinator, of course. That should be a bit of fun. You know how much I like that sort of fun.' He grimaced.

* * * *

Their overnight shift had been unusually quiet. Although the CRT had received one child around midnight, no adults had arrived. Otisk and Francel had spent their shift quietly updating their records. Towards the end of their shift, Otisk had looked at the Administrative Centre Directory and noted the number of the Administrative Coordinator's room.

'Room 1/20,' he said. 'I'm going straight into the lion's den,' he grinned, 'I hope you're coming with me!'

'It was the Dragon yesterday,' she quipped, 'yes, I'll come with you and hold your hand.'

By 0900 hours, their handover to ART3 was complete. They collected their belongings and the transporter took them to Room 1/20. They stepped forward towards the door but, unlike most doors in the Administrative Centre, this one did not open as they approached.

'Please state your business.' The voice was flat and metallic.

'Otisk, accompanied by Francel, ART9. We wish to speak to the Administrative Coordinator.'

'Please state the time of your appointment.' the voice said.

'We do not have an appointment. Our business will be brief.'

'It is not possible to see the Administrative Coordinator without an appointment.' the voice stated.

'Yes, it is. Open this door.'

'Please wait.' Silence for twenty seconds. 'It is not possible to see the Administrative Coordinator without an appointment. Do you wish to make an appointment?'

'Open this door immediately.' Otisk was becoming annoyed.

'It is not possible to see the Administrative Coordinator without an appointment.' the voice repeated irritatingly.

'Open this door or I shall file a Negative Comment about the procedures of this department.'

Silence for thirty seconds, then the door swung open to reveal a large room with many young men and women sitting quietly at small, cramped desks, poring over data screens. None looked up as Otisk and Francel entered.

Francel approached the nearest desk. 'Excuse me, could you tell me where I would find the Administrative Coordinator?' Her tone was very friendly and informal.

The girl at the desk did not respond.

'Excuse me, I'm sorry to interrupt. Where is the Administrative Coordinator?' Francel asked again.

Without looking up, the girl spoke very quietly. 'I am not permitted to speak to anyone without official authorisation.'

Otisk stepped forward. 'Who is in charge here?' he said loudly.

After a long pause, a young man in the centre of the room stood up. 'I am the Room Supervisor.' he said nervously, looking at Otisk with distinct dread.

'What is the answer to our question?'

'I am sorry, Otisk. The answer is: "She is not here".' The young man spoke almost inaudibly.

'Can you give her a message from me?'

Ten seconds passed. 'Well, I suppose I can, but I'm not...'

'The message is: "Otisk and Francel, ART9, wish to meet with Counsellor Begiet as soon as possible." Can you deliver that to her and ask that she contacts me?'

'Yes, I have recorded what you say and I will do my best.' The young man sat down and bowed his head to his data screen.

Otisk and Francel left.

* * * *

Back at home, they discussed the visit to the Administrative Coordinator's Department.

'What did you think of our visit this morning?' Otisk asked.

'Dreadful! All these young people packed into that room and not allowed to speak. I would have thought that was against the rules of Pazoten.'

'Yes, that's a good point, Francel. Everywhere else we have gone, people are invariably helpful and kind. And they seem to be happy in their jobs, too. Why should people employed in the Administrative Centre be treated any differently?'

'Well, I can't think of any reason, can you? I feel quite strongly about it. Maybe we should bring it up when we meet Counsellor Begiet? I mean, I don't want to cause trouble, but what appeared to be going on there does not seem acceptable. These young people looked so cowed. I feel really sorry for them.'

'I'll make a note, Francel, and we can bring it up if the opportunity arises. The trouble is, we will be asking Counsellor Begiet for explanations about very complex matters—fundamentals of the being and reality of Pazoten, no less! So to focus down from that to a small-scale internal organisational problem might be a bit tricky.'

She smiled. 'Yes, I see that. We'll see how it goes, then. Meanwhile, let's get some rest. Keep your phone handy, however, because you'll probably get a call about our appointment with the Counsellor.'

They slept until mid-afternoon.

'No calls about our appointment, eh?' Otisk said. 'Perhaps the Administrative Coordinator is having a busy day. Or maybe a day off… I'll put in a call and see what's happening. Got to keep the pressure up, eh?'

The call was connected. 'Hello. Administrative Coordinator's Office? Who are you, please? Secretary to the Coordinator? Right. This is Otisk and Francel, ART9. We have been awaiting a call from the Coordinator about a meeting with Counsellor Begiet. Could we speak to the Coordinator, please? What's that? We can't? She's in a meeting? When will the meeting be finished? You don't know? Well, as soon as it is, tell the Coordinator that we expect a call from her. Thanks. Goodbye.'

It was almost two hours later before the phone bleeped, indicating a call from the Administrative Coordinator.

'Hello, Otisk here.'

'This is the Coordinator's Secretary here, Otisk. I am afraid the Administrative Coordinator is unable to speak to you today. There is a problem and she is fully committed.'

'What's happening? Our request is important, you know.'

'Yes, we are aware of that but, unfortunately, nothing can be done today. As I say, there is a problem and the Coordinator is fully committed.'

'Yes, I know. You told me that before. What is the nature of this problem?'

'I am sorry, Otisk. I am not allowed to divulge that. However, I can confirm it is a serious problem. The Coordinator says that she will speak to you tomorrow.'

Otisk sighed and shook his head as a signal to Francel. 'We are on duty in RR5 from 0900 to 1500 hours tomorrow. Would you tell the Coordinator that, please? So we will expect to see her after our shift. We will come to Room 1/20. Please book the appointment for 1530 hours.'

'Otisk, I will do my best but you must understand…'

'Fine, thanks for your help. See you then. Goodbye.'

'What was all that about?'

'There's a "serious problem" in the Administrative Department—so they say. Anyway, whatever the truth, the Dragon isn't speaking to us today. As you heard, I booked an appointment for tomorrow after our shift. Goodness knows what will happen when we turn up.'

'Well,' she smiled, 'we'll just have to look forward to that, then.'

He kissed her. 'I'm hungry. Let's go and have dinner. Let's really relax!'

They had ordered a lavish dinner and sat in the balmy evening air outside the café.

'I've received the enlarged pictures, Francel.' The proprietor stood beside the table. 'I've brought you a bottle of our best vintage wine to have with your meal. Is that acceptable to you? We keep this wine for our very best customers, you know.'

'Ah, good evening, Purserf. I told the photographer to send the pictures over to you when he had done the job. Are they satisfactory?'

'Exactly what I want. Tomorrow, I'll get them framed and then they can go up on the wall over there. I'm sure they will enhance the room and give it a very artistic feel.'

Otisk smiled up at the man. 'And, Purserf, regarding that splendid bottle of wine you have in your hand, the answer is "yes, we'll have it with pleasure." Thanks.'

* * * *

The following morning, their handover from ART11 had been uncomplicated.

'We had one incomer early in our shift,' they reported. 'Absolutely no problem. Arrived serenely and was very calm and content when I settled him in his house. We'll see him this afternoon. I'm sure he will be happy and there should be no problem. His Monitoring Team can probably have him later today if we're happy he's fully settled. Nice to have an easy one.'

'Have you been having some problems recently?' Francel asked.

'Not many,' the woman replied, 'but then you only need one problem case and it can worry you for weeks after. We did have a difficult one a couple of weeks ago. A girl, not very old—can't remember her age, now—she arrived very upset. It took me a long time to get to the bottom of the problem. She needed a huge amount of reassurance. It was quite exhausting.'

'What was the problem?'

'It seems she was afraid of pain. And that's why she couldn't settle down. She kept saying that she was waiting for the pain. She knew it would start, she said, and it would be terrible. It took us some time but eventually we convinced her that we don't have pain in Pazoten. After we convinced her, she cheered up a great deal and began to settle down.'

'Yes,' the man said, 'that was a distressing one. I wonder why she was so fixated on pain. It's a bit of a mystery, that.'

They paused for a moment. 'Right, then,' the woman said briskly, 'over to you. We'll get off for some rest. Goodbye.' Waving, they faded away as they relocated to their home.

Francel and Otisk settled down in their Reception Area and updated their statistics as they kept an eye out for any arrival notifications. About an hour later, the familiar soft chime took their full attention to the screen.

'Wow, Francel, look at this.' They looked at the screen with some concern:

```
Incomer procedure is commencing.
Two adult manifestations are proceeding.
Note that manifestations are simultaneous,
repeat simultaneous.

Data will follow.
```

'A new one for us, eh? Simultaneous! We've had two come quite close together in the past but simultaneous is an unusual coincidence, I reckon. Anyway, we'll need to go to Single Reception Procedures, won't we?

'Certainly, and, Otisk, we had better be aware of something else. If any more incomers start to manifest while we are dealing with these two, we will need to consider calling in the Standby Reception Team.'

'Yes, Francel, you're quite right. That is the procedure. But if we are in the latter stages of our receptions, it might be possible for one of us to return to deal with the next incomer. That's what we're supposed to do, if we can. Standby Teams are called in only very rarely. It's a last resort.'

Suddenly, Otisk sat down at the system communicator. 'I've just had another thought, Francel. We should arrange for the incomers to be in adjacent pods. The system may do that anyway but there was no mention of that in the training.'

'Why should they...'

'So that we can support each other more easily if either becomes a problem.'

She looked at him with affectionate admiration. 'You're brilliant, Otisk! If that isn't in the Standard Procedures, you should report in and get it added. We must check up on that—sometime when we're a lot less busy than this.'

He nodded and linked with the system:

```
AAT9 Command:
simultaneous incomers to be manifested in
adjacent capsules... Acknowledge.
```

His command appeared on the display with the immediate system response:

> Command recorded and accepted. Data will follow

'Right, that's done. Now we wait.' Around ten minutes later, the next message displayed:

> Two manifestations are now at Stage 6
> Name of incomer: GRYSEW
> Data: Male, Age 34 years
> Arrival Location: RC7
>
> Name of incomer: MOONG
> Data: Male, Age 15 years
> Arrival Location: RC8

As the screen confirmed the locations of RC7 and RC8 in the room, the physical display indicators lit up to confirm the information.

'Right, Francel. Which one do you want to take?'

'I think I would be better with the younger one. Mother him, you know.'

'Fine. So I'm RC7 and you're RC8. There's likely to be a variation in the awareness developments—we know that can vary quite a bit. After another ten minutes, the system chimed and displayed:

> Incomer MOONG, Male, 15
> Awareness has reached Level 10
> PI is now appropriate. RC8

Immediately, Francel stood up. 'See you at the RC banks,' she said as she left. It was another eight minutes before Otisk was alerted:

> Incomer GRYSEW, Male, 34
> Awareness has reached Level 10
> PI is now appropriate. RC7

Otisk immediately went to the capsule. As he passed RC8, Francel caught sight of him and gave a smiling "thumbs up" sign. He waved back, relieved that there were no apparent problems with her incomer.

Grysew was a handsome, muscular man, fully aware and looking around him calmly.

'Oh, hello,' he said, as Otisk entered the room. 'I didn't expect to see you.'

Otisk was rather taken aback. 'Ah… hello,' he responded. 'I'm Otisk. I'm your Reception Team member. I'm here to look after you and sort everything out.'

'Well, that's good to hear. Otisk, eh? That's not the name I know you by! You're…' he stopped and furrowed his brow. 'You know, I don't know why but I can't remember your name! That's ridiculous, because I know it very well. Anyway, you know me, don't you?'

'Well, yes. You're Grysew.'

'Grysew? I don't think so. Why do you call me that?'

'Look at your bracelet, Grysew. It's printed on there. Look, I've got one exactly the same, except that it's got my name on it.' Otisk displayed his bracelet.

The man looked confused. 'Listen, ah…, *that* isn't your name. I know you. We're friends. I know you.'

Otisk paused and wondered what to do.

'Right,' he said finally, 'but here I'm called Otisk and you're called Grysew. You're in a land called Pazoten and here, things are a bit different. You'll have a great time here—everyone does. And, as I've already said, I'm here to make sure you have a smooth arrival. Now look, I know you will be feeling hungry and thirsty—you are, aren't you?'

The man nodded. 'You're right, I am. OK, I'll go along with what you say about names and we'll see what happens. Anyway, it's really nice to see you again. You look well.'

'Thanks, Grysew. Here's a tray with a meal. It's your favourite food and drink. Just relax, eat and drink and I will be back very soon. I've just got a few things to organise for you. Is that all right?'

Grysew nodded happily, already eating his meal. Otisk left the capsule.

'Everything OK?' He had called into RC8. Francel smiled. 'Yes, we're getting on fine. Moong is just relaxing and having something to eat. I was just going to propose we settle him into a student block. That will be perfect for him, I think. How is your incomer?'

'Yes, he's fine. He's eating also. But there's something strange, Francel. He insists he knows me. Keeps trying to remember my name. It's a bit worrying.'

'Hm, that's strange. We'll see how it develops. Shall we go down to the Duty Admin Office together?'

'Yes, let's. I'm sure these two will be fine. I expect them to be asleep when we return and then we can get on with the transfers.'

It was soon established that Moong would move into a student block and Grysew would have a house near the centre of the Town. When they returned, Moong was deeply asleep and clearly ready to be transported. However, Grysew was awake and could be seen waving to them. They both entered RC7.

'Hello!' Grysew's voice was extremely cordial. 'Another surprise. Always a pleasure to see you.' He was looking squarely at Francel with a wide smile on his face. 'Looking good, too.'

'I'm Francel,' she said, distinctly disquieted, 'I'm the other half of the Reception Team. Otisk and I work together.'

'What did you say your name was?' Grysew asked.

'Francel.'

He became serious. 'No, that's not it.' He clutched his forehead. 'Just a minute, I'll remember it in a minute... I know, you're...' he paused, 'no, it's gone. But I know it, I really do.'

'Let's not worry about that at the moment, Grysew. Francel has someone else to look after and she must go off and attend to him. I'm going to settle you into your new home. You'll really like it there.'

Moments later, Otisk and Grysew were in a pleasant, sunny room.

'Goodness, this is nice,' the man said. 'Lovely view out the window, too.' He sank down on a comfortable chair. 'I must say, I'm pretty tired now. Seems like a long day, this one. I don't normally get as tired as this in the middle of the day.'

'Just come through here and lie down on the bed, Grysew. A good sleep will soon sort you out. Francel and I will come to see you tomorrow. You'll find everything you need here in the house. I'll leave you now unless there's anything else you want me to do.'

Grysew, eyes already closed, said: 'No I'm fine. See you tomorrow. Maybe I'll have remembered your name by then. Thanks for all your help.'

As Otisk arrived back in RR5, the system chimed once more and the display announced that another incomer procedure was starting. 'Just in time,' he grinned, pouring a cup of coffee and sitting down to monitor the screen. 'If Francel isn't back when PI is required, I'll need to go Single Reception again. At least I will be familiar with the procedures.' The "Level 6 Awareness" display appeared around fifteen minutes later, advising that the incomer was a lady of 63. Ten minutes later, Level 10 awareness was reached. Just as Otisk was preparing to leave for RC2, Francel appeared.

'Wow, we're being tested tonight! Just one this time?'

'Yes. Welcome back.' He kissed her. 'Come on, Team Member, let's get started. It's lovely to have you back at my side.'

* * * *

It was 1445 hours and ART6 looked impressed.

'We haven't experienced three on a shift—and surely, a "simultaneous" pair must be very rare. You must be feeling a bit tired?'

'No, we aren't, are we, Francel? It's good to be pushed sometimes and it reassures you that the procedures work when you're at the limit. The adrenalin keeps you going.'

'Did the Single Reception Procedures serve you well?'

'Yes, they all worked perfectly. Although the third incomer followed on just as I returned, Francel was back just as Level 10 was reached, so we switched back to normal procedures for the third one.'

'Right, we'll take over. I'm sure you're more than ready for that.'

Their meeting with the Administrative Coordinator was not for another 45 minutes, so Otisk and Francel left the building to take a short walk.

'Although we haven't had any confirmation, I'm assuming the meeting with the Dragon is still on for 1530. I'll complain if we go there and are unable to see the Co-ordinator. That would be pretty annoying.' Otisk's jaw was set.

As they walked on, he turned to Francel: 'So Grysew recognised you as well, Francel—or so he says. What did you think about that?'

'It felt very peculiar. Like a cold shadow had fallen across me. I could see the recognition in his eyes. It gave me quite a jolt. Was he the same with you?'

'Yes, it really took me aback and I didn't know what to say. In the end, I just insisted that Otisk was my name here in Pazoten. I said that things were a bit different here and that's the way it was. He did accept it but, at the same time, he didn't capitulate. Even when I left him at the house, his last words to me were a hope that he would be able to remember my name when we next met.'

They sat down on a bench. 'You know, Francel, I think he must have known us in our previous life and, unlike all the others we have met, somehow he still has a memory of it. We certainly don't, anyway! We've tried to make headway with that several times, haven't we?'

'Yes, we certainly have. Well, we're seeing him tomorrow. We'll see what he has to say then. I must say, if he comes out with either of our names, it will be a great shock. Will we be able to recognise them? It's quite worrying.'

'I really don't know, Francel. And if we did, where would that take us?'

They looked at each other, trying to imagine their thoughts. 'OK,' she said finally, 'we'll just have to see what he says tomorrow. Meanwhile I think it's time to go and see the Dragon.'

* * * *

'Please state your business.' The annoying metallic voice again.

'ART9, Otisk and Francel to see the Administrative Coordinator.'

'Please state the time of your appointment.'

'1530 hours.'

Pause. 'Please enter.'

The door swung open to reveal the crowded room, filled with silent, young workers crouching over their data screens. The Supervisor approached them on noiseless feet.

'Please sit here,' he said, indicating a padded bench against one wall.

Otisk looked at his watch. 'It is 1530 hours. I hope that the meeting is to commence promptly.'

The man looked stricken. 'The Administrative Coordinator is very busy. There are many problems...'

'Please inform the Coordinator that we are waiting and that we will be brief.'

A few moments later the man returned. 'The Administrative Coordinator will see you now. She says it can only be for a few minutes.'

Otisk was stony-faced as he marched into a large, lavish office. A stern, elderly woman was writing at a very large desk. She did not look up.

'Yes? I only have a minute.'

'So do we. When can we see Counsellor Begiet?' Otisk's voice was sharp with annoyance.

'You cannot.'

'What?'

Now she looked up, unsmiling. 'You cannot.'

'Why not?'

'Because she is not here.'

'Not here? What do mean, "not here"?'

'She has left.'

Otisk's jaw dropped open. 'Wha...' he spluttered.

'Do you mean, "left Pazoten"?' Francel's soft question.

'Yes. She has departed. This is the problem I'm trying to solve. Is there anything else you wanted to ask? If not...'

'There is.' Francel's response was immediate. 'We would like to know why the young people who work in your Department are cowed and working in unpleasantly cramped conditions.'

The woman's head jerked up and her gaze was piercing. 'I require consistent and excellent work from them. Their conditions allow that to be achieved. There is nothing wrong with their treatment.'

'We think there is.' Francel's reply was polite but implacable. 'We will pursue this with the relevant authorities in due course. Goodbye.'

They left the building silently and sat down on a bench outside.

'Counsellor Begiet has left.' His tones were of bemused disbelief. 'I can't believe it!'

Francel was more practical. 'Yes, it is a shock. But, listen, Darling, it does happen. People do leave Pazoten all the time. You know that.'

'Yes,' he said in a whisper, 'but Counsellor Begiet...'

* * * *

They sat at breakfast, both deep in thought.

'Otisk?'

'Yes?'

'We've got three inductions to do this morning, haven't we?'

'Oh, yes! You're right. I'm afraid my mind was elsewhere. We have a serious responsibility to these three incomers. I'm sorry. I got side-tracked.'

'I think we should use Single Induction for Moong and Grysew. What do you think?

'Yes, I agree. Otherwise we'll be arriving rather late. Our third incomer knows we're coming to her around mid-morning.'

'Let's do that, then. I'm sure that's the most efficient way.'

Thirty minutes later they were on their way. Francel found that her young incomer Moong was delighted with his flat. Like most students, he had already made contact with some of the other young people and was mixing well. Francel sat down with him and gave the initial briefing, finishing up with the recommendation that he should go out exploring.

'Tack yourself on to some of your new friends,' Francel told him, 'they will soon set you straight on all the things you need to know. You will be going to the College with them and the College Office will sort out your studies. You'll have a lovely time here. Also, you'll meet your Monitoring Team soon. They are your first port of call if you want help or advice. And I'll be keeping an eye on you too.'

'Thanks a lot, Francel. Everything is so perfect here. I'm sure I'll really enjoy it.'

Otisk had been a little worried as he approached Grysew's house. What would the man say about his name? He felt distinctly nervous because this information might open up new worries for him. Grysew opened the door to him with a big smile.

'Otisk! Welcome. I'm having a lovely time here! I've already met the young lady next door and we've had breakfast together. She says she has an absolutely wonderful life here.'

'That's really good, Grysew. I trust you had a good sleep?'

'Yes, I didn't awaken until 0800. Then I've been familiarising myself with the house. It's so well designed and fitted out.'

'Right, let's sit down. I've come to give you the initial briefing. Then it will be up to you to stroll around and check the Town out. You'll find that everyone wants to help you.' Otisk then gave the standard briefing and handed over the info-reader. 'So that's it, Grysew, you'll meet your Monitoring Team later today but Francel and I will always take an interest in you as well. Do you have any questions?'

'Well, no, actually. I think you've covered everything, Otisk. It's great, here.'

Otisk got up to go. 'Ah, Grysew, when you arrived yesterday, you started saying that we had met before…'

Grysew looked at him in puzzlement. 'Did I? Don't remember that, Otisk. I remember you being there and helping me. Being really kind and reassuring. But knowing you before? I don't think so. I can't imagine why I would have said that.'

Otisk smiled. 'I must have misunderstood you, Grysew. Sorry about that.'

'No, that's fine, Otisk. Maybe I was just rambling. Anyway, I certainly know you now.'

Francel and Otisk met shortly afterwards.

'What did Grysew have to say about your name?' she asked, rather anxiously.

'Couldn't remember a thing about it,' he smiled. 'Just like we can't remember his age now, can we? It's the way Pazoten works! As I said to him yesterday: "things are different here".'

* * * *

That evening, they were relaxing after dinner in the café.

'Your photographs in the café certainly look good, Francel. You're a real genius.'

'No, I think genius is too strong, Otisk—but thanks for the compliment. The proprietor says he's very pleased with them. Many customers comment on how interesting they are, he says.'

He stretched back. 'You know, Francel, we've got a clear day tomorrow. The last two days have been pretty full. We could just have a relaxing day but I'm wondering whether we could gather another bit of essential information as well.'

'What are you planning, Otisk?'

'Well, we know we can't get through the hedge or the woodland beside the farm out west.'

'Yes?'

'I suddenly thought—what if we went southwest or south? Maybe we could we access the mountain from a different angle. Get over to the range of hills and walk along until we come to the mountain. When we get back home, we can have a look at the map. However, I think the map only works for Pazoten—and the mountain with the building seems to be outside Pazoten. But we could make it a nice, relaxing picnic out that way and see what the conditions are like. Good idea?'

'Yes, why not. It will be a nice day out and it might further our investigation.'

Chapter 14

They had examined the map over breakfast.

'Look, Francel, the South Road leads to some low hills and there are a few picnic areas indicated there. Further south, on the other side of a low ridge, there is some flat ground followed by a belt of woodland. After that, the map shows a sort of ill-defined "no-man's land" before the high mountain range is indicated without detail. We can drive as far south as we can—I'll get a 4-wheel drive car that will cope with rough terrain—then we can search for paths that lead over the ridge, across the low ground and through the woods. It would be nice to survey the no-man's land beyond, wouldn't it? Once we've seen what that's like, we will be able to assess whether we could hike across it and then proceed along the foot of the mountain range to "our" mountain. We won't manage that today, even if we make good progress, but we'll know where we're going when we return the next time for a serious attempt on the mountain.'

'Right, let do that. I'll get a picnic ready. Let's not forget to take our boots and rucksacks—we might wind up doing a bit of serious hiking today.'

'Right. I'll be off to Town Auto One and get a suitable vehicle for us.'

* * * *

'Hi, Morseb, here I am again. One of your best returning customers.'

Morseb did not smile as he shook Otisk's hand. 'I know you're joking, but, here, we think you *are* one of our best customers. You always know what you want and you're usually pretty knowledgeable about it. It's a pleasure to have you as a customer.'

Otisk smiled. He recognised a salesman when he met one! 'Thanks a lot you're a pleasure to deal with too! I'm looking for a nice roomy 4-wheel drive just for Francel and me. I was thinking of a Range Rover maybe?'

'Good choice;' (Otisk knew that Morseb would have said that whatever his proposal!) let's go over and have a look at the selection. These are lovely to drive and they'll go anywhere, you know—well, almost anywhere, if you know what I mean.'

'Yes, I know the capabilities of the car. I reckon this sophisticated black metallic one will do us fine.'

'Right, we'll get that outside for you. It'll be ready shortly. Come and have a quick coffee with me.'

They sat in Morseb's comfortable office. 'You've been here quite some time, Morseb?'

'Yes, you're right. This place needed a bit of reorganisation when I took over but I soon sorted that out. Since then, we've been meeting all our customer's needs—whatever they want. I introduced our motto "100% satisfaction is guaranteed", you know.'

'So what happened to the previous manager?'

'Oh, he left, you know. The usual thing.' Morseb spoke offhandedly.

'Did you know him?'

'No. He left. I came. I took over. I have to say that the place wasn't up to scratch. It took me a little while but I'm very good at organisation and sales matters. And I know my vehicles.'

'So was that your previous job? You know, the one you had before you came to Pazoten?'

Morseb suddenly looked quite uncomfortable. 'Ah Otisk, I can't answer that. I don't know. I don't know anything about it. No point in asking me.' The man was becoming increasingly agitated.

'Oh, that's fine, Morseb. I think it must have been what you did. You're so good at it.'

Morseb smiled with relief. 'That's very kind of you to say that. But, yes, you are right. I am very good at it. Everyone says so. Now, I believe your car is ready...'

* * * *

There it is, Francel: a Range Rover. Beautiful to drive. Superb all-terrain vehicle. Sophisticated 3-litre diesel engine—six-cylinder, you know, very smooth—permanent 4-wheel drive, eight-speed automatic transmission, dynamic, responsive suspension; it's got everything.'

'I'm sure it has,' Francel said, looking at him attentively but mentally checking off all the items they should be taking, 'it looks lovely.'

Everything was soon loaded into the Range Rover and they were ready to depart.

'Do you want to drive, Francel? It's really nice. You should try it.'

'No thanks, you drive, I'll just luxuriate in this lovely leather passenger seat here.'

They set off from the Town Square in high spirits. South Road was not far around the Ring Road and they were soon driving towards the southern mountain range that could be seen in the distance. There was very little traffic on the long straight road and Otisk was able to maintain a steady 60 to 70mph. Eventually he slowed down as the road began to bend smoothly around the rising contours of the ground. Soon after, a road sign indicated a cross-roads just ahead and, as they approached the intersection, Otisk pulled in to the side of the road to consult the map.

'Ah, yes,' he said. 'I had forgotten there is a sort of outer ring road that links at least some of the radial roads. We're on South Road; if we turned right it would take us to Southwest Road and then to West Road (you remember we saw that turnoff when we were there on our quad bikes?), while if we turned left we would eventually intersect with Southeast Road. However, since we want to continue south, we'll go straight on.'

Just after they had crossed the intersection, a large information sign advised them:

"Picnic areas several miles ahead. Warning—road narrows and surface deteriorates."

'Good test for our Range Rover,' Otisk said joyfully.

'Don't break it, though. We need to get it back in one piece!'

'Of course I won't. As you know, my speed will always be matched to the conditions.' Otisk was proud of his driving skill.

Several miles later, the road had become quite narrow, the corners sharper and the hills steeper. The Range Rover coped with this change of conditions splendidly, its automatic systems recognising the changed conditions, selecting the correct gear ratios and adjusting the suspension settings to deal with bumpier road surfaces. Just before a steep rough track, a sign stated:

"THIS ROAD SHOULD ONLY BE ATTEMPTED BY OFF-ROAD VEHICLES".

'Now our wonderful vehicle comes into its own,' Otisk smiled happily.

The track was negotiated slowly and eventually they reached the highest and most remote picnic spot, a remote grassy clearing approached by a final, very steep, rocky track. The Range Rover tackled this obstacle with contemptuous ease, switching smoothly to appropriate extreme systems. All Otisk had to do was keep his foot on the accelerator and steer around the biggest boulders.

'Wow!' he said admiringly, 'this is an awesome car; it can handle anything. What an engineering masterpiece! It really has got everything right.'

'Well, they do have that reputation, don't they, darling,' Francel replied serenely.

He parked the Range Rover on level ground at a convenient spot. 'We can set up just there, where we have that delightful view over a large part of Pazoten. By the way, Francel, how did you know about the Range Rover's reputation?' He grinned at her.

'You're teasing me, Otisk! It's yet another demonstration of us knowing things but having no specific memories to call upon. It's all rather annoying, isn't it?'

'Some day, we'll solve all of this, Francel. I feel we're getting closer. Let's have an early lunch and then we can walk over the ridge behind us and explore the wooded area located on the map. It can't be too far away.'

They set out lunch and began to eat.

'You know, Otisk, I've been thinking about the departure of Counsellor Begiet and our situation. I think we had a very good relationship with her but, logically, there's no reason why another

Counsellor shouldn't be as good. Maybe they are all like Counsellor Begiet. I imagine we're quite likely to meet another Counsellor, perhaps even Counsellor Begiet's replacement. Back at the Administrative Centre, the Dragon (sorry, the Coordinator) said she was trying to sort out the problem that Counsellor Begiet's departure had produced. As far as we can see, the Counsellors are kept extremely busy and I am sure they need to be operating with their full complement. We know there are only six Counsellors plus the Leader. We know that the Counsellors have to support the whole population of Pazoten and sort out problems—day and night, it would seem. We don't know how much the Leader is involved in the day-to-day running of Pazoten but we have no reason to believe that he functions the same as the Counsellors. I would say he supports the Counsellors and functions like a high-level executive authority. A sort of Chief Executive, you know, sitting somewhere in a very lavish office.'

'I agree with your analysis, Francel. The thing is, we've proved that we are very different from the vast majority of people here. We ask questions that they don't. Indeed, they don't want to have anything to do with the subjects we raise. As you know, they become quite agitated. So I think we need to continue our personal investigations into the mountain-top building while pursuing our questions through another Counsellor, if we ever get to see one. We'll see what information today brings and consider things after that.'

Soon, they had finished lunch and donned their boots and rucksacks. The path up to the ridge behind them was steep and it proved to be quite a tiring climb. When they reached the top, they could see the woodland below. Beyond it, they could see the bulk of the mountain ridge but their angle of view did not allow them to see the flat no-man's land area between the wood and the foothills of the mountain. Otisk was disappointed. 'Hm, I was hoping we might get a clue about that no-man's land from this viewpoint but we're not high enough to see it.'

A narrow and precipitous path led down to the flat area in front of the wood and they climbed down this very carefully. At last, they reached the bottom and were able to walk the several hundred yards towards the woodland. As they came closer and closer, the trees seemed to grow in height and become more and more dense. The effect was of a barrier solidifying in front of them. Finally, they arrived, looking with incredulity at the densely-tangled wall of trunks, branches and large leaves before them.

'I don't think I've ever seen trees like these.' Francel was examining a leaf. 'They look tropical. It's like the most dense rain forest that exists. But this can't be a rain forest, can it?'

Otisk had been prowling up and down, attempting to penetrate the mass of green and brown before him. However, when he parted the large outer leaves, the dense mass of vegetation just inside gave no prospect of further vision. 'This is just the same as at the farm,' he said finally, 'except that it was like a thorn hedge with a dense woodland immediately behind it. Here, it's just like the thickest woodland you have ever seen. There's absolutely no prospect of finding a path through this.'

'This is not natural, Otisk. Not natural in the way we understand. This is a deliberate barrier to stop anyone going through. I think that there is no way a resident of Pazoten can break out of this land. The only way out of here is when you "leave"—and no inhabitant has any control over that, as far as I can see.'

'That's right, Francel—and the people here are programmed not to want to leave. We've certainly discovered that. We, however, are different for some reason. We don't know why—and maybe we never will. Anyway, let's return to our picnic spot, there's absolutely nothing we can do here. We'll need to think about this.'

Before they left, Francel took a series of photographs, including some close-ups of the dense woodland. As she was packing her camera away, they were both startled to hear the sharp noise of an engine, clearly coming closer. They looked around to identify the source of the sound and finally spotted a powerful quad bike racing across the uneven field, coming from the east directly towards them. As it came closer, they could see the single rider, wearing a full-head helmet that completely obscured his face.

The quad bike jolted to a very noisy halt in front of them. Otisk noted that it was a much bigger machine than they had rented from Town Auto One, with much larger wheels and very deeply ridged tyres capable of gripping any terrain. Switching the engine off, a large powerful man swung himself off the machine. They waited rather nervously as he lifted the darkened visor of his helmet.

'Howdy, folks!' The voice was friendly enough and his face wore a slight smile. 'Saw you out here and came over in case I could help. I'm the farmer of this stretch of land, all along the south side. Don't see many people over here. You're Otisk and Francel?'

'Yes, we are.' The man did not respond with his name and neither of them could sense it. However, they noticed that he was wearing the familiar bracelet. There was silence as the man waited for them to speak, his expression unchanged.

'We were just leaving,' Otisk said rather hesitatingly, gesturing towards the north.

'Leaving, are you? OK. So is there anything I can do for you before you go?'

'Well, yes, there is.' The man turned to Francel and cocked his head in an attitude of listening. 'Is there a path through this dense woodland?'

The smile disappeared. 'A path?' The tone was one of surprise.

'Yes.' Francel nodded encouragingly.

'What do you want a path for?'

'To walk through. Then to climb the mountains we can see down south. We're very keen on climbing mountains.'

The man was silent as he looked from one to the other, a distinctly puzzled expression on his face.

'There's no path,' he said finally. 'Anywhere. It isn't possible. It's not allowed. No-one ever goes through here. It doesn't go anywhere.' The silence lengthened.

'Right, thanks,' Otisk said. He turned to go then turned back. 'By the way, what do you farm here?'

The man became silent and motionless again and they thought he was not going to answer. Then: 'Various crops. I have some animals, too.' This was forced out with great reluctance.

Otisk looked around. 'There's nothing growing here,' he commented lightly.

'Fallow this year,' the man responded briefly. 'You want anything else before you go?'

'No. Thanks again for your help.'

Gratefully, they left. It took some time to climb back up the steep cliff path but, finally, they made it to the top. The farmer sat on his quad bike and observed their progress narrowly. After Francel had taken some more photographs from the top of the ridge, they made their way back to the picnic spot and were glad to sit down. As they sat, they looked across the perfection that was Pazoten.

'He's like the other one out west, I reckon,' Otisk said. 'I don't think they're farmers. I think they're frontier guards, patrolling the boundary and making sure that no-one gets out of Pazoten; not in our physical state, anyway.'

'Physical state, Otisk? What do you mean?'

'Well, we don't know where we were before we came to Paz-oten but we do know we were in a different physical state then. We could suffer pain. We could become ill. We needed medicines and doctors.'

Francel nodded thoughtfully and was silent for a while. 'We tried, didn't we, Otisk? We tried out hardest to accept Pazoten as everyone else seems to do. But, in the end, we couldn't do it.'

'Yes. You're absolutely right. I think I was the one to break first, Francel. I just couldn't do it. It was seeing that mysterious building that did it for me. Obviously, no-one else sees it, except you, that is. That certainly makes us different, eh?'

'You weren't the first one to break, Otisk. You were just the first one of us to mention it. I was with you all the way.'

They sat silently, deeply grateful for the other's presence.

It was approaching evening as they cleared away all their picnic items into the car. Soon they were driving smoothly along South Road, heading for the Town. On arrival, they drove around to the Town Square and offloaded their equipment.

'I'll take the car back to Town Auto One,' Otisk said, 'I'll tell Morseb it was perfect: he will be so pleased—and I'll be telling the truth!'

Soon after, lavish words of praise accompanied the return of the Range Rover.

'I knew you had chosen well, Otisk. You always do.' Morseb was very pleased! 'These Range Rovers are known as the best off-roaders, you know. The engineering is superb!'

'Well, we didn't do anything too extreme. Just went south to the highest picnic spot there. You need a good off-roader to get there and the Range Rover took it all in its stride; its sensor and control systems are awesome. Much better than any other off-roader I've driven.'

'Are you a very experienced off-road driver, Otisk?'

Otisk grinned at the man. 'Who knows, Morseb? I can't remember anything before Pazoten. Bet you can't, either.'

Morseb considered this seriously. 'Of course you're right, Otisk. But I've been thinking about what you said earlier today—about my job before Pazoten. I'm pretty sure I was doing this sort of job. I am really comfortable doing this and I have extensive knowledge of it, too.'

Otisk looked at the man thoughtfully. 'Do you ever wish you could know the past with more certainty, Morseb?'

'What do you mean?' The man looked confused.

'What you did before Pazoten. What your life was like. Who you were. How you were brought up as a child. Who your parents were.'

Morseb's face had gone ashen. 'Certainly not, Otisk. We're not supposed to know these things—or even think about them. You know that, don't you? It's contrary to Pazoten life. It's what we're taught, you must know that. It's what everyone is taught.'

'OK, Morseb. Don't look so worried. I won't mention it again. I just think it's interesting, that's all. Harmless, too.'

Morseb shuddered visibly. 'Not harmless, Otisk. Harmful, worrying,' he whispered.

Otisk was taken aback by the man's extreme reaction. 'That's fine, Morseb,' he said, 'you're right, of course.' Morseb looked relieved and began to regain his normal colour. Otisk continued. 'I'll see you again soon. You know I wouldn't go anywhere else.'

Morseb had now regained his normal composure. 'You're always welcome here,' he said warmly. '100% satisfaction is guaranteed.' They shook hands and Otisk left.

* * * *

Back at the house, Otisk reported on his conversation with Morseb. 'We weren't taught that, were we? We weren't taught that trying to think about the past would be harmful to us?'

She shook her head. 'Definitely not. But that raises something very interesting, Otisk. We think that our Reception Procedure and the subsequent Initial Briefing we give are the only formal induction processes that take place here. That's all we are instructed to do and then we tell them to go exploring to find out the rest. That's a nice, gentle way of acquiring the knowledge of Pazoten that they need. But there could be a direct teaching process, too. Something that we are completely unaware of. For instance, something that happens during manifestation in which the "Rules" or "Laws" of Pazoten are implanted. Everyone I know—except you—seems to obey these rules and apply them to their life. And that would explain why people become so upset when we wish to explore forbidden knowledge. Your first experience of this was at the chemist shop, wasn't it?'

'Yes, that's right, Francel. And, either we didn't get that teaching or we got it just like everyone else but, for some reason, it didn't work on us.' He thought for a moment. 'Yes, I think the second idea is much more likely because we were sufficiently taught—or should I say "programmed"—to forget our previous life, weren't we? We can't even remember what age we are!'

As they sat silently, thinking about this, the phone trilled. Otisk answered.

'Hello. This is Counsellor Corneg.' A rich, plummy voice. 'I have been contacted by the Administrative Coordinator and I understand that you wish to speak to a Counsellor. Could we meet tomorrow at 1000 hours?'

Otisk switched on the phone loudspeaker so that Francel could hear. 'Well, we wished to speak to Counsellor Begiet,' Otisk replied, 'but we understand that she has left. So, yes, Francel and I would like to have a meeting with you. 1000 hours tomorrow would be fine. What location, please?'

'I could come to your house?'

'That would be splendid, thank you.'

'I will look forward to that,' the voice said unctuously, 'goodbye.'

They looked at each other. 'We had better plan our approach, Otisk. We want to make maximum use of this meeting. I hope this Counsellor has at least some of Counsellor Begiet's excellent qualities.'

They looked at each other with extreme seriousness. Then Otisk leapt up, seized Francel around the waist and swung her around joyously. 'Meanwhile,' he said breathlessly, 'let's have a lovely evening together and think of something else. We deserve a break. We'll get up early and sort it out tomorrow. But now, let's eat, drink, sleep and enjoy!'

* * * *

Breakfast eaten, they were deep in discussion. Otisk was speaking earnestly. 'I think we ought to take this opportunity to speak about the staff situation in the Administrative Coordinator's Office.'

'Ah, yes, Otisk. I had forgotten about that. I've been concentrating on how we can best express our wider Pazoten concerns. You're right, though, we should raise that. Would that be a good starting item?'

'Yes, I think it would be best at the beginning. It's a relatively simple one. Either it will be taken on board and something done about it or it will be rejected and nothing will happen.'

Francel nodded. 'I think we should put our case strongly. The conditions in that room are terrible and I think it's against the rules of Pazoten. Everyone here is supposed to enjoy themselves! These poor young men and women were not doing that.'

'Right! I'll put that as Item 1. Will you state our case and 1'll support? The feminine touch, you know... Take him off his guard!' He smiled at her.

She smiled back. 'Fine, I'll start us off. What's next?'

'I think we could go on to the proposal (heard from Morseb) that attempting to find out about your history is "harmful". Presumably, this also applies to attempts to go beyond Pazoten boundaries, physical or otherwise. I can raise that one, since I was the one he spoke to.'

'That's Item 2, then.'

'What about Item 3 being our failure to penetrate both woodlands? We would like an explanation of that, wouldn't we?'

'Fine. Shall I lead in on that one?'

'Yes, Please, Francel. Then I think Item 4 should be a discussion about the Leader, to see if we can acquire any more information about him. It may or may not be appropriate to reveal our belief – or is it a suspicion? – that Zadorb is the Leader. Personally, I think he is.'

'OK, then. You lead on that, Otisk. But what about the man we met yesterday? Could he be the Leader?'

Otisk thought. 'He could be, Francel, but somehow I think not. Somehow, he didn't seem to have the qualities that Zadorb has. And, I've just remembered, he didn't make the sign and say the words that Zadorb did as we were parting. To my mind, that was significant.'

'Well, let's just keep both of them in mind.'

They sat quietly for a moment. Finally Otisk said: 'We might want to talk about the building on the mountaintop. Without knowing what this Counsellor will be like, it's difficult to know how we should approach this—or even whether to approach it at all. I suggest we list that as Item 5, to be raised or not depending on the circumstances.'

'Yes, let's do that, Otisk. If we're getting nowhere with this Counsellor (you know what I mean, don't you?) we would be wasting our time if we brought this up. Let's be flexible at that point.'

They sat back. 'I guess we're ready, Francel?'

She flashed a smile. 'Ready for anything, eh?'

Counsellor Corneg had arrived, a large, bluff, middle-aged man, who strode briskly into their house surrounded by an invisible aura of confidence and energy.

'How are you both?' he said in joyful tones. 'Unfortunate about Counsellor Begiet. But when it's your time to go—you go! So, that's that.'

Francel poured coffee for them all and they sat down around the table.

Otisk started. 'Thanks for coming, Counsellor, I know you will be very busy...'

'Think nothing of it, Otisk. We're always busy—it's part of the job.'

'Right, we won't waste your time. We have noted down a few matters that we wanted to discuss with Counsellor Begiet. May we now discuss these with you?'

'Shoot,' the man trumpeted, 'I'm all ears!'

Francel consulted her notes. 'Counsellor, Otisk and I are concerned about the staff in the Administrative Coordinator's Department. We have visited there twice and have been appalled by the working conditions imposed on the junior staff. Physically, they are very cramped but, worse still, they appeared to be severely supressed, forbidden to speak, for instance. We think this is a totally inappropriate situation for Pazoten, where everyone is supposed to enjoy themselves. In fact, it isn't an appropriate situation for anywhere.'

'Anywhere?' The Counsellor shot this sharp query at her with a raised eyebrow.

'Anywhere else. Places other than Pazoten.' Francel's reply was calm and firm.

'I'll look into it.' He made a note. 'Next?'

'Just a minute, Counsellor,' Otisk interjected. 'If the situation is as we described, what are your thoughts?'

The Counsellor was silent, his eyes now fixed on Otisk's. Finally, he said: 'It shouldn't be like that. I'll let you know.'

Otisk nodded and made a note. Then he spoke. 'Counsellor, are you aware that Francel and I have attempted to acquire information about our previous existence?'

'I am aware of that,' the man said. 'It was in Counsellor Begiet's review. It has been discussed.'

'And that we have been exploring the boundaries of Pazoten?'

'Yes.'

'Recently, it has been suggested to me that such attempts and activities are personally harmful. Is that true?'

The man was silent again, this time looking down at the table. Without looking up, he said quietly: 'It is true for most people here.'

'But not for us?'

'It would seem so.'

'Francel and I would like to understand this fully, Counsellor. Are you saying that Pazoten is set up to harm its inhabitants if they step out of line – is that it?' Otisk's voice had hardened.

The Counsellor sighed. 'That is a very harsh interpretation of the situation, Otisk. It is never the intention of the Leader or the Administration to harm anyone in Pazoten. Indeed, you know very well there is no pain or suffering here. However, in order to protect our inhabitants optimally, they are taught to stay within the boundaries that we know are safe. It is for their own good that they feel some unease about this subject. That is merely part of the mechanism we use for their protection.'

'Boundaries? What are these boundaries, Counsellor?'

'I mean boundaries in every sense, physical, psychological, apparent.'

'But we are different?' Francel's quiet enquiry.

'Yes.'

'Why?'

'We don't know. You completed the full induction processes, just like everyone else.'

'Is this a cause for concern?'

'Well... we think the situation isn't ideal.'

'OK, Counsellor,' Francel continued, 'you know we've been to the edge of the woodland on two occasions in different locations?'

'Yes, I know all about that.'

'How do you know?'

'These activities are monitored for the good of the inhabitants.'

'Why is it impossible to get through?'

The man paused for a moment. 'That is a difficult question to answer specifically, Francel. I can say that it is not safe for any inhabitant of Pazoten to penetrate the woodland areas.'

'Why? What would happen? Otisk intervened.

'Because the woodland is the effective boundary of Pazoten.'

'But what would happen?' Otisk insisted.

'I cannot say. No-one can penetrate the woodland. No-one. I do not have any further information about that. That information is not known by anyone.'

'Counsellor, as a Reception Team, we brief the incomers, telling them about the basics of Pazoten.' The man nodded, relieved that the conversation was turning to more familiar ground. 'We tell them about the six Counsellors and the Leader. I imagine almost everyone has contact with at least one Counsellor in due course?'

'Yes, they do, I'm sure,' the man acknowledged.

'But they never meet the Leader or get to know anything more about him.'

'That's true, they don't.'

'Why?'

'There is no need for the inhabitants to have any contact with the Leader. His function is beyond the day-to-day activities of any local Pazoten matter. His role is strategic.'

'But *you* know who the Leader is, Counsellor—and you are an inhabitant of Pazoten.' Otisk was triumphant: now he was making progress!

There was silence for some moments. Then the Counsellor turned his gaze upon Otisk.

'You're wrong about that, Otisk,' he said very quietly, 'I don't know the Leader. I don't know who he is. Neither I nor any of the other Counsellors have ever met the Leader. You can ask them. They will all say exactly the same thing as I have just done. We recognise that it is not something we need to know.'

Otisk was incredulous. 'You don't know the Leader? How does that work, Counsellor? How is that possible? You and your fellow Counsellors are the Leader's executive staff. He works directly through you. You must know who the Leader is!'

'We don't. We report to him. We receive orders and we carry them out. The Leader works at a much higher level than we Counsellors do. We are mere foot soldiers. He is the Commanding Officer.'

'But I hear that you know the Leader to be a *man*, don't you?' Otisk was incisive!

'Why do you say that?'

'You refer to him as "he"—so you know that the Leader is a man.'

The Counsellor shook his head. 'No, Otisk, you're wrong about that. Calling the Leader "he" and "him" is just a convention. The

Counsellors don't know whether the Leader is a man or a woman. It simply doesn't matter to us. We say "he" because saying "he or she" every time would be unacceptably clumsy.'

Now there was silence and stillness in the room. As the seconds ticked by, Francel rose and refreshed the coffee cups. Then she left the room for a moment and returned with a large photograph which she laid in front of Counsellor Corneg.

'May we have your opinion on this, Counsellor?' Her question was quiet and gentle.

After a moment, the man lifted the photograph and took it to the brighter light near the window where he examined it meticulously. Francel and Otisk waited at the table without sound or movement, hardly daring to breathe. At last, the Counsellor returned to his seat and placed the photograph back on the table.

'I have no idea where this is,' he said, puzzlement clear in his eyes, 'It looks like one of the mountain peaks that surround Pazoten; there are quite a number of these. However, the low angle of the sun's rays indicate that the photograph was taken either in the early morning, when the sun was rising or in the evening when the sun was setting. As the sun in Pazoten rises in the east and sets in the west, this mountain is either in the northeast or in the southwest of our Land. It's a nice, professional photograph, Francel—but why are you showing it to me?'

Otisk and Francel looked at each other with astonishment, unsure how to respond. Then Francel replied. 'What do you think about the construction that is built on the mountain peak?'

The Counsellor lifted the photograph up and re-examined it for a moment or two. 'What construction? Where? I do not see any construction. The mountain peak looks perfectly natural, rocky and bleak.' He put the photograph down on the table and looked quizzically at them in turn.

Otisk and Francel were dumbfounded as they looked at the photograph, the large brooding building clearly pictured on the peak. Otisk leaned forward and placed the tip of his pencil in the centre of the building. 'Could you tell me what I am pointing to here?' he asked the Counsellor.

The Counsellor looked carefully. 'The tip of your pencil is placed exactly on the summit of the mountain,' he said, 'jagged rock below and sky above with near-horizontal sun rays.'

'Are you sure that's all you see?'

'Of course.'

'That is not what we see.' Francel's soft interjection.

'Really? What do you see?'

'Watch, please.' Otisk moved the tip of his pencil around the image of the building. 'We see a large dark grey building inside the lines I have just traced.'

The silence in the room thickened the air, muffling all sound, preventing all motion. Several minutes trundled by on silenced wheels. The Counsellor sat with eyes closed. Finally, he spoke. 'We know that you are very unusual inhabitants of Pazoten. Counsellor Begiet recognised this and communicated it to the other Counsellors and to the Leader. This meeting with you has indicated that you are even more unusual than we thought.'

Now the Counsellor tapped the photograph. 'I am sure that no-one else in Pazoten would see what you have described to me, even though you have been able to photograph it for yourselves. I certainly do not see what you describe to me. The reality you see in this photograph is triggered by the reality that you saw when you were there. That image is your reality, projected upon your situation. This mountain, and all the mountains we can see, are beyond the boundary of Pazoten. No inhabitant of Pazoten can access areas beyond the boundary—these areas do not exist for us. I can say no more than that to you. You need to think deeply about what I have said. I hope that my comments will be useful to you both when you are doing so. Thank you for consulting me on all these unique questions. I am afraid I have answered them in the only way I can.

So here is my serious recommendation. Just accept the situation, Otisk and Francel. Yes, you are different. But you are still bound by the reality of Pazoten. You cannot change that. So, relax and enjoy your life here, because you know it will come to an end for you sometime in the future. And, as you know, your future is unknown, as all futures are.' The man sat back and waited for their response.

After some silent moments, Otisk took Francel's hand and looked into her eyes. 'We've done all we can here, Francel. I suggest we thank the Counsellor for his time and for his advice—and leave it at that.'

Tears in her eyes, she nodded and he turned to the Counsellor. 'So thank you, Counsellor Corneg for your advice and for this meeting. We have listened very carefully to all you have said.'

'That's good!' The man was relieved, smiling warmly at them. 'I must go now, I'm afraid, as I am urgently required elsewhere.' He shook their hands and faded away almost immediately.

They sat unmoving for some time. Then Francel looked at Otisk sadly. 'So it's over, darling. Finished. We're different—but actually we're the same as everyone else. It's just that our perception makes everything much more difficult for us. There's nothing else we can do, is there?'

He looked at here seriously before his face was lit up by a cheeky grin. 'Of course there is, Francel. Tomorrow, we have a daytime shift to do, then we are clear for the following two days. During that time, we're going to visit the Leader at his farm out west and ask him to let us through the boundary so that we can climb the mountain and ascertain precisely what the meaning of that building is. Of course we're not stopping now; how can we?'

Silence for ten seconds. 'You're a star,' she said finally.

Chapter 15

Their shift was 1500 to 2100 hours. They planned an artistic morning, she reviewing her photographs and he fine-tuning his painting. As they worked in harmonious contentment, periodically flashing arrows of love across to each other, the phone trilled.

Francel answered. 'This is the Administrative Coordinator's Office. I am the Supervisor of Room 1/20. We met briefly when you were visiting the Administrative Coordinator.'

'Why, yes, I remember you.'

'I am informed that you and Otisk are on duty this afternoon in the Reception Centre?'

'Yes, that is correct.'

'The Administrative Coordinator asks if you would visit Room 1/20 before you go to your own department. Would that be possible, please?'

'Can you tell me what this is about?'

'I'm just passing on her message, Francel. Will you be able to come?'

'Well, all right, we will. See you later, possibly around 1430 hours.'

'Thank you very much, Francel. I will communicate your response to the Administrative Coordinator. We'll see you then.'

'Yes, goodbye.'

She ended the call. 'Hi, Otisk, the Dragon is asking us to call in to Room 1/20 before we go on duty. That was the young Supervisor we met the other day. He couldn't tell me why she wants to see us. Anyway, I said we would. We might as well get to know what it's all about. I suggested we should be there around 1430 hours.'

'OK, Francel. Maybe we're going to be *severely reprimanded*.'

'Well, I doubt whether she will have heard anything yet about our complaint. It was only yesterday we saw the Counsellor and, obviously, he needs to investigate—with care, I would imagine— assuming, that is, that he's going to do anything about it. However, maybe the Dragon has found something else to reprimand us about. Anything is possible from Room 1/20! She'll go through the roof when she hears we've been criticising her organisation!'

'Yes, I imagine there will be an explosion or two when the news filters down to her. Let's hope it doesn't arrive while we're actually there.'

'Well, Otisk, what we said was really needed. The working conditions for the junior staff there are absolutely disgusting. So, whatever happens, I will always be glad we raised our heads above the parapet.'

'Do you think the Counsellor will actually do anything about it? He did seem a bit reluctant, I thought.'

'Yes, that's true. I think he seemed to be glossing it over but you jumped in and pushed it a bit harder, didn't you? In the end, he admitted and conditions shouldn't be like that. But, maybe significantly, he didn't actually say he was going to do anything about it. We'll see.'

Otisk nodded. 'We won't give up, anyway,' he said shortly, 'we don't do that.'

Hand in hand, they had strolled gently to the Administration Centre and arrived there shortly after 1430 hours. As the entered the transporter, Otisk said. 'Here we go, Francel, into the lion's den. Stiffen your sinews!' He grinned cheerfully at her.

To their surprise, the door of Room 1/20 opened smoothly as they left the transporter and they were astonished at what was revealed inside. The room was twice the size it had been before. There was a pleasant hum of quiet conversation as the young men and women attended to their work at new and spacious desks. The atmosphere was happy and positive. There was a reception desk just inside the door and one of the girls rose from her desk and came forward with a smile.

'Otisk and Francel? Welcome to the Administrative Coordinator's Department. The Administrative Coordinator is waiting to see you. Will you come with me, please?'

As they walked across the room, the Supervisor stood up at his desk and waved a greeting to them. 'Hello,' he called, 'things have a changed a little bit, as you can see.' The man was smiling proudly as he looked around at his staff.

'It's very nice to see everyone so happy,' Francel said in response.

As they entered the Coordinator's room, she immediately rose from her desk and extended a hand of welcome to each of them. 'I'm so glad you could spare the time to call in,' she said smilingly, 'I have to thank you for what you did. You know, when you're busy—and, I must say, this job tends to be busy most of the time— it's very easy to take your eye off the ball. When I heard yesterday what you had said to Counsellor Corneg, I realised immediately that I had a disaster on my hands. I immediately reviewed the situation here, agreed with you completely and changed everything right away, in consultation with my Room Supervisor. I thought you would like to see the good effect that your intervention has had. I hope you're pleased with what you have seen. As you said, everyone in Pazoten should be happy. There was no doubt that my staff were far from happy—but they certainly are now.'

Francel had tears in her eyes as she responded. 'Coordinator, we are not only pleased but astonished at your undoubted wisdom, which is a lesson for us both. Thank you for inviting us here to see the happy result of your reorganisation which, I am sure, will bring not only happiness but greatly increased effectiveness.'

Otisk stepped forward. 'I agree with every word Francel has said. But I want to say something else. We are humbled by your attitude, how you responded immediately and what you have done here. This is not only a demonstration of wisdom but also of pure love. Thank you for teaching us this. We thank you from the bottom of our hearts.'

They shook hands with her and walked through the happy atmosphere of Room 1/20. No words were spoken as they transported to R55. They were strangely silent as they took over from ART2. Finally, they were alone in their reception area, sightlessly surveying the display in front of them.

After some minutes, Otisk spoke. 'Wow! I think I'm speech-less—that's a lesson for me. About humility, about wisdom, about love. Something I really needed to see, hear and know about.'

Francel did not answer. She just leaned over and kissed him very gently. Just then, a familiar chime made them turn their full attention to the display in front of them to assimilate the news of a new incomer on their way to the land of Pazoten.

* * * *

2145 hours found them sitting at the café in the Town Square, eating dinner. Their shift had been quiet. Their single incomer, a young lady in her twenties had arrived calmly and been dealt with by Francel without problem. They would visit her the next morning at 0900 hours to complete her induction and expected to pass her over to her Monitoring Team by mid-morning.

'Otisk, I been thinking, it's nearly two weeks since we've spoken to Lonei. We seem to have been so busy—causing trouble, some would say, no doubt. If he was free tomorrow afternoon, we could all go boating once again. He enjoys it so much and it seems to be the only pleasure he has, as far as I can see.'

'Thank for reminding me. I'll contact him right now and see if he's free tomorrow. I would be very pleased to do that. You're right, Lonei does enjoy it so much but—you know what—so do I!'

Minutes later, Lonei had been contacted and, as luck would have it, was free the following afternoon. 'Juno II and I would love to go to the Lakes,' he said. 'You know that we always enjoy it there.'

'OK, let's do it.'

'There's just one thing. Otisk, I want you to control the boat tomorrow. You've never actually sailed her and it's very important that you do.'

Otisk was mystified. 'Why should that be so important?' he asked, 'I don't really understand.'

Lonei was silent for a moment. 'Because you'll enjoy it so very much,' he said quietly. 'It's such a wonderful thing to do. And there's something else, too. It's always a good thing to acquire a new skill.'

'Right, Lonei; you've convinced me. I'm happy to have a go. But you'll have to teach me. I'll sail her and then you can take over. You're the expert, you know. You're the person they all come to see.'

'No, I'm sure that's not true.'

'You know it is. We'll pick you up at 1300 hours…'Bye.'

* * * *

The incomer induction was carried out smoothly and the transfer to her Monitoring Team was completed by 1030 hours. While Francel went home to prepare their picnic lunch, Otisk went off to Town Auto One.

'Back again, Morseb!' he called out gaily on arrival. 'Going over to The Lakes for a bit of sailing. Need a covered pickup with double cab.'

'Let's go over and see what takes your fancy today. You always know what you want, Otisk, I can depend on that.' Morseb was his usual polite and helpful self.

'Let's go Mitsubishi this time,' Otisk said, sweeping his eyes across the range on offer. Could I have the Warrior Manual?'

'Yes, of course. We have red or white.'

'The red looks nice. I'll have that, please.'

'Yes, darling, it's very nice,' Francel said mechanically, though with a smile. 'Let's get all the picnic stuff loaded.'

Lonei was ready and waiting. The tugboat was carried out carefully and strapped down in the covered load area of the pickup.

'Red one this time, Otisk? And a different model. What do you think of it?'

'Rather like the Hilux we had the first time. 2.5 diesel, manual gearbox and 4-wheel drive. Nice, comfortable cab, too. But listen, Lonei, Francel and I had a Range Rover some days back. We went south to a really remote picnic spot in the hills. The roads up there get really bad. They're just tracks, really. The Range Rover tackled the steepest, roughest roads you could imagine. It was really awesome. Of course we don't need anything like that for this trip. And I'm not sure we could have packed everyone and everything into a Range Rover, either. The rear load area probably wasn't big enough for the boat and the rest of the equipment.'

Soon they were on the familiar road to The Lakes and it wasn't long before they had reached their usual parking spot beside the model boat lake. The picnic table and chairs were unloaded from the pickup and set up on a piece of level ground set above lake. While Francel began to set out the picnic, Otisk and Lonei carried the tugboat to the water's edge, set it down on its hall rests and removed its protective cover.

'Boys,' Francel called with a broad smile, 'let's have some lunch first. If you two get absorbed in sailing the boat it will be tea-time before you resurface! I've got everything ready. Come and get it now.'

Otisk looked at Lonei with a smile. 'We had better do as we're told, Lonei. Otherwise we'll not be popular and I'll be blamed.'

'We can't have that,' Lonei replied. 'Anyway, I'm more than ready for lunch.'

They sat around the table, enjoying their lunch and watching the various model boats sailing on the lake.

'There really are some very nice traditional yachts there,' Otisk commented. 'Some of these have quite a complex sail pattern. Must be quite tricky to trim these sails and get the best out of the boat. You must need to know what you're doing.'

'Yes, I see what you mean,' Lonei sounded rather doubtful, 'but, you know, there's nothing like a good powerboat, especially if it has a really manoeuvrable system of control. You know, our tugboat...'

'You mean, *your* tugboat!' Otisk interjected.

'... our tugboat,' Lonei continued, ignoring Otisk's interruption, 'is easily the most manoeuvrable model power boat on the lake. Did you realise that?'

'Well,' Francel said with a smile, 'I believe you've told us that before, Lonei.'

'Ah, Francel, I may have mentioned it before but the question is: "why is it the most manoeuvrable power boat on the lake?"'

'Of course I know why; it's the way it has been designed!'

'Not good enough,' now Lonei was teasing her, 'you haven't mentioned the Voith Schneider Propeller System. That the secret of it all. The Voith...'

Otisk interrupted. 'Yes, you keep talking about that every so often. What's it all about? Surely a propeller system is a propeller system? You know, that bladed thing that spins around at the back of the ship? It "screws" the boat through the water.'

'Sorry, Otisk, you're completely wrong about that!' Lonei was triumphant. 'Juno II does not have a conventional propeller, the sort you have just described. It has something much better! The Voith Schn...'

'Yes, fine, but how does it work? Surely there has to be a propeller?'

'Of course there has to be, but it doesn't need to be a conventional screw. You can propel a ship in a different way. You know, I'm always having to explain the Voith Schneider System to the people down by the lake.'

'OK,' Otisk said resignedly, 'now is the time. Explain it to us— in words of one syllable, please.'

'OK. Vertically-mounted hydrofoil blades...'

Francel held up an imperious hand. 'Just a minute. You've just started and already I don't know what you're talking about! What's a hydrofoil, Lonei?'

He sighed. 'A hydrofoil is a blade shaped like an aircraft wing,' he said, drawing the appropriate shape in the air. 'OK?' he looked at them. 'May I continue?' They nodded.

'Right, a circle of vertically-mounted hydrofoil blades are driven to spin around a vertical axis, with each blade capable of turning on its own axis. When you cause the blades to turn on their axis at one point of the general rotation, you provide thrust in any chosen direction. You see? It's absolutely brilliant. And much better than a conventional screw and rudder!'

'You've lost me,' Francel said despairingly. 'I'm switching off now.'

'Don't see it, Lonei. How can that possibly provide thrust in any direction?' Otisk's brow was furrowed.

'Otisk? Do you by any chance know how a helicopter rotor works?'

Otisk screwed up his face. 'Yes,' he said slowly, 'I think I do. When you increase the rotor blade angle uniformly, the helicopter goes up because there's a downward thrust. But when you make the rotor angle increase even more just when it's passing the rear part of the rotation, the helicopter goes forward as well, because there's a rearward thrust as well as a downward thrust.'

'Bravo!' Lonei smiled. 'The Voith Schneider Propulsion system works like that, except that there is only a need for horizontal thrust. Look, I'll show it to you in a diagram...'

'We don't have them in Pazoten, though.' Francel was looking introspectively across the boating lake.

'What don't we have?' The men were puzzled.

'Aircraft, helicopters. We don't have them in Pazoten. I've never thought of that. Not once.'

There was silence. 'You're right, Francel.' Otisk's voice was full of puzzlement. 'Why is that? What do you think, Lonei?'

Lonei thought for a moment. 'The answer is obvious,' he said, 'there's nowhere to go. I mean there's nowhere to go that needs you to fly in the air. I reckon that's the reason, wouldn't you think?'

Otisk and Francel looked at each other significantly. Then they nodded thoughtfully. 'I expect you're right, Lonei,' they said.

They finished their lunch. 'Time for you to sail the boat, Otisk,' Lonei said, rising resolutely to his feet with excitement on his face.

'Are you sure you want me to do this, Lonei? I'm quite happy sitting here watching the expert at work. Maybe I'll make a mess of it and become a laughingstock to your admiring crowd.'

Lonei was adamant. 'You really should experience control of Juno II, Otisk. You never know when such an experience is going to come in handy. Please come and gain some experience. You'll be fine. I know you—you're a fast learner.'

'Right, Lonei, I'm coming.'

Francel smiled. 'I'll just enjoy clearing up here and then I will watch you perform.'

'No laughing, Francel, if it all goes wrong. You know how sensitive I am!'

The boat was prepared meticulously and launched—but not before Lonei had shown Otisk the Voith Schneider Propulsion System projecting below the hull towards the back of the craft.

'Wow, Lonei, I'm really surprised by that. That is certainly different from the norm. I'm just used to seeing conventional propellers and there's absolutely no sign of one here. Do many ships have this very different system?'

'Yes, Otisk, a lot of modern tugboats use this, as do many ferries—in fact, it's ideal for ships that need to manoeuvre precisely, as you will soon appreciate. With this system, you can rotate the ship in a very small space.'

The moment had arrived. Otisk stood at the water's edge with the complex control unit strapped around him.

Lonei pointed. 'You control the steering with this joystick. It controls the pitch of the rotating blades in the propulsion system. It's very sensitive and precise. The power from your two engines is controlled by these sliders here. You just ease up the power and steer where you want to go. Try it now.'

Otisk was very impressed. The tugboat was clearly very powerful and the steering proved to be wonderfully light and precise.

'Listen, Otisk, there's quite a strong, turbulent wind in the middle of the lake, so you'll need to reduce power a bit, to cope with the rough sea out there. Just take her over towards the opposite bank. Then, just watch her carefully as she deals with the stormy waves. Get yourself familiar with the behaviour of the steering in a storm like that. Notice how you need to correct for the wind and wave flow. That's really good: now bring her back and practice docking here by the edge.'

Otisk's attempts at handling and docking the tugboat were visibly clumsy at first but he soon mastered the sensitivity and lightness of touch required. Eventually, despite the fresh wind and waves on the lake, he found he could keep a smooth control and confidently bring Juno II in, docking it very neatly at the lake edge.

After several repeats, he had perfected the docking manoeuvre and Lonei was satisfied. 'Finally, Otisk, I want you to take her out to the stormy water and execute a very tight rotation, turning her virtually within her own length. This would be impossible for a ship with a normal propeller system, but you'll see it can be done with care by our boat, even when the water is as stormy as this.'

Obediently, Otisk took the tugboat out to the centre of the lake and, in the stormiest part, brought it to a halt. Then, with the most sensitive of touches on the controls, he turned the craft around as Lonei had instructed. Having completed this manoeuvre perfectly, he increased the power and sailed at full speed back towards them, finally bringing it competently and smoothly to rest alongside the bank.

Lonei clapped his hands loudly and all the spectators joined in. 'I knew you would be good at this, Otisk; I told you! You've passed all the tests with flying colours and I'm giving you your Master's Ticket,' he said. 'You have proved to me that you can captain a tugboat perfectly and that's a skill you will always retain. Skills are important things to have, Otisk, and you'll never regret having this one.'

'Thanks a lot, Lonei. Sorry I was a bit reluctant at first—I was a bit afraid the unknown, you know. But I've enjoyed this experience very much and I feel really good that I've acquired another skill. So thanks very much.' He put his arm around the older man's slight shoulders. 'You're a real expert at all this, aren't you? I think you're a real star!'

Lonei flushed with pleasure. 'It's nothing, Otisk. You and Francel, you're so kind to me...'

'Back to the real Captain, then.' Otisk handed over the control console. 'Your public is awaiting a demonstration of your skill. I'll go back to Francel, now. I'm gasping for a cup of her excellent tea.'

'It was really good, Francel. Extremely interesting and really tricky to get right. I'm very glad that Lonei insisted. He obviously knows me better than I do myself. I was holding back but he knew I would really enjoy it! So I've got my Master's Ticket to captain a model tugboat now—that's what Lonei says. You know, doing the work of a tugboat captain must be really difficult. Just imagine pulling and manoeuvring a ship many times larger than you – it must need a huge amount of skill.'

Francel kissed him lightly. 'It doesn't surprise me at all that you were good at sailing a tugboat. I know that you're good at everything.' Now it was Otisk's turn to blush!

'After I've finished this excellent cup of tea, should we go off and rent a boat on the big lake, Francel?'

'I think it's a bit windy for that today. It might be a bit too bumpy on the boat. Anyway, you might spoil the Boat Master's day if you turned up again. He probably dreads meeting you again after all your awkward questions.'

'He needn't worry, because I wouldn't ask him anything like that again. As we know, all the boats he needs are effectively produced out of thin air, in a process that is screened from view within that derelict boathouse. We know that is just another Pazoten mystery. We don't know how the mechanism works and I suspect we never will. Unlike us, he and all the others just accept the process as a "routine miracle" of Pazoten. For some reason, we can't. Anyway, the Boat Master is quite safe—I'm just a pussy cat now!'

Francel was silent for a moment or two. 'You know, I've never thought about that. That's another thing we don't have,' she said quietly.

'What don't we have?'

'Pussy cats.'

They looked at each other in some astonishment. 'You're right,' he paused. 'But, wait a minute, I've seen a couple of pet shops in the Town. I'm sure you must be able to get pet cats from them, don't you think?'

'Probably. But, the point is, we never see any, do we? Walking around. Lying, curled up asleep in the sun. If there are any cats—or dogs—they seem to be kept indoors by the people who have them. The animal lovers, I expect.'

'Hm,' he said, 'Later on, I'll try to remember to ask Lonei about pets. Chances are, he will know about this.'

* * * *

It was late afternoon and Juno II had been lifted from the water and prepared for its journey home.

'Have we packed away all the picnic items, Francel?' Otisk called.

'Yes, I've checked around and we've got everything.'

'Let's go, then.'

Soon, they were bowling along the road to the Town.

'Lonei? Something just occurred to Francel and me when we were talking earlier. Where are all the cats and dogs in Pazoten? Do you know?'

'Cats and dogs? Yes, there are cats and dogs for the people who want them. Most people don't, I think. You can get them from pet shops. I imagine you can get other animals, too. I don't know, I've never been in a pet shop because I never wanted to keep an animal.'

'Right. But don't people walk their dogs? Let their cats out to roam around? For instance, do you have to clean up any dog mess, for instance?'

'No, Otisk, I don't. Pazoten streets are always very clean. It's only necessary to empty the litter bins. When people unwrap something, a bar of chocolate, for instance, they always put the wrapper in a bin.'

OK. But what about dogs? Do dog owners take them to the parks or to the countryside for exercise?'

'No, they don't.'

'I don't understand how you can have a dog and never take it out.' Francel was puzzled.

Lonei was silent for a time. 'That's just the way it is here on Pazoten, Francel.'

Soon, they arrived at the Town.

'Otisk, could we go by our house first and offload our picnic equipment. We could all have a nice cold drink and then you can take Lonei home and drop off the pickup.'

'No problem, Francel. Is that all right with you, Lonei? It's time you visited us, anyway.'

'Yes, that would be nice. It's kind of you to ask me.'

As they were relaxing with their drinks, Lonei looked around admiringly. 'Nice place you have here. Spacious and comfortable and you get a good view of the Town Square...' His voice faded away as he focussed upon Otisk's painting on its easel beside the window. Silently, he got up and went over to examine it very carefully for some minutes. Finally, he spoke. 'It's yours, isn't it, Otisk?'

'Yes, it is.'

The man did not reply but continued to look searchingly at the painting. After some more minutes, he returned to his seat beside them and appeared to be deep in thought. Finally, he raised his head and looked at both of them. 'Francel and Otisk? Would it be all right if I spoke to you about your lives in Pazoten?'

'Well, it depends what you say,' Otisk replied jocularly. Then, seeing the serious expression on Lonei's face, said quickly: 'Sorry, Lonei, I was only teasing you. Of course we're more than happy to hear anything you want to say about our lives in Pazoten. Please go ahead, we're listening carefully.'

Now Lonei looked at the floor. 'You see, you two people have been so nice to me. Much nicer than anyone else on Pazoten. I just want to offer you a bit of advice. Especially now that I have seen that painting.'

They were puzzled by his words and looked at each other blankly. 'That's fine. Speak with complete freedom. We're happy to hear your advice—but why do we need advice? Are we doing something wrong here? And what has my painting got to do with it?'

'Well,' Lonei said very quietly, 'it's just that you ask so many difficult questions.'

'I'm sorry about that, Lonei. I'm sorry if we're worrying you, but...'

Lonei lifted his head and interrupted gently. 'It's not me you're worrying, it's you. You're worrying yourselves.'

The man was silent for a few moments. He seemed to be marshalling his thoughts with difficulty. 'You see, Pazoten is different...'

Otisk could not help interrupting. 'Yes,' he said very gently, 'we've had deep conversations about that with no less than two Counsellors. We know Pazoten is different. We even know some of the ways in which it's different. Also,' he added, 'we know we're different.'

Lonei was silent. 'What is the subject of your painting?' His voice was almost a whisper.

'It's a landscape scene out west. A mountain top. Shown late in the day when the sun was very low in the sky.'

'This mountain. Is it the one with the building?'

Otisk looked at him with surprise. 'You remember my question weeks ago?'

'Yes.' There was a long pause. 'And what did I reply?'

'You said it was a trick of the light.'

The man nodded. 'Yes, Otisk. You're right. That's exactly what I answered and that's exactly what it was.' He looked towards the painting, glowing by the window. 'And that's exactly what you have painted, isn't it? You've managed to paint a trick of the light that somehow suggests the faint outline of an imaginary building. You have an incredible skill there.'

Otisk leaned forward. 'Listen, Lonei...' He stopped abruptly as he caught sight of Francel, who was shaking her head at him. He understood her message. Of course it wasn't appropriate to argue with this nice elderly man, who spent his life carrying out a simple cleaning job in the Town. After all, as he had already said, hadn't they argued their case with no less than two Counsellors—and obtained some valuable information? Counsellor Corneg had revealed that only they could see the building. He had admitted that the mountain was outside Pazoten and could not be reached because the boundary of the Land was impervious. Both Counsellors had advised acceptance of their situation in Pazoten.

Otisk started again. 'Listen, thank you very much for your praise and concern. Francel and I appreciate that very much and we are really glad that you are our friend. And, of course, we will always remember your advice.'

The man looked at them and smiled rather sadly. 'Thanks for that, both of you. You're lovely people. Actually, though, you won't be able to remember my advice.'

Otisk looked at him in surprise and concern. 'Why is that, Lonei?'

'Because I haven't given you any advice yet!'

Francel smiled gently. 'Better do it now. We promise to be quiet.'

'It isn't much,' he said. 'Just accept your life here and enjoy it. I just hope that's your destiny.'

* * * *

'That was a bit of a surprise, Otisk, wasn't it?' He had returned from delivering Lonei to his home and returned the pickup to Town Auto One.

'Yes. It seemed to be the painting that set him off. Anyway, that was pretty clever of him to link it with our question about the building. That was a few weeks back, wasn't it?

'Yes, it was on the way home from one of our boating sprees, weeks ago.'

'Well, in any case, maybe we'll know a lot more at the end of tomorrow after we've talked to the Leader. At first, I thought we might just relocate over there but then I had second thoughts. It might be useful if we rode out on quad bikes again; I would like to see if we can spot anything as we make the journey. More information, you know. So I've arranged with Morseb at Town Auto One that we'll pick up our bikes first thing tomorrow. Agreed?'

'Yes, of course. I'll make sure we take everything with us, including my trusty camera. Tomorrow could be a very big day for us, couldn't it?

'Certainly. It isn't every day that you meet the Leader. In fact, as far we know, it will be a first. Even the Counsellors don't meet him. We'll just have to see what happens when we confront him. Maybe we will be in possession of everything we need to know by tomorrow evening.'

They were preparing for bed and Otisk was cleaning his teeth in the bathroom:

"589 times 741?"
'436,449.'

"72,756 divided by 129?"
'564.'

The maths test was over in a flash, his responses instantaneous, as always. Ruefully, he looked at himself in the mirror. 'I wouldn't mind so much if they were new tests. But these repeats drive me mad!' His thought flashed across his consciousness and disappeared.

Chapter 16

In the interest of maximising their day, they decided to relocate with their quad bikes to the clearing at the western edge of the forest where they had parked before.

'We know we can't see much of the mountain range from the road before that,' Otisk had said. 'It tends to be screened by trees or blocked by some closer higher ground areas. It's only after the forest that that we get a clear view of the mountain range and, of course, "our" mountain comes into view as we continue west. It will be really interesting to see if the building appears on the mountain at any other time of the day.'

Francel agreed. 'That sounds like a good plan. I'll be ready to take photographs if we see anything untoward happening on the mountain—or, indeed, anywhere else.'

So there they were, standing beside their machines in the forest clearing and preparing to ride down a track to join West Road.

* * * *

The previous evening, they had tried to map out a strategy for the day to come.

Otisk began with a statement of their intention. 'Right, Francel, our principal goal is to speak to the Leader, who has introduced himself to us as Zadorb. The sooner we can find him and initiate that conversation the better. Of course, if he's not at the farm, we'll just have to wait around and hope he arrives before evening. If the worst comes to the worst, we'll need to give up and return on another day.'

Francel had nodded. 'So what do we say when we finally find him?'

Otisk thought about this. 'Well, after the greetings, etc., I suggest we start by telling him that we know he is the Leader. Obviously, we have no idea how he will react to that. I hope he isn't too shocked. I think his most likely reaction is to try to persuade us to keep his identity secret. I can imagine him telling us that such knowledge would greatly unsettle the "normal" people of Pazoten. He would stress how they are content with the situation as it is. What do you think, Francel?'

'Yes, I think that's quite a likely scenario. If he does that, how should we respond?'

'I think that's our opportunity. Of course, we'll agree to his proposal—it would be churlish not to—but we will agree on condition that he answers our fundamental questions about Pazoten. You know, the ones we keep asking ourselves. What is Pazoten all about? Why are we here? Where were we before? Where do we go to when we leave? And, of course, we will want the mystery of the building on the mountain explained.'

Francel thought for a bit. 'I think we've got to start with the building. All the rest, the really fundamental things, will follow on. It was the appearance of the building that was the last straw for us, wasn't it? Don't you think we should start with that?'

Otisk pondered this and then replied. 'Well, yes, Francel, maybe you're right; I see the logic of that approach. Now, let's think about his response. If he explains the building to us, that's fine. Then we can then go on and ask him all the other questions. However, if he cannot explain the building to us—or denies all knowledge of it—we can ask him to let us climb the mountain and investigate personally! As the Leader, he must be able to arrange that, don't you think? Allow us to go through the boundary? If he agrees to that, would you be happy to do that?'

She considered this. 'Yes, I agree, because we really want to know the answer. But, listen, he might say "no" to climbing the mountain. He might tell us it's just too dangerous for anyone to do that, especially since it means leaving the Land and penetrating into the "no-man's land" around it. At the moment, we have absolutely no idea about the reality of that building, do we? It could be an extremely dangerous place. Or it could be a totally imaginary place. He might insist that there is absolutely nothing there and that what we have seen is just a product of our imagination. That would link up with what Counsellor Corneg told us.'

'In that case, we'll have to ask ourselves if we believe him. He could just be telling us that to stop us solving the mystery, couldn't he?' Otisk paused and thought some more. 'OK, if he proposes that we don't explore it, we should only accept that recommendation if he promises to reveal the truth about Pazoten. How about that?'

'Yes, but if he does, how will we ever know it's the truth?'

Silence for several minutes. 'We won't,' Otisk admitted finally. 'Anyway, we think this is the only way we can make progress. We must talk directly to the Leader. There may be problems and dangers in what we're doing but we have agreed that we cannot just sit back and accept the Pazoten situation like everyone else seems to. For some reason, and we cannot imagine what it is, we are being shown that building on the mountain top. We know it is real—well, real to us, anyway. You have taken photographs of it. Whoever or whatever is showing us the building knows that we are bound to investigate. That's just the way we are. So we must go, meet the Leader, and ask him all our questions.'

She nodded. 'I think that's right, Otisk. I'm convinced we must do that.'

* * * *

They made good progress along the smooth surface of West Road. When they reached the intersection that turned off to link with Southwest Road, Otisk called a halt.

'I've been keeping a good watch on the mountains but I haven't seen anything yet. Have you seen anything, Francel?'

'No. Now that we can see "our" mountain in the distance, I'll take the opportunity to shoot off a few frames. Just give me a minute or two.'

A few moments later, she was back. 'Look at this, Otisk.' She held up her camera. 'When I used my telephoto lens and zoomed in, I found that there's a little bit of wispy cloud on top of the mountain. And sometimes, as it moves, it suggests the shape of our building. Have a scan through; I took a series of shots.'

He gasped. 'You're absolutely right, Francel!' They looked at each other, wide-eyed. 'It looks really different today. And there's no doubt that the cloud seems to form the shape of the building that we have seen twice in reality and many times more in your photographs. Something has changed, or maybe something *is* changing. We'll need to keep a sharp eye on this. Maybe the Leader will be able to explain this. If anyone knows, he should.'

They remounted their quad bikes and drove rather more slowly along the narrowing road. By the time they reached the point where it was appropriate to go on foot, they had observed that the cloud on the mountain was thickening. Now they parked their bikes and donned walking boots and rucksacks. As they walked west, they observed that the mountain top was increasingly obscured by a cap of thick cloud.

'Mountain tops do get covered with cloud at times, Francel. I think it happens when the air becomes more moist and flows up the slope of the mountain. The moisture condenses and becomes cloud. At least, I think that's how it works. So this may just be a natural thing that's happening.'

'Well, yes, Otisk. That works for real mountains—but is "our" mountain real? It's outside the Land of Pazoten—that's all we know about it at the moment. Remember what Counsellor Corneg said? He said that the mountain was outside the boundary of Pazoten and that areas outside the boundary do not exist for those inside the Land. He said that what we saw on the mountain was only a projection of our reality, which, it would appear, is very different from other people's reality. I cannot claim to understand the full implication of what he said but his recommendation to us was adamant. Basically, it was: "forget it and enjoy!" Lonei said that, too, didn't he? In fact, that's what everyone seems to say to us every time we query things.'

'What you have just said certainly complicates the issue, Francel. If the mountain is real, we could believe that a natural weather process was taking place. Cloud had formed in a normal weather sequence and it's probably raining up there. But if it's just a projection of our reality, where does that take us? Does that mean we are making up this cloud—and the rain, if there's any rain. I'm certainly not aware of any reason why we should do that. And if it's an unconscious action, that makes it even more puzzling. Obviously, this is another thing we'll have to discuss with the Leader!'

Half an hour had passed and now they were approaching the area where the farmhouse was located. Soon, they would pass the track that ended with the thorn hedge barrier they knew so well.

'Francel, I've just had an idea. If the reality of the mountain has changed, maybe the reality of the barrier has changed, too. I suggest we relocate down there and check. We know that relocation works here, provided you can define your area and we've actually done this particular relocation before.'

'Good idea, Otisk. It certainly is worth a check before we meet the Leader.'

Seconds later, they both stood at the bottom of the track, next to the wall of thorn hedge. Francel stood close to it and examined it carefully. 'I can't see any difference in it, can you? It looks completely impenetrable, just like last time.'

Otisk parted some outer leaves with difficulty. 'No, you're right. I can't see a thing through here. Let's walk to the left this time and check it as we go. You never know, we might get lucky...'

They didn't. The hedge continued to be dense, dark and completely impenetrable. After several hundred yards, they stopped. 'I think we're wasting our time here, Francel. This is absolutely solid and, looking ahead, I cannot see any variation. Somehow, it seems to get even more dense as you approach it. That happened with the other part of the barrier that we explored beyond South Road, didn't it? I think we should relocate back up to the road, now.'

'I agree,' she said and they held hands for the relocation.

Back on the road, they looked carefully around them and listened for sounds of activity. They were surprised to hear nothing. Also, it was absolutely still around them. The sun shone. The air was still. Even the small sounds of nature were quieted.

'We would hear his tractor coming if he was out driving that,' Otisk murmured, overcoming a strong feeling of reluctance to break the silence. 'Maybe he's in his cottage or he could be in one of the barns or outhouses up there. We'll walk up the track to the farmhouse and knock at the door. With a bit of luck, he'll be there. Also, he must have office work to do, so we'll look for a building used as an office, too.'

As they started to walk up the steep track towards the farm buildings, the noise of their footsteps sounding appallingly loud. Each of the larger rounded stones set in the track seemed to resonate under their boots, while the rattle and scatter of the smaller gravel provided an accompanying snare drum percussion. Apart from the noises they were making, everything was worryingly still.

Francel shuddered. 'This silence is quite eerie.' She couldn't help whispering.

'Yes, I feel it too. Why is it like this, I wonder? I feel as if we're making more noise than a stampeding buffalo herd!'

Almost tiptoeing (a difficult feat in stout walking boots!), they arrived at the spacious farmyard and stopped, restoring absolute silence around them. Otisk had intended to call out but found that he could not; the silence demanded that he made no sound.

'Let's go over to the farmhouse and knock on the door,' he whispered, taking Francel's hand. As they walked slowly towards the farmhouse, Otisk automatically responded to a three-calculation maths test without losing his focus on the door they were approaching, although he grimaced in an irritated scowl for a moment.

His knock was deafening and Francel jumped inadvertently.

'Sorry,' Otisk whispered, 'no point in knocking softly. If he's in here, we want him to hear us.'

They waited as silent seconds cumulated. No reply. Otisk knocked again and they waited.

'Nobody in here,' he said finally. They looked around. A number of farm buildings surrounded the farmyard, barns, sheds of various sizes, many open-fronted.

'Let's check through these outbuildings. He could be working in any of these.'

There were several large barns, piled with bales of hay and neatly stacked plump sacks. Otisk paused and placed his hands on a sack. 'Feels like harvested grain,' he said. 'Where does it grow? How does he harvest it and process it? He says he works here alone. Surely that is impossible?'

They passed on to the next large barn where there were various items of farm machinery. They recognised ploughs and cutters but did not recognise the purpose of many other pieces of equipment. Then they came to a smaller wooden building, clearly used as an office. They knocked on the door and peered through the windows. There was no-one inside. At last they came to a very large, closed barn. The heavy double doors were closed and locked shut with a large brass padlock.

'Look at this, Francel, this barn is securely locked, so I imagine he can't be in here. Whatever is in here must be valuable, secret, or both. Interlopers like us are not allowed to see inside. I wonder what is stored in here.'

Ever practical, Francel examined the door. 'It's not locked, you know. Look, the padlock is locked around the ring part of the fastening but the locking flap is still free. That flap part has to be behind the padlock, hasn't it? I don't know the technical names for these parts.'

'Wow, Francel, you're right. You're really observant. Yes, I think the bits are called the "staple"—that's the ring part—and the hinged bit is the "hasp". The door would only be locked if the staple was through the slot in the hasp and the padlock secured in front of it. So the door is unlocked.' They looked at each other, suddenly guilty conspirators. 'Shall we investigate?' he proposed with a little nervous grin.

She looked worried. 'Do you think we should? I mean, it's private, isn't it? Maybe it's something that the Leader has to keep secret.'

'Well, if it's so very secret, he would be sure to keep it locked all the time, wouldn't he? I really think there would be no harm in us taking a little peep!'

She still looked doubtful. 'Well, let's just open the door and have a quick look inside. We needn't go in. The Leader might not want "ordinary people" to go inside his secret place. I don't want to make him sad or angry by acting selfishly.'

'Right, I'll open the door and we'll take a look. After all, the Leader might be working in here. I'll call him when I've opened the door.'

Rather unhappily, she nodded and watched nervously as he opened the door wide.

'Zadorb?' he called into the dimness inside. No reply. 'Zadorb?' he called again, more loudly this time. Still no response. 'I'm going in!' he said decisively. He waved gaily to Francel and then disappeared into the dark interior of the barn.

She waited at the door, looking around nervously and counting the seconds until he would return. The seconds became minutes and she became increasingly alarmed. Finally, she could stand the tension no longer and called his name through the open door. Silence. Alarmed, she repeated her call, craning her head into the barn. Silence.

'Otisk, where are you?' Her voice now a scream of panic.

'Here I am.' His familiar figure came out from the darkness. 'I was just having a look around. It's a big place. Sorry if I took too long.' He was surprised when she clung to him. 'It's all right, Francel, I was just taking a good look. There's lots of things in there.'

'I thought you had gone. I called and you didn't answer,' she whispered, clinging to him. 'I was afraid. I felt so alone in this empty place. I don't like it here.'

'There's nothing to worry about,' he comforted her. 'This is just a vast storehouse for all the farm produce. Come on in. Your eyes will soon get used to the dim light and I'll show you what's here.'

'I'm not sure,' she held back. 'It doesn't feel right…'

He put his arm around her. 'Come on, Francel, it's OK, it's just an unlocked storehouse. Come and see.'

She was persuaded to enter the barn and he took her around, showing her the racks of farm produce. Every sort of vegetable, all cleaned and ready to cook, racks and racks of fresh fruit, milk in large containers, large bales of shorn wool and even meat from various types of animals kept cool in large refrigerators.

'There's absolutely everything here. This must be where the produce is picked up. But how is it all produced? Where are the animals in the fields? Where are the people to look after them? Where are the crops grown? How is it all collected and processed? It's impossible, incomprehensible!'

'No, it isn't.' As these words reverberated around the walls, every part of the barn became brightly illuminated as many large bright lights were switched on with the explosive click of a high-voltage relay switch. And there, standing just inside the doorway, was the powerful figure of Zadorb, the farmer, his face impassive, eyes fixed unblinkingly upon Otisk and Francel. In their surprise and shock, Otisk and Francel clung together as the burly farmer strode forward. They both had to fight the desire to turn and flee but they knew that escape was impossible. The man planted himself directly in front of them and examined them closely.

'Francel and Otisk.' His voice was quiet and uninflected, almost a comment to himself. 'I wasn't expecting visitors today but I had the feeling you would be back.'

'I hope we're not trespassing?' Francel's voice was conciliatory.

Zadorb turned slowly and looked at her. 'No,' he said, after a moment. 'The door is normally locked, not for security but to keep animals out. Wild animals, you know. I must have left it open this morning by mistake.'

With the diminution of his fear, Otisk's natural curiosity was becoming re-established.

'Is this where all the farm produce is stored before being transported to the Town?' he asked. The farmer nodded briefly. 'And you work the farm alone, do you?' Again the man nodded. 'I'm sorry, Zadorb. I have to repeat what I said a short time ago—it's impossible. One man cannot do all this. And, in any case, where are all the crops, the orchards, the fields for the animals, the processing plants, the dairies?'

'These things do exist. You have seen only a very small part of this farm.'

'So where are all your workers, then? You cannot possibly do all this alone.'

'I farm here alone.'

'But, Zadorb, this store alone would take many men to organise.' He swept his arm around to encompass all the tall racks of vegetables, fruit, etc. 'What you claim is really impossible. I'm sorry.'

Zadorb sighed. 'You are wrong, Otisk. You want to attach your own sense of reality to everything—and this is the wrong thing to do.'

'Explain it all to me, then.' Otisk looked at the man with intensity.

'I will. All this is possible because we are in Pazoten. That is the explanation.' The man turned round. 'Let us go to the farmhouse for refreshment. I have the sense that you have more to say.'

When they left the storehouse, Otisk and Francel were astonished to see Zadorb's large tractor parked just outside.

'But how...' Otisk began.

'This is Pazoten,' the man repeated with a slight smile.

Soon they were sitting around the large table in the farmhouse, food and drinks before them. Zadorb had said nothing, apart from offering them refreshment and placing what they chose in front of them. Now he sat silently and waited for them to speak. For the first time, they both noticed that he was wearing a bracelet. They could see that there was printing on it but were unable to make out anything else.

Now Otisk looked at Francel, trying desperately to remember what they had agreed at the end of their strategic discussion the night before. Now, in the tension of the moment, his mind had gone blank. Was he to confront the man with their conviction that he was the Leader? He didn't think so, although he could remember proposing that very thing! He desperately tried to recreate their discussion in his mind. Francel looked into his eyes and, with their special bond of love, knew that he needed a nudge in the appropriate direction; but how to do it? As he looked at her in despair, she turned her head and looked through the window at the mountain. When she looked back, she saw grateful recognition in his eyes.

'We need to talk to you again about the mountain.'

The man looked sad. 'Listen,' he said with a distinct tinge of impatience, 'why are you so fixated on this? Last time, I told you everything I know, which isn't a great deal. You wanted to know if there was a path through the woods. There isn't! I know you've been down there yourselves, so you know that I'm telling the truth. No-one goes through these woods. No-one goes to that mountain. Anyway, what's so special about the mountain? There are hills, small mountains, in Pazoten for you to climb. Why not go and climb these? What you're suggesting makes no sense at all.'

'We know about the building.'

'The building? What building, where?'

'The big grey building on top of that mountain peak.' He pointed out the window to the mountain, with its cap of dense cloud clearly visible.

Zadorb looked at the mountain and then at each of them in turn. 'I'm sorry, he said finally, 'I don't know what you're talking about. There's no building on that mountain. Such a thing makes no sense. Who would build on top of a high mountain?' He was incredulous.

'Well, there are many monasteries and temples built on mountain peaks, for instance.' Otisk was surprised to hear his voice saying this.

The man shook his head. 'Sorry, Otisk, I don't know what you're talking about. Shouldn't you be discussing this sort of thing with a Counsellor? They get to know a lot of things that normal people don't.'

'We have already done that, Zadorb. We've been told that the mountain is outside the boundary of Pazoten and that no-one from Pazoten can go there because it doesn't exist in Pazoten reality. It has also been suggested that the building we have seen was merely a projection of our reality and that no-one else sees it.' He paused briefly. 'We cannot accept this. We don't believe it and we want to solve the mystery that is the building and, with it, the mystery that is Pazoten.'

There were minutes of silence during which no-one at the table moved. Each person seemed to be absorbed totally with their own thoughts.

Finally, Zadorb stirred. 'I don't understand,' he said. 'I don't understand why you come to me with this.'

Francel leaned forward and spoke softly. 'Zadorb, we come to you because it is obvious that you are different. You are one man working here on a huge productive farm, doing what is impossible in normal reality. You have explained to us that what you do *is* possible because this is Pazoten and we can just about grasp what you mean by that. However, that marks you out as a special person and we also believe that you have a guardian function, too. You are the guardian of the Pazoten boundary here, are you not?'

The man shifted uncomfortably. 'There is never any need to guard the boundary,' he muttered in reply, 'because the boundary is impenetrable.'

'We would question that.' Francel's assertion was gentle but firm.

He looked up. 'No, Francel, you must not question that. I am speaking about fact here. The boundary is impenetrable.'

'Zadorb?' An incisive tone in Otisk's voice. 'We know who you are.'

The man looked at him with surprise. Finally, he answered: 'Yes? I'm Zadorb, the farmer of the West Zone.' As he spoke, he held up his arm and they could read "ZADORB" printed on his new bracelet. 'I remember when I met you for the first time, you commented that I had no bracelet on my wrist and I explained it had been destroyed by machinery on the farm. As you can see, I have since obtained a replacement, knowing it to be a requirement for life on Pazoten.' Now he smiled broadly. 'So, Otisk, you are right—now you know who I am. Didn't you believe me before?'

Now Otisk spoke slowly and in uninflected tones. 'We know that you are the Leader.'

Slowly, the man appeared to crumple before them. He turned deathly pale and looked at them with shock in his eyes. Unmoving, Otisk and Francel waited for his response. When it came, the voice was thin, wavering. 'You are wrong. Completely wrong. I am not.'

Minutes passed and no-one moved. Then Zadorb rose slowly to his feet. 'You must excuse me for a few minutes,' he said, almost inaudibly. Francel and Otisk were left sitting at the table as he disappeared from the room.

Otisk took Francel's trembling hand. 'This isn't getting us very far, is it, Francel?' She shook her head in response. 'We'll see what he says when he comes back but I intend to continue our questioning about the mysteries of Pazoten. I must say I don't feel very optimistic, though.'

'I'm confused now, Otisk. We were sure he was the Leader but he denies it. I can't help feeling that he wouldn't deny it if he *really* was the Leader. At the moment, I don't know what to think!'

The inner door opened and Zadorb re-entered the room briskly. 'Right,' he said with his former forcefulness, 'Now I'm going to show you something. Come with me, please. We'll use my tractor.'

Moments later, they had climbed into the cab of the tractor. Zadorb started it up and they bumped down the steep track to the road where he turned left to head eastwards.

'Where are we going?' Otisk had to shout above the noise of the tractor engine.

'I'm going to show you something that you'll want to see.' As Zadorb said these words, he turned the tractor right onto the track between the fields and headed down the hill towards the dense thorn hedge that guarded the woodland behind. The tractor stopped with a jerk in the clearing at the bottom of the track. Without a word, Zadorb climbed down and gestured to Otisk and Francel to follow him. He walked towards the wall of thorn hedge and stopped, facing it squarely. Down at this lower elevation, the air was still and it was stiflingly hot.

At first, the sound was barely perceptible, but then it increased steadily in volume, building to become as deafening as a sub-bass pulsation, at the lowest end of the human aural range. As the sound volume became even louder, Francel and Otisk noticed a startling change in the area of thorn hedge just in front of them. A semicircle of leaves, twigs and branches were quaking violently and dissolving in front of their eyes. A dark tunnel was opening up in front of them, leading through the hedge into the dense woodland beyond. As they watched this happening, they were beset with primeval pangs of fear at the sight of an awesome, stygian cavern opening up before them. Both could not help recoiling in horror at the thought of approaching this terrifying, incomprehensible leafy maw. They were extremely relieved when Zadorb produced a large, powerful hand torch and directed its powerful beam into the blackness, lighting up the steadily dissolving wall of vegetation, already fifty metres or so from where they were standing.

'What is happening?' Otisk's voice was a shocked whisper.

'You are about to see what very few people have ever seen,' the farmer said, without looking around. 'I, myself, have seen it only once before. Now you will see it—and then you will know. Come, follow me, it is time for us to proceed.'

The man strode into the dark tunnel, shining his light forward. Otisk and Francel held hands tightly as they scuttled on his heels, speechless and with eyes wide with fear. The tunnel appeared to be extending at walking pace, because they continued to see the wall of woodland vegetation dissolving well ahead of them. As unmarked time passed, Otisk tried to clear his head and re-establish rationality. Had they walked for ten minutes? Possibly—but he had to admit that each minute could have represented an eternity as far as he was concerned. He recognised that all concept of time and distance had been lost at the instant they had entered this mind-numbing environment. He hoped fervently that it would come to an end as soon as possible! For humanity, the fear of the unknown is all-pervading, almost paralyzing.

Then, with the heart-stopping suddenness of a soundless explosion, the tunnel broke through into blessèd daylight. Otisk felt Francel duplicate his inadvertent forward thrust towards the light as they both felt a strong surge of relief deep within them.

'Out of the darkness into the light,' he heard Francel murmur, 'haven't people been saying that since time immemorial?' It was a rhetorical question but he squeezed her hand in response.

They had to narrow their eyes as they emerged into the warm, incandescent sunlight. Otisk looked back at the wall of dense woodland towering over them, hoping that their small tunnel, now looking so insignificant, would remain a lifeline for their return. Then he turned his eyes forward. They were walking on level, grass-covered ground. Directly ahead of them was the mountain, clearer now but still a significant distance away. He focussed his eyes on its surface, seeking any indication of a path leading upwards towards the rocky peak. At this distance, he was unable to discern anything, although, to his experienced eyes, he thought that the mountain looked reasonably scalable.

As Zadorb continued to lead them forward, Otisk noticed that the grass under his feet had given way to mostly bare, smooth rock. He scanned the ground ahead and it seemed they were walking directly towards the edge of a cliff.

'Are you all right, Francel?'

'Yes, but I'm glad to be out of that tunnel.' A small voice.

'So am I. It looks as if we're coming to a cliff edge just up ahead. It will be interesting to see what sort of land there is between here and the base of the mountain. We can see the mountain a lot more clearly now, can't we? On an initial look, I would have thought it should be possible to climb it. Nothing too precipitous, as far as I c cloud is still capped over the peak. That's a pity, because we might have been able to see more detail from here.'

Within minutes, they were approaching the cliff edge and Zadorb stopped. They stopped beside him.

'How high is the cliff just ahead, Zadorb?' Otisk asked.

'I don't know,' the man answered immediately.

'What sort of land is at the bottom?'

'I don't know that either.'

'Not to worry, I'll be able to see that when I look over the edge.'

'You won't be able to do that, Otisk, because you can't go to the cliff edge. The ultimate boundary is here, just in front of us. I've brought you here so that you can see it for yourself—and, if you want, experience it, too.'

'Sorry, Zadorb, I don't understand. Why shouldn't I look over the edge?'

In answer, the man picked up a weighty stone at his feet. 'Watch,' he said and threw the stone powerfully into the air towards the cliff edge. Almost immediately, the stone rebounded back towards them, landing near their feet with a loud clatter. At the same time, the picture of the mountain before them distorted and shivered violently before gradually settling back to immobility.

Francel and Otisk were astonished. 'What…'

'Nothing can possibly pass through this barrier. It is the ultimate barrier.' The man said calmly and waited for their response.

After a moment or two, Francel turned to him. 'I don't understand. What is it?'

'I don't know what it is,' the man said. 'It could be field of force. It could be some sort of physical entity. It could be a figment of imagination, a personally conceived reality. I don't know what it is—and I don't need to know. All I need to know is that it is absolutely impenetrable.'

'I want to go closer to it,' Otisk said. 'I want to touch it, to experience it. Is it dangerous to do that?'

'I don't know whether it is dangerous or not,' the man replied. 'It is up to you to act as you see fit. I am not your keeper.' As he said this, he stood aside and waited.

Without pause, Otisk started to walk forward purposefully.

'Be careful, darling, I don't want lose you. Don't you think you should…?'

'I must do it, Francel. You know I must.'

He walked forward very slowly, arms outstretched ahead of him. Very soon, he began to feel a retardation against his body. Progressively, it was becoming more and more difficult to make forward progress. He leaned his weight forward and managed another metre or so. Finally, still ten metres or so from the cliff edge, he could make no further forward movement; the force of retardation had become so strong that his strength was completely overpowered. As he accepted defeat and fought to turn around to come back, he was suddenly projected towards Francel and Zadorb as if a giant gust of wind had caught him.

'Wow,' he said breathlessly as he skidded to a stop beside them. 'You're right, Zadorb; nothing gets through there!'

'Zadorb?' Francel asked a question. 'What do you see on the mountain top?'

The man glanced at the mountain briefly. 'Cloud,' he said in a disinterested voice.

'Have you ever seen anything else?'

'Nothing else. I told you before.' The man sat down and closed his eyes.

At their request, they did not go back through the woodland right away. They sat and studied the mountain carefully. Francel took many photographs. At last they were ready to leave.

'Follow me,' Zadorb said.

'Can't we just relocate?' Otisk thought this would be much quicker.

'Relocation doesn't work here. It only works in Pazoten. This is not Pazoten.'

He led the way to the black tunnel and they entered into its darkness.

* * * *

They had returned to the farmyard and Zadorb had offered them refreshments once again. Once again they sat around his kitchen table. Inevitably, Otisk had started the questioning again.

'You say you are not the Leader, Zadorb. If you are not the Leader, who is?'

'I don't know who the Leader is. I only know that there is a Leader and that he is the one who gives me instructions occasionally.'

Otisk sat forward. 'When did he last give you an instruction,?'

'Today.'

'When? And what was it?'

Zadorb said nothing for a few moments, then he looked up. 'Normally, I would not answer these questions, because my communication with the Leader is strictly private business between us. However, in this case, I will make an exception.'

'Why?'

'Because the subject of the instruction concerned you and Francel.'

Startled, they were silent. After a moment, the man continued. 'I was in communication with the Leader when I left you alone earlier. It was then that he instructed me to show you the ultimate boundary. It was he who created the tunnel.'

'But we heard no sounds of communication when you were not with us?'

'Of course not. All my contacts with the Leader are by direct thought transference.'

'So who is the Leader?'

'I do not know—and, furthermore, I do not wish to know. It is not appropriate for me to know who the Leader is. My task is to do my work and to carry out his instructions.'

Chapter 17

They had left Zadorb's farm and were walking back to their quad bikes. Francel glanced at her watch. 'Goodness, Otisk, it's only midday. I know we started our day very early and used relocation to speed things up but I would have thought it was very much later than that.'

He agreed. 'So much has happened to us this morning, Francel. In fact, I think we need to slow down and try to grasp it all. I know: when we get back to the bikes, we can soon ride back to our favourite picnic spot—you know, the one where we had our first glimpse of the building on the mountain. Then we can sit down and start to rationalise our experiences. We might as well see how much or how little progress we have made.'

'That sounds a great idea, Otisk. In any case, I think we're beginning to need a good rest, don't you?'

The quad bikes were retrieved and soon they were driving towards their picnic area, increasing speed as the track surface became smoother.

'Calling Francel. Nearly there. Over'

'Acknowledge. I can see the area coming up ahead of us. We can turn in and park there. Over and out,' she grinned.

Minutes later, they were lying on the soft grass, hands interlinked, staring at the clear blue sky above. After several minutes of silence, Francel was the first to speak. 'I wouldn't like to call it a failure, Otisk, but I think we've come to a dead end. Of course we now know so much more about the boundary of Pazoten than we did this morning but what we have discovered has shown us the impossibility of solving our mystery—the mystery of the building on the mountain peak.'

'That's true, Francel, I can't think of any way we can reach that mountain, can you? For some reason, the mysterious Leader, who is hidden away somewhere unknown, has allowed us to see and experience the "ultimate barrier" just before what appears to be some sort of cliff or steep drop in the land. However, there's no way that we could even begin to get through the woodland barrier before it. We now know that the woodland barrier is a sort of initial system—a pre-barrier that needs to be breached before you can reach the ultimate barrier near the cliff. We've checked out that first woodland barrier in two separate places in Pazoten and there's no doubt it is impenetrable to us and, by implication, to all the other residents of Pazoten. I'm absolutely convinced we would find exactly the same impenetrable woodland barrier if we investigated it anywhere else in the peripheral regions of Pazoten.'

'I'm sure you're right, Otisk. As I see it, Pazoten is like an island, isn't it? Instead of a land surrounded by water, it's a land surrounded by something else, or maybe nothing else. Maybe what we can see beyond the boundary of Pazoten is just a sort of mirage?' She smiled and held up a hand as Otisk opened his mouth to speak. 'Don't say it – I know that "mirage" is the wrong word to use but you know what I mean, don't you?'

He returned her smile and closed his mouth again. They thought some more.

'Otisk? Do you think that there is anyone in Pazoten who knows the secret of the building? Because I think that's the only way we can get at the truth now. Someone who knows has to be persuaded to tell us.'

Otisk shook his head slowly. 'I'm pretty sure that none of the "normal" people in Pazoten can help us. We've tried before and, on every occasion, they react with complete incomprehension and are also very reluctant, fearful, even, to pursue the subject. The nearest we got to it was with Counsellor Corneg. He was willing to talk about the boundaries of Pazoten but could not, or would not, enlighten us about areas outside the boundaries. It's a pity that we never managed to discuss it with Counsellor Begiet—I felt we had a very good rapport with her. She might have revealed more; if she knew any more, that is.'

'What about Zadorb? He seems to be very close to the Leader. He had direct communication with him just this morning. Would he know any more?'

'I really doubt it, Francel. When we were at the ultimate barrier he gave me the impression that he was telling us all the information he knows. When you asked him about the mountain top he insisted there was nothing there. I'm sure he would just repeat that. I think we can now give up the idea that Zadorb is the Leader. We confronted him on that subject and he denied it. Although we have no direct, independent proof that he is not the Leader—only his word—I agree with your judgement that Zadorb would be unlikely to deny being the Leader if he really was. It just does not seem to be the sort of thing the Leader would do. Now Zadorb certainly knew about the way through the initial woodland barrier. He said he had seen the ultimate barrier once before. That certainly makes him a very unusual person in Pazoten but it doesn't make him the Leader; especially since he told us that he was showing us the barrier on the Leader's instructions.'

'Maybe there isn't a Leader at all; have you thought of that as a possibility?'

Otisk pondered this. 'Maybe there isn't,' he said finally, 'it's impossible to say. But I can't help feeling that someone or something has to be in charge of Pazoten. He, she or it may not be called the Leader but I feel there must be a coordinated control somewhere, somehow... Maybe this controlling entity is not in Pazoten at all. But we certainly have Counsellors here and these Counsellors have to be selected and coordinated somehow. There must be a controller.'

'So we'll just have to withdraw and regroup, won't we?'

'Looks like it,' he said, putting his arms around her. Rather exhausted, they drifted off to sleep.

* * * *

They were still sleeping when they heard it. A peculiar, rattling noise. An alien sound that somehow had no place in this tranquil countryside. Yet, it was a noise that they had heard before; somehow familiar. Slowly they ascended through their layers of sleep, becoming more aware of the noise, their brains registering and analysing its disturbing, jarring tones. Finally, Otisk levered himself up. 'What's that noise? Do you hear it?'

She joined him in a sitting position. 'You mean that strange resonant, rattling sound?'

'Yes.' Now he stood up. 'I can't make out what it is. Is there a bird that makes that sort of noise?'

She listened. 'Not one I can recognise. It's strange, though. I seem to have heard that noise before. I can't think where.'

'I feel that way too. It is a noise that could come from a bit of farm machinery?'

'Could be; we don't know all the noises that Zadorb's machines make.'

He swung his head around, sensing the sound's direction. 'I think it's getting closer. I would say it's approaching us from the east. From somewhere down the West Road, in the direction of the Town.'

Rigid, they listened carefully. There was no doubt that the rattling, resonant noise was becoming louder. 'I think we'll see Zadorb coming round the bend any minute, driving one of his farm machines. We'll give him a wave as he passes.' Now the sound had become quite dominant and they both focussed their eyes on the nearest bend in the road. Suddenly, a flash of something orange coloured could be seen flickering through the roadside bushes.

'Here he comes, Francel.' They waited, poised in eager anticipation. A moment later they were frozen in utter disbelief as Lonei came into view, pushing his small litter cart ahead of him. Instantly, they remembered that resonant, rattling sound. It was the sound of Lonei's cart bumping along. Absolutely riveted, they watched as the little man continued to approach them, carefully scanning each side of the road for any sign of litter. As they watched, he stopped and removed something from the roadside, dropping it into one of his cart containers. The lid closed with its familiar clang.

Francel and Otisk continued to be speechless with surprise. Their eyes followed Lonei and his cart as he came closer. At last, he came to the short track that led up to the picnic spot and parked his cart neatly by the side of the road. Only then did he raise his eyes and meet theirs.

'Hello, Francel and Otisk,' he called out and walked up the track to stand beside them.

Otisk's eyes were wide with astonishment. 'Are you real, Lonei?' he gasped. 'Am I dreaming this?'

The man smiled. 'No. It really is me and I really am here.'

'But, why... how?' Otisk spluttered in total confusion.

Lonei responded with calm quietness. 'Occasionally, I come out to check the outlying roads. I told you before, remember? Today, it was the turn of the West Road.'

Francel fought down her sense of unreality. 'It's lovely to see you, Lonei,' she said gaily, as if he was an expected guest, 'Let's all sit down and have a nice cold drink.'

Silent minutes passed as they sipped their drinks and munched upon some sandwiches.

'So that's your mountain, is it?' Lonei's eyes were fixed on the cloud-shrouded peak, clearly visible from this raised viewpoint.

'Yes.' Otisk turned his gaze upon Lonei. 'What do you see when you look at it?'

'I see a mountain, capped by white cloud.'

Otisk turned to look at the mountain. 'What else do you see, Lonei?'

'Nothing else.'

Otisk turned to Francel. 'What do you see, Francel?'

'I see cloud, swirling around and sometimes taking the shape of a large square building.'

Otisk looked at Lonei. 'That's what I see, too.'

Lonei sat perfectly still for several minutes and then he sighed deeply. 'I had hoped that you two excellent young people would become Counsellors here in Pazoten,' he said, very quietly.

Francel and Otisk looked at each other, dumbfounded. 'Counsellors?' Otisk said, faintly.

'Yes. You would be perfect.'

There was silence as Otisk and Francel looked at the mountain, their thoughts completely in turmoil.

Unmeasured minutes of silence rolled by. At last, a very thoughtful Francel turned to Lonei. 'It's you, isn't it?' Her voice was very soft.

'Yes, it is.' Lonei's equally quiet reply.

Otisk was confused. 'Sorry...?' He looked from one to the other. 'I don't...'

Francel took Lonei's hand. 'It's you. You are the Leader.' The words were spoken as a statement of fact, not a question.

'Yes.' A very quiet reply, completely uninflected.

There was utter silence for some time as Otisk tried to come to terms with this new and astounding turn of events. Gradually, his confusion diminished and, inevitably, he found his curiosity rising. 'Lonei, do you choose to manifest yourself as the Pazoten Town litter collector? Is that your free choice?'

Lonei smiled briefly at him. 'Yes, Otisk, of course it is. It's the perfect disguise that allows me to go everywhere and see everything. Some people, actually, a lot of people, don't even see me—that's why I am ignored—but I see them. I see everything and it gives me all the information I need to run Pazoten and direct my Counsellors.'

Otisk now looked at Lonei with a degree of awe. 'So are you some sort of superior being, then?' he asked in a faltering voice.

Lonei laughed. 'No, I certainly am not! I'm exactly like you. But I came to Pazoten a very long time ago and I was appointed to carry out this function.'

'Immediately, Lonei? As soon as you came?'

'Yes, immediately. I don't know for sure but I think it was because they knew I would be here for a very long time—and that has proved to be correct!'

Francel turned to him. 'So is there a higher authority than you, Lonei?'

'Of course there is. But I have no idea who, what or where he, she or they are. Furthermore, I don't want to know. That's not my business. I'm kept too busy running Pazoten.'

Astounded and overwhelmed by it all, Otisk shook his head in wonderment. However his brain soon re-engaged to plan a forward strategy. Otisk was always focussed on the task in hand. Now he recognised that he and Francel were with the person who knew everything. The Leader himself. The person who could answer all their questions about Pazoten and the building on the mountain. Now they were getting somewhere. He felt his excitement rise. Best make a start right away!

'Lonei?'

'Yes, Otisk.'

'Can I ask you some questions?'

'I've just been waiting for you to start.'

Otisk smiled, knowing that Lonei would have predicted his strategy perfectly. 'Well... could you explain the barrier around Pazoten, please? It's very puzzling. We don't understand it.'

Lonei smiled. 'I knew you would ask me that, Otisk. Listen, it's quite simple—and you know the answer already. That's why I arranged for you to penetrate the inner barrier and see the ultimate barrier at the cliff. Unless you saw it for yourself and experienced it, I knew that you would never believe it.'

'Yes, Lonei, thank you. You arranged for us to see the barriers. We saw their reality and their impervious nature—but why are they there at all?'

'Counsellor Corneg told you why, Otisk. They are there because that is the boundary of Pazoten—the edge of Pazoten, if you like. Beyond the ultimate barrier, Pazoten doesn't exist. Pazoten reality stops there, exactly at that point.'

'But why have two barriers, Lonei? Why not only one?'

'Because the ultimate barrier would worry people too much. They wouldn't be able to understand it. So the inner barrier of woodland is to present people with a natural barrier, one that is much more comprehensible to them.'

Otisk nodded. 'Hm, I see that. Thanks, Lonei.'

Now Francel spoke. 'Tell us about the mountain, and the building on the mountain.'

Lonei looked at the ground. 'I was waiting for that one, and you're not going to be satisfied by my answer. I don't know. Because I don't know anything about the situation outside the boundary of Pazoten. There is absolutely no need for me to know anything about that. You see, that's why I don't see this building on the mountain.' He paused. 'Why you should see it, I don't know.'

'But you can see the mountain?'

'Yes.'

'Why? It's outside Pazoten and you say you know nothing about the situation beyond the boundary.'

'Sorry, Francel, obviously, I haven't explained my situation well enough. When I said I know nothing about the reality outside Pazoten, I meant I could not explain that reality. Obviously, I can see the mountain, along with the mountain ranges that are visible all around Pazoten. Everyone in Pazoten can see the mountain ranges that surround the Land. However, we all see that landscape just as a backdrop. You know, like a pictorial projection.'

Otisk had been listening carefully and looked rather unconvinced. Now he leaned forward purposefully. 'So, for instance, you don't know what the land is like between the ultimate boundary and the foothills of the mountain range?'

Lonei turned his eyes to him. 'Yes, I do, although I only saw it once for a very brief moment. Just once, not long after I came here and became the Leader, I was allowed to be outside the ultimate barrier and glance over the cliff. What I saw was not land at all. It's water. A sort of sea. Very stormy, it was. I can only assume it's still like that today, although I don't know for certain.'

As Otisk drew breath to pose his next question, Lonei held up a hand. 'Don't ask me any more questions about that. I've told you all I know—almost more than I know, in fact. Now I must leave you, because I have much thinking to do. I'll be in touch soon.' As the man said this, he faded from their view and disappeared. When they looked down the track, they saw that the litter cart had disappeared also. Obviously, Lonei had relocated with his cart.

Otisk hugged Francel tightly. 'Wow,' he shouted, 'what a day! Never in my wildest dreams did I think we would find out so much. Let's go home right away. We have a great deal to think about.'

They had relocated back to Town Auto One with the quad bikes. Morseb was pleased to see them. 'Hello, I didn't expect to see you until much later.'

Otisk explained. 'We were out beyond the West Road and found we had done everything we wanted to do by early afternoon. So we just came back and now we plan to relax for the rest of the day.'

* * * *

Of course, it was impossible for them to relax. Both were flushed with the excitement of all their discoveries of the day. They decided to walk along the river path and exchange their thoughts.

'Just imagine!' Francel squeezed his arm, 'Lonei! Lonei as the Leader. I can't believe it. And yet… I can believe it, so easily. Although I don't think it would ever have crossed our minds that Lonei was the Leader, we knew, deep down, there was something very different about him. There was the unprinted bracelet, for instance. That might have given us a clue.'

'Yes but we were never anywhere near to thinking that Lonei was a very important person.' Then he grimaced. 'Goodness, I've just had a worrying thought, I must have given him a serious problem by taking up his case. There he was, happily doing his work every day, all day, keeping a close eye on everyone in Pazoten and then I stampeded in and brought him to the attention of the authorities. Before I did that, all the Maintenance Managers thought that he worked for one of the other managers—and I ruined that for him! And when I talked to Counsellor Begiet, she obviously had never heard of him and I catapulted him into the limelight. He was discussed in a Counsellor's Meeting. He must have thought I was a real problem. A bull in a china shop!'

'Well, yes but it actually worked out all right, didn't it? We became Lonei's friends and we got Juno the tugboat and went sailing at the Lakes. Lonei may be the Leader but I'm convinced he was delighted with Juno II. He really enjoyed sailing her and making contact with all those people who were interested in model boating. I think we were able to introduce some welcome relaxation into Lonei's life, don't you?'

'Well, yes, I hope so. However, I'd better apologise to him for causing him so much trouble. I must remember to do that. Incidentally, should we be treating him differently now?'

Francel considered this. 'I don't think so, Otisk, because we might make the mistake of identifying him to others as the Leader. Anyway, I can't think of him as anything other than "Lonei."'

'Maybe we should be more respectful. Or, perhaps I should say, maybe *I* should be more respectful.'

'I am sure we have always respected Lonei, haven't we? I think we should continue just as we are, although I admit we are bound to regard him in a completely different light now.'

'You know, Francel, we should discuss this with Lonei. We don't want to spoil anything for him, do we? We'll tell him we'll do whatever he advises.'

'Yes, I think we should do that,' Francel nodded.

They walked in silence for a while. Suddenly Otisk stopped dead and looked at Francel with a shocked expression.

'What's the matter, Darling?'

'Francel, it's just occurred to me. We've got to think about this the other way around.'

She was confused. 'Sorry, I don't understand...'

'It's us. We are the problem now!'

'Problem? What problem?'

He looked intensely into her eyes. 'We are the only people in Pazoten who know the identity of the Leader. No-one else does. Not the Counsellors, Not the Farmer/Guardians. Just us. We are the problem now. The identity of the Leader should not be known by anyone in Pazoten. That is perfectly clear. That is the way Pazoten is organised. And now *we* know who it is.'

She looked at him, her eyes sightless now as her brain tried to grasp all the implications of what he had just said. He was right. This was a serious problem. By finding out who the Leader was, they had gone against the rules of Pazoten.

'What do we do?' she asked. 'What can we do? The damage is done now.'

'There's nothing we can do, Francel. It's all in Lonei's hands now, or maybe in the hands of whoever is above him. It's possible that we cannot smore, isn't it? I really don't know. We must talk to Lonei about this. This must be the first thing we raise with him.'

The rest of their day was filled with a growing concern. They spent an anxious evening together and then prepared for their overnight shift at the Administration Centre. Although they tried very hard to be their normal focussed selves, both knew that the reception work they carried out was done with a certain abstraction. Fortunately, their experience meant that they could deal with their single incomer professionally. The elderly lady was serene when she arrived and they were able to keep her in a calm and happy state; in due course, she was settled into her new home in the Town. They would visit her for the induction process around lunchtime, after they had rested at home.

Mid-afternoon found them very quiet and thoughtful, walking in the sunshine, silently hand-in-hand.

'Hello, Francel and Otisk.' Lonei's voice. They looked around in surprise, to find him standing just behind them. Although he was wearing his familiar orange jacket, there was no sign of his litter cart. 'We need to get together,' he said, 'we need to talk.'

They looked at him blankly, thoughts racing. Otisk was the first to recover. 'We could go to our house, Lonei. Would that be suitable?'

'Very suitable.'

Ten minutes later, they were back at home with Lonei, sitting around the table with cups of coffee before them. As soon as they were settled, Otisk spoke with urgency. 'Listen Lonei, I just want to start with an apology...'

Lonei held up a hand. 'Listen, Otisk, my friend, you have nothing to apologise for.'

'That's not true, Lonei. I have caused you a lot of trouble...'

Lonei smiled at him. 'You have nothing to apologise for,' he repeated gently, 'however, I have something to say before we get down to business. You two young people have been wonderful friends to me and your kindness and generosity mark you out as very special people. The fact that you have found out the truth about me does not change that in any way. I have been honoured to have you as my friends. And, as I think you know, your gift of Juno II has greatly enhanced my life here. So I thank you from the bottom of my heart.'

Francel took his hand. 'Lonei, it's lovely of you to say that. It's just that we're so sorry that we've ruined it all for you. Nobody here is supposed to know the identity of the Leader. We know that is a rule of Pazoten—and we have broken that rule. Now we have to face the consequences.'

'There are no consequences, Francel. Pazoten does not work like that. However, the situation does require a decision to be made and that is what I have been concentrating on since our conversation yesterday.'

Otisk could not keep silent. 'Lonei, Francel and I understand if it is not possible for us to stay here any longer. We are completely in your hands and await your decision. Whatever it is, we will of course comply.'

'It isn't like that, Otisk, my friend. Yes, there is a decision to be made but you and Francel will make it. My purpose here is to explain the options you have. Before I do that, I just want to remind you that you two young people are unlike anyone else here. You alone have been asking questions that no-one else asks. Although you have received some of the answers from various sources, like the Counsellors or myself, you have not received an answer to your most important query of all. That query concerns the building that you can see on the mountain top; a building that no-one else—including me—can see. Now, at this point, you have three options to consider and here they are:

First option: you can become Counsellors and continue your life here.

Second option: you can choose the *status quo* and continue your work as ART9.

Third option: you can climb the mountain and personally investigate what is built on top—or perhaps find that there is nothing built on top.'

The little man paused. 'Now, I am sure you will have questions to ask me about these options.' He sat back and waited.

Otisk and Francel turned to each, speechless with astonishment. In total silence, they sat frozen, unseeing eyes locked together as they fought for understanding and comprehension.

Without moving, Francel finally spoke in a strangely normal voice. 'But it is impossible to climb the mountain, Lonei. We have seen that there is no way through the ultimate barrier. You have shown us that.'

'For you, Francel and Otisk, a way will be found, if this is your choice.'

'Will we be able to return?' Otisk's small, shocked voice.

'I don't know. I have no control over that. I think it may depend upon what you find.'

Now there was silence for some time before Otisk eventually turned to Lonei. 'Surely Francel and I cannot stay in Pazoten, as Counsellors or as a Reception Team, if we are the only people here who know the identity of the Leader? Does that not obviate these two options?'

'No, it doesn't. If you chose to stay in either function, your training would be arranged to solve that particular problem. You would merely know me as your friend the model boat enthusiast and litter collector.'

They thought about this and then nodded slowly, remembering how efficient and direct their Reception Team training had been.

'I imagine you need us to make this decision as soon as possible, Lonei?' Francel was calm.

'Yes, I'm afraid so. The current situation does require action.'

'Can you give us a short time to discuss your options and make our decision?' Otisk asked.

'Yes, Otisk, of course I can. Shall I return here in one hour?'

'Yes, Lonei. And—thank you very much for your consideration.'

The man smiled gently and faded as he relocated away.

'Let's just sit and think for a while, Francel. Then we can tell each other our thoughts and work our way towards the decision. We must be ready when Lonei comes back.'

'When we've come to our own conclusions, Otisk, let's write it down. When we've both done that, we can see what independent choice each of us has made and then have an open discussion to reach a final decision before Lonei comes back.'

'That's a very good idea, Francel. That way, we're making sure that we're considering everything.'

They parted company deliberately. Otisk sat in front of the window, surveying the scene outside as he considered in fine detail each of the three options they had been given. Francel sat in a deep chair in their bedroom, totally engrossed in thought. After about ten minutes, she stood up and wrote on a piece of paper. Then, she returned to the main room where Otisk was still motionless by the window. Folding her paper carefully, she placed it in the centre of the table, then sat down and waited. She did not have long to wait.

'Here I am,' he smiled, 'returned to the land of the living.' He placed a folded piece of paper on the table beside hers. 'The moment of truth!'

They looked at the squares of paper, mundane everyday objects that now had acquired paramount status in their lives. They both felt breathless with tension.

Francel gulped and whispered: 'Let's unfold them both at the same time.'

Otisk lined them up beside each other and, at his quiet command "NOW", they unfolded the two papers simultaneously. One said "Climb Mountain"; the other said "Mountain".

They looked at each other wordlessly and fell into a tight embrace.

'That makes the decision very easy,' he whispered in her ear.

They sat down beside each other. 'Why?' he said to her.

'I concluded that I must find out the truth,' she said simply, 'for some reason, that's the way I am.'

'I felt that too. And I didn't want to be re-programmed, because that's what must happen to us if we choose to stay here, isn't it?'

'Yes, you're right, Otisk. We have to be made to forget that Lonei is the Leader. Presumably also, we would be made to forget about the building on the mountain. And we would no longer ask awkward questions about Pazoten.'

'Doesn't sound like us, does it?' he said with a slight smile.

'Definitely not!'

'So are we ready to call Lonei back?'

'Definitely yes.'

Lonei sat before them. He had been informed of their decision. He was silent and impassive.

'Is that OK, Lonei?' Otisk was a little nervous.

The small man smiled gently at them. 'Of course it is. I was fairly sure that would be your choice but I had to present the other options to you. These were my instructions.'

'Who instructs you, Lonei?' Otisk could not help himself!

'Even if I knew, do you think I would answer that, Otisk?'

Otisk smiled ruefully. 'Sorry, Lonei, I shouldn't have...'

'You go tomorrow,' Lonei interrupted gently. 'Kit yourself out for climbing. You need to take climbing gear.'

'Yes, Lonei, but how are we going to get through the barriers? How are we going to get to the foot of the mountain? You said...'

'It will all be arranged, Otisk. It will not be easy but I think you will succeed. Just look after each other. Here are your initial instructions. Tomorrow morning at 0800 precisely you are to relocate west to the thorn hedge barrier at the foot of Zadorb's farm track. You know where I mean?' They nodded. 'When the tunnel opens, pass through and wait near the ultimate barrier. I expect you to be there by 0815 hours. Do you understand?'

They nodded, dumbly.

'Do you have any questions?'

'What about our work here, Lonei?' Francel asked.

'You need not do anything about that. That will be arranged.'

'Will you be there, Lonei? At the barrier?' Otisk's question.

'Possibly. But, in any event, someone will be there.' The man stepped forward and hugged them both powerfully. Then he stood back and made a complex sign with his right hand. 'May you be safe and in power.' At that, he faded from their sight as he relocated.

They were silent for a while.

'Now that we've done it, do you have any regrets, Otisk?'

'Regrets? No, none at all. It's what we must do. We've always known that.'

'I feel exactly the same. I have only one worry, though.'

'What's that, Francel?'

'Losing you. When we leave here, we are going into the unknown.'

His face darkened. 'I know, Francel. I worry about that, too. But people don't stay in Pazoten for ever, do they? That's when they go into the unknown. The only difference with us is that we're choosing when to leave Pazoten and we're going to be together. I think there must be a reason that we're being shown the building that no-one else can see—even the Leader can't see it! That's why we must go.'

She embraced him. 'Whatever happens, Darling, I believe we belong together and, wherever we are, I'll use my whole power to achieve that.'

'So will I.'

They looked out of their window. 'Francel, why don't we go to the café for a really splendid meal, then come back and prepare our kit for tomorrow's departure? That sounds like the right thing for us to do on this very special day.'

'Let's do that,' she murmured.

Chapter 18

Perhaps surprisingly, they had both slept very well. Their dinner at the café had been excellent and, on return to the house, it had not taken very long to prepare their kit for the day (or days) to come.

'We'll need to take really warm clothing, Francel. Since we'll be outside Pazoten, we may have to cope with bad weather. Lonei has already told us to take climbing gear, so we need ropes and helmets. Fortunately, we have all that equipment to hand. Also, we need to take food rations, high-energy packs, etc. We may need to cover our food and drinks requirement for a number of days. However, we mustn't take anything we don't need because we can't afford to carry unnecessary weight.'

Francel nodded. 'The only extra I must take is my camera. We need it to record our experience.'

'Yes, of course. Why don't you carry the camera with its standard lens and give me the telephoto lens?'

'Thank you, I accept your kind offer. It will fit easily into your rucksack. What are we doing about shelter?'

'I've got that "covered", Francel,' he said with a smile. 'I have a very small, lightweight tent that folds away and fits into my rucksack. If we need to use it, we'll just have to snuggle close—very close.'

'Well, you know I would want to do that anyway.'

By 2200 hours they were fully prepared and they sat down close together to think about the next day.

'Otisk, we know how to get to the final barrier—I assume we'll go through the woodland tunnel again. How do you think we'll get through the ultimate barrier?'

'I don't know, Francel, but Lonei says he can arrange that. If it's a sort of force field, I assume it can somehow be switched off for a time. I really don't know—we'll just have to do as we're told. Lonei says it's possible.'

'We know there's some sort of cliff there. You couldn't get near it but Lonei said he looked over once. He said there was rough sea at the bottom, didn't he?'

'Yes—but he only had a glimpse of it. Again, we'll just have to do as we're told. I assume we'll need to climb down the cliff. After that, if there really is water there, I hope nobody is going to suggest we swim. I can swim but not for very long!'

'What we're going to need is a boat. A little motor boat should do us fine, eh?' She laughed. 'After all, there are plenty motor boats produced from thin air up at the Lakes.'

They snuggled together, each thinking their own thoughts. Then Otisk stirred. 'Time for bed. We need to be well rested for tomorrow.'

* * * *

They were up at 0600 hours and soon eating a very hearty breakfast. 0730 hours found them checking all their kit meticulously. By 0755 they were fully prepared and kitted up. At 0800 they were standing before the impenetrable thorn hedge.

'You're very prompt.' A cheerful Zadorb greeted them. 'I believe that the access tunnel through the woodland will begin to manifest in about five minutes.'

They stood in quiet anticipation until they began to hear the mysterious pulsating sound that preceded the birth of the tunnel. Once more, Francel and Otisk watched in wonder as the dense vegetation melted away, giving them a shaft of access through the impenetrable darkness.

'Shall we go, Zadorb?' Otisk stood back to allow the man to precede him.

'No, Otisk, you are going without me. Here's a powerful light-weight torch. It's probably a good idea to take it with you if you don't have one of your own. If you don't want it, just leave it near the cliff and it'll make its way back to me somehow.'

They were rather appalled that they had to go through the tunnel without Zadorb's reassuring presence. 'Ah... thanks, Zadorb. I suppose we'll mange on our own.' Otisk didn't sound very confident. 'Will there be anyone at the other end of the tunnel?'

'I don't know that, Otisk. I'm just carrying out my instructions.'

Rather nervously, they prepared to enter the tunnel. As they did so, Zadorb made a sign with his right hand. 'May you be safe and in power,' he said as he watched them disappear into the blackness.

Of course the first time of any alien experience is always the worst, because the totally unknown procedure fills the mind with a myriad of negative possibilities. This time, although progress through the tunnel was still unnerving, they knew it would come to an end in due course. Meanwhile, the intense beam from the torch illuminated their increasingly confident steps forward. However, the sudden appearance of a disc of daylight at the end of the tunnel presented a very welcome sight and they both breathed easier as they emerged into the bright sunlight of a beautiful day. Otisk clicked off the torch and fitted it into his rucksack.

At first they could see no-one but, as they walked forward towards the cliff, they found Lonei sitting on a large boulder not far from the edge of the cliff, wearing his familiar orange jacket.

'Hello, my friends, I see you have followed my instructions carefully. That's very good, because getting through the barrier and making your way to the foothills of the mountain requires great precision and expertise. When the time comes, I will enable you to pass through the barrier and then you must climb down the cliff alone. Be very careful, because it is very steep and it will be very slippery in places. Also, the gusty wind will be an additional hazard. The weather outside Pazoten is much more inclement.'

'How do we get across to the foot of the mountain, Lonei? You said stormy water...?' A faltering question from Otisk.

'That is correct, Otisk. Since I last spoke to you about this, I have established positively that a sea crossing has to be made.'

'How will we do that, Lonei?'

'You will find a boat and you must use that. There is no other way to cross the water.'

Otisk opened his mouth to ask the next question but Lonei held up a hand and rose to his feet.

'The time approaches,' he said. 'You have only a very short time to cross the barrier and we must go to the crossing point immediately. Follow me.'

As they walked forward, they felt the barrier's power acting increasingly against their progress. Lonei continued until the retardation power was very strong. 'Otisk and Francel, now you must stand completely still.' They obeyed with some difficulty as they fought against the barrier's repelling power. Seconds later, with heart-stopping suddenness, they were catapulted forward through the barrier towards the cliff top and came to a skidding halt about four metres from the edge. When they turned around, they were astonished to find that the barrier was now a gigantic opaque wall extending up into the sky. They were alone on one side of the barrier and Lonei was on the other.

'Lonei, are you there?' Otisk shouted, his voice seemingly absorbed by the wall before them.

There was a pause before Lonei's voice answered. 'Yes, I am here in Paradise Zone Ten where I belong. Good fortune, Francel and Otisk. May you be safe and in power. May you discover all that you should know. Goodbye.'

Francel and Otisk turned to each other, now filled with dismay at the enormity of their situation. Finally, Otisk spoke in a faint voice. 'Are you all right, Francel?'

She thought for a moment. 'Yes,' she said very quietly, 'but all that was a bit sudden. I wasn't expecting that to happen to us!'

'Neither was I. Somehow, the repelling power was switched off at that point and we exploded through the barrier like a champagne cork popping from a bottle. I would have preferred something a bit less extreme!' He paused and looked out across the sea. 'Now we know another fact,' he said introspectively.

'What's that?'

'Paradise Zone Ten.'

She was silent for a moment, then she smiled. 'It makes sense, doesn't it? As far as we can understand it, that is.'

Now it was time for action and they looked around to take stock. They were standing quite close to the cliff edge, buffeted by a cold, unpleasant, blustery wind. Down below, there was the distinct sound of powerful waves dashing themselves against the base of the cliff. They crouched down and moved forward gingerly to peer cautiously over the edge. The cliff was sheer and perhaps a hundred feet high. Black, stormy water boiled below. They raised their sight to look across at their destination. They could see that the stormy water extended across to the foot of the mountain. Otisk estimated that there were two to three kilometres of water to cross.

'I hope this boat is capable of making the crossing in these conditions,' he said worriedly, 'that sea is pretty rough.'

'Look, Otisk, there's a narrow path just along there that leads down the face of the cliff. That looks like the only way down. It looks possible but dangerous.'

'Lonei said it was dangerous. I think we had better use our ropes, Francel. I'll get them sorted out and ready.'

Their decision to use the ropes proved to be fully justified. In places, the path was very narrow and there were precipitous drops to the sea below. They rigged up the ropes at the appropriate points and worked their way down the cliff as safely as they could. Eventually, they approached the base of the cliff where the going became easier. Reaching a wide ledge, they stopped to rest and review their situation.

'We've got to find this boat, Otisk. I think it must be round that tall rock projection that's just along the path here. We can see quite a long way in the other direction and there's no sign of an inlet that could harbour a boat. I think it must be around this headland. The boat could be on a beach, waiting to be launched.'

Otisk squinted worriedly. 'I hope we don't find a rowing boat around there. Indeed, I'm not sure that any small open boat would be able to make it across this sea in these stormy conditions. I hope that whoever has set this up for us has taken the storm into consideration. If it is a small open boat, we may have to wait for a calmer day.' Otisk was rapidly losing his optimism.

Francel remained positive and reasonable. 'Listen, we'll soon find out. Whatever it is, they must have reckoned that it can weather this storm. No point in arranging all this for us and then giving us a boat that won't do the job, is there?'

'I just hope you're right, Francel,' he muttered darkly.

After a short rest, they kitted up and started to make their way towards the headland. At this point, the path was not far above the water and the going was relatively easy. Finally, they started to work around the tall, rocky headland and the small bay on the other side began to be revealed. Here, sheltered by the land, they were very grateful to observe that the sea was considerably calmer.

As they continued to work around the headland, more and more of the bay was revealed to them until they could see all of it. They stopped, nonplussed. There was no sign of a boat anywhere. Just an empty stretch of sand.

Otisk brow became deeply furrowed. 'Where is it?' he cried, panic tinging his voice. 'I hope they haven't screwed this up; sent us through the barrier and down a precipitous cliff on a wild goose chase! Listen, it won't be easy to get back up that cliff—and how on earth do we get back into Pazoten? This is turning into a disaster!'

'Just a minute, let's try to keep calm. Isn't that another indentation in the rock along here on the right? I think that's where the boat must be.'

'Well, we can't make this crossing in a blasted canoe, that's for certain.' Otisk was becoming increasingly despondent.

They turned around a sharp corner of rock and there before them was a small, narrow inlet. The path led forward to some steps hewn from the rock, leading down to a small jetty. Tied up at the jetty was a squat, powerful tugboat, bobbing gently in the calm water. As they descended the steps in stunned silence, both read the name on the tugboat's bow—it was "Juno II".

'Francel, I'm sorry, I think I have to sit down for a moment.' Otisk sank down on the bottom step and looked at the vessel with tears in his eyes. 'This is why Lonei insisted that I learned how to sail the tugboat. That's truly encouraging...' He was overcome with relief.

Francel sat down beside him and put her arms around him. 'It's the perfect craft, isn't it? Highly manoeuvrable, powerful and incredibly tough. A bit like you, eh?'

'You are incredible, Francel. I'm so glad I met you. I believe we are made to be together and I'm going to insist that, whatever happens, we stay together. I promise.'

'Let's go aboard and see how the boat is controlled. It might be quite different from the model of Juno II. We don't know if this boat has that special driving system that Lonei was always banging on about.'

Taking all their equipment, they crossed the short gangway and stood on the wide, low deck where the many winches and capstans were wound with stout ropes and chains. Beside them, a steep companionway led up to the elevated bridge deck above. They climbed this and entered the spacious bridge house through a sturdy watertight door.

'Wow, Francel. Just look at this. This is really high-tech.'

In the spacious and airy bridge, two raised controller seats were surrounded by equipment banks and information screens while the very large windows gave a panoramic view outside. Otisk stepped forward, sat down in one of the seats and swept his eyes over the control panels. After a moment, he looked up happily. 'Although I have no idea what many of these switches are for, I can see immediately that the principal controls are just like those on Lonei's control panel. Look, here are the power control levers for the two engines and this joystick control will control the Voith-Schneider Propulsion Unit. That gives us very precise directional control.'

'How do you know that this boat is fitted with this Voith-Whatever thing?' Francel asked doubtfully.

He grinned at her. 'Because this main control panel identifies it! Look, it says "Voith Schneider" here at the top.' Anyway, we know that Lonei has somehow provided us with the full-scale version of his tugboat, because the name is the same. Isn't that just marvellous?'

'The engines aren't running, are they, Otisk?'

'No, I don't think so. I'm sure we would hear them or feel the vibrations.'

'Do you know how to start the engines? Don't you need an engineer in the engine room?'

'I think you would on most tugboats, Francel. But this is a special tugboat, isn't it? So I'm hoping I will be able to do everything from here.' He pointed to the panel that included the two engine power levers. 'I see there are two buttons marked "Start Engines". I'm hoping that they will do just that when I press them. If they don't, I'll have to find out what else I have to do.'

'We're ready to go, aren't we, Otisk?'

'Yes, we are. Here goes.' He pressed the first button. At first, nothing seemed to happen except that a red light began flashing on the panel. Then he noticed that one of the displays was reporting that the port engine had started and the revolutions were climbing. As this happened, they felt a vibration through the boat. When the value had steadied, he released the first button and pressed the second "Start" button. They were pleased when the display showed that the second engine had also started. Otisk advanced the port engine's power lever and they heard the engine respond. He repeated this with the starboard engine. He turned to Francel. 'We seem to be in business,' he said with great satisfaction, 'I'll go down to the deck and cast off.'

Thick ropes at bow and stern tethered the boat to the jetty, coiled around winches on the deck. First at the stern and then at the bow, he was able to operate the winches to slacken the ropes sufficiently to lift them clear and toss them on to the jetty. The boat was now free to start its journey across the sea. Quickly, he returned to the bridge and they settled into the control seats.

'Ready?' he smiled at her.

'Yes, I am. I do hope Lonei's blessing works for us.'

He nodded thoughtfully and then advanced the engine power levers before easing the joystick forward and a little to starboard. The tugboat moved very slowly away from the jetty and headed towards the centre of the bay and the open sea beyond. Once the open sea was reached, Otisk adjusted the engine power and the forward thrust of the propulsion system to minimise the effect of the rough sea and the wind that was blowing across their bows. Pointing the prow of the boat at the mountain, they started to make steady progress across the sea towards it.

'You're doing so well,' Francel said. 'You're making it really smooth.'

He smiled. 'Thank you, Francel. It's all due to Lonei's training with the model boat. He knew this was what would happen to us.'

'How do you think he knew?'

'Either because he's the Leader and he knows everything that will happen on Pazoten, or because the authorities above him briefed him. I don't suppose we will ever know. I wonder what will happen to him: will *he* ever leave Pazoten?'

'Do you think he's happy, Otisk?' Francel sounded sombre.

'I really don't know, Francel. I've thought about that before. Before we came along and got to know him, it seems he did nothing except work as the Leader. You know, I think he must have done his special Leader's work at night, maybe all night, every night. Then, during the day, he was out and about as the Litter Bin Man, largely unseen but monitoring everything and directing the Counsellors. That may be wrong but it's the only way I can understand his position.'

'It was nice when he had time off and we went sailing the model boat. But, of course, now we know that even that had a purpose—this purpose—so, in that sense, Lonei was never free of his responsibilities. That makes me sad.'

'I feel the same way, Francel. But, when you think about it, there is no way that the Leader can ever be free. That's what being the "top person" is like. You're always on duty. You're always responsible—and culpable.'

Now they were silent as they thought about Lonei, his life and their lives on Pazoten. Meanwhile Juno II muscled purposefully through the storm, bringing the mountain closer and closer, its peak still capped by thick dark cloud.

Francel examined the navigation map displays shown on screen before them. 'Look at this, Otisk. Do you think that's a harbour area there? Just a minute, I'll zoom in on this aerial photograph on the screen next to it. Maybe it will show us where we can land.' A few moments later she became excited. 'Look at this. It's definitely a harbour—and, look, there's quite a large pier. And it's located at the foot of the mountain. I think this could be ideal for us.'

'Well done, Francel. I'll head for there.'

Within half an hour, Juno II sailed into a spacious harbour and slowly headed for the pier. There were no other vessels in the bay and absolutely no sign of life on the pier or anywhere on the shore-line. There were no buildings of any kind and the whole area looked as if it had been deserted for a very long time. Remembering his docking lessons with the model boat, Otisk manoeuvred Juno II smoothly and expertly alongside the pier and brought his craft to a precise stop so close to it that he could step ashore and toss two heavy cables from the tug around the mooring points on the dock. Returning to the deck, he operated the tug's winches and secured the boat alongside the pier. Finally, he slid the gangway across and Francel disembarked.

'I'll just go and power down,' he told her. 'If, for any reason, we need to come back, we'll need Juno II to return to Pazoten.'

'Good idea, Otisk. I'll start to offload our equipment on to the pier.'

It was then that Otisk discovered that he could not stop Juno II's engines. Although there were buttons for starting the engines, there were no "Stop" buttons to be seen. He tried switching off other switches on the control panels but the engines were unaffected by this and continued to run. Finally, he descended to the Engine Room and examined the control panels there. Eventually finding a red-painted lever beside each engine he operated one of these and was pleased when he heard the engine slowing and stopping. 'Possibly a fuel valve,' he thought. He repeated the manoeuvre for the other engine and then left a silent engine room.

'Managed to stop them,' he told Francel when he emerged on deck. 'There were red levers to pull and they stopped the engines. That must be how it's done. I probably cut off the fuel supply.'

It was cold and unpleasant on the pier, fully exposed to the wind. 'Let's find some shelter,' Francel suggested. 'We should have a short break before starting the climb, I think.'

A little way up the lower slope of the mountain, they found a small dry cave and were grateful to shelter in there from the wind. They rested for a while and fortified themselves with some food and drinks. After a time, Francel walked to the mouth of the cave and looked out. He heard her involuntary cry as she looked out.

'What's wrong, Francel,' he cried as he leapt to his feet.

'Look,' she gasped, her voice a shocked whisper. He followed her gaze towards the harbour. Both became transfixed in disbelief. Juno II was sailing purposefully towards the mouth of the harbour. Motionless, they continued to watch her as she began to buffet her powerful way across the sea, retracing their journey, a ghost ship with no-one on board.

They watched the boat until she had disappeared into the spray and then turned to each other with a mixture of dismay and resignation.

'It seems we have chosen the way,' he said quietly, 'and there is only one way to go. Forward.'

'This must be our destiny, Otisk. There can be no other explanation.'

"45,521 divided by 23?"
'1,979.1739.'

"298 times 64?"
'19,072.'

"27 times 4,751 plus 320?"
'128,597.'

"4,378.95 divided by 37?"
'118.35.'

'Problem?' she asked, seeing his face tense.

'No, just the usual maths test. A repeat, of course. So I'm still getting them here, outside Pazoten. I thought they stop in this alternative world. It's annoying that they're still here!'

She pressed his hand in sympathy and they busied themselves with their preparations for the climb to come.

The lower slopes of the mountain were covered with trees and scrub—not dense like the woodland barrier on Pazoten but rather difficult to make progress through. At times, they had to cut a path through the undergrowth, so progress was slow. As they gained height, the bushy vegetation thinned and progress became easier. Finally they emerged to a view of the mountain above them, just as the thick cloud began to clear from the top.

'Look, Francel, the cloud is dissipating.' Otisk was jubilant. 'At last, we'll get a clear view of the mountain top. Maybe we'll get a closer view the mysterious building.'

They stopped and watched attentively as the curtain of cloud thinned and lifted, revealing the bare rock of the peak that Francel had so often recorded with her telephoto lens. Their view was now unobstructed. They strained their eyes to make out any sign of the building they had come so far to investigate.

'I can't see anything,' she said. 'No sign of the building. Just bare rock. May I have my telephoto lens, please?'

They examined her images at full resolution and magnification. The rocky summit was now strongly illuminated by the sun. Every detail of the rocks could be seen but there were absolutely no vestiges of the building to be seen.

'Nothing!' Francel said disappointedly. 'I thought we might see something at this close range.'

Otisk was thoughtful. 'Maybe it's not so surprising, Francel. When we were in Pazoten, we looked at the mountain many times and saw only the bare rock of the peak, just as it is now. We saw the building only a very few times—and always when the sun was low. Also, when the cloud came down on the mountain, we sometimes saw the shape of the building in the swirling cloud, or maybe it was through the swirling cloud. If we keep on climbing, we should be near the peak by the time the sun is low. That's when we'll need to be at our most vigilant.'

Francel put her camera away. 'I see what you mean, Otisk. Let's keep going so that we're in the right place when the sun is going down.'

They were soon approaching the upper part of the mountain where the ground became much steeper and it was necessary to pick their way carefully along steeply-sloping rock spurs. The scree underfoot meant that each step had to be tested carefully. By mid-afternoon, they had reached the base of some near-vertical cliffs.

'I suggest you sit down and rest here, Francel. I'm going to scout around and see whether there are any easy ways up this cliff section. I shouldn't be long.'

He worked his way around the base of the first cliff and eventually found a fissure that sloped upwards. 'We can certainly use this,' he muttered, 'with a bit of luck it may extend upwards for quite a way. Much easier than tackling a vertical face!'

He returned to Francel and threw himself down beside her. 'I've found a good way up this big cliff. It shouldn't be too bad; there's a usable fissure around that way.' He pointed. 'We'll need to use the ropes for extra safety but it looks quite a reasonable climb. I suggest we start in about half an hour.'

They spent the next few hours working their way very carefully up a series of fissures in the mountain rock. On two occasions, they had to climb a section of exposed rock face. By early evening, they had made very good progress and were not very far below the summit. Here, although the rock surfaces were broken and jagged, the slopes were not so great and they could progress quite quickly. Finally, a flatter area was reached and Otisk called a halt.

'Whew,' he said, 'that was quite a climb wasn't it? Good thing we are experienced climbers, eh?' he grinned at her.

'Yes,' she smiled back, 'we're experienced but we can't remember anything about it! Very peculiar, isn't it?'

'Well, that's exactly why we're here, isn't it? To find out what all this is about. We have long had an ambition to come to this mountain and here we are, nearly at the top. We've succeeded in our ambition!'

'Otisk, I've been thinking. We had better not climb up to the peak; that's the location of the building we have seen, isn't it? It might not be a good idea to have the building manifest itself on top of us.'

Otisk looked at her with startled admiration. 'Wow! You're absolutely right, Francel. I hadn't thought of that. We should stay here as the sun gets lower in the sky and keep a careful watch. That's when we should see the building—certainly that's when we've seen it in the past.'

'Let's make camp here, Otisk. We can keep our eyes on the peak and see what happens. If the building appears, we don't want to try and investigate it in darkness, do we? We can investigate it tomorrow in daylight. At least we'll know it's there—in some dimension of reality, that is.'

'Excellent strategy, Francel. Let's do that. I'll set up the tent and at least one of us can keep watch for the building. Surely it must appear when the sun gets low enough?'

They positioned themselves precisely with the mountain peak clearly in view, Francel with camera in hand ready to record the events. The sun sank lower and lower in the sky and its rays became more and more horizontal, extending strange shadows across the summit area. Time passed and, eventually, the disc of the sun began to dip below the horizon, progressively reducing the output of its electromagnetic radiation to the mountain. In response, light levels decreased and dusk arrived as the inevitable precursor of night. Even when the sun finally dipped below the horizon, it still sent its reflected light to the mountain for a time. Inevitably, however, deepening dusk gave way to darkness. And nothing had happened. Absolutely nothing.

They sat staring into the darkness long after their eyes were capable of discerning anything. Neither could believe their failure to see the building. After all, in Pazoten they had seen it appear several times; Francel had many photographs of it—of its detail, too. There was no doubt that it existed—or existed to them in some reality. There was no doubt that the building was real to them. These and many other thoughts swirled around their consciousness as they sat motionless in the cooling darkness.

'Let's get warm in our tent, Francel. We can talk about it there.' Otisk was despondent.

'Maybe it can only be seen from Pazoten?' Francel's first tentative suggestion.

He considered this. 'Hm. I don't think so, because we could still see the mountain and its cap of cloud *after* we had passed through the ultimate barrier. We were outside Pazoten then and there was no change to the mountain scene before us.' He thought some more. 'Maybe the building doesn't appear every time. Maybe it will appear tomorrow night or the next.'

'Well, yes, that's possible, although I can't think why it would do that.'

'Well, it may not be given to us to understand. Anyway, we're here now. There must be a reason why we've been allowed to come all this way. So, all we can do is wait and try again tomorrow night. We have plenty of food. I reckon we can last up here for five days—longer, if we find a source of water.'

'Hm. I hope we make progress long before that,' she murmured sleepily.

'So do I,' he whispered and closed his eyes.

* * * *

They awoke just as it was getting light and turned eager eyes up to the mountain peak. The pointed summit was disappointingly unchanged.

'Today, Francel, you and I are climbing up to that peak. When we get there we'll search meticulously for any evidence of the building. Does that sound like a good idea?'

'Yes, it does. Let's get ourselves prepared and have a good breakfast. Then we can start. How long do you think it will take us to get up to the summit?'

He assessed the climb. 'It really isn't too bad, Francel. As far as I can see, we don't have any cliffs to climb. It could be a bit steep in places, though, and the surface may be quite loose here and there. We'll rope ourselves together and just take it slowly. I would say one or two hours.'

'Presumably we're striking this camp?'

'Yes, I would think that's sensible. I'm sure we'll find another suitable camping spot somewhere further up the slope. If not, we can always come back here.'

Within the hour they were on the move, securely roped together and moving steadily upwards. An hour later they came to the top of a minor ridge and the roughly conical peak of the mountain was fully revealed before them. They were surprised to see that the ground ahead changed from broken, fissured rock to a much smoother and bare slope that angled quite steeply upwards towards the point of the peak. They stopped.

'This looks rather strange from here, doesn't it, Francel. Suddenly, there's no split or splintered rock; no vegetation either, not even rock lichens in any of the narrow cracks. Up to the summit looks peculiar; lifeless, unreal, somehow.'

'Yes, I see it too—and I feel the strangeness. But there's still no sign of any building, is there? It's impossible to imagine that there would be.' As she spoke she assembled her camera and was now examining the very top of the peak at full magnification. 'The rock looks completely smooth at the top, rising to a single pointed summit,' she said. Then she moved forward a few steps to stand on a flat rock, swinging her camera up in front of her face to fine-tune the focus. They were both completely dumbfounded when the image of the mountain peak before them distorted and shimmered in front of them. They both rubbed their eyes, thinking they must have been affected by some strange eye focus problem. Gradually, the picture before them steadied and became still once again.

Otisk leapt forward and pulled Francel back. 'Come back,' he said urgently, 'there may be something dangerous there. What happened? What did you do?'

'Nothing. I was just checking the focus and suddenly everything started distorting and pulsating. Did you see it?'

'Yes, I certainly did. That's why I pulled you back.'

'Has something gone wrong with our eyes?' she said. They looked all around them, checking their eye focus again but all appeared to be normal. Then Francel gripped his arm. 'Wait a bit, I've just remembered. What we saw was just like…' she stopped and looked at him, wide-eyed, rendered speechless by her thought.

'Like what?'

'Like that time Zadorb threw the stone at the Pazoten barrier,' she breathed. 'Do you remember?'

'You're right! Yes, it was like that—but that was caused by a stone and the stone rebounded back to us. He was doing that to prove to us that the barrier, although invisible, was impassable. And—that barrier had a powerful repelling force that meant you couldn't get near to it. This is different. I don't understand what is going on here.'

'I think we've come to a critical point, Otisk. We've got to solve this mystery. This must be the key. I'll walk over there again and…'

'No, let me go this time, Francel. Let's see if we can establish where this effect starts. I'll take my rucksack and hold it out in front of me. Then, no part of me will be in danger.'

As Francel watched carefully, Otisk edged very slowly towards the flat stone that Francel had stood upon. When he arrived there, he held his rucksack forward and was astonished to see the end of it disappearing through a now distorted image of the mountain. Alarmed, he pulled it back and, once again, the wavering, distorted image of the mountain before them took around thirty seconds to become still.

Otisk retreated back to Francel. 'Did you see that? The end of my rucksack went through the image we are seeing and partially disappeared. And, as it went through, the whole image distorted again. After I pulled the rucksack back, the stillness of the image was gradually restored. The rucksack is undamaged, as far as I can see.' He held it forward for her inspection.

'Yes, I saw all that, Otisk. We need to think about this. We'll have some lunch.'

They sat down together, glad to busy themselves with the routine of eating and drinking. As they ate, each of them grappled with what they had just experienced.

After a while, Otisk turned to her. 'Here's what I'm thinking, Francel. I think this invisible entity is fundamentally the same sort of barrier that surrounds Pazoten. But, for some reason, maybe this one is not set up as a barrier. It has no repelling function. When you think about the Pazoten situation, the barrier there has two functions. It marks the limit of Pazoten and it prevents anyone—almost anyone, that is, from getting out. But its second function is sort of pictorial. It shows the people inside Pazoten a picture of what is beyond the barrier. Now, we came through the barrier and discovered that the mountain we could see from Pazoten was real. Or, should I say, as real as we can determine. But, uniquely, when we lived in Pazoten, we saw another reality that no-one else seemed to see. We saw the incongruous building on this mountain as a sort of secondary reality.' He stopped. 'That's as far as I've got. How am I doing?'

'Yes, I think all that you've said is right, Otisk. And that's made me think about something that I'm struggling to put into words.' He waited for her to speak again. 'OK, here it is. Basically, I think the building might be on the other side of that barrier. Now, I don't think this is a barrier at all—at least, not for us. You've already proved that this boundary—let's call it that—can be penetrated freely, haven't you? So now we've got to test my theory—and I know a way we can test it without danger to us, without involving our bodies penetrating the boundary.'

'Wow, Francel. That's an awesome thought. How does your test work, then?'

'We know where the boundary is, don't we? Or, at least, we know where one small section of it is. It's just over there, just in front of that flat stone. So we both go over there and stand on that stone. Then I switch my camera on and I move it forward very slowly while we both watch the viewing screen. If my theory is right, the camera will start off showing the mountain and then, as it passes through the boundary, it will show whatever is on the other side of the division. If I'm right, it will show us the building or some part of it. In any case, it should show us something different than we see now. And—the only thing penetrating into the "other side" is the front part of my camera lens!'

'Francel, that is absolutely brilliant. Let's go and do that right away!'

They stood together on the flat stone. The camera was switched on and advanced forward very slowly. At first, the familiar image of the mountain peak was pictured on the display. Then the screen went blank for a brief moment and now they were looking at an image of a blank grey wall perhaps twenty metres away from the camera. Francel angled the camera down a little and a flat, black surface could be seen; it looked like a roadway. She panned the camera upwards very slowly and, as higher portions of the wall were shown, they recognised the blank wall of the building with what looked like a few small windows set in its surface. Undoubtedly, this was the mountain-top building they had seen and photographed when they were in Pazoten! Slowly, she withdrew the camera and the scene in the viewing screen reverted to the mountain.

Silently, they returned to their camping area and sat down.

'I think that proves it,' she said simply.

'I agree,' he nodded gravely, 'and you know what must happen now, don't you?'

It was her turn to nod. 'We pack up here and we walk through there.'

He looked around. 'Do you think we should take everything with us, Francel, or leave some of it here?'

'I think it would be safer to take everything. We don't know whether we can come back.'

'You're right, we had better take everything.'

They packed everything up and carried out a final check. 'Ready?' he said.

'Yes.'

He took her in his arms. 'Before we go, Francel, I just want to tell you that I love you and I never want to be apart from you—ever. Whatever happens, I want you always to remember that.'

'I love you, too, Otisk. You know that. And I never want to be apart from you, either.'

Chapter 19

There was only one way to do it. They linked hands tightly, closed their eyes and stepped forward two tentative paces. They felt nothing as they passed through the boundary. Their eyes flicked open and the huge building towered over them. A series of 180 degree visual scans in a range of forward planes revealed that they were standing on an asphalt road surface that stretched all the way to the building and extended to left and right along its massive wall. The building itself was a very tall, grey block. Above its roofline, bright blue sky could be seen. From where they stood, they could not see the horizontal extent of the building either to left or right. The small, square indentations that relieved the uniform wall appeared to be small windows, either blanked out or possibly glazed with some sort of translucent material.

Two seconds had passed. Now they turned around and looked behind them to see a high brick wall close behind. Still linked together, they couldn't resist attempting to retrace the two paces that had brought them to this different world. The solid brick wall soon thwarted their attempt and they stood, touching the rough vertical brick surface with their backs. Complete silence continued to reign; no life noise, no wind caresses, no bustle of nature.

He touched her arm and brought his mouth close to her ear. 'We've arrived, Francel—and we've just proved that we can't go back. I think this is where we're meant to be. It must be.' His voice was a very quiet whisper.

'I wonder why we couldn't see the building when we were on the mountain?' she mused introspectively, 'after all, we could see it from Pazoten.'

'Yes, that's true—but we only saw it occasionally and only at a special time of day, didn't we? Maybe they knew we would find the reality of it when we climbed to the top, so we didn't need to see it beforehand. Anyway, whatever the truth of it, here we are!'

They were quiet for a few minutes as they continued to scan the scene before them.

'We need to enter that building, Otisk. That must be our next move. At the moment, I can't see how we can do it, though, can you?'

He scanned the base of the building carefully. 'Beats me,' he said, 'but there must be a way in—and we'll find it. Maybe we'll have to go around to the other side of the building. Anyway, there must be a way in. No point having a building if you can't enter it!'

'Listen, Otisk, I think we'll need to sneak in. Big buildings like this usually have some sort of restricted access. (I don't know how I know that but I'm convinced that's true!) Even if it's for the general public, you have to be going in for a purpose and there will usually be security or reception staff to receive you and send you to the right part of the building. We don't know what we want, do we? We just want to enter the building. We want to snoop around to find out what we need to know and then work out what it is we have to do.'

'I suppose so,' he agreed. 'So let's just stay here out of sight and see if any action happens. Hopefully, no-one will notice we're here and ask us what we're doing or what we want. That would be a bit awkward, because, as you say, we don't know what we want!'

'Maybe we should be prepared for that, Otisk. The trouble is, we don't know what happens inside this building.' She thought for a moment. 'I know, if anyone asks, let's just say we've been told to go to the sixth floor. That way, we might be told how to get there and then left alone.'

'That's really clever, Francel. What happens if they ask us why we have to go to the sixth floor?'

'We'll just say we don't know. We'll act a bit stupid!'

He grinned at her. 'I'm not going to say anything.'

So they stood in the shadows beside the brick wall and waited in the profound silence. Suddenly, they were both startled by a very loud noise. As they tried to identify its origin, a massive covered truck charged across their field of vision from right to left, its powerful diesel engine roaring lustily at high revs. As they watched, its brakes shrieked deafeningly before it turned sharply right towards the base of the building and disappeared into the surface of the road. The engine noise diminished and died away completely. Then a low rumbling sound was heard before absolute silence was restored.

They looked at each other in shock and dismay. What had happened? How could a large truck disappear into the ground? Was this place magic? Was this another Pazoten?

'Otisk, I've just had a thought. Maybe relocation works here like it did in Pazoten. Let's do an experiment. Let's relocate over to the wall of the building.'

He agreed and they applied the familiar technique. Nothing happened. 'I'm not surprised,' he commented, 'relocation only works in Pazoten. Zadorb told us that.'

'Well, it was worth a try,' she replied. 'It would certainly have made our investigations easier.'

'We've got to get closer to the building and see how the "disappearing truck" illusion was done,' Otisk said, 'Let's hope nobody sees us as we run across the road. Once we're close to the building, it'll be easier to hide.'

Moving as quickly as they could, they ran across the wide stretch of asphalt and soon reached the building, flattening themselves into the shadows.

'So far so good.' Otisk was pleased. 'Now let's work our way along until we come to that area where the truck disappeared.' They had not gone far when the mystery was solved very simply. Ahead of them was a steep ramp which led down from the road surface to a very large industrial roller shutter door. Otisk smiled widely at Francel. 'The inexplicable explained!' he said.

She laughed in response. 'Why didn't I think of that? A wide ramp down to the basement area and a big roller shutter door. And we thought we might have been seeing magic!'

'Well, Francel, from where we were standing, it really did look as if that truck disappeared into the ground! It certainly looked like magic! And, of course, we're familiar with magic; we've experienced plenty of it in Pazoten!' Now he examined the ramp and the door. 'Listen, Francel, this is our way in. When they open this shutter door to let someone in or out, we should be able to slip in unnoticed—or, at least, I hope we can. When they next open the door, we'll try to get a look inside, because we need to plan our move carefully. We can't afford to get caught at the very first hurdle, eh? We can crouch down here beside the bottom of the ramp where no-one can see us. Then, when we've worked out the best plan, we'll creep inside and hide.'

They didn't have long to wait. They heard a strident warning buzzer sounding from behind the door and then it started to open. Inside, they saw several large loading bays located at the back of a very large, manoeuvring area. A large truck was moving slowly away from one of the bays and heading for the exit. Craning his neck, Otisk could just see the beginning of a metal staircase leading upwards just inside the roller shutter door.

'That's a good entry point, Francel, because that staircase and whatever is at the top of it will be in deep shadow when the door is open. Provided we can slip inside, I shouldn't think anyone will see us once we're on the staircase.'

The truck passed close by them and climbed up the ramp to road level where it turned and accelerated away. Meanwhile, the roller shutter door rumbled back down to close with a loud metallic clang.

'When do you think is our best chance of sneaking in?' Francel asked.

'When the next vehicle comes, we can crouch down close behind it as it goes through the door, provide it's big enough to conceal us. Then we can scamper up the stairs as fast as our legs can carry us. What do you think?'

'Let's try that. If we get caught, we'll just have to talk our way out. Just leave it to me, Otisk. I'll play the little lost girl. They'll be sorry for me and we might get in that way!'

In fact they had over two hours to wait but, eventually, they heard the noise of an approaching engine and the roller shutter door began to rattle up slowly. Disappointingly, this vehicle proved to be a rather small fork-lift truck.

'No good for us, Francel. Too small.' They watched as the fork-lift truck entered the loading bay area. The door rumbled down behind it.

A further hour passed and they heard another vehicle approaching. This time it was a large box van which edged its way down the steep ramp.

'Get ready, Francel. When I say "go", we'll crouch down behind the van as it enters and then dash up these stairs in the darkness.'

The plan worked beautifully and, seconds later, they were through the doorway and tiptoeing up the stairs as fast as they could. Unfortunately, the staircase was not in darkness because overhead lights now illuminated it brightly.

'Keep down low,' Otisk hissed, 'Hopefully no-one will see us through the mesh.' They paused at the top of the stairs and peered down fearfully. There were several men in white overalls gathered around the van, quite a distance below them. Fortunately, none of the men looked up towards them.

'Success!' Otisk whispered, 'but we've got to get out of here before they spot us.'

There was a heavy metal door ahead of them and Otisk tried the handle. The door opened quietly and smoothly and they slipped through, closing it carefully behind them. Then they turned around slowly. They were standing on a high walkway that led across the side wall of an enormous room that appeared to be a hive of activity. Under bright lights, large stainless steel machines buzzed and hummed, while smaller machines moved around the passageways between them. While they examined the scene before them, Francel and Otisk stood absolutely still, so that they would not attract the attention of the operators of all this equipment.

'Can you see any people down below, Francel?' Otisk's voice was a hoarse whisper.

'No, I can't. I think all these machines are running automatically, whatever they're doing.'

'Right. Let's take advantage of the absence of human operators and move on.' They scuttled across the high walkway, finally reaching a door at the other side. There was no challenge from below.

The high-level walkway continued through the next few rooms. In each room, a metal stairway led down from the walkways to floor level. It was obvious that these were storerooms, all fitted with very tall racking. A number of high-reach forklift trucks plied the corridors between the racks; all were automatic machines, run by a central computer somewhere. The high-level walkway stopped in a final storeroom and stairs led down to floor level. This room was obviously a large food store, with high racks stacked with many items of food and drink.

They paused at the top of the stairs, hidden in the upper shadows, and waited to see if anyone was likely to see them as they descended. There appeared to be no movement in the room so they made their way down, careful to make no noise.

'Well Francel, it looks like we won't starve, anyway. There is everything here,' Otisk whispered. 'We'll carry on using our own supplies and then we'll start eating some of theirs. We'll need to be careful, though. What we need to find is a secure place to rest and sleep, so we need to keep exploring.'

They saw that there was a small office at one end of the room, with one or, possibly, two people inside, dressed in white clothes. Their stairway had deposited them at the other end of the room so they were unseen as they walked towards an exit nearby. Through the doorway, they found themselves standing in a long, empty corridor.

'This way, I think,' Francel said, pointing away from the area behind them. They walked quickly along the corridor, hoping they wouldn't meet anyone.

'We need white coats,' Otisk whispered, 'then we can pretend to be one of them.'

After they had walked for a while, they became aware of a growing humming noise. Eventually, they reached a large metal door. A notice identified it as "B32 Power Room". Otisk placed an ear on the metal. 'The humming noise definitely comes from in here,' he said.

Just then, they heard the distinct sound of approaching footsteps from along the corridor. They looked around wildly for a hiding place. There was a small hatch door inset in the main door of Room B32 and Otisk released the catch to swing the door open. A blast of heat and noise enveloped them.

'Quick, Francel, in here!' he hissed. They scrambled through the small door and closed it softly behind them. He placed his ear on the door and heard the footsteps coming worryingly close before passing by and diminishing down the corridor.

'Phew, that was a bit close. What is this place?'

They looked around gingerly and, as far as they could assess, there was no-one in the large room. It was very hot and the humming noise was loud and obtrusive. They saw there was some sort of a control position on one wall showing many lights, dials and data screens. Apart from that area, the large room was dimly lit.

'This is a Power Generation and Distribution Room, I reckon,' Otisk said quietly. 'It probably supplies heat, light and power to the building above. That panel down there will be a control point but it looks as if the system normally runs on automatic. Over there, there are several large furnace units to produce heat, which is the reason it's so hot in here. There are also several big generators for electricity. Now if we could find a nice corner to fit into, this would be an ideal place for us to live. Let's have a good look around.'

They soon found the ideal place. A small office at the other end of the long room, air conditioned and with a soundproof door that reduced the rather strident hum in the main room to a pleasant whisper. Inside, there were desks and comfortable reclining chairs, while a door in one corner gave way to a small bathroom. Everything was thick with dust, indicating that the office was not in general use. And, most importantly, a clear glass window gave them a wide view of the Power Room.

'This meets all our needs, Otisk. We can sleep and eat in here and use this as our base to go exploring. If anyone comes, we can hide in the bathroom.'

In reply, he threw himself into one of the large chairs. 'This is really comfortable, Francel. I think it folds flat, too. A couple of these will be excellent beds for us.'

'We need a break now, Otisk. Let's have lunch and review what we've learned so far.'

They had collected their thoughts and Otisk began. 'Well, I think the first thing to say is that we are actually in the basement of the mysterious building that we saw so intriguingly when we were in Pazoten. After a great deal of investigation and discovery, we were allowed to leave Pazoten and given the means to arrive here—however "they" didn't make it easy for us to get here; quite the reverse, I think. I am still astounded that our friend Lonei was—is—the Leader.'

'Yes, but we were up to it, weren't we? Here we are in a secure base, with access to food, drink, washing and toilet facilities—and, we have each other. What more could we want? It's perfect. It seems to me that only a small number of people work down here in this basement area. Everything seems to be automated as far as possible. In that first big room, the one with all the machines, we saw small robot machines attending to the big machines. Presumably human beings only become involved with engineering maintenance and repairs—although it's possible to cover even these things by automation, too. We thought we saw only one or two people in a very large area.'

'That suits us just fine, Francel. What we need to do is find our way out of this basement and investigate the rest of the building to find out what it is all about. I think we should start on that this afternoon, once we've taken it easy for a bit.'

By mid-afternoon, they were ready to start. They had changed into some lightweight shoes they had brought with them, grateful to take off their heavy climbing boots. They searched the cupboards for white coats but there were none. 'We'll just have to keep ourselves hidden if anyone comes,' Francel said, 'even if we were wearing white coats, they may well recognise us as intruders and challenge us. We would have a bit of difficulty talking our way out of that! Anyway, our dark clothes will make us more difficult to spot.'

Now they had left the office room. 'We don't want anyone finding evidence of our presence here,' Otisk said as he carefully locked the door behind them. A cautious scan out the hatch door revealed a long empty corridor.

'Left or right, Francel?'

'Let's try right. We came from the left, didn't we, so right will be new territory for us.'

'Yes. We'll just go slowly and very carefully. If we hear anyone coming, we'll have to find somewhere to hide.' As they walked along, they were pleased to see that other corridors branched off the main corridor. 'We can hide down one of these if we hear anyone,' Francel whispered.

They felt it was rather like being in the bowels of a very large ship. The area was vast and windowless and the deep hum and constant slight vibration added to that impression. Then a new, additional sound reached their ears. It was a loud clanking noise overlaid by loud, echoing voices. The volume of the noise was increasing steadily.

'Quick, Otisk, into this corridor. There's a supporting pillar on one side. We can hide behind that and hope they'll continue on up the main corridor.'

The loud noise became positively strident and then they saw a large stainless steel trolley being pushed by two men in white coats. They were talking loudly to each other. Otisk and Francel tuned their ears to hear what the men were saying—and then looked at each other in some dismay. They couldn't understand what the men were saying! They were talking in an unknown language.

'Let's follow them at a safe distance, Francel. They may be taking that trolley to the upper floors of the building.'

They followed the loud clanking noise stealthily. At one point they had a severe shock when a woman suddenly appeared from one of the side corridors but, just as she was turning towards them, a voice from the corridor called her back causing her to turn away and re-enter the corridor.

'Wow! That was lucky. I thought she must see us but she was distracted just in the nick of time by that other voice calling her back.' When they came to the side corridor they peeped around the corner cautiously and, seeing two women deep in conversation some distance away, they tiptoed across without being seen.

Now they hurried to re-join the men with the trolley. Soon they were near enough to make out snatches of their loud conversation. Both listened carefully. There was no doubt about it—the men were conversing in a completely unknown language. Again, Francel and Otisk looked at each other and raised their eyebrows. 'I don't recognise that language,' he said. She shook her head. 'Neither do I,' she agreed. 'It's going to make it pretty difficult for us here if we can't speak the language.'

At last they heard the loud clanking noise fall silent. They stole a look around an angle in the corridor. The two men, still talking in their incomprehensible language, stood by large metal doors. Seconds later, the doors slid open and they saw the men pushing the trolley into what was obviously a large elevator.

'Look, Francel, the indicator above the doors shows eight floors above the basement. You would have been all right with your "sixth floor",' he smiled.

She returned his smile. 'What can we do now?' she asked.

'There must be stairs, Francel. We can't use the elevator, because people get in an out all the time and we would be in danger of being recognised as intruders. But there must be stairs. They're usually for emergency only so they are likely to be largely unused. There's usually an emergency stairway associated with a lift. Look, there's a door to the left of the lift entrance. That's probably it. With a bit of luck, the stairway might extend to all the floors above and we can use it to get ourselves up and down secretly.'

They waited and listened carefully. When all seemed quiet and calm, they scuttled across the lift hall and pushed at the door. It wouldn't budge! Otisk pushed at the door with all his might—still without success. Then horror of horrors, they heard voices approaching.

'It won't move, Francel.' Otisk's face was flushed with the effort of trying.

'Try pulling it,' she hissed, her voice betraying rising panic.

He pulled—and the door opened freely! In an explosion of relief, they dashed inside and pulled the door shut behind them. He leaned against the wall, panting and speechless with relief. After a few minutes, they recovered and began to examine their surroundings. The stairway was wide and rudimentary, everything constructed in plain grey concrete, apart from the non-slip material on the steps and the tubular handrails. Everything was very dusty. It was obvious that this stairway was largely unused.

'Perfect for our purposes,' Otisk was jubilant, 'we can use this to go from floor to floor. Let's go up and see what we can find at ground level.'

They climbed the stairs gingerly, keeping themselves vigilant for the presence of others.

'Here's the first door coming up now,' she said. 'Look, it identifies the floor level as "0".

'Right,' he said, 'Let's see what we can find out.'

They stood close to the door and listened. They could hear a noise on the other side but it was impossible to identify what it was.

'I think this door is pretty soundproof, Francel. I'll ease it open a little way and we'll see what we can see and hear.' They put their heads close together as Otisk pushed the door open a few centimetres. A shocking blast of light and sound immediately assaulted their unprepared senses. The light was intense and appeared to be a blend of bright daylight and artificial illumination. The noise was a confused, very loud hubbub, clearly emanating from the large crowd of people who filled the enormous room.

There were people of every type and age there, men, women and children, some standing, sitting or walking about. Almost everyone was talking loudly; many were gesticulating for emphasis. Francel and Otisk tried to attune their ears to hear at least one thread of conversation but it proved to be impossible to disentangle any specific conversation from the all-pervading cacophony of sound.

Otisk eased the door shut. The light was cut off and the noise diminished to a confused rumble. They went down the stairs and turned the corner out of sight; then they sat down.

'What did you make of that?' she said, shaking her head in puzzlement.

'Whatever this place is, it's a place that a lot of people come to,' he answered. 'Who they are and why they come here is a complete mystery, though. Furthermore, I couldn't make out anything anyone was saying. I think we've landed in a foreign country, Francel. Somewhere far away, it seems to me, where they speak some obscure language. I can't imagine what we're doing here. It doesn't make sense to show us this building as an additional reality of Pazoten and then let us come here with no prospect of return. It just doesn't make sense.'

'Maybe we shouldn't be so hasty, Otisk. Maybe we're reading too much into the slim evidence we've managed to collect so far. But, like you, I'm totally confused and I think we should do no more today. After all, we've found out how we can access the rest of the building through this stairway, so we can "retire gracefully" and start again tomorrow.'

He sighed. 'I'm really confused, Francel. I was expecting to make a lot more progress than this. Yes, I agree, let's call it a day and think the whole thing over.'

Fifteen minutes later, they had managed to return to their secret base in Room B32 without trauma. 'I've got a suggestion, Otisk. It's 1700 hours now—I checked a clock near the elevator and set my watch by it. I think that all the "Day Workers" will go home soon and then there will be even less people down here. Let's wait for another hour and then do some more exploring around the basement. It would be useful to build up our knowledge of the geography of this place.'

Otisk nodded. 'That's a good plan. The sooner we find out about this building, the sooner we will discover why we're here. So let's do that.'

An hour later, they ventured out of their base. The main corridor was deserted and they turned left to retrace their steps back to the areas they first passed through after they had entered through the loading bay area. They did not climb up to the high walkway but stayed at floor level. Once or twice, they had to hide from the robot machines that were moving around purposefully. They did not want the machines to "see" them because their systems might report or record their presence. They found no human presence in any of the rooms they had passed through earlier, even in the food store office where they reckoned they had seen at least one worker earlier.

'Everything seems to be switched to total automation,' Otisk commented. 'We're happy enough about that, aren't we?'

When they reached the back of the loading bay, they found a small office staffed by two security guards. They were busy eating a meal and watching a small television screen.

Francel and Otisk continued past the loading bay, finding suites of storage rooms and the occasional corridor of offices. All were empty. They then struck deeper into the building, discovering more storage areas and a range of machine rooms, workshops and offices. Every so often, there were large elevators, similar to the one they had seen earlier. On two more occasions, they found a staffed security office, similar to the one behind the loading bays, and passed by silently.

As they explored, they were careful to keep their sense of direction and finally reckoned they had covered a large rectangle around the basement area.

'This is certainly a vast place, Francel. By my assessment, we should soon come out near "our" stairway. Then we will only have a short walk back to base.'

'That's what I think, too, Otisk. I think we've seen a lot of the basement. It hasn't told us very much about the purpose of this building, though. There was certainly a huge number of people on the ground floor above when we investigated earlier. Maybe we should make a quick check as we pass. It would be interesting to see if all these people are still there.'

'That's a great idea! We'll soon be there and we can have a quick look.'

They soon found their stairway and, minutes later, they were at the door leading to Floor "0". Otisk eased it open a little and they both looked into the vast bright room. There were still a significant number of people but fewer than there had been earlier. The noise, though still present, was more muted. Again, they tried to make out what people were saying but they were unable to distinguish anything comprehensible. They closed the door and withdrew to their base, where they prepared their evening meal.

'Well, my beautiful Francel, we've had a pretty tiring day today—it isn't every day you pass through boundaries into a new reality and then break into a place you're not supposed to be! And—nearly get caught a few times, too. So, why don't we relax together and call it a day?'

'You don't need to suggest that twice,' she smiled at him. 'Would you make sure you lock the door? We don't want to be disturbed, do we?'

* * * *

They awoke the next morning and were startled to see that the room outside their observation window was brightly lit; intense spotlights shone down on the many items of machinery and equipment. The large metal entrance door was wide open and a number of equipment trolleys had been brought into the room. They looked through their observation window carefully but could not see any sign of activity anywhere.

'This looks like major maintenance,' Otisk whispered, 'maybe we're waiting for the team to turn up. I hope they're not expecting to get into this office.'

'They won't be able to, will they? You locked the door.'

As Francel spoke, their attention was drawn to movement at the entrance door. A man entered the room, dressed all in white and wearing a large helmet that completely covered his head. He moved towards the furnace area of the room. As the figure approached, it became obvious that it was not walking but rolling forward smoothly. It also became clear that this figure was very tall, much taller than a man, with very long arms that ended in complex mechanical hands.

'It's a robot,' Otisk whispered. 'It's probably designed to withstand furnace heat. I think it will check and service the furnaces. Let's watch it closely.'

The robot worked for several hours in the furnace areas, after collecting various tools and equipment from the trolleys in the room. Finally it returned all equipment to the trolleys and made its way to the control panel where it set various switches and levers.

'Francel, I'm going to go out. I know a bit about robots and I think this robot will ignore me. It will only have been programmed to avoid me if it meets me. We can't sneak around here avoiding everyone and everything for ever.'

'Otisk, do you think you should? What if it recognises you as an intruder…?'

'Listen, Francel, we'll probably be meeting robots all the time, so we may as well get to know how they react to us, don't you think? After all, we're bound to be spotted, sooner or later.'

She still looked doubtful but he was resolute. 'Wish me luck, Francel. Watch and see what happens.'

He unlocked the door and walked towards the robot, which was still checking settings on the control panel. He stopped beside it, several feet away. After a few moments, the robot turned around to face him. He felt his face flush as it held its position immobile. Then it turned away and began organising the trolleys, all of which he could see were automatically controlled. Otisk turned away and came back to the office.

'Quick, Francel, let's follow the robot when it leaves. It would be useful to know where it goes. If we meet anyone, we'll pretend to be engineers on maintenance. Quickly, let's go. I think it's about to leave.'

The automatic trolleys began to leave the room one by one. The robot made one final check around the room, ignoring Otisk and Francel as it passed by them quite closely. Then it made a final check of the control panel and left the room, operating the switch to close the large metal door. They exited by the door hatch and followed the robot as is whirred along several corridors, eventually turning into a large room filled with inert robots standing in racks around the walls. They followed and stood in front of a wall of lockers. The robot rolled towards an empty bay and reversed into it neatly; then, with a series of clicks, it powered itself down.

'So this is the robot room,' Otisk said quietly. 'We'll just note that. Now we know that the robots don't "see" us—and that's a very useful thing to know. It's only the human workers we need to avoid as best we can.'

As he said that, something extremely shocking happened. The robot they had followed into the room suddenly split apart with a loud metallic click and a muscular man stepped out, looking fixedly at them. Involuntarily, they shrank back against the array of lockers behind them as he strode towards them, his face set in a grim but strangely incurious stare. Otisk and Francel were paralysed with fear, a fear that was turned into a physical pang of absolute terror as the man raised a muscular arm and swung a powerful, tightly-clasped fist directly towards Otisk's face; even worse, a large cylinder lock key jutted forward from between a powerful finger and thumb, transforming the large fist into a terrifying, sharply-pointed dagger with jagged serrations along each edge.

At such moments, time expands to become an eternity. Intense fear blasted through Otisk's body and paralysed his every sense. Nevertheless, a small part of his brain remained active and it made an observation and asked a question: 'This large clenched fist will deliver an extreme crushing and damaging blow to facial tissue and bone structure but what additional damage will the jagged metal key do to human skin, muscle and bone?' In almost the same instant, the answer was provided: 'A very considerable amount of facial and cranial damage,' the brain replied.

Then the horrific weapon, the powerful hand and following arm passed through Otisk's head and the appalling dagger-like weapon was plunged into a key slot on the locker door surface directly behind his head.

A blankness of unknown length ensued before a vivid realisation of total incredulity preceded such a huge surge of relief that Otisk struggled to remain conscious. A great many leaden-footed seconds lumbered by before he was able to speak.

'We're invisible—*that's* what we are!' he gasped. 'We're in a different reality plane from everyone here.' The words whispered thickly through flaccid, bloodless lips.

Francel, a deathly white spectre beside him, was incapable of speech or movement.

* * * *

"45,521 divided by 23?"

...

"298 times 64?"

...

"27 times 4,751 plus 320?"

...

"4,378.95 divided by 37?"

...

For once, there was no response to the maths test calculations.

Chapter 20

'**W**ell, that certainly makes it a whole lot easier!'

They had returned to base and were gradually recovering from their ordeal. With a rather pale smile, he repeated his final words. '…a whole lot easier.'

'Do you think no-one sees us—no-one at all?' she asked.

'Well, if I'm right—and I think I am—there's no way that anyone can see us, touch us, or experience us in any way. And that means we have been creeping around and hiding in corners for nothing. That's why no-one saw us when we sneaked in at the loading bay, or when we crept along the high walkway, or when the woman suddenly came out of a side corridor and turned back without noticing us. She didn't see us because there was nothing to see.'

'OK, Otisk. I hope you're right. I think we've just got to go out and test the theory. That will be a bit nerve racking, but I think we need to be assured that we really are invisible.'

He sat quietly for a bit, becoming more thoughtful. 'We'll need to test our new selves out and find out what this building is all about—and find out what foreign country this is as well. We can do all of that today. But—I've just thought—that's really only the start. If we aren't like all these other people, then what are we? What reality are *we* living in? And why are we here, anyway? You see, it's just the start. I think maybe we're still Pazoten people. We know they are different; no pain, no illness, no problems, instant manifestation of what you wanted, physical relocation... but I reckon we might not have these things now. For instance, we know we can't relocate...' His voice died away with the complexity of it all.

Francel became briskly practical. 'Listen, Otisk, all you say is true but we've just got to approach it step by step. The first step is action right now. We go out to confirm we're non-existent to the people here and then we'll try to find out what this building is all about.'

Suddenly, he got up and walked over to the door and bumped into it rather noisily.

'What are you doing, Otisk? You're supposed to open the door if you want to go out!'

He turned to her, smiling rather sheepishly. 'I was just checking, Francel. If we have no existence here—we know that man's hand went straight though me—then why can't we walk though solid objects here? Strangely, it seems we can't.'

She thought about this. 'If we could walk through their walls, Otisk, doesn't that mean that we couldn't be in here at all? We wouldn't be able to stand on their floors, would we?' We need to use their structures if we are to operate in this Land. We can be ephemeral to them, so they don't experience us—presumably they have no need to do so. But we need their structures to stand on, don't we?'

He looked at her in admiration. 'That's brilliant, Francel. You really are superb. That's an excellent explanation of our situation and you expounded it so very well.'

She flushed with pleasure. 'It's just logic, you know.'

He hugged and kissed her. 'You are just so wonderful, Francel. I don't ever want to be apart from you. Promise you won't ever leave me. I want to be with you forever.'

'And I want to be with you always.'

They left their base, somewhat tentatively, and started to walk along the corridor. Inevitably, they met no-one. They arrived in the area where the elevator doors were.

'Let's wait here, Francel and see if anyone reacts to us.'

They stood right in the middle of the hallway. After ten long minutes, there was the rattling sound of an approaching trolley garnished with loud voices. They recognised the two men they had seen the day before, still in loud animated conversation but speaking in their unknown language. The trolley and the men passed closely by them without a glance and one of the men pressed the button to call the elevator.

Otisk stepped forward. 'Excuse me,' he said loudly, speaking just behind the two men. There was no reaction; the men continued their conversation. 'Excuse me.' This time, Otisk's voice was extremely loud and Francel covered her ears. Again the men did not react. Just then, two women appeared and paused beside the elevator door. Like the men with the trolley, they ignored Otisk also. He turned to them. 'Excuse me,' he said loudly. They did not react but continued to speak quietly to each other. He shrugged his shoulders and was turning back to Francel when something astounding occurred to him. He could understand their conversation: They were speaking in English!

'Come closer, Francel and listen to them. They're speaking English.'

'Yes, you're right! This means that we've been fooled by these two men. They must be friends who come from a foreign country. When they speak to each other, they use their own language. That's a very common thing for people to do when they come from another country. We've been completely duped by that, Otisk.'

'That solves an important problem. And I think we've proved that we do not exist to the people in this building. Or, at least, we haven't found anyone yet who can see and hear us.'

The elevator came and went. They had decided it would best if they used the stairs. Soon, they were standing at the door marked "0".

'Are you ready for this, Francel?'

'Yes. Let's do it!'

Seconds later they had slipped through the stairway door and were standing in the vast hall that they had glimpsed before. Again, there were many people present, all ages, some sitting on rows of seats placed around the hall. They now saw that there was a very large reception desk along one side of the room. Many arrivals reported to this desk when they entered through the wide glass doors at the front of the building. There were a number of receptionists behind the desks and the newcomers had long and detailed conversations with them, while computer screens were examined gravely and document files manipulated. However, they also noticed that other people entered the hall and made their way directly to the row of elevators located on the back wall.

As they had noticed the day before, the hall was very brightly lit; now they saw that this was due to its dramatic atrium structure. The hall rose to the full height of the building and the ceiling consisted of very large glass panels, through which the sunshine streamed unimpeded.

'What do you think, Francel? Is this a hotel? Is this the vestibule of a performance hall, or maybe a library or a museum? Certainly, it looks like a building to which the public have free access.'

She looked around. 'I think the furniture would be more luxurious if it were any of these things, Otisk. I would say this is a building that the general public come to for some sort of service, some sort of advice, maybe. Let's go closer to the Reception Desks and see if we can pick anything up from what's being said.'

It proved rather difficult to eavesdrop, because people were called to the receptionists one by one and spoke in very low voices. They went as close as possible and strained their ears without success. Suddenly, Francel laughed out loud and Otisk looked at her with surprise.

'What fools we are,' she smiled. 'No-one can see us. We can go as close as we like. We can go behind the Reception Desks and peer at the computer screen and folders. We can go where we like and do what we like!'

As she was about to move forward, he grasped her arm. 'I've got it, Francel. Look at these notices. Why didn't we think of that before?'

The notice was an information board. It said: "Wards 1-6" and a direction arrow pointed the way, then "Wards 7-12" and the arrow pointed in the other direction.

'This is a hospital. A very large one by the look of it. I wonder what we are supposed to find here. This could take us a very long time.'

They withdrew from the rather noisy reception hall and found a quiet room with comfortable settees. 'If anyone comes in, we can move out and find somewhere else,' Francel said. 'Meanwhile, I think we need to start working out what we should do. At the moment, I'm overcome by the unknown nature of the task.'

'Right, Francel, let's just review it all quickly. Now we know we are in a large hospital. We don't know where it is and we find that we are in a different reality from everyone else—so no-one sees or hears us.' He stopped and looked enquiringly at Francel.

'Agreed, Otisk. And you've suggested what we need to do next, you know.'

'Have I? What is it?'

'Well, we know the purpose of this building and no doubt we will find out more. But we don't know where it is and I think that's our next task. We'll go outside and see where we are.'

'Wow, I didn't know I was that clever! You're right, though. Let's go ahead and do that right now.'

It proved to be a very pleasant day outside. They examined all the signs as they walked down smooth roads and pathways between well-tended gardens. The signs directed people to the various departments of the hospital and it seemed that every type of illness or ailment was catered for. Various notices identified the hospital by name; that name meant nothing to either Francel or Otisk.

At last, they reached the main entrance to the hospital, a wide system of gates that gave access into the hospital from a very busy road full of traffic. There was a very large sign board setting out many details of the hospital. They examined the board for further clues, hoping that the sign would reveal more about the location and administrative structure of the hospital. It did reveal more— but none of the information was helpful. The place names were all unknown to them.

'Maybe we don't know these place names because we're in a different reality, Francel. There's lots of information on this board— not only the name of the hospital but its location and region. Even if we didn't know the specific name of the hospital, surely we would have heard of the location? Surely we would know what region it was in: we know that the people here are English-speaking and the accent is not unfamiliar to us, is it?'

'You mean we're still programmed as Pazoten people—and Pazoten people would know nothing about any details of this other dimension?'

He nodded vigorously. 'Precisely.'

'Well, it certainly is possible,' she said slowly, 'maybe we will be able to prove it in due course. Right now, however, I suspect we can't.'

'Let's go out the gates and go for a walk along this road. Stretching our legs will do us good and we may see something that will jog our memories. Maybe we'll recognise something from our previous lives.'

She agreed and they were soon striding along the broad pavement that flanked the busy road. They met a few people, most of whom were walking towards the hospital.

'It looks as if these people are walking from a town nearby,' Francel said. 'That would make sense. A large hospital built on the edge of a town and serving the surrounding region.'

After a mile or so they came to the town boundary. Again, the name meant nothing to them. They continued to walk and eventually arrived at the main square of the town, a pleasant green park where there were benches to rest upon. There were many people in the park area and children played in areas designated solely for them.

'Do you have any feeling of recognition, Otisk?' she asked, looking around.

'Absolutely none at all,' he said. 'I reckon I've never been here before. I must admit it's very pleasant, though.'

'As nice as Pazoten Town?'

He thought about this, looking around carefully. 'Probably not,' he said eventually.

'Yes, I agree, Otisk. Pazoten is very special, isn't it?'

After a while, they walked back to the hospital, both thinking of their remarkable lives in Pazoten.

'I wonder if we'll ever be there again, Francel. We did have a fantastic time.'

'I doubt it,' she replied flatly, 'we chose here, didn't we?'

He nodded. 'Anyway, Francel, I don't care where I am as long as I am with you.'

They turned into the hospital gates and found a pleasant bench to sit on.

'We've got to plan our actions, now, Francel. We need to visit all parts of the hospital and see what happens—see if anything jumps out at us, you know?'

She frowned. 'I have a feeling that's not going to work.'

'A feeling?'

'Yes. Somehow, I feel that's not what we are supposed to do.'

He became a little irritated. 'OK, Francel, but listen. If we search the whole hospital, surely we've got to find what we're looking for? I mean, when we get there, it should be revealed to us. Otherwise we would not have been allowed to come here. We've just got to search.'

Her eyes were downcast. 'Sorry, Otisk. I don't think we are supposed to do that.'

He sighed. 'So what do you think we are supposed to do?'

'I don't know.'

He recognised that logic was not going to win the day and sat silently.

Suddenly: 'I think I've got it!' Her voice was low and quiet.

'Got what?'

'I think I know where we're supposed to go.'

He sat forward intently. 'Where?'

'The Sixth Floor! Do you remember I talked about the Sixth Floor when we were outside the building?'

'Well, yes, you were saying that if anyone challenged us, you would say we had been told to go to the Sixth Floor. But that was…'

'That was a message. I know it now. I feel it.'

'What's on the Sixth Floor?'

'I've no idea. But, at the moment, I am convinced that's where we need to go.'

'Well, OK, if you're so sure. I just hope we get better directions once we get there. All the floors of this building must be extensive. There must be a large number of different departments on each floor.'

'We can look at a directory and find out what is on the Sixth Floor.'

'Right, let's do that.' He leapt to his feet, characteristically quivering with enthusiasm at the action to come. Soon, they stood in the Reception Hall and looked around for a directory.

'There's a display over there, Otisk.' They walked over and examined the display very carefully. The Sixth Floor listed many wards, offices and laboratories, some identified by function, others just by a number.

'At the moment, nothing speaks to me,' Francel said. 'We'll need to go up there and see what happens.'

This time, they had secretly joined a group of people in an elevator and, within a minute, were standing in the spacious central area of the Sixth Floor. Reception desks lined the walls of this area and wide corridors led away from it, with signs indicating the various departments and room numbers that would be found along each corridor.

She touched his arm. 'Let's go and sit over there on these seats in that alcove.' Although she knew that no-one but Otisk could hear her, she couldn't help whispering!

They sat down. 'What are you thinking, Francel?'

She closed her eyes and was silent for a few moments. 'I don't know. I'm just trying to react to something here. I feel that we're going to be directed to where we must go.'

He took her hand. 'You know, I feel it, too. Not so strongly as you do, I think. You must be more sensitive, more tuned in, to whatever is communicating with us at this point. I've got an idea, though. Why don't we walk around the periphery of this central area, past each of the corridor entrances and see whether we are drawn to go in a particular direction?'

She looked rather worried. 'Well, yes, we can do that, Otisk. But that isn't how we have been directed up till now. We've just been left to work everything out by ourselves, haven't we?'

'Not quite, Francel. We were shown the building, this building, while we were living on Pazoten. Whoever showed us this knew we would choose to come here and attempt to solve the mystery. Maybe they're ready to give us a bit more direction, now that we're here? In any case, it can't do any harm to try my strategy, can it?'

She still looked unconvinced. 'OK, let's try it. I suppose it might be helpful,' she said.

They worked their way around the area very slowly, pausing at the entrance to each corridor and peering into it, while searching their senses for anything unusual. After some time, they arrived back at their starting point.

'Anything?' he asked.

She shook her head. 'Nothing. You?'

'No, I didn't feel anything. Maybe we'll have to do it the hard way. Search everywhere, you know? It's been the hard way up till now, hasn't it?' They sat down again in the alcove seats and were silent.

Gradually, the light faded outside as dusk fell. Internal lighting was switched on. The people who had filled the central area gradually dwindled away, their business completed. One by one, almost all of the reception desks closed and the staff withdrew. While the area was never totally deserted, Otisk and Francel were now almost alone and silence reigned for most of the time.

'Blue lights.' she said suddenly.

He, dozing, jerked upright. 'What?'

'Blue lights,' she repeated. 'I've just had a message. "Blue lights".'

They looked at each other, wide awake. 'What can it mean?' he asked.

She looked around. There were no blue lights to be seen. 'It definitely was a message,' she said.

'Let's walk around the area again,' he said, 'we can't see everything from here.'

They retraced their earlier steps. Pausing at each corridor mouth and scanning carefully along the new vistas presented. The first three corridors revealed no hint of blue lights. This was repeated at the fourth corridor. Then, just as they were turning away, Francel thought she saw a brief flash of blue along the corridor.

'Just a minute, Otisk. There may be something here...'

They stood still and focussed down the corridor once again. They stood motionless for several minutes but nothing happened. Then, as they were about to turn away again, they both saw it. Some way down the corridor, there was a small column of different coloured lights, mounted high on the wall near the ceiling; in this column, a soft blue light flashed briefly.

'A blue light,' she breathed. 'That's it! What are these lights for, Otisk?'

'Probably some sort of signalling system. Quite likely used for calling particular staff members when there is an emergency. But I think the system is being used to call us, now.' He looked at her, nodding happily. 'I think you've connected, Francel. All because of your sensitivity.' As he finished speaking, the blue light winked briefly at them again.

Immediately, they started to walk along the corridor, passing the column of lights. Round a bend in the corridor, they came upon another column of lights; this eventually winked its beckoning blue call. The corridor they were walking along was wide and well-lit, although completely deserted. On either side, doors led to offices. Some had identifiable notices on them, designating their function; others had incomprehensible strings of letters. They walked slowly, scanning everything carefully so that they would not miss their tracking blue lights. At one point, the corridor branched and there was a column of lights a little way along each.

'I'll watch this one,' Otisk suggested, 'and you watch that one.'

Minutes later, Otisk touched Francel's arm. 'I think it's this way,' he said, pointing. 'I just saw the blue light flash.'

'We'll just confirm that, Otisk. Let's watch until it flashes again. Meanwhile, I'll keep my eye firmly on this other one.'

'Yes, there it is again, Francel. Anything happening with yours?'

'No, it definitely hasn't flashed. So we go down your corridor.'

He kissed her gently. 'Let's call it "our" corridor, shall we,' he smiled.

The corridor curved around and the soon exited into another hallway area. There were a few reception desks around the walls but all were unmanned. Five other wide corridors led away from the central area.

'Our path must take us down one of these corridors,' Francel said, 'let's go and find our blue light.'

As they looked around, they noticed illuminated information signs at each corridor. The corridor they had just come from was identified as "Main Reception and Way Out" Signs at the next two corridors said "Operating Suites A" and Operating Suites B". Unsurprisingly, both of these corridors had additional notices stating "No Admittance: Authorised Personnel Only." The remaining corridors led to "Wards 56-60 High Dependency" and "Wards 52-55 Intensive Care"; they were additionally annotated "Strictly No Entry Without Authorisation".

They walked around the area and stopped at the entrance of each corridor, looking carefully for the familiar columns of coloured lights. There were none to be seen.

'Well, Francel, at least we've narrowed it down to this area of the hospital.'

'Yes. And I would doubt that our destination would be down the Operating Suites corridors. There is a constant flow of patients, nurses and doctors through these when they are in use.'

'Yes, I agree. But we've got to examine all the corridors for our blue light.'

Half an hour later, they had scanned each of the corridors meticulously and even penetrated along them for a little way in case their blue light was concealed behind something or hidden around a bend. Now they sat on a bench seat to discuss their failure.

'Right, Francel. We've been guided by the light columns up till now but the blue light must take another form now.'

'Could it just be something that's blue in colour?' Francel asked. 'You know, not a light, just a blue item?

'Well, it could be, but I can't see anything that strikes me as a possible, can you? Some of these seats are upholstered in blue, aren't they? But there are blue seats all around as well as other colours. Some of the walls of this reception area are blue, too. Does that help?'

She looked around. 'Not really. If one of the corridors was painted blue and the others weren't, that would be a good indicator, but none are.'

He closed his eyes. 'We must be very near, now. It's frustrating. As you say, we need a good indicator.' He was greatly startled as Francel jumped up and clapped her hands loudly.

'A blue indicator, Otisk, look! We've got one!' She pointed. The illuminated sign indicating the way to the "Intensive Care" wards had bright yellow letters on a blue background. He jerked his head around to look at the other illuminated signs. The two "Operating Suite" signs had a red background and the "High Dependency" ward sign had a green background.

'You're absolutely amazing!' he said, embracing her. 'You've solved it. Let's collect ourselves and follow the blue light as we are instructed to do.'

The first part of the corridor was obviously offices and equipment rooms; all appeared to be unoccupied. Then they reached the wards. Here efficient, white-coated staff occupied many monitoring stations where there were large screens of graphs and data displays, all being constantly updated. Other staff members were checking or attending to the patients, all of whom were lying in beds that were located in wide bays around the periphery of the wards. Some patients were inside various forms of life-support capsules. All were festooned with tubes and electric cables that led to various pieces of complex equipment that surrounded each bed. It was a strange environment, superficially calm, controlled and safe, yet overlaid with a tension that suggested catastrophe could occur at any time.

Otisk and Francel had stopped, taken aback, disquieted and bewildered by the scene before them.

'I knew these functions exist in hospitals,' Otisk said, very quietly, 'but I've never been in the middle of one. I feel so vulnerable, I don't know why. I feel so worried.'

'You don't think our presence here could be harmful to anyone, do you?' Francel's voice was a shocked whisper.

'No, Francel. I really don't think so. We're in a different reality plane. But I still feel worried.'

They stood there, in the middle of one of the wards, baffled, awed, confused. Frozen.

Suddenly she seized his arm. 'Look there, Otisk.' She pointed along the corridor to the next ward.

'What is it? I don't see anything.'

'Didn't you see her? It was a child, a little girl—*she waved and smiled at me*. She went through that doorway.'

'Are you sure, Francel? It might have just been your imagination.'

'No, no,' she cried, 'I saw where she went, I'm going to investigate. She must be in the same reality plane as us!' She released his hand and dashed off along the corridor.

'Just a minute,' he called after her but she paid no attention and disappeared through the doorway she had indicated.

'She'll be back in a minute,' he muttered, 'she knows where I am. It was probably just her imagination. It would be easy to imagine things in this environment.'

He forced himself to move and walked closer to the patient beds. The sight of the inert patients was distinctly unnerving. Some were attached to mechanical devices that pulsated in various ways to keep them alive. The pulse of heartbeats could be heard, creating complex rhythmic patterns as they interacted with artificial breathing equipment operating at a different frequency. The sound was disturbing, yet oddly musical.

'I wonder whether they're really alive?' he thought. 'Will any of them will ever live a normal life again.'

Looking at them, he was inclined to think not. This thought made him very sad. He had passed four completely inert patients now and was about to turn away from the fifth when something strange caught his eye. The fifth bed had a bold notice hooked on to the rail at the foot. The notice stated in large, bold letters: "STIMULATE WITH MATHS". Astonished, he approached this bed quickly and found that the notice was a folder containing sheets of mathematical calculations. *He recognised them all: every one!*

His eyes snapped up to the small notice on the wall above the bedhead. In clear, medium-sized black characters, this gave the name of the patient. As he read: "KARL OTIS", his eyes widened in shock and disbelief. Lowering his gaze, he saw that the inert figure in the bed was wearing on his left wrist a hospital bracelet made of clear plastic. Apparently without volition, he moved close enough to be able to read it. The name printed on the bracelet was clear to see—it was "OTISK". He looked at his own wrist. His bracelet was gone. He bent down and looked into the patient's face; it was his own face, pale, immobile, lifeless, an impassive holo-gram representation of himself.

His eyes unfocussed. Reality diminished. Consciousness fled.

* * * *

She dashed through the wide doorway, her eyes searching for the little girl who had waved to her so gaily just seconds before. There was absolutely no movement in the large room. The staff were motionless as they examined their monitoring equipment or gave attention to bulky folders on their desks. Their patients, cocooned and festooned, were still. Equipment hummed, chattered and pulsated in muted tones. She focussed on the nearest patient, recognising, with some difficulty, the little girl who had waved to her—except that this little girl was just a lifeless doll. A white, almost translucent facsimile of the joyful person she had seen such a short time before.

Whispering to herself, she started to walk around the other beds in the ward, looking sadly at these husks of humanity, each clearly named above their heads by a notice on the wall. Seeing them like this, she could hardly imagine that they once were living, independently breathing people, loved by others who were no doubt devastated by their current state. As she approached the next bed, she heard signs of activity behind her and saw that a number of staff were now clustered around the little girl's bed.

'Oh dear,' she thought, 'I hope nothing bad is happening to that little girl.' She looked again and didn't think so. The staff were smiling. 'Good,' she muttered and turned to read the name of the next motionless patient. It was "LISA FRANCE".

Chapter 21

There was pain but it wasn't too bad; more an awareness of pain, distant, almost like it belonged to someone else. A dull ache? He wondered if that described it. He couldn't remember much about the previous hours (days?) but he thought that a series of kindly people had come to talk to him, to attend to his needs (what were his needs?). He had felt their hands on his body and their breath on his skin. Did they change his position on the bed? Possibly; but why would they do that? He knew he hadn't opened his eyes much; everything out there was so bright and fast moving. The images confused him and tired him out, so he was quite glad to keep his eyes closed and continue to rest. Was it rest or just existence? He didn't know. He gave up trying to work it out.

Somehow, he was aware that he had lost some of the tubes that had been attached to his body, coiled around him, he thought. Some of the electric cables had disappeared, too and he thought that some of the machinery around him had been switched off. He wondered if this was good or bad and concluded that he didn't know—maybe these tubes and cables didn't do anything, anyway. Probably there for show? Show can be very important in life, can't it?

Unmeasured time flowed past, coloured grey, he decided. Like a rather sluggish industrial river—that's what it was like. Lazy whorls of oily water, viscid, hardly moving. Battleship grey, that was the colour, he concluded (what was a battleship, anyway?).

And unmeasured time still flowed on. It still flowed on because it was impossible to measure. It was just there and he was embedded in it, buoyed up by it, carried along. Gradually he began to respond to some of the people who approached him. They asked him questions, difficult questions; questions that needed a lot of thought. After a while, he tried his best to make some response. It wasn't easy. He felt as if his brain had been pickled in treacle. Treacle? He couldn't help smiling. Did he smile? He didn't know. He did answer but he was sure that his answers were unsatisfactory. Not adequate for their purpose. He was rather sorry about that. He would have liked to explain but he couldn't work out the strategy to begin to formulate the solutions that were needed to solve the equations that he knew would be there, waiting. Equations were always there, waiting.

How was he feeling? He didn't know. All right, he supposed. Maybe. Did he want to sit up a bit more? Difficult question! He didn't know. He just went along with whatever was suggested. It seemed to please them when he did that. He thought that the fluids they gave him were quite nice. He usually managed to drink some of the liquid through the tube they offered to his lips. He thought they were pleased by this, too, so he tried his hardest. And—he did start to smile at some of the younger nurses—just a little, just occasionally!

Now he knew that days were passing and, with every day, he was improving. His brain began to function again with steadily increasing normality. Where was he? Eventually, he was able to grasp that he was in a hospital. Why was he here? What had happened to him? Was he seriously ill, damaged? Gravely, he had studied all parts of his body (well, the bits he could see, anyway) and concluded that all looked reasonable, except, that is, for some rather dramatic scars and evidence of contusions on various parts of his limbs and body. Dreamily, he recalled that the body was a wonderful thing. 'Just heals itself – incredible!' he murmured to himself. But now he began to want his specific questions answered.

He tried asking the nurses. They shook their heads. 'You'll have to ask the doctors. They have access to all the files. They should be able to tell you what happened to you.'

'Can you tell me what happened to put me in here?' A grave senior doctor had come to examine him. The doctor had looked in his file.

'It seems that you had a climbing accident, Mr Otis,' he said briefly.

'Can you tell me a bit more about it, please?'

'Well, there isn't much more here. You were climbing a high cliff face in the Northern Mountains and you fell a long way. It was a miracle you survived, especially since you were very seriously injured. You needed a rescue helicopter to bring you here. We didn't know whether you would survive. You had very few vital signs when you were first examined.'

'Will I have any disability from my injuries?'

'We don't think so. Since you've awakened, your recovery has been very good and we can't detect any permanent damage. I think you've been very lucky.'

'So do I. Thanks for telling me what happened. By the way, how long have I been here?'

The doctor consulted the file. 'You've were in a coma for three months.'

'Three months: whew! That's a long time.'

'Yes, we thought so, too. That's why we're so pleased to see you recovering.'

'What about my family, Doctor? I'm remembering that I live in the town near this hospital but I can't recall any family...'

'Your parents live abroad, Mr Otis. They have come to see you several times while you were in a coma. We have informed them of your progress and they will visit you soon.'

In the following hours, Karl was able to recall more details of his life. He was a Lecturer in Mathematics at a nearby university and was rather famous for his gift of instant numerical calculation. He lived alone in a flat near the centre of the town, overlooking the very pleasant Central Square. He was physically very active and played a number of sports. In particular, he was very keen on climbing. 'My downfall, it would seem' he concluded, with a little private smile at the apt use of the word.

The following day, he was encouraged to leave his bed, supported on either side by nurses. He could only manage this for very brief periods at first—the world would start to spin around him—but, quite quickly, he became better. He was soon able to walk around the ward, increasingly unsupported but always monitored. Now he was impatient to progress to the next step.

'It's the corridor for me next,' he muttered determinedly. He had observed that a few patients from other wards were allowed to extend their walks into the corridor for brief periods. He began to negotiate with his nurses for these extended walks.

'Knowing you, you'll walk right out of Intensive Care if you keep on going like this,' they joked, 'then we'll know that you're not ill enough for us and we'll kick you out!'

Nevertheless, the great day soon arrived.

'We're going to take you out to the corridor today,' they told him, 'but you have to promise us that you won't overdo it.'

'I won't,' he promised, 'anyway, how could I? You're always there to stop me.'

It was a great thrill to step out into the corridor and Karl's eyes gleamed with pleasure. They walked slowly towards the other wards. He was walking largely unaided and he felt his balance was much improved.

'I think that's quite enough for your first time,' the nurse said. 'Stop and turn around slowly.'

'No, really. I think we could go a little further,' he pleaded.

'No. This is enough. Do as you're told. Turn yourself around.'

Obediently, he negotiated the turn smoothly. 'Just look how well-coordinated I am,' he joked with the nurse. 'You see, I'm absolutely sure we could have gone all...' His voice died away as his eyes focussed over the nurse's shoulder to rest upon an incredibly beautiful girl who was walking slowly down the corridor towards them. *Although she looked happy enough, he sensed a degree of nervousness and uncertainty about her. As she came closer, he was increasingly transfixed by her beauty and natural elegance.* His nurse was forgotten, totally wiped from his consciousness. His surroundings had disappeared, switched off.

As the girl came close, he stepped forward and held out his hand. 'Hello, I'm Karl Otis.' These words gasped breathlessly. 'Who are you?'

She stopped and met his soft gaze of admiration, respect and love. In response, a fierce wave of emotion swept through her. Wow, he's really nice. A thought which catapulted joyfully through her senses. Love always recognises love! 'I'm Lisa France,' she responded softly.

He smiled with huge pleasure. 'What a beautiful name,' he cried in joyful, ringing tones.

The nurse looked at them, both standing transfixed. She turned away with a knowing smile. 'Who would have thought it would happen in the corridor of an Intensive Care ward? Love at first sight! Now I've seen everything.'

* * * *

They became inseparable, spending as many as possible of their waking hours together, sometimes in his ward, sometimes in hers, sometimes in the corridor. He told her all about his life and she listened with rapt attention. When he had finished he asked. 'What about you?'

'I'm a photographer,' she replied. 'I have my own studio in the town and I work commercially for a number of newspapers and magazines. I live in a flat in the town, not very far from you.'

'It's surprising that we never have met,' he said.

'Maybe we don't move in the same circles,' she smiled, 'you know, you'll be with all the intellectuals while I'm just with the ordinary people. Anyway, Karl, you haven't told me why you're here. What happened?'

When he recounted the sketchy details of his climbing accident, her face had clouded with concern. 'That must have been terrible, Karl. Are you all right now? You must never do such a dangerous thing again... although,' she added, 'I have to admit to doing a little bit of climbing myself.'

He smiled. 'Listen, Lisa, if you are a climber you already know what my answer will be! Life isn't meant to be lived in caution and fear. Life is for living the way you want and if climbing mountains attracts you, then that's what you'll do. But, don't worry, I'll certainly be extremely careful in future—and I'll be equally careful crossing the road!' he grinned. He was surprised when she didn't smile back.

'So will I,' she said seriously, 'that's why I'm in here. I was in a hurry to cross the road and I didn't take enough care. I was knocked down by a car. It was all my fault.'

He was aghast. 'Oh, Lisa, are *you* all right,' he said, putting his arms around her, 'are you fully recovered now?'

'Yes, I am. But the collision knocked me unconscious and I was in a coma for weeks.'

'Oh dear! Your family must have been so worried.'

'I don't have any family, Karl. My parents died in a road accident many years ago. I have no brothers or sisters so I'm all alone.'

He sat quietly for a moment and then put his arms around her again. 'You're not alone, you know. And you needn't ever be. I never want to be parted from you, no matter what happens. I really mean it. I always want to be with you, now that I've found you. I love you. Will you marry me when we get out of here?'

'I will,' she responded instantly.

* * * *

Two days later, they were both informed by the doctors that they were being discharged from Intensive Care.

'We're transferring you to an ordinary ward downstairs,' they were told, 'We're sending you to the same ward for your final recuperation. Is that all right?'

They held hands, eyes locked together. 'It's more than all right,' Karl said, 'it's superb!'

Later that day, they were seated in wheelchairs for the journey to the new ward. After they had said their fond goodbyes, they were wheeled along the corridor towards the Reception Area. Suddenly, Lisa was aware of a very powerful desire to stop.

'Could we stop for a moment, please?' The entourage came to a halt opposite the open door of a small side ward with a sole patient motionless on a bed inside. The room was filled with the hum, pulsation and gentle chatter of life-sustaining equipment. She turned to the Doctor. 'Sorry. I must ask. Why is that patient isolated in a single room?'

The doctor looked puzzled. 'Well, he has been in a coma for a very long time. He's our longest serving patient. He's quite an elderly man. We keep thinking he won't survive but we've managed to stabilise him. We just keep hoping that one day he will waken up and tell us who he is.'

'You don't know who he is? That's very sad.' She paused. 'Does anyone ever visit him?'

'Never. He was brought in by the Emergency Services. They found him lying in the street. We tried many times to find out who he was but we were unsuccessful. So no one ever visits.'

She sat immobile for a moment. Then she spoke in a voice of quiet introspection.

'So he's like me. No visitors.' Then she spoke more loudly. 'I want to visit him, please. Can I do that? I really think he should have a visitor. You never know, I might know him. I might be able to tell you who he is. Will you come with me, Karl?'

'Of course I will. Is that acceptable to you?' the last words spoken to the doctor.

'Of course. Just go in. We'll join you in a few minutes.'

'Doctor?'

'Yes, Lisa?'

'Is there a chance he might be aware but unable to communicate?'

'We have investigated that. We keep monitoring him carefully. Up till now, there has been no sign of any response. His coma is very deep and we need to do everything to keep his body alive. There is a very low level of activity in the brain—that's why we haven't given up on him. We keep hoping he might improve but there's been nothing as yet.'

'Thank you, Doctor. Let's go in, Karl.'

They wheeled themselves into the room and stopped by the cluttered bedside, keenly aware of the familiar clicking and pulsating sounds emitted by the systems that were keeping this unfortunate man alive. Lisa placed her soft, slim hand on the man's gnarled fingers, feeling the surprising, pulsating warmth generated mechanically by the life-sustaining machines.

'Look at this, Karl. He has a bracelet on his wrist but it has no name printed on it! It's absolutely blank. They have to call him something, don't they? They need to identify his files. I do hope they don't just put a number on it. That would be awful.'

It was when they looked up that they noticed the small printed notice above the bedhead, displaying the man's name. The notice said: "LONEI".

'Lonei.' She held his hand and spoke the name softly. 'We have come to visit you today. I'm Lisa and this is Karl. We hope that you will come out of your coma soon and recover fully from your injuries. We'll come back and visit you again, if we can.'

'I wonder why they gave him that peculiar name,' Karl said. 'we must ask about that.'

In due course, the doctor and nurses joined them. 'Any recognition?' the doctor asked.

'None at all,' they replied. 'Why is he called LONEI?'

'Oh, that was one of the nurses. He didn't have a name for quite a while and she said that was wrong. She said he was "The Lone One" and started calling him "LONEONE". When the notice was printed, the number "LONE1" we had submitted for printing had been changed to the letter "I" and, when we got the display card back, we thought that "LONEI" was a much better idea for him! We thought it suited him better; our very own "lone mystery"!'

Otisk and Francel smiled: 'Well, we hope he comes back to life soon. Can we visit him again?'

'Certainly. Come anytime you like. Just book in at Intensive Care Reception. I'll authorise it.' As they prepared to go, the doctor added. 'So you're quite sure you don't know him?'

'We don't think so. We didn't look closely at his face. We were afraid to go too close in case it was bad for him.'

'Oh, you needn't worry about that. You can go as close as you like. He's breathing through his respirator. You can't hurt him by going close.'

She stood up and bent across the bed. She saw an elderly, lined face, impassive and expressionless. She felt a rush of intense sadness as she scanned his every feature carefully. Then she spoke into his ear in a quiet whisper, her words unheard by the others in the room. Eventually, she straightened up and moved aside without a word, motioning Karl to take her place.

He examined the small, lined face, so clearly kept alive by external intervention. Then he placed a hand on the elderly man's fingers and whispered: 'Lonei, if you can hear me, make some response, anything, no matter how small.' He waited and watched carefully. Nothing happened. Finally he stood up and stepped back.

'Any luck?' the doctor asked.

Karl shook his head sadly. 'I am afraid not,' he replied, 'I very much wish that I did know him.'

The doctor looked at Lisa quizzically. 'I'm sorry. I've never seen him before either,' she said, 'but I feel we should keep visiting him. I do hope he'll come out of his coma soon.'

* * * *

Unfortunately, the elderly man called Lonei never improved. They had visited him periodically until the awful day came several months later. The doctor asked them to come and speak to him after their visit. Now they sat in his office.

'Mr and Mrs Otis, I'm sorry to tell you that Lonei is now completely brain-dead. He deteriorated about a week ago and his brain scans have shown absolutely no activity for the last five days. We have checked him many times over this period.'

After a long pause, Lisa spoke in a very small voice. 'What does this mean?'

'It means that he is dead, I'm afraid. He's gone. We need to switch off our life support systems because there is now no life left to support.'

'Is there any possibility of error?' Karl asked, 'couldn't you just...'

The doctor shook his head. 'There is no possibility of error,' he replied, 'Lonei is dead.' After a pause, he continued. 'The reason I asked you to come to see me is to ask you a question. You see, in a real sense, you are Lonei's nearest relatives, his only "family", in fact. My question to you is: "Do you wish to be present when we switch off?"' He waited for their reply.

They looked at each other and nodded in unison. 'I think we must,' Lisa said quietly.

The doctor spoke quietly. 'Shall we go in now?'

Inevitably shocked by the suddenness of the event, they nodded dumbly...

The appallingly simple procedure was soon over. Fortunately, it was so obvious that there had been absolutely no spark of life left in that small elderly body. As soon as the crude, noisy elements of artificial life were withdrawn, the physical body that had contained Lonei became the recognisable corpse that it already had been for the previous five days.

* * * *

Meanwhile, in other realities, there had been considerable activity. The Leader had been transferred from Pazoten to Pazo-one five days previously. Pazoten had a new Leader, already hard at work. And LIFE, in all its other planes, dimensions and realities, continued—as it always does.

However, although all these elements appear to be fundamental and self-contained, there is one constant, overarching force that links them all powerfully; that force is love, which transcends all. For love is the prevailing force; constant, incredible, indestructible, and totally unconfined.

Meanwhile, the singularity that is *"love at first sight"*, which so powerfully shaped the destiny of Karl and Lisa Otis (as it does, routinely, for myriads of others), is the mere iceberg tip of the boundless totality that is love. In our perceived world, the phenomenon of "love at first sight" is generally considered to be based upon chance, one-off contacts. However, the truth is much more elegant. The story of Karl and Lisa, with its *repeated* example of "love at first sight", serves to illuminate that with precision.

Epilogue

(Chapter 2 page 18 vs. Chapter 21 page 302)

"LOVE AT FIRST SIGHT. IN HUMAN LIFE, IT HAPPENS REMARKABLY OFTEN! AND WHEN THE LOVE AT FIRST SIGHT IS RECIPROCATED, IT CAN BLOSSOM AT TRULY LIGHTNING SPEED, BECOMING A TOTALLY ARRESTING EVENT FOR THE TWO PEOPLE INVOLVED."

"IN OUR PERCEIVED WORLD, THE PHENOMENON OF "LOVE AT FIRST SIGHT" IS GENERALLY CONSIDERED TO BE BASED UPON CHANCE, ONE-OFF CONTACTS. HOWEVER, THE TRUTH IS MUCH MORE ELEGANT. THE STORY OF KARL AND LISA, WITH ITS REPEATED EXAMPLE OF "LOVE AT FIRST SIGHT", SERVES TO ILLUMINATE THAT WITH PRECISION."

(Chapter 2 page 21, repeated at Chapter 21 page 297)

"IN RESPONSE, A FIERCE WAVE OF EMOTION SWEPT THROUGH HER. 'WOW, HE'S REALLY NICE.' A THOUGHT WHICH CATAPULTED JOYFULLY THROUGH HER SENSES. LOVE ALWAYS RECOGNISES LOVE!"